TREASURED
STORIES of
CHRISTMAS

TREASURED
STORIES of
CHRISTMAS

Edited by Sarah Anne Stuart

BRISTOL
PARK
BOOKS

First Bristol Park Books edition published in 2010

Bristol Park Books
252 W. 38th Street
NYC, NY 10018

Bristol Park Books is a registered trademark of Bristol Park Books, Inc.

Library of Congress Control Number: 2010930875

ISBN: 978-0-88486-466-0

Text and jacket designed by Cindy LaBreacht

Printed in the United States of America

CONTENTS

THE GIFT OF GIVING

THE GIFT OF JOY

Introduction

Sarah Anne Stuart

Christmas is a special time of year. It's a season of faith and hope; a season of love and joy; a season of giving. We celebrate Christmas by gathering with loved ones—family, friends, and neighbors. We remember those special moments of our Christmases past and embrace the new joys we discover in our present Christmas. It is our hope that *The Treasured Stories of Christmas* can be a part of your Christmas celebrations and help you and your loved ones fully enjoy the spirit of the season this year and for many years to come.

The stories selected for this collection include family classics that can be shared and returned to again and again: excerpts from "A Christmas Carol" by Charles Dickens, Hans Christian Anderson's "The Fir Tree," Eugene Fields' "The First Christmas Tree," and O. Henry's "The Gift of the Magi."

Many of our most noted modern writers have contributed to this volume. Here you will find John Cheever's "Christmas is a Sad Season for the Poor,"

Ray Bradbury's "Bless Me Father, For I Have Sinned," and Willa Cather's "December Night," plus wonderful stories from Dostoyevsky, Bret Harte, Pearl Buck, and Cleveland Amory.

And no collection could be complete without stories from favorite children's authors such as Laura Ingalls Wilder, author of The Little House® series, Beatrix Potter, Louisa May Alcott, and Lucy Maud Montgomery.

Each story included in this volume reflects the gifts of Christmas—faith, hope, love, and joy. It is our hope that, as you re-read old favorites and discover wonderful new gems, your own Christmas will be enriched by those gifts.

May this *Christmas Treasury* become a Christmas tradition to be shared with loved ones year after year and passed on from generation to generation. This is our wish for you—our gift of Christmas.

Merry Christmas!

Sarah Anne Stuart

TREASURED
STORIES of
CHRISTMAS

The Gift of
FAITH

Born in Bethlehem

(St. Luke 2:1–16)

And it came to pass in those days, that there went out a decree from Caesar Augustus, that all the world should be taxed.

(*And* this taxing was first made when Cyrenius was governor of Syria.)

And all went to be taxed, everyone into his own city.

And Joseph also went up from Galilee, out of the city of Nazareth, into Judæa, unto the city of David, which is called Bethlehem (because he was of the house and lineage of David); to be taxed with Mary, his espoused wife, being great with child.

And so it was, that, while they were there, the days were accomplished that she should be delivered.

And she brought forth her firstborn son, and wrapped him in swaddling clothes, and laid him in a manger; because there was no room for them in the inn.

And there were in the same country shepherds abiding in the field, keeping watch over their flock by night.

And, lo, the angel of the Lord came upon them, and the glory of the Lord shone round them: And they were sore afraid.

And the angel said unto them, "Fear not. For, behold, I bring you good tidings of great joy, which shall be to all people.

For unto you is born this day in the city of David a Saviour, which is Christ the Lord.

And this *shall* be a sign unto you. Ye shall find the babe wrapped in swaddling clothes, lying in a manger."

And suddenly there was with the angel a multitude of the heavenly host praising God, and saying,

"Glory to God in the highest, and on Earth peace, goodwill toward men."

And it came to pass, as the angels were gone away from them into heaven, the shepherds said one to another, "Let us now go even unto Bethlehem, and see this thing which is come to pass, which the Lord hath made known unto us."

And they came with haste, and found Mary, and Joseph, and the babe lying in a manger.

The Three Wise Men

(St. Matthew 2:1–14)

Now when Jesus was born in Bethlehem of Judæa in the days of Herod the king, behold, there came wise men from the East to Jerusalem.

Saying, "Where is he that is born King of the Jews? For we have seen his star in the East, and are come to worship him."

When Herod the king had heard these things, he was troubled, and all Jerusalem with him.

And when he had gathered all the chief priests and scribes of the people together, he demanded of them where Christ should be born.

And they said unto him, "In Bethlehem of Judæa: for thus it is written by the prophet:

And thou Bethlehem, in the land of Juda, art not the least among the princess of Juda: for out of these shall come a Governor, that shall rule my people Israel."

Then Herod, when he had privily called the wise men, enquired of them diligently what time the star appeared.

And he sent them to Bethlehem, and said, "Go and search diligently for the young child; and when ye have found him, bring me word again, that I may come and worship him also."

When they had heard the king, they departed; and lo, the star, which they saw in the East, went before them, till it came and stood over where the young child was.

When they saw the star, they rejoiced with exceeding great joy.

And when they were come into the house, they saw the young child with Mary his mother, and fell down, and worshipped him. And when they had opened their treasures, they presented unto him gifts; gold, and frankincense, and myrrh.

And being warned of a God in a dream that they should not return to Herod, they departed into their own country another way.

And when they were departed, behold, the angel of the Lord appeareth to Joseph in a dream, saying, "Arise, and take the young child and his mother, and flee into Egypt, and be thou there until I bring thee word: for Herod will seek the young child to destroy him."

When he arose, he took the young child and his mother by night, and departed into Egypt.

The First Christmas Tree

* * * * * * *

Eugene Field

Once upon a time, the forest was in a great commotion. Early in the evening, the wise old cedars had shaken their heads ominously and predicted strange things. They had lived in the forest many, many years; but never had they seen such marvelous sights as were to be seen now in the sky, and upon the hills, and in the distant village.

"Pray tell us what you see," pleaded a little vine. "We who are not as tall as you can behold none of these wonderful things. Describe them to us, that we may enjoy them with you."

"I am filled with such amazement," said one of the cedars, "that I can hardly speak. The whole sky seems to be aflame, and the stars appear to be dancing among the clouds; angels walk down from heaven to the earth, and enter the village or talk with the shepherds upon the hills."

The vine listened in mute astonishment. Such things never before had happened. The vine trembled with excitement. Its nearest neighbor was a tiny tree, so small it scarcely ever was noticed; yet it was a very beautiful little tree, and the vines and ferns and mosses and other humble residents of the forest loved it dearly.

"How I should like to see the angels!" sighed the little tree. "And how I should like to see the stars dancing among the clouds! It must be very beautiful."

As the vine and the little tree talked of these things, the cedars watched with increasing interest the wonderful scenes over and beyond the confines of the forest. Presently they thought they heard music, and they were not mistaken, for soon the whole air was full of the sweetest harmonies ever heard upon Earth.

"What beautiful music!" cried the little tree. "I wonder whence it comes."

"The angels are singing," said a cedar; "for none but angels could make such sweet music."

"But the stars are singing, too," said another cedar; "yes, and the shepherds on the hill join in the song, and what a strangely glorious song it is!"

The trees listened to the singing, but they did not understand its meaning: It seemed to be an anthem, and it was of a Child that had been born; but further than this they did not understand. The strange and glorious song continued all the night; and all that night the angels walked to and fro, and the shepherd folk talked with the angels, and the stars danced and caroled in high heaven. And it was nearly morning when the cedars cried out, "They are coming to the forest! The angels are coming to the forest!" And, surely enough, this was true. The vine and the little tree were very terrified, and they begged their older and stronger neighbors to protect them from harm. But the cedars were too busy with their own fears to pay any heed to the faint pleadings of the humble vine and the little tree. The angels came into the forest, singing the same glorious anthem about the Child, and the stars sang in chorus with them, until every part of the woods rang with echoes of that wondrous song. There was nothing in the appearance of these angel hosts to inspire fear; they were clad all in white, and there were crowns upon their fair heads, and golden harps in their hands; love, hope, charity, compassion, and joy beamed from their beautiful faces, and their presence seemed to fill the forest with a divine peace. The angels came through the forest to where the little tree stood, and gathering around it, they touched it with their hands, and kissed its little branches, and sang even more sweetly than before. And their song was about the Child, the Child, the Child that had been born. Then the stars came down from the skies and danced and hung upon the branches of the tree, and they, too, sang that song—the song of the Child. And all the other trees and the vines and the ferns and the mosses beheld in wonder; nor could they understand why all these things were being done, and why this exceeding honor should be shown the little tree.

When the morning came the angels left the forest—all but one angel, who remained behind and lingered near the little tree. Then a cedar asked: "Why do you tarry with us, holy angel?" And the angel answered: "I stay to guard this little tree, for it is sacred, and no harm shall come to it."

The little tree felt quite relieved by this assurance, and it held up its head more confidently than ever before. And how it thrived and grew, and waxed in strength and beauty! The cedars said they never had seen the like. The sun seemed to lavish its choicest rays upon the little tree, heaven dropped its sweetest dew upon it, and the winds never came to the forest that they did not forget their rude manners and linger to kiss the little tree and sing it their prettiest songs. No danger ever menaced it, no harm threatened; for the angel never slept—through the day and through the night the angel watched the little tree and protected it from all evil. Oftentimes the tree talked with the angel; but of course they understood little of what he said, for he spoke always of the Child who was to become the Master; and always when thus he talked, he caressed the little tree, and stroked its branches and leaves, and moistened them with his tears. It all was so very strange that none in the forest could understand.

So the years passed, the angel watching his blooming charge. Sometimes the beasts strayed toward the little tree and threatened to devour its tender foliage; sometimes the woodman came with his axe, intent upon hewing down the straight and comely thing; sometimes the hot, consuming breath of drought swept from the south, and sought to blight the forest and all its verdure: The angel kept them from the little tree. Serene and beautiful it grew, until now it was no longer a little tree, but the pride and glory of the forest.

One day the tree heard someone coming through the forest. Hitherto the angel had hastened to its side when men approached; but now the angel strode away and stood under the cedars yonder.

"Dear angel," cried the tree, "can you not hear the footsteps of someone approaching? Why do you leave me?"

"Have no fear," said the angel; "for He who comes is the Master."

The Master came to the tree and beheld it. He placed His hands upon its smooth trunk and branches, and the tree was thrilled with a strange and glorious delight. Then He stooped and kissed the tree, and then He turned and went away.

Many times after that the Master came to the forest, and when He came it always was to where the tree stood. Many times He rested beneath the tree and enjoyed the shade of its foliage, and listened to the music of the wind as it swept through the rustling leaves. Many times He slept there, and the tree watched over Him, and the forest was still, and all its voices were hushed. And the angel hovered near like a faithful sentinel.

Ever and anon men came with the Master to the forest, and sat with Him in the shade of the tree, and talked with Him of matters which the tree never could understand; only it heard that the talk was of love and charity and gentleness, and it saw that the Master was beloved and venerated by the others. It heard them tell of the Master's goodness and humility—how He had healed the sick and raised the dead and bestowed inestimable blessings wherever He walked. And the tree loved the Master for His beauty and His goodness; and when He came to the forest it was full of joy, but when He came not, it was sad. And the other trees of the forest joined in its happiness and sorrow, for they, too, loved the Master. And the angel always hovered near.

The Master came one night alone into the forest, and His face was pale with anguish and wet with tears, and He fell upon His knees and prayed. The tree heard Him, and all the forest was still, as if it were standing in the presence of death. And when the morning came, lo, the angel had gone.

Then there was a great confusion in the forest. There was a sound of rude voices, and a clashing of swords and staves. Strange men appeared, uttering loud oaths and cruel threats, and the tree was filled with terror. It called aloud for the angel, but the angel came not.

"Alas," cried the vine, "they have come to destroy the tree, the pride and glory of the forest!"

The forest was sorely agitated, but it was in vain. The strange men plied their axes with cruel vigor, and the tree was hewn to the ground. Its beautiful branches were cut away and cast aside, and its soft, thick foliage was strewn to the tenderer mercies of the winds.

"They are killing me!" cried the tree. "Why is not the angel here to protect me?"

But no one heard the piteous cry—none but the other trees of the forest; and they wept, and the little vine wept too.

Then the cruel men dragged the despoiled and hewn tree from the forest, and the forest saw that beauteous thing no more.

But the night wind that swept down from the City of the Great King that night to ruffle the bosom of distant Galilee, tarried in the forest awhile to say that it had seen that day a cross upraised on Calvary—the tree on which was stretched the body of the dying Master.

A Little Boy at
Christ's Christmas Tree

Fyodor Dostoyevski

From *The Diary of a Writer*

B ut I am a novelist, and it seems that one "story" I did not invent myself.
Why did I say "it seems," since I know for certain that I did actually
invent it; yet I keep fancying that this happened somewhere, once upon a
time, precisely on Christmas Eve, in *some* huge city during a bitter frost?

I dreamed of a little boy—very little—about six, or even younger. This
little boy woke up one morning in a damp, cold basement. He was clad in
a shabby dressing gown of some kind, and he was shivering. Sitting in the
corner on a chest, wearily he kept blowing out his breath, letting escape from
his mouth, and it amused him to watch the vapor flow through the air. But
he was very hungry.

Several times that morning he came to the bedstead, where his sick mother lay on bedding thin as a pancake, with a bundle of some sort under her head for a pillow.

How did she happen to be here? She may have come with her little boy from some faraway town, and then suddenly she had fallen ill.

Two days ago the landlady of this wretched hovel had been seized by the police; most of the tenants had scattered in all directions—it was the holiday season—and now there remained only two. The peddler was still there, but he had been lying in a drunken stupor for more than twenty-four hours, not even having waited for the holiday to come. In another corner of the lodging, an eighty-year-old woman was moaning with rheumatism. In days past she had been a children's nurse somewhere. Now she was dying in solitude, moaning and sighing continuously and grumbling at the boy so that he grew too frightened to come near her. Somehow he had managed to find water in the entrance hall, with which to appease his thirst; but nowhere was he able to discover as much as a crust of bread. Time after time he came up to his mother, trying in vain to awaken her. As it grew dark, dread fell upon him. Though it was late evening, the candle was not yet lit. Fumbling over his mother's face he began to wonder why she lay so quiet, and why she felt as cold as the wall. "It's rather chilly in here," he said to himself. For a moment he stood still, unconsciously resting his hand on the shoulder of the dead woman. Then he began to breathe on his tiny fingers in an attempt to warm them, and, suddenly, coming upon his little cap that lay on the bedstead, he groped along cautiously and quietly made his way out of the basement. This he would have done earlier had he not been so afraid of the big dog upstairs on the staircase, which kept howling all day long in front of a neighbor's door. Now the dog was gone, and in a moment he was out in the street.

"My God, what a city!" Never before had he seen anything like this. There, in the place from which he had come, at night, everything was plunged into dark gloom—just a single lamp-post in the whole street! Humble wooden houses were closed in by shutters; no sooner did dusk descend than there was no one in sight; people locked themselves up in their homes, and only big packs of dogs—hundreds and thousands of them—howled and barked all night. Ah, but out there it was so warm, and there he had been given something to eat, while here... "Dear God, I do wish I had something to eat!" And here—what a thundering noise! What dazzling light! What crowds of people and horses and carriages! And what biting frost! What frost! Vapor, which at once turned cold, burst forth in thick clouds from the horses' hot-breathing muzzles. Horseshoes tinkle as they strike the stones through the fluffy snow. And men pushing each other about... "But, good heavens, how hungry I am! I wish I had just a tiny bit of something to eat!" And suddenly he felt a sharp pain in his little fingers.

A policeman passed by and turned his head away, so as not to take notice of the boy.

"And here is another street. Oh, how wide it is! Here I'll surely be run over! And how people shout and run and drive along! And what floods of light! Light everywhere! Look, what's this? Oh, what a huge window and, beyond it, a hall with a tree reaching up to the ceiling. It's a Christmas tree covered with gleaming lights, with sparkling bits of gold paper and apples, and all around are little dolls, toy horses. Lots of beautifully dressed, neat children running about the hall; they laugh and play, and they eat and drink something. And see, over there, that little girl—now she starts to dance with a boy! What a pretty little girl she is! And just listen to the music! You can hear it from inside, coming through the window!"

The little boy gazes and gazes and wonders; he even starts laughing, but… his toes begin to hurt, while the little fingers on his hand have grown quite red—they won't bend any longer, and it hurts to move them. And when at last he became fully aware of the sharp pain in his fingers, he burst into tears and set off running.

Presently, through another window, he catches sight of a room, with trees standing in it, and tables loaded with cakes, all sorts of cakes—almond cakes, red cakes, yellow cakes!… Four beautifully dressed ladies are sitting in the room; whoever enters it is given a cake… Every minute the door opens, and many gentlemen come in from the outside to visit these ladies.

The boy stole up, quickly pushed the door open, and sidled in. Oh, how they started shouting at him and motioning him out! One of the ladies hurried toward him, thrust a small copper coin into his hand, but she opened the door into the street. How frightened he was! The coin rolled from his hand, bouncing down the steps; he was just unable to bend his little red fingers to hold on to it.

Very fast, the little boy ran away, and quickly he started going, but he himself did not know whither to go. Once more he was ready to cry, but he was so frightened that he just kept on running and running, and blowing on his cold little hands. How dreadfully lonesome he felt, and suddenly despair clutched at his heart.

But lo! What's going on in here? In front of a window people are standing crowded together, lost in admiration… Inside they see three tiny dolls, all dressed up in little red and green frocks, so real that they seem alive! A kindly looking old man is sitting there, as if playing on a big violin; and next to him— two other men are playing small violins, swinging their heads to the rhythm of the music; they look at each other, their lips move, and they talk—they really do, but one simply can't hear them through the window pane.

At first the little boy thought that these moving figures were alive, but when at last he realized that they were only small puppets, he burst into laughter. He had never seen such figurines, and he didn't even know that such existed! He felt like crying, and yet the dolls looked so funny to him— oh, how funny!

Suddenly he felt as if somebody grabbed him by his dressing gown: a big bully of a boy, standing close by, without warning, struck him on the head, tore off his cap and kicked him violently. The little fellow fell down, and the people around began shouting. Scared to death, he jumped quickly to his feet and scampered off. All of a sudden he found himself in a strange courtyard under the vault of a gateway, and leaped behind a pile of kindling wood. "Here they won't find me! Besides, it's dark here!"

He sank down and huddled himself up in a small heap, but he could hardly catch his breath for fright. But presently a sensation of happiness crept over his whole being: His little hands and feet suddenly stopped aching, and once more he felt as comfortable and warm as on a hearth. But hardly a moment later, a shudder convulsed him: "Ah, I almost fell asleep. Well, I'll stay here awhile, and then I'll get back to look at the puppets" the little boy said to himself, and the memory of all the pretty dolls made him smile. "They seem just as though they're alive!" And all of a sudden he seemed to hear the voice of his mother, leaning over him and singing a song. "Mother dear, I'm just dozing. Oh, how wonderful it is to sleep here!"

Then a gentle voice whispered above him: "Come, little boy, come along with me! Come to see a Christmas tree!"

His first thought was that it might be his mama still speaking to him, but no—this wasn't she. Who, then, could it be? He saw no one, and yet, in the darkness, someone was hovering over him and tenderly clasping him in his arms... The little boy stretched out his arms and... an instant later... "Oh, what dazzling light! Oh, what a Christmas tree! Why, it can't be a Christmas tree," for he had never seen such trees.

Where is he now? Everything sparkles and glitters and shines, and scattered all over are tiny dolls—no, they are little boys and girls, only they are so luminous, and they all fly around him; they embrace him and lift him up; they carry him along, and now he flies, too. And he sees: yonder is his mother; she looks at him, smiling at him so happily. "Oh, Mother! Mother! How beautiful it is here!" exclaimed the little boy, and again he begins to kiss the children; he can hardly wait to tell them about those wee puppets behind the glass of the window.

"Who are you, little boys? Who are you, little girls?" he asks them, smiling, and he feels that he loves them all.

"This is Christ's Christmas Tree," they tell him. "On this day of the year Christ always has a Christmas Tree for those little children who have no Christmas tree of their own."

And then he learned that these little boys and girls were all once children like himself, but some of them have frozen to death in those baskets in which they had been left at the doors of Petersburg officials; others had perished in miserable hospital wards; still others had died at the dried-up breasts of their famine-stricken mothers (during the Samara famine); these, again, had choked to death from stench in third-class railroad cars. Now they are all here, all like little angels, and they are all with Christ, and He is in their midst, holding out His hands to them and to their sinful mothers... And the mothers of these babes, they all stand there, a short distance off, and weep: Each one recognizes her darling—her little boy, or her little girl—and they fly over to their mothers and kiss them and brush away their tears with their little hands, begging them not to cry, for they feel so happy here...

Next morning, down in the courtyard, porters found the tiny body of a little boy who had hidden behind the piles of kindling wood, and there had frozen to death. They also found his mother. She died even before he had passed away.

Now they are again united in God's Heaven.

And why did I invent such a story, one that conforms so little to an ordinary, reasonable diary—especially a writer's diary? And that, after having promised to write stories preeminently about actual events! But the point is that I keep fancying that all this could actually have happened—I mean, the things which happened in the basement and behind the piles of kindling wood. Well, and as regards Christ's Christmas Tree—I really don't know what to tell you, and I don't know whether or not this could have happened. Being a novelist, I have to invent things.

December Night

Willa Cather

From *Death Comes for the Archbishop*

Father Vaillant had been absent in Arizona since midsummer, and it was now December. Bishop Latour had been going through one of those periods of coldness and doubt which, from his boyhood, had occasionally settled down upon his spirit and made him feel an alien, wherever he was. He attended to his correspondence, went on his rounds among the parish priests, held services at missions that were without pastors, superintended the building of the addition to the Sisters' school; but his heart was not in these things.

One night about three weeks before Christmas he was lying in his bed, unable to sleep, with the sense of failure clutching at his heart. His prayers were empty words and brought him no refreshment. His soul had become a barren field. He had nothing within himself to give his priests or his people.

His work seemed superficial, a house built upon the sands. His great diocese was still a heathen country. The Indians traveled their old road of fear and darkness, battling with evil omens and ancient shadows. The Mexicans were children who played with their religion.

As the night wore on, the bed on which the Bishop lay became a bed of thorns; he could bear it no longer. Getting up in the dark, he looked out of the window and was surprised to find that it was snowing; that the ground was already lightly covered. The full moon, hidden by veils of cloud, threw a pale phosphorescent luminousness over the heavens, and the towers of the church stood up black against this silvery fleece. Father Latour felt a longing to go into the church to pray, but instead he lay down again under his blankets. Then, realizing that it was the cold of the church he shrank from, and despising himself, he rose again, dressed quickly, and went out into the court, throwing on over his cassock that faithful old cloak that was the twin of Father Vaillant's.

They had bought the cloth for those coats in Paris, long ago, when they were young men staying at the Seminary for Foreign Missions in the rue du Bac, preparing for their first voyage to the New World. The cloth had been made up into caped riding cloaks by a German tailor in Ohio, and lined with fox fur. Years afterward, when Father Latour was about to start on his long journey in search of his Bishopric, that same tailor had made the cloaks over and relined them with squirrel skins, as more appropriate for a mild climate. These memories and many others went through the Bishop's mind as he wrapped the trusty garment about him and crossed the court to the sacristy, with the big iron key in his hand.

The court was white with snow, and the shadows of walls and buildings stood out sharply in the faint light from the moon muffled in vapor. In the deep doorway of the sacristy he saw a crouching figure—a woman, he made out, and she was weeping bitterly. He raised her up and took her inside. As soon as he had lit a candle, he recognized her, and could have guessed her errand.

It was an old Mexican woman, called Sada, who was a slave in an American family. They were Protestants, very hostile to the Roman Church, and they did not allow her to go to Mass or to receive the visits of a priest. She was carefully watched at home—but in winter, when the heated rooms of the house were desirable to the family, she was put to sleep in a woodshed. Tonight, unable to sleep for the cold, she had gathered courage for this heroic action, had slipped out through the stable door and had come running up an alley way to the House of God to pray. Finding the front doors of the church fastened, she had made her way into the Bishop's garden and come round to the sacristy, only to find that, too, shut against her.

The Bishop stood holding the candle and watching her face while she spoke her few words; a dark brown peon face, worn thin and sharp by life and sorrow. It seemed to him that he had never seen pure goodness shine out of human countenance as it did from hers. He saw that she had no stockings under her shoes—the cast-off rawhides of her master—and beneath her frayed black shawl was only a thin calico dress, covered with patches. Her teeth struck together as she stood trying to control her shivering. With one movement of his free hand the Bishop took the furred cloak from his shoulders and put it about her. This frightened her. She cowered under it, murmuring, "Ah, no, no Padre!"

"You must obey your Padre, my daughter. Draw that cloak about you, and we will go into the church to pray."

The church was utterly black except for the red spark of the sanctuary lamp before the high altar. Taking her hand, and holding the candle before him, he led her across the choir to the Lady Chapel. There he began to light the tapers before the Virgin. Old Sada fell on her knees and kissed the floor. She kissed the feet of the Holy Mother, the pedestal on which they stood, crying all the while. But from the working of her face, from the beautiful tremors which passed over it, he knew they were tears of ecstasy.

"Nineteen years, Father, nineteen years since I have seen the holy things of the altar!"

"All that is passed, Sada. You have remembered the holy thing in your heart. We will pray together."

The Bishop knelt beside her, and they began, *O Holy Mary, Queen of Virgins...*

More than once Father Vaillant had spoken to the Bishop of this aged captive. There had been much whispering among the devout women of the parish about her pitiful case. The Smiths, with whom she lived, were Georgia people, who had at one time lived in El Paso del Norte, and they had taken her back to their native State with them. Not long ago some disgrace had come upon this family in Georgia, they had been forced to sell all their Negro slaves and flee the State. The Mexican woman they could not sell because they had no legal title to her, her position was irregular. Now that they were back in a Mexican country, the Smiths were afraid their charwoman might escape from them and find asylum among her own people, so they kept strict watch upon her. They did not allow her to go outside their own *patio*, not even to accompany her mistress to market.

Two women of the Altar Guild had been so bold as to go into the *patio* to talk with Sada when she was washing clothes, but they had been rudely driven away by the mistress of the house. Mrs. Smith had come running out into the court, half dressed, and told them that if they had business at her *casa* they were to come in by the front door, and not sneak in through the stable to frighten a poor silly creature. When they said they had come to ask Sada to go to Mass with them, she told them she had got the poor creature out of the clutches of the priests once, and would see to it that she did not fall into them again.

Even after that rebuff, a very pious neighbor woman had tried to say a word to Sada through the alley door of the stable, where she was unloading wood off the burro. But the old servant had put her finger to her lips and motioned the visitor away, glancing back over her shoulder the while with such an expression of terror that the intruder hastened off, surmising that Sada would be harshly used if she were caught speaking to anyone. The good woman went immediately to Father Vaillant with this story, and he had consulted the Bishop, declaring that something ought to be done to secure the consolations of religion for the bond-woman. But the Bishop replied that the time was not yet; for the present it was inexpedient to antagonize these people. The Smiths were the leaders of a small group of low-caste Protestants who took every occasion to make trouble for the Catholics. They hung about the door of the church on festival days with mockery and loud laughter, spoke insolently to the nuns in the street, stood jeering and blaspheming when the procession went by on Corpus Christi Sunday. There were five sons in the Smith family, fellows of low habits and evil tongues. Even the two younger boys, still children, showed a vicious disposition. Tranquilino had repeatedly driven these two boys out of the Bishop's garden, where they came with their lewd companions to rob the young pear trees or to speak filth against the priests.

When they rose from their knees, Father Latour told Sada he was glad to know that she remembered her prayers so well.

"Ah, Padre, every night I say my Rosary to my Holy Mother, no matter where I sleep!" declared the old creature passionately, looking up into his face and pressing her knotted hands against her breast.

When he asked if she had her beads with her, she was confused. She kept them tied with a cord around her waist, under her clothes, as the only place she could hide them safely.

He spoke soothingly to her. "Remember this, Sada: In the year to come, and during the Novena before Christmas, I will not forget to pray for you whenever I offer the Blessed Sacrifice of the Mass. Be at rest in your heart, for I will remember you in my silent supplications before the altar as I do my own sisters and my nieces."

Never, as he afterward told Father Vaillant, had it been permitted him to behold such deep experience of the holy joy of religion as on that pale December night. He was able to feel, kneeling beside her, the preciousness of the things of the altar to her who was without possessions: the tapers, the image of the Virgin, the figures of the saints, the Cross that took away indignity from suffering and made pain and poverty a means of fellowship with

Christ. Kneeling beside the much enduring bond-woman, he experienced those holy mysteries as he had done in his young manhood. He seemed able to feel all it meant to her to know that there was a Kind Woman in Heaven, though there were such cruel ones on earth. Old people, who had felt blows and toil and known the world's hard hand, need, even more than children do, a woman's tenderness. Only a Woman, divine, could know all that a woman can suffer.

Not often, indeed, had Jean Marie Latour come so near to the Fountain of all Pity as in the Lady Chapel that night—the pity that no man born of woman could ever utterly cut himself off from—that was for the murderer on the scaffold, as it was for the dying soldier or the martyr on the rack. The beautiful concept of Mary pierced the priest's heart like a sword.

"*O Sacred Heart of Mary!*" she murmured by his side, and he felt how that name was food and raiment, friend and mother to her. He received the miracle in her heart into his own, saw through her eyes, knew that his poverty was as bleak as hers. When the Kingdom of Heaven had first come into the world, into a cruel world of torture and slaves and masters, He who brought it had said, "*And whosoever is least among you, the same shall be first in the Kingdom of Heaven.*" This church was Sada's house, and he was a servant in it.

The Bishop heard the old woman's confession. He blessed her and put both hands upon her head. When he took her down the nave to let her out of the church, Sada made to lift his cloak from her shoulders. He restrained her, telling her she must keep it for her own, and sleep in it at night. But she slipped out of it hurriedly; such a thought seemed to terrify her. "No, no,

Father. If they were to find it on me!" More than that, she did not accuse her oppressors. But as she put it off, she stroked the old garment and patted it as if it were a living thing that had been kind to her.

Happily Father Latour bethought him of a little silver medal, with a figure of the Virgin, he had in his pocket. He gave it to her, telling her that it had been blessed by the Holy Father himself. Now she would have a treasure to hide and guard, to adore while her watchers slept. Ah, he thought, for one who cannot read—or think—the Image, the physical form of Love!

He fitted the great key into its lock, the door swung slowly back on its wooden hinges. The peace without seemed all one with the peace in his own soul. The snow had stopped, the gauzy clouds that had ribbed the arch of heaven were now all sunk into one soft white fog bank over the Sangre de Cristo mountains. The full moon shone high in the blue vault—majestic, lonely, benign. The Bishop stood in the doorway of his church, and lost in thought, looking at the line of black footprints his departing visitor had left in the wet scurf of snow.

Bless Me, Father, for I Have Sinned

Ray Bradbury

I t was just before midnight on Christmas Eve when Father Mellon woke, having slept only for a few minutes. He had a most peculiar urge to rise, go, and swing wide the front door of his church to let in the snow and then go sit in the confessional to wait.

Wait for what? Who could say? Who might tell? But the urge was so incredibly strong it was not to be denied.

"What's going on here?" he muttered quietly to himself, as he dressed. "I am going mad, am I not? At this hour, who could possibly want or need, and why in blazes should I..."

But dress he did and down he went and opened wide the front door of the church and stood in awe of the great artwork beyond, better than any painting in history, a tapestry of snow weaving in laces and gentling to roofs and shadowing the lamps and putting shawls on the huddled masses of cars waiting to be blessed at the curb. The snow touched the sidewalks and then his eyelids and then his heart. He found himself holding his breath with the fickle beauties and then, turning, the snow following at his back, he went to hide in the confessional.

Damn fool, he thought. Stupid old man. *Out* of here! Back to your bed!

But then he heard it—a sound at the door, and footsteps scraping on the pavestones of the church, and at last the damp rustle of some invader fresh to the other side of the confessional. Father Mellon waited.

"Bless me," a man's voice whispered, "for I have sinned!"

Stunned at the quickness of this asking, Father Mellon could only retort:

"How *could* you know the church would be open and I here?"

"I prayed, Father," was the quiet reply. "God *made* you come open up."

There seemed no answer to this, so the old priest, and what sounded like a hoarse old sinner, sat for a long cold moment as the clock itched on toward midnight, and at last the refugee from darkness repeated:

"*Bless* this sinner, Father!"

But in place of the usual unguents and ointments of words, with Christmas hurrying fast through the snow, Father Mellon leaned toward the lattice window and could not help saying:

"It must be a terrible load of sin you carry to have driven you out on such a night on an impossible mission that turned possible only because God heard and pushed me out of bed."

"It *is* a terrible list, Father, as you will find!"

"Then speak, son," said the priest, "before we both freeze…"

"Well, it was this way…" whispered the wintry voice behind the paneling. "Sixty years back…"

"Speak up! Sixty?" The priest gasped. "The *long* past?"

"Sixty!" And there was a tormented silence.

"Go on," said the priest, ashamed of interrupting.

"Sixty years this week, when I was twelve," said the gray voice, "I Christmas shopped with my grandmother in a small town back East. We walked both ways. In those days, who had a car? We walked, and coming home with the wrapped gifts, my grandma said something, I've long since forgotten what, and I got mad and ran ahead, away from her. Far off, I could hear her call and then cry, terribly, for me to come back, come back, but I wouldn't. She wailed so, I knew I had hurt her, which made me feel strong and good, so I ran even more, laughing, and beat her to the house and when she came she was gasping and weeping as if never to stop. I felt ashamed and ran to hide…"

There was a long silence.

The priest prompted, "Is that *it*?"

"The list is long," mourned the voice beyond the thin panel.

"Continue," said the priest, eyes shut.

"I did much the same to my mother, before New Year's. She angered me. I ran. I heard her cry out behind me. I smiled and ran faster. Why? Why? Oh God, why?"

The priest had no answer.

"Is that it, then?" he murmured, at last, feeling strangely moved toward the old man beyond.

"One summer day," said the voice, "some bullies beat me. When they were gone, on a bush I saw two butterflies, embraced, lovely. I hated their happiness. I grabbed them in my fist and pulverized them to dust. Oh, Father, the shame!"

The wind blew in the church door at that moment and both of them glanced up to see a Christmas ghost of snow turned about in the door and falling away in drifts of whiteness to scatter on the pavings.

"There's one last terrible thing," said the old man, hidden away with his grief. And then he said:

"When I was thirteen, again in Christmas week, my dog Bo ran away and was lost three days and nights. I loved him more than life itself. He was special and loving and fine. And all of a sudden the beast was gone, and all his beauty with him. I waited. I cried. I waited. I prayed. I shouted under my breath. I knew he would never, never come back! And then, oh, then, that Christmas Eve at two in the morning, with sleet on the sidewalks and icicles on the roofs and snow falling, I heard a sound in my sleep and woke to hear him scratching at the door! I bounded from bed so fast I almost killed myself! I yanked the door open and there was my miserable dog, shivering, excited, covered with dirty slush. I yelled, pulled him in, slammed the door, fell to my knees, grabbed him and wept. What a gift, what a gift! I called his name over and over, and he wept with me, all whines and agonies of joy. And then I stopped. Do you know what I did then? Can you guess the terrible thing? I beat him. Yes, beat him. With my fists, my hands, my palms, my fists again, crying: 'How dare you leave, how dare you run off, how dare you do that to me, how dare you, how dare?' And I beat and beat until I was weak and sobbed and had to stop for I saw what I'd done, and he just stood and took it all as if he knew he deserved it; he had failed my love and now I was failing his, and I pulled off and tears streamed from my eyes, my breath strangled, and I grabbed him again and crushed him to me but this time cried: 'Forgive, oh please, Bo, forgive. I didn't mean it. Oh Bo, forgive…'

"But, oh, Father, he couldn't forgive me. Who was he? A beast, an animal, a dog, my love. And he looked at me with such great dark eyes that it locked my heart and it's been locked forever after with shame. *I* could not then forgive *myself.* All these years, the memory of my love and how I failed him, and every Christmas since, not the rest of the year, but every Christmas Eve, his ghost comes back, I see the dog, I hear the beating, I know my failure. Oh, God!"

The man fell silent, weeping.

And at last the old priest dared a word: "And that is why you are here?"

"Yes, Father. Isn't it awful. Isn't it terrible?"

The priest could not answer, for tears were streaming down his face, too, and he found himself unaccountably short of breath.

"Will God forgive me, Father?" asked the other.

"Yes."

"Will *you* forgive me, Father?"

"Yes. But let me tell you something now, son. When I was ten, the same things happened. My parents, of course, but then—my dog, the love of *my* life, who ran off and I hated him for leaving me, and when he came back I, too, loved and beat him, then went back to love. Until this night, I have told no one. The shame has stayed put all these years. I have confessed all to my priest-confessor. But *never* that. So…"

There was a pause.

"*So*, Father?"

"Lord, Lord, dear man. God will forgive us. At long last, we have brought it out, dared to say. And I will forgive you. But finally…"

The old priest could not go on, for new tears were really pouring down his face now.

The stranger on the other side guessed this and very carefully inquired, "Do you want *my* forgiveness, Father?"

The priest nodded, silently. Perhaps the other felt the shadow of the nod, for he quickly said, "Ah, well. It's *given*."

And they both sat there for a long moment in the dark and another ghost moved to stand in the door, then sank to snow and drifted away.

"Before you go," said the priest. "Come share a glass of wine."

The great clock in the square across from the church struck midnight.

"It's Christmas, Father," said the voice from behind the panel.

"It's the finest Christmas ever, I think."

"The finest."

The old priest rose and stepped out.

He waited a moment for some stir, some movement from the opposite side of the confessional.

There was no sound.

Frowning, the priest reached out and opened the confessional door and peered into the cubicle.

There was nothing and no one there.

His jaw dropped. Snow moved along the back of his neck.

He put his hand out to feel the darkness.

The place was empty.

Turning, he stared at the entry door and hurried over to look out.

Snow fell in the last tones of far clocks late-sounding the hour. The streets were deserted.

Turning again, he saw the tall mirror that stood in the church entry.

There was an old man, himself, reflected in the cold glass.

Almost without thinking, he raised his hand and made the sign of blessing. The reflection in the mirror did likewise.

Then the old priest, wiping his eyes, turned a last time and went to find the wine.

Outside, Christmas, like the snow, was everywhere.

A Christmas Story

Katherine Anne Porter

An episode in the short life of the author's niece,
who died at the age of five and a half years.

When she was five years old, my niece asked me why we celebrated Christmas. She had asked when she was three and when she was four, and each time had listened with a shining, believing face, learning the songs and gazing enchanted at the pictures which I displayed as proof of my stories. Nothing could have been more successful, so I began once more confidently to recite, in effect, the following:

The feast in the beginning was meant to celebrate with joy the birth of a Child, an event of such importance to this world that angels sang from the skies in human language to announce it and even, if we may believe the old painters, came down with garlands in their hands and danced on the broken roof of the cattle shed where He was born.

"Poor baby," she said, disregarding the angels, "didn't His papa and mama have a house?"

They weren't quite so poor as all that, I went on, slightly dashed, for last year the angels had been the center of interest. His papa and mama were able to pay taxes at least, but they had to leave home and go to Bethlehem to pay them, and they could have afforded a room in the inn, but the town was crowded because everybody came to pay taxes at the same time. They were quite lucky to find a manger full of clean straw to sleep in. When the baby was born, a good-hearted servant girl named Bertha came to help the mother. Bertha had no arms, but in that moment she unexpectedly grew a fine new pair of arms and hands, and the first thing she did with them was to wrap the baby in swaddling clothes. We then sang together the song about Bertha the armless servant. Thinking I saw a practical question dawning in a pure blue eye, I hurried on to the part about how all the animals—cows, calves, donkeys, sheep—

"And pigs?"

Pigs, perhaps, even had knelt in a ring around the baby and breathed upon Him to keep Him warm through His first hours in this world. A new star appeared and moved in a straight course toward Bethlehem for many nights to guide three kings who came from far countries to place important gifts in the straw beside Him: gold, frankincense, and myrrh.

"What beautiful clothes," said the little girl, looking at the picture of Charles the Seventh of France kneeling before a meek blond girl and a charming baby.

It was the way some people used to dress. The Child's mother, Mary, and His father, Joseph, a carpenter, were such unworldly simple souls they never once thought of taking any honor to themselves nor of turning the gifts to their own benefit.

"What became of the gifts?" asked the little girl.

Nobody knows, nobody seems to have paid much attention to them, they were never heard of again after that night. So far as we know, those were the only presents anyone ever gave to the Child while He lived. But He was not unhappy. Once He caused a cherry tree in full fruit to bend down one of its branches so His mother could more easily pick cherries. We then sang about the cherry tree until we came to the words *Then up spake old Joseph, so rude and unkind.*

"Why was he unkind?"

I thought perhaps he was just in a cross mood.

"What was he cross about?"

Dear me, what should I say now? After all, this was not *my* daughter; whatever would her mother answer to this? I asked her in turn what she was cross about when she was cross. She couldn't remember ever having been cross but was willing to let the subject pass. We moved on to *The Withy Tree,* which tells how the Child once cast a bridge of sunbeams over a stream and crossed upon it, and played a trick on little John the Baptist, who followed Him, by removing the beams and letting John fall in the water. The Child's mother switched Him smartly for this with a branch of withy, and the Child shed loud tears and wished bad luck upon the whole race of withies forever.

"What's a withy?" asked the little girl. I looked it up in the dictionary and discovered it meant osiers, or willows.

"Just a willow like ours?" she asked, rejecting this intrusion of the commonplace. Yes, but once, when His father was struggling with a heavy piece of timber almost beyond his strength, the Child ran and touched it with one finger and the timber rose and fell properly into place. At night His mother cradled Him and sang long, slow songs about a lonely tree waiting for Him in a far place; and the Child, moved by her tears, spoke long before it was time for Him to speak and His first words were, "Don't be sad, for you shall be Queen of Heaven." And there she was in an old picture, with the airy jeweled crown being set upon her golden hair.

I thought how nearly all of these tender medieval songs and legends about this Child were concerned with trees, wood, timbers, beams, crosspieces; and even the pagan north transformed its great druidic tree festooned with human entrails into a blithe festival tree hung with gifts for the Child, and some savage old man of the woods became a rollicking saint with a big belly. But I had never talked about Santa Claus, because myself, I had not liked him from the first, and did not even then approve of the boisterous way he had almost crowded out the Child from His own birthday feast.

"I like the part about the sunbeam bridge the best," said the little girl, and then she told me she had a dollar of her own and would I take her to buy a Christmas present for her mother.

We wandered from shop to shop, and I admired the way the little girl, surrounded by tons of seductive, specially manufactured holiday merchandise for children, kept her attention fixed resolutely on objects appropriate to the grown-up world. She considered seriously in turn a silver tea service, one thousand dollars; an embroidered handkerchief with lace on it; five dollars; a dressing-table mirror framed in porcelain flowers, eighty-five dollars; a preposterously showy crystal flask of perfume, one hundred twenty dollars;

a gadget for curling the eyelashes, seventy-five cents; a large plaque of col-ored glass jewelry, thirty dollars; a cigarette case of some fraudulent material, two dollars and fifty cents. She weakened, but only for a moment, before a mechanical monkey with real fur who did calisthenics on a crossbar if you wound him up, one dollar and ninety-eight cents.

The prices of these objects did not influence their relative value to her and bore no connection whatever to the dollar she carried in her hand. Our shop-ping had also no connection with the birthday of the Child or the legends and pictures. Her air of reserve toward the long series of bleary-eyed, shapeless old men wearing red flannel blouses and false, white-wool whiskers said all too plainly that they, in no way, fulfilled her notions of Christmas merriment. She shook hands with all of them politely, could not be persuaded to ask for anything from them, and seemed not to question the obvious spectacle of thousands of persons everywhere buying presents instead of waiting for one of the army of Santa Clauses to bring them, as they all so profusely promised.

Christmas is what we make it and this is what we have so cynically made of it: not the feast of the Child in the straw-filled crib, nor even the homely winter bounty of the old pagan with the reindeer, but a great glittering commercial fair, gay enough with music and food and extravagance of feeling and behavior expense, more and more on the order of the ancient Saturnalia. I have nothing against Saturnalia, it belongs to this season of the year: But how do we get so confused about the true meaning of even our simplest-appearing pastimes?

Meanwhile, for our money we found a present for the little girl's mother. It turned out to be a small green pottery shell with a colored bird perched on the rim which the girl took for an ashtray, which it may as well have been.

"We'll wrap it up and hang it on the tree and *say* it came from Santa Claus," she said, trustfully making of me a fellow conspirator.

"You don't believe in Santa Claus anymore?" I asked carefully, for we had taken her infant credulity for granted. I had already seen in her face that morning a skeptical view of my sentimental legends. She was plainly trying to sort out one thing from another in them; and I was turning over in my mind the notion of beginning again with her on other grounds, of making an attempt to draw, however faintly, some boundary lines between fact and fancy, which is not so difficult; but also further to show where truth and poetry were, if not the same being, at least twins who could wear each other's clothes. But that couldn't be done in a day, nor with pedantic intention. I was perfectly prepared for the first half of her answer, but the second took me by surprise.

"No, I don't," she said, with the freedom of her natural candor, "but please don't tell my mother, for she still does."

For herself, then, she rejected the gigantic hoax which a whole powerful society had organized and was sustaining at the vastest pains and expense, and she was yet to find the grain of truth lying lost in the gaudy debris around her, but there remained her immediate human situation, and that she could deal with, or so she believed: Her mother believed in Santa Claus, or she would not have said so. The little girl did not believe in what her mother had told her, she did not want her mother to know she did not believe, yet her mother's illusions must not be disturbed. In that moment of decision her infancy was gone forever; it had vanished there before my eyes.

Very thoughtfully I took the hand of my budding little diplomat, whom we had so lovingly, unconsciously prepared for her career, which no doubt would be quite a successful one; and we walked along in the bright sweet-smelling Christmas dusk, myself for once completely silenced.

The Miraculous Staircase

✳ ✳ ✳ ✳ ✳ ✳

Arthur Gordon

O n that cool December morning in 1878, sunlight lay like an amber rug across the dusty streets and adobe houses of Santa Fe. It glinted on the bright tile roof of the almost completed Chapel of Our Lady of Light and on the nearby windows of the convent school run by the Sisters of Loretto. Inside the convent, the Mother Superior looked up from her packing as a tap came on her door.

"It's *another* carpenter, Reverend Mother," said Sister Francis Louise, her round face apologetic. "I told him that you're leaving right away, that you haven't time to see him, but he says..."

"I know what he says," Mother Magdalene said, going on resolutely with her packing. "That he's heard about our problem with the new chapel. That he's the best carpenter in all of New Mexico. That he can build us a staircase to the choir loft despite the fact that the brilliant architect in Paris who drew the plans failed to leave any space for one. And despite the fact that five master carpenters have already tried and failed. You're quite right, Sister; I don't have time to listen to that story again."

"But he seems such a nice man," and Sister Francis Louise wistfully, "and he's out there with his burro, and…"

"I'm sure," said Mother Magdalene with a smile, "that he's a charming man, and that his burro is a charming donkey. But there's sickness down at the Santo Domingo pueblo, and it may be cholera. Sister Mary Helen and I are the only ones here who've had cholera. So we have to go. And you have to stay and run the school. And that's that!" Then she called, "Manuela!"

A young Indian girl of 12 or 13, black-haired and smiling, came in quietly on moccasined feet. She was a mute. She could hear and understand, but the Sisters had been unable to teach her to speak. The Mother Superior spoke to her gently: "Take my things down to the wagon, child. I'll be right there." And to sister Francis Louise: "You'd better tell your carpenter friend to come back in two or three weeks. I'll see him then."

"Two or three weeks! Surely you'll be home for Christmas?"

"If it's the Lord's will, Sister. I hope so."

In the street, beyond the waiting wagon, Mother Magdalene could see the carpenter, a bearded man, strongly built and taller than most Mexicans, with dark eyes and a smiling, wind-burned face. Beside him, laden with tools and scraps of lumber, a small gray burro stood patiently. Manuela was stroking its nose, glancing shyly at its owner. "You'd better explain," said the Mother Superior, "that the child can hear him, but she can't speak."

Goodbyes were quick—the best kind when you leave a place you love. Southwest, then, along the dusty trail, the mountains purple with shadow, the Rio Grande a ribbon of green far off to the right. The pace was slow, but Mother Magdalene and Sister Mary Helen amused themselves by singing songs and telling Christmas stories as the sun marched up and down the sky. And their leathery driver listened and nodded.

Two days of this brought them to Santo Domingo Pueblo, where the sickness was not cholera after all, but measles, almost as deadly in an Indian village. And so they stayed, helping the harassed Father Sebastian, visiting the dark adobe hovels where feverish brown children tossed and fierce Indian dogs showed their teeth.

At night they were bone-weary, but sometimes Mother Magdalene found time to talk to Father Sebastian about her plans for the dedication of the new chapel. It was to be in April; the Archbishop himself would be there. And it might have been dedicated sooner, were it not for this incredible business of a choir loft with no means of access—unless it were a ladder.

"I told the Bishop," said Mother Magdalene, "that it would be a mistake to have the plans drawn in Paris. If something went wrong, what could we do? But he wanted our chapel in Santa Fe patterned after the Sainte Chapelle in Paris, and who am I to argue with Bishop Lamy? So the talented Monsieur Mouly designs a beautiful choir loft high up under the rose window, and no way to get to it."

"Perhaps," sighed Father Sebastian, "he had in mind a heavenly choir. The kind with wings."

"It's not funny," said Mother Magdalene a bit sharply. "I've prayed and prayed, but apparently there's no solution at all. There just isn't room on the chapel floor for the supports such a staircase needs."

The days passed, and with each passing day Christmas drew closer. Twice, horsemen on their way from Santa Fe to Albuquerque brought letters from Sister Francis Louise. All was well at the convent, but Mother Magdalene frowned over certain paragraphs. "The children are getting ready for Christmas," Sister Francis Louise wrote in her first letter. "Our little Manuela and the carpenter have become great friends. It's amazing how much he seems to know about us all..."

And what, thought Mother Magdalene, is the carpenter still doing there?

The second letter also mentioned the carpenter. "Early every morning he comes with another load of lumber, and every night he goes away. When we ask him by what authority he does these things, he smiles and says nothing. We have tried to pay him for his work, but he will accept no pay..."

Work? What work? Mother Magdalene wrinkled up her nose in exasperation. Had that soft-hearted Sister Francis Louise given the man permission to putter around in the new chapel? With firm and disapproving hand, the Mother Superior wrote a note ordering an end to all such unauthorized activities. She gave it to an Indian pottery maker on his way to Santa Fe.

But that night the first snow fell, so thick and heavy that the Indian turned back. Next day at noon the sun shone again on a world glittering with diamonds. But Mother Magdalene knew that another snowfall might make it impossible for her to be home for Christmas. By now the sickness at Santo Domingo was subsiding. And so that afternoon they began the long ride back.

The snow did come again, making their slow progress even slower. It was late on Christmas Eve, close to midnight, when the tired horses plodded up to the convent door. But lamps still burned. Manuela flew down the steps, Sister Francis Louise close behind her. And chilled and weary though she was, Mother Magdalene sensed instantly an excitement, an electricity in the air that she could not understand.

Nor did she understand it when they led her, still in her heavy wraps, down the corridor, into the new, as-yet-unused chapel where a few candles burned. "Look, Reverend Mother," breathed Sister Francis Louise. "Look!"

Like a curl of smoke the staircase rose before them, as insubstantial as a dream. Its top rested against the choir loft. Nothing else supported it; it seemed to float on air. There were no banisters. Two complete spirals it made, the polished wood gleaming softly in the candlelight. "Thirty-three steps," whispered Sister Francis Louise. "One for each year in the life of Our Lord."

Mother Magdalene moved forward like a woman in a trance. She put her foot on the first step, then the second, then the third. There was not a tremor. She looked down, bewildered, at Manuela's ecstatic, upturned face. "But it's impossible! There wasn't time!"

"He finished yesterday," the Sister said. "He didn't come today. No one has seen him anywhere in Santa Fe. He's gone."

"But *who* was he? Don't you even know his *name?*"

The Sister shook her head, but now Manuela pushed forward, nodding emphatically. Her mouth opened; she took a deep, shuddering breath; she made a sound that was like a gasp in the stillness. The nuns stared at her, transfixed. She tried again. This time it was a syllable, followed by another. "Jo-sé." She clutched the Mother Superior's arm and repeated the first word she had ever spoken. "José!"

Sister Francis Louise crossed herself. Mother Magdalene felt her heart contract. José —the Spanish word for Joseph. Joseph the Carpenter. Joseph the Master Woodworker of…

"José!" Manuela's dark eyes were full of tears. "José!"

Silence, then, in the shadowy chapel. No one moved. Far away across the snow-silvered town Mother Magdalene heard a bell tolling midnight. She came down the stairs and took Manuela's hand. She felt uplifted by a great surge of wonder and gratitude and compassion and love. And she knew what it was. It was the spirit of Christmas. And it was upon them all.

AUTHOR'S NOTE: You may see the inexplicable staircase itself in Santa Fe today. It stands just as it stood when the chapel was dedicated over a hundred years ago—except for the banister, which was added later. Tourists stare and marvel. Architects shake their heads and murmur, "Impossible." No one knows the identity of the designer-builder. All the Sisters know is that the problem existed, a stranger came, solved it and left.

The 33 steps make two complete turns without central support. There are no nails in the staircase; only wooden pegs. The curved stringers are put together with exquisite precision; the wood is spliced in seven places on the inside and nice on the outside. The wood is said to be a hard-fir variety, nonexistent in New Mexico. School records show that no payment for the staircase was ever made.

Keeping Christmas

Henry Van Dyke

It is a good thing to observe Christmas day. The mere marking of times and seasons when men agree to stop work and make merry together is a wise and wholesome custom. It helps one to feel the supremacy of the common life over the individual life. It reminds a man to set his own little watch, now and then, by the great clock of humanity.

But there is a better thing than the observance of Christmas day, and that is, keeping Christmas.

Are you willing to forget what you have done for other people and to remember what other people have done for you; to ignore what the world owes you and to think what you owe the world; to put your rights in the background and your duties in the middle distance and your chances to do a little more than your duty in the foreground; to see that your fellow men are just as real as you are, and try to look behind their faces to their hearts, hungry for joy; to own that probably the only good reason for your existence is not what you are going to get out of life, but what you are going to give to life; to close your book of complaints against the management of the universe and look around you for a place where you can sow a few seeds of happiness—are you willing to do these things even for a day? Then you can keep Christmas.

Are you willing to stoop down and consider the needs and the desires of little children; to remember the weakness and loneliness of people who are growing old; to stop asking how much your friends love you and ask yourself whether you love them enough; to bear in mind the things that other people have to bear on their hearts; to try to understand what those who live in the same house with you really want, without waiting for them to tell you; to trim your lamp so that it will give more light and less smoke, and to carry it in front so that your shadow will fall behind you; to make a grave for your ugly thoughts and a garden for your kindly feelings, with the gate open—are you willing to do these things even for a day? Then you can keep Christmas.

Are you willing to believe that love is the strongest thing in the world— stronger than hate, stronger than evil, stronger than death—and that the blessed life which began in Bethlehem nineteen hundred years ago is the image and brightness of the Eternal Love? Then you can keep Christmas.

And if you keep it for a day, why not always?

But you can never keep it alone.

The Gift of
HOPE

The Fir Tree

Hans Christian Andersen

Out in the woods stood a nice little Fir Tree. The place he had was a very good one; the sun shone on him; as to fresh air, there was enough of that, and round him grew many large-sized comrades, pines as well as firs. But the little Fir wanted so very much to be a grown-up tree.

He did not think of the warm sun and of the fresh air; he did not care for the little cottage children that ran about and prattled when they were in the woods looking for wild strawberries. The children often came with a whole pitcherful of berries, or a long row of them threaded on a straw, and sat down near the young tree and said, "Oh, how pretty he is! What a nice little Fir!" But this was what the Tree could not bear to hear.

At the end of a year he had shot up a good deal, and after another year he was another long bit taller; for with fir trees one can always tell by the shoots how many years old they are.

"Oh, were I but such a high tree as the others are!" sighed he. "Then I should be able to spread out my branches and with the tops look into the wide world! Then would the birds build nests among my branches; and when there was a breeze I could bend with as much stateliness as the others!"

Neither the sunbeams, nor the birds, nor the red clouds which morning and evening sailed above him gave the little Tree any pleasure.

In winter, when the snow lay glittering on the ground, a hare would often come leaping along and jump right over the little Tree. Oh, that made him so angry! But two winters were past, and in the third the Tree was so large that the hare was obliged to go round it. "To grow and grow, to get older and be tall," thought the Tree. "That, after all, is the most delightful thing in the world!"

In autumn the woodcutters always came and felled some of the largest trees. This happened every year; and the young Fir Tree, that had now grown to a very comely size, trembled at the sight. For the magnificent great trees fell to the earth with noise and cracking, the branches were lopped off, and the trees looked long and bare—they were hardly to be recognized—and then they were laid in carts, and the horses dragged them out of the wood.

Where did they go to? What became of them?

In spring, when the Swallows and the Storks came, the Tree asked them, "Don't you know where they have been taken? Have you not met them anywhere?"

The Swallows did not know anything about it; but the Stork looked musing, nodded his head, and said, "Yes, I think I know. I met many ships as I was flying hither from Egypt. On the ships were magnificent masts, and I venture to assert that it was they that smelt so of fir. I may congratulate you, for they lifted themselves on high most majestically!"

"Oh, were I but old enough to fly across the sea! But how does the sea look in reality? What is it like?"

"That would take a long time to explain," said the Stork, and with these words off he went.

"Rejoice in thy growth!" said the Sunbeams. "Rejoice in thy vigorous growth and in the fresh life that moveth within thee!"

And the Wind kissed the Tree, and the Dew wept tears over him, but the Fir understood it not.

When Christmas came, quite young trees were cut down, trees which often were not even as large or of the same age as this Fir Tree who could never rest but always wanted to be off. These young trees—and they were always the finest-looking—retained their branches; they were laid on carts, and the horses drew them out of the wood.

"Where are they going to?" asked the Fir. "They are not taller than I. There was one indeed that was considerably shorter—and why do they retain all their branches? Whither are they taken?"

"We know! We know!" chirped the Sparrows. "We have peeped in at the windows in the town below! We know whither they are taken! The greatest splendor and the greatest magnificence one can imagine await them. We peeped through the windows and saw them planted in the middle of the warm room, and ornamented with the most splendid things—with gilded apples, with gingerbread, with toys and many hundred lights!"

"And then?" asked the Fir Tree, trembling in every bough. "And then? What happens then?"

"We did not see anything more. It was incomparably beautiful."

"I would fain know if I am destined for so glorious a career," cried the Tree, rejoicing. "That is still better than to cross the sea! What a longing do I suffer! Were Christmas but come! I am now tall, and my branches spread like the others that were carried off last year! Oh, were I but already on the cart! Were I in the warm room with all the splendor and magnificence! Yes; then something better, something still grander will surely follow, or wherefore should they thus ornament me? Something better, something still grander *must* follow—but what? Oh, how I long, how I suffer! I do not know myself what is the matter with me!"

"Rejoice in our presence!" said the Air and the Sunlight. "Rejoice in thy own fresh youth!"

But the Tree did not rejoice at all. He grew and grew, and was green both winter and summer. People who saw him said, "What a fine tree!" and toward Christmas he was one of the first that was cut down. The ax stuck deep into the very pith; the tree fell to the earth with a sigh. He felt a pang— it was like a swoon; he could not think of happiness, for he was sorrowful at being separated from his home, from the place where he had sprung up. He well knew that he should never see his dear old comrades, the little bushes and flowers around him, anymore, perhaps not even the birds! The departure was not at all agreeable.

The Tree only came to himself when he was unloaded in a courtyard with other trees, and heard a man say, "That one is splendid. We don't want the others." Then two servants came in rich livery and carried the Fir Tree into a large and splendid drawing room. Portraits were hanging on the walls, and near the white porcelain stove stood two large Chinese vases with lions on the covers. There, too, were large easy chairs, silken sofas, large tables full of picture books and full of toys worth hundreds and hundreds of crowns—at least the children said so. And the Fir Tree was stuck upright in a cask that was filled with sand; but no one could see that it was a cask, for green cloth was hung all around it, and it stood on a large, gaily colored carpet. Oh, how the Tree quivered! What was to happen? The servants as well as the young ladies decorated it. On one branch there hung little nets cut out of colored paper, and each net was filled with sugarplums; and among the other boughs gilded apples and walnuts were suspended, looking as though they had grown there, and little blue and white tapers were placed among the leaves. Dolls that looked for all the world like men—the Tree had never beheld such before—were seen among the foliage, and at the very top a large star of gold tinsel was fixed. It was really splendid—beyond description splendid.

"This evening!" said they all. "How it will shine this evening!"

"Oh," thought the Tree, "if the evening were but come! If the tapers were but lighted! And then I wonder what will happen! Perhaps the other trees from the forest will come to look at me! Perhaps the Sparrows will beat against the windowpanes! I wonder if I shall take root here and winter and summer stand covered with ornaments!"

He knew very much about the matter! But he was so impatient that for sheer longing he got a pain in his back, and this with trees is the same thing as a headache with us.

The candles were now lighted. What brightness! What splendor! The Tree trembled so in every bough that one of the tapers set fire to the foliage. It blazed up splendidly.

"Help! help!" cried the young ladies, and they quickly put out the fire.

Now the Tree did not even dare tremble. What a state he was in! He was so uneasy lest he should lose something of his splendor that he was quite bewildered amid the glare and brightness, when suddenly both folding doors opened and a troop of children rushed in as if they would upset the Tree. The older persons followed quietly; the little ones stood quite still. But it was only for a moment; then they shouted so that the whole place re-echoed with their rejoicing. They danced round the Tree, and one present after the other was pulled off.

"What are they about?" thought the Tree. "What is to happen now?" And the lights burned down to the very branches, and as they burned down they were put out one after the other, and then the children had permission to plunder the Tree. So they fell upon it with such violence that all its branches cracked. If it had not been fixed firmly in the cask it would certainly have tumbled down.

The children danced about with their beautiful playthings. No one looked at the Tree except the old nurse, who peeped between the branches; but it was only to see if there was a fig or an apple left that had been forgotten.

"A story! A story!" cried the children, drawing a little fat man toward the Tree. He seated himself under it and said, "Now we are in the shade, and the Tree can listen too. But I shall tell only one story. Now which will you have: that about Ivedy-Avedy, or about Klumpy-Dumpy who tumbled downstairs, and yet after all came to the throne and married the princess?"

"Ivedy-Avedy," cried some. "Klumpy-Dumpy," cried the others. There was such a bawling and screaming. The Fir Tree alone was silent, and he thought to himself, "Am I not to bawl with the rest—am I to do nothing whatever?" for he was one of the company and had done what he had to do.

And the man told about Klumpy-Dumpy that tumbled down, who notwithstanding came to the throne and at last married the princess. And the children clapped their hands and cried out, "Oh, go on! Do go on!" They wanted to hear about Ivedy-Avedy, too, but the little man only told them about Klumpy-Dumpy. The Fir Tree stood quite still and absorbed in thought; the birds in the wood had never related the like of this. "Klumpy-Dumpy fell downstairs, and yet he married the princess! Yes, yes! That's the way of the world!" thought the Fir Tree, and believed it all, because the man who told the story was so good-looking. "Well, well! Who knows, perhaps I may fall downstairs, too, and get a princess as a wife!" And he looked forward with joy to the morrow, when he hoped to be decked out again with lights, playthings, fruits, and tinsel.

"I won't tremble tomorrow!" thought the Fir Tree. "I will enjoy to the full all my splendor! Tomorrow I shall hear again the story of Klumpy-Dumpy, and perhaps that of Ivedy-Avedy, too." And the whole night the Tree stood still in deep thought.

In the morning the servant and the housemaid came in.

"Now, then, the splendor will begin again," thought the Fir, but they dragged him out of the room, and up the stairs into the loft; and here in a dark corner, where no daylight could enter, they left him. "What's the meaning of this?" thought the Tree. "What am I to do here? What shall I hear now, I wonder?" And he leaned against the wall, lost in reverie. Time enough had he, too, for his reflections, for days and nights passed on, and nobody came up; and when at last somebody did come it was only to put some great trunks in a corner out of the way. There stood the Tree, quite hidden; it seemed as if he had been entirely forgotten.

"'Tis now winter out-of-doors!" thought the Tree. "The earth is hard and covered with snow. Men cannot plant me now, and therefore I have been put up here under shelter till the springtime comes! How thoughtful that is! How kind man is, after all! If it only were not so dark here and so terribly lonely! Not even a hare. And out in the woods it was so pleasant when the snow was on the ground, and the hare leaped by; yes, even when he jumped over me—but I did not like it then. It is really terribly lonely here!"

"Squeak! Squeak!" said a little Mouse, at the same moment peeping out of his hole. And then another little one came.

They snuffed about the Fir Tree and rustled among the branches.

"It is dreadfully cold," said the Mouse. "But for that it would be delightful here, old Fir, wouldn't it?"

"I am by no means old," said the Fir Tree. "There's many a one considerably older than I am."

"Where do you come from," asked the Mice, "and what can you do?" They were so extremely curious. "Tell us about the most beautiful spot on the earth. Have you never been there? Were you never in the larder where cheeses lie on the shelves and hams hang from above, where one dances about on tallow candles; that place where one enters lean and comes out again fat and portly?"

"I know no such place," said the Tree. "But I know the wood, where the sun shines, and where little birds sing." And then he told all about his youth; and the little Mice had never heard the like before; and they listened and said, "Well, to be sure! How much you have seen! How happy you must have been!"

"I!" said the Fir Tree, thinking over what he had himself related. "Yes, in reality those were happy times." And then he told about Christmas Eve, when he was decked out with cakes and candles.

"Oh," said the little Mice, "how fortunate you have been, old Fir Tree!"

"I am by no means old," said he. "I came from the wood this winter; I am in my prime, and am only rather short for my age."

"What delightful stories you know!" said the Mice, and the next night they came with four other little Mice, who were to hear what the Tree recounted. And the more he related, the more plainly he remembered all himself; and it appeared as if those times had really been happy times. "But they may still come—they may still come. Klumpy-Dumpy fell downstairs, and yet he got a princess!" And he thought at the moment of a nice little Birch Tree growing out in the wood; to the Fir that would be a real charming princess.

"Who is Klumpy-Dumpy?" asked the Mice. So then the Fir Tree told the whole fairy tale—for he could remember every single word of it—and the little Mice jumped for joy up to the very top of the Tree. Next night two more Mice came, and on Sunday two rats, even; but they said the stories were not interesting, which vexed the little Mice; and they, too, now began to think them not so very amusing, either.

"Do you know only one story?" asked the Rats.

"Only that one," answered the Tree. "I heard it on my happiest evening; but I did not then know how happy I was."

"It is a very stupid story! Don't you know one about bacon and tallow candles? Can't you tell any larder stories?"

"No," said the Tree.

"Then good bye," said the Rats, and they went home.

At last the little Mice stayed away also, and the Tree sighed. "After all, it was very pleasant when the sleek little Mice sat round me and listened to what I told them. Now that, too, is over. But I will take good care to enjoy myself when I am brought out again."

But when was that to be? Why, one morning there came a quantity of people and set to work in the loft. The trunks were moved, the Tree was pulled out and thrown—rather hard, it is true—down on the floor, but a man drew him toward the stairs, where the daylight shone.

"Now a merry life will begin again," thought the Tree. He felt the fresh air, the first sunbeam—and now he was out in the courtyard. All passed so quickly, there was so much going on around him, that the Tree quite forgot to look to himself. The court adjoined a garden, and all was in flower; the roses hung so fresh and odorous over the balustrade, the lindens were in blossom, the Swallows flew by and said, "Quirre-vit! My husband is come!" but it was not the Fir Tree that they meant.

"Now, then, I shall really enjoy life," said he, exultingly, and spread out his branches. But alas! They were all withered and yellow. It was in a corner that he lay, among weeds and nettles. The golden star of tinsel was still on the top of the Tree, and glittered in the sunshine.

In the courtyard some of the merry children were playing who had danced at Christmas round the Fir Tree and were so glad at the sight of him. One of the youngest ran and tore off the golden star.

"Only look what is still on the ugly old Christmas tree!" said he, trampling on the branches so that they all cracked beneath his feet.

And the Tree beheld all the beauty of the flowers and the freshness in the garden; he beheld himself and wished he had remained in his dark corner in the loft. He thought of his first youth in the wood, of the merry Christmas Eve, and of the little Mice who had listened with so much pleasure to the story of Klumpy-Dumpy.

"'Tis over! 'Tis past!" said the poor Tree. "Had I but rejoiced when I had reason to do so! But now 'tis past, 'tis past!"

And the gardener's boy chopped the Tree into small pieces—there was a whole heap lying there. The wood flamed up splendidly under the large brewing cauldron, and it sighed so deeply! Each sigh was like a shot.

The boys played about in the court, and the youngest wore the gold star on his breast which the Tree had had on the happiest evening of his life. However, that was over now—the Tree gone, the story at an end. All, all was over; every tale must end at last.

Merry Christmas

Stephen Leacock

From *Frenzied Fiction*

M y dear Young Friend," said Father Time, as he laid his hand gently upon my shoulder, "you are entirely wrong."

Then I looked up over my shoulder from the table at which I was sitting and I saw him.

But I had known, or felt, for at least the last half hour that he was standing somewhere near me.

You have had, I do not doubt, good reader, more than once that strange, uncanny feeling that there is someone unseen standing beside you—in a darkened room, let us say, with a dying fire, when the night has grown late, and the October wind sounds low outside, and when, through the thin curtain that we call Reality, the Unseen World starts for a moment clear upon our dreaming sense.

You *have* had it? Yes, I know you have. Never mind telling me about it. Stop. I don't want to hear about that strange presentiment you had the night your Aunt Eliza broke her leg. Don't let's bother with *your* experience. I want to tell mine.

"You are quite mistaken, my dear young friend," repeated Father Time, "quite wrong."

"*Young* friend?" I said, my mind, as one's mind is apt to in such a case, running to an unimportant detail. "Why do you call me young?"

"Your pardon," he answered gently—he had a gentle way with him, had Father Time, "the fault is in my failing eyes. I took you at first sight for something under a hundred."

"Under a hundred?" I expostulated. "Well, I should think so!"

"Your pardon again," said Time, "the fault is in my failing memory. I forgot. You seldom pass that nowadays, do you? Your life is very short of late."

I heard him breathe a wistful hollow sigh. Very ancient and dim he seemed as he stood beside me. But I did not turn to look upon him. I had no need to. I knew his form, in the inner and clearer sight of things, as well as every human being knows by innate instinct the Unseen face and form of Father Time.

I could hear him murmuring beside me—"Short—short, your life is short"—till the sound of it seemed to mingle with the measured ticking of a clock somewhere in the silent house.

Then I remembered what he had said.

"How do you know that I am wrong?" I asked. "And how can you tell what I was thinking?"

"You said it out loud," answered Father Time; "but it wouldn't have mattered, anyway. You said that Christmas was all played out and done with."

"Yes," I admitted, "that's what I said."

"And what makes you think that?" he questioned, stooping, so it seemed to me, still further over my shoulder.

"Why," I answered, "the trouble is this. I've been sitting here for hours, sitting till goodness only knows how far into the night, trying to think about something to write for a Christmas story. And it won't go. It can't be done—not in these awful days."

"A Christmas story?"

"Yes. You see, Father Time," I explained, glad with a foolish little vanity of my trade to be able to tell him something that I thought enlightening, "all the Christmas stuff—stories and jokes and pictures—is all done, you know, in October."

I thought it would have surprised him, but I was mistaken.

"Dear me!" he said, "not till October? What a rush! How well I remember in Ancient Egypt—as I think you call it—seeing them getting out their Christmas things, all cut in hieroglyphics, always two or three years ahead."

"Two or three years?" I exclaimed.

"Pooh," said Time, "that was nothing. Why in Babylon they used to get their Christmas jokes ready—all baked in clay—a whole Solar eclipse ahead of Christmas. They said, I think, that the public preferred them so."

"Egypt?" I said, "Babylon! But surely, Father Time, there was no Christmas in those days. I thought—"

"My dear boy," he interrupted gravely, "don't you know that there has always been Christmas?"

I was silent. Father Time had moved across the room and stood beside the fireplace, leaning on the mantel. The little wreaths of smoke from the fading fire seemed to mingle with his shadow outline.

"Well," he said presently, "what is it that is wrong with Christmas?"

"Why," I answered, "all the romance, the joy, the beauty of it has gone, crushed and killed by the greed of commerce and the horrors of war. I am not, as you thought I was, a hundred years old, but I can conjure up, as anybody can, a picture of Christmas in the good old days of a hundred years ago—the quaint old-fashioned houses, standing deep among the evergreens, with the light twinkling from the windows on the snow—the warmth and comfort within—the great fire roaring on the hearth—the merry guests grouped about its blaze and the little children with their eyes dancing in the Christmas firelight, waiting for Father Christmas in his fine mummery of red and white and cotton wool to hand the presents from the Yuletide tree. I can see it," I added, "as if it were yesterday."

"It was but yesterday," said Father Time, and his voice seemed to soften with the memory of bygone years. "I remember it well."

"Ah," I continued, "that was Christmas indeed. Give me back such days as those, with the old good cheer, the old stage coaches and the gabled inns and the warm red wine, the snap-dragon and the Christmas tree, and I'll believe again in Christmas, yes, in Father Christmas himself."

"Believe in him?" said Time, quietly. "You may well do that. He happens to be standing outside in the street at this moment."

"Outside?" I exclaimed. "Why won't he come in?"

"He's afraid to," said Father Time. "He's frightened and he daren't come in unless you ask him. May I call him in?"

I signified assent, and Father Time went to the window for a moment and beckoned into the darkened street. Then I heard footsteps, clumsy and hesitant they seemed, upon the stairway. And in a moment a figure stood framed in the doorway—the figure of Father Christmas. He stood shuffling his feet, a timid, apologetic look upon his face.

How changed he was!

I had known in my mind's eye, from childhood up, the face and form of Father Christmas as well as that of Old Time himself. Everybody knows, or once knew him—a jolly little rounded man, with a great muffler wound about him, a packet of toys upon his back and with such merry, twinkling eyes and rosy cheeks as are only given by the touch of the driving snow and the rude fun of the North Wind. Why, there was once a time, not yet so long ago, when the very sound of his sleigh bells sent the blood running warm to the heart.

But now, how changed.

All draggled with the mud and rain he stood, as if no house had sheltered him these three years past. His old red jersey was tattered in a dozen places, his muffler frayed and raveled.

The bundle of toys that he dragged with him in a net seemed wet and worn till the cardboard boxes gaped asunder. There were boxes among them, I vow, that he must have been carrying these three years past.

But most of all I noted the change that had come over the face of Father Christmas. The old brave look of cheery confidence was gone. The smile that had beamed responsive to the laughing eyes of countless children around unnumbered Christmas trees was there no more. And in the place of it there showed a look of timid apology, of apprehensiveness, as of one who has asked in vain the warmth and shelter of a human home—such a look as the harsh cruelty of this world has stamped upon the face of its outcasts.

So stood Father Christmas shuffling upon the threshold, fumbling his poor tattered hat in his hand.

"Shall I come in?" he said, his eyes appealingly on Father Time.

"Come," said Time; and added, as he turned to speak to me, "Your room is dark. Turn up the lights. He's used to light, bright light and plenty of it. The dark has frightened him these three years past."

I turned up the lights and the bright glare revealed all the more cruelly the tattered figure before us.

Father Christmas advanced a timid step across the floor. Then he paused, as if in sudden fear.

"Is this floor mined?" he said.

"No, no," said Time soothingly. And to me he added in a murmured whisper—"He's afraid. He was blown up in a mine in No Man's Land between the trenches at Christmastime in 1914. It broke his nerve."

"May I put my toys on that machine gun?" asked Father Christmas timidly. "It will help to keep them dry."

"It is not a machine gun," said Time gently. "See, it is only a pile of books upon the sofa." And to me he whispered: "They turned a machine gun on him in the streets of Warsaw. He thinks he sees them everywhere since then."

"It's all right, Father Christmas," I said, speaking as cheerily as I could, while I rose and stirred the fire into a blaze. "There are no machine guns here and there are no mines. This is but the house of a poor writer."

"Ah," said Father Christmas, lowering his tattered hat still further and attempting something of a humble bow. "A writer? Are you Hans Andersen, perhaps?"

"Not quite," I answered.

"But a great writer, I do not doubt," said the old man, with a humble courtesy that he had learned, it may well be, centuries ago in the Yuletide season of his northern home. "The world owes much to its great books. I carry some of the greatest with me always. I have them here."

He began fumbling among the limp and tattered packages that he carried—"Look! *The House that Jack Built*—a marvelous, deep thing, sir— and this, *The Babes in the Wood*. Will you take it, sir? A poor present, but a present still—not so long ago I gave them in thousands every Christmastime. None seem to want them now."

He looked appealingly toward Father Time, as the weak may look toward the strong, for help and guidance.

"None want them now," he repeated, and I could see the tears start in his eyes. "Why is it so? Has the world forgotten its sympathy with the lost children wandering in the wood?"

"All the world," I heard Time murmur with a sigh, "is wandering in the wood." But out loud he spoke to Father Christmas in cheery admonition: "Tut, tut, good Christmas," he said, "you must cheer up. Here, sit in this chair—the biggest one—so—beside the fire—let us stir it to a blaze—more wood—that's better—and listen, good old Friend, to the wind outside— almost a Christmas wind, is it not? Merry and boisterous enough, for all the evil times it stirs among."

Old Christmas seated himself beside the fire, his hands outstretched toward the flames. Something of his old-time cheeriness seemed to flicker across his features as he warmed himself at the blaze.

"That's better," he murmured. "I was cold, sir, cold, chilled to the bone. Of old I never felt it so; no matter what the wind, the world seemed warm about me. Why is it not so now?"

"You see," said Time, speaking low in a whisper for my ear alone, "you see how sunk and broken he is? Will you not help?"

"Gladly," I answered, "if I can."

"All can," said Father Time. "Every one of us."

In the meantime, Christmas had turned toward me a questioning eye, in which, there seemed to revive some little gleam of merriment.

"Have you, perhaps," he asked half timidly, "schnapps?"

"Schnapps?" I repeated.

"Aye, schnapps. A glass of it to drink to your health might warm my heart again, I think."

"Ah!" I said. "Something to drink?"

"His one failing," whispered Time, "if it is one. Forgive it him. He was used to it for centuries. Give it to him if you have it."

"I keep a little in the house," I said, reluctantly perhaps, "in case of illness."

"Tut, tut," said Father Time, as something as near as could be to a smile passed over his shadowy face. "In case of illness? They used to say that in ancient Babylon. Here, let me pour it for him. Drink, Father Christmas, drink!"

Marvelous it was to see the old man smack his lips as he drank his glass of liquor neat after the fashion of old Norway.

Marvelous, too, to see the way in which, with the warmth of the fire and the generous glow of the spirits, his face changed and brightened till the old-time cheerfulness beamed again upon it.

He looked about him, as it were, with a new and growing interest.

"A pleasant room," he said, "and what better, sir, than the wind without and a brave fire within!"

Then his eye fell upon the mantel piece, where lay among the litter of books and pipes a little toy horse.

"Ah!" said Father Christmas, almost gaily. "Children in the house!"

"One," I answered. "The sweetest boy in all the world."

"I'll be bound he is!" said Father Christmas, and he broke now into a merry laugh that did one's heart good to hear. "They all are! Lord bless me! The number that I have seen, and each and every one—and quite right, too—the sweetest child in all the world. And how old, do you say? Two and a half all but two months except a week? The very sweetest age of all, I'll bet you say, eh, what? They all do!"

And the old man broke again into such a jolly chuckling of laughter that his snow-white locks shook upon his head.

"But stop a bit," he added. "This horse is broken—tut, tut,—a hind leg nearly off. This won't do!"

He had the toy in his lap in a moment, mending it. It was wonderful to see, for all his age, how deft his fingers were.

"Time," he said, and it was amusing to note that his voice had assumed almost an authoritative tone, "reach me that piece of string. That's right. Here, hold your finger across the knot. There! Now, then, a bit of bee's wax.

What? No bee's wax? Tut, tut, how ill-supplied your houses are today. How can you mend toys, sir, without bee's wax? Still, it will stand up now."

I tried to murmur my best thanks.

But Father Christmas waved my gratitude aside.

"Nonsense," he said. "That's nothing. That's my life. Perhaps the little boy would like a book too. I have them here in the packet. Here, sir, *Jack and the Bean Stalk*, a most profound thing. I read it to myself often still. How damp it is! Pray, sir, will you let me dry my books before your fire?"

"Only too willingly," I said. "How wet and torn they are!"

Father Christmas had risen from his chair and was fumbling among his tattered packages, taking from them his children's books, all limp and draggled from the rain and wind.

"All wet and torn!" he murmured, and his voice sank again into sadness. "I have carried them these three years past. Look! These were for little children in Belgium and in Serbia. Can I get them to them, think you?"

Time gently shook his head.

"But presently, perhaps!" said Father Christmas. "If I dry and mend them. Look, some of them were inscribed already! This one, see you, was written *'With father's love.'* Why has it never come to him? Is it rain or tears upon the page?"

He stood bowed over his little books, his hands trembling as he turned the pages. Then he looked up, the old fear upon his face again.

"That sound!" he said. "Listen! It is guns—I hear them!"

"No, no," I said, "it is nothing. Only a car passing in the street below."

"Listen," he said. "Hear that again—voices crying!"

"No, no," I answered, "not voices, only the night wind among the trees."

"My children's voices!" he exclaimed. "I hear them everywhere—they come to me in every wind—and I see them as I wander in the night and storm—my children—torn and dying in the trenches—beaten into the ground—I hear them crying from the hospitals—each one to me, still as I knew him once, a little child. Time, Time," he cried, reaching out his arms in appeal, "give me back my children!"

"They do not die in vain," Time murmured gently.

But Christmas only moaned in answer, "Give me back my children!"

Then he sank down upon his pile of books and toys, his head buried in his arms.

"You see," said Time, "his heart is breaking, and will you not help him if you can?"

"Only too gladly," I replied. "But what is there to do?"

"This," said Father Time, "listen."

He stood before me grave and solemn, a shadowy figure but half seen though he was close beside me. The firelight had died down, and through the curtained windows there came already the first dim brightening of dawn.

"The world that once you knew," said Father Time, "seems broken and destroyed about you. You must not let them know—the children. The cruelty and horror and the hate that racks the world today—keep it from them. Someday *he* will know—" here Time pointed to the prostrate form of Father Christmas—"that his children, that once were, have not died in vain; that from their sacrifice shall come a nobler, better world for all to live in, a world where countless happy children shall hold bright their memory forever. But for the children of today, save and spare them all you can from the evil hate and horror of the war. Later they will know and understand. Not yet. Give them back their Merry Christmas and its kind thoughts, and its Christmas charity, till later on there shall be with it again Peace upon Earth, Good Will toward Men."

His voice ceased. It seemed to vanish, as it were, in the sighing of the wind.

I looked up. Father Time and Christmas had vanished from the room. The fire was low and the day was breaking visibly outside.

"Let us begin," I murmured. "I will mend this broken horse."

Valley Forge
24 December 1777

F. Van Wyck Mason

C orporal Timothy Maddox of Smallwood's Maryland Cavalry, presently detailed to the Commander-in-Chief's bodyguard, stood disgustedly considering the armful of fir boughs he had dropped at the rear of the General's weather-beaten marquee. In evident disappointment Sergeant Hiram Toulmin considered the fruits of his corporal's labors.

"And is that all ye have to show for a half hour's rummagin'?"

"Yer cussed right," the Corporal grunted, retying the length of cotton cord serving him in place of a belt. "I had to get mighty 'cute to find as much. Only two days here and there ain't an evergreen within a mile o' here but's been stripped clean."

The Sergeant blew on grimy, reddish-blue fingers. "I believe ye, Maddox, but I'd been hopin' fer more. That much won't bank above five feet of the marquee. Wish to God we could come across some hay. The wind beats in cruel sharp under them canvas bottoms, and tonight bein' Christmas Eve His Excellency will be expectin' guests, no doubt."

"Even so," Maddox observed, "the General'd never let us use them boughs for banking, Christmas Eve or no Christmas Eve—not with a third o' the army settin' up all night around fires for lack o' beddin'."

Mechanically, Sergeant Toulmin's smoke-reddened eyes sought the camp-fires of the Blue Hen's Chickens—General Billy Maxwell's Delaware troops. In the fading yellow-gray sunset he could see that the smoke of their camp-fires veered ever more sharply away to the southwest. A veteran of White Plains and Brandywine, he noticed subconsciously that the fires they had built were too big and hot by far. Even now the huddled soldiers began to move away—roasted on one side and half frozen on the other.

Beyond the trampled fields to his right, Conway's and Huntington's ragged battalions were faring better. Quite a few rough huts had been near enough completed for occupancy, and a dogwood grove afforded them a measure of shelter.

Despite the plans of Colonel Duportail, that competent if irascible Frenchman, for a permanent arrangement, there was no order about the way in which the campfires had been kindled; dozens upon dozens of them glowed within easy eyeshot, and farther across the weed-tufted expanse of meadows more fires winked and blinked. These marked the camp's outer line of defenses.

The snowy ground between the General's marquee and the outer defenses had, during the day, become heavily criss-crossed by caisson and forage wagon wheels, splashed with dark groups of horse droppings, and trampled by the feet of nearly nine thousand men.

A gust of wind stirred sere brown leaves clinging doggedly to the branches of some oaks growing between the temporary headquarters and an old schoolhouse standing at the intersection of Gulph and Baptist roads.

The Corporal sniffed a clear drop back into his nose. "Lay you two to one, Sergeant, if that blasted wind holds out o' the northeast we'll get a three-day blizzard. As if we ain't been nipped raw already."

"Don't want an easy bet, do ye?" Though his effort was hardly more than a gesture, Sergeant Toulmin knelt, commenced carefully to arrange the fir boughs along the base of the marquee's windward side. So few branches would not go very far toward dispelling the frost-laden wind now beginning to dislodge remnants of old snow from the tops of tall oaks.

Plague take it! Why did the General persist in being so careless of his own comfort? Why, Generals Varnum, Wayne, Patterson, and even tough old Teufel Piet Muhlenberg had long since ensconced themselves, more or less comfortably, in various sturdy stone or wood farmhouses of the neighborhood. Lord, how the General's aide, Major Alexander Hamilton, had cursed—out of his superior's earshot—when the General had refused courteously but firmly to occupy Mrs. Deborah Hewes's well-constructed mansion. Under no conditions, the General had declared, would he occupy a comfortable billet while his rank and file chattered their teeth in this uncommonly bitter December air.

The Corporal's attention became attracted by a flight of belated crows flapping along in a ragged formation. Above them heavy whitish-gray clouds were commencing to scud furiously across the darkening sky. A regimental clerk appeared at the marquee's flap. He was rubbing ink-stained fingers in an effort to warm them and ended by tucking them under his armpits.

"Maddox! Why in Tunket you loafin' out here? Yer wanted—take a message to Weedon's command."

The Corporal's sharp young features contracted. Weedon? Weedon's brigade was camped about as far as it was possible to go within the new encampment—a generous two miles away. Well, maybe he could warm himself there—the Virginians had been putting the finishing touches on the huts they had built so quickly and according to specification. Old soldiers, they were mighty handy at contriving shelters, didn't stand helplessly about like the city men of Lachlan McIntosh or Knox's Artillery.

The Corporal began making his way toward a side entrance of the marquee. A faint and querulous outcry drew his attention to an attenuated V of Canada geese fleeing on rhythmically beating wings before what must certainly be an oncoming storm.

At this familiar discordant music from the sky Tim Maddox's eyes filled, so poignant was the reminder of his home at the mouth of the Patuxent. Why, only a year ago this very Christmas Eve he, Brother John and Billy Stumpp had conducted a mighty successful hunt for just such mighty honkers.

Even inside the marquee, and out of the rising wind, it remained perishingly cold. The chief clerk was still writing, so Maddox seized the opportunity to blow his nose on the dull blue cuff of his stained gray uniform. Those pewter buttons which once had decorated its revers long since had been lost and so did not scratch his nose. Mechanically, the Corporal's stiff red fingers tugged his tunic into a few less wrinkles. He then kicked his feet together, but gently, because the sole of his right shoe was held in precarious security by only two or three oaken pegs and the good Lord knew he didn't want to get his feet full of snow. Of course they had been wet and aching for time out of mind, but still the stout wool of his socks lent a considerable protection.

From beyond a canvas partition separating the orderly room from the rest of the tent rose a deep voice which, somehow, always started a tremor tumbling the length of Tim Maddox's spine.

"You must try to be patient, Wayne. For the moment nothing more can be done than has been done. All this week I have written to every imaginable authority, begging and imploring assistance."

"Then, sir, can we expect no supplies for certain?" Major-General Anthony Wayne's voice was hoarse as the rasping of a grindstone against a sword blade.

"Nothing, I fear, within five days."

"Five days!" The Pennsylvanian exploded. "God in heaven! The army will long since have mutinied and dispersed."

Maddox heard the Commander-in-Chief fetch a slow sigh, indescribably descriptive of fatigue. "You are convinced there is danger of mutiny?"

"As surely as I stand on this spot!" came the immediate reply. "What else can be in the minds of men so betrayed, so victimized by the petty jealousies and greeds of Congress?"

At the far end of the marquee beyond the General's quarters rose angry voices. Maddox recognized them as belonging to various commanding officers.

They were lodging complaints and making requisitions which were bound to prove fruitless. The voices grew more strident. One rose above the rest. "'Fore God we've had no meat in five days, no flour for two! Half of my third platoon wear women's clothes! You don't believe that?" The speaker's accents were shaking with fury. "Then I'll show you. Send in Private Hacker."

Tim Maddox couldn't help peeking around the canvas door in time to behold the shambling entrance of a sunken-eyed, unshaven fellow. He came to an uneasy halt in the midst of a semicircle of red-faced officers. He wore but a single boot; his other foot being clumsily swathed in what looked like a length of lace-edged window curtain. The wrapping was foul, stained with mud and horse manure. Just above his ankle glowed a damp red spot. Private Hacker's breeches hung in tatters, and beneath filthy crossbelts supporting his cartridge box and bayonet was wound a woman's bright-red woolen petticoat.

Because he had no sleeves the soldier's arms remained hidden and useless beneath the folds of the petticoat. About his gaunt neck had been twisted an indescribably ragged and worn gray woolen stocking. A woman's dark-green calash hat was set on the back of the soldier's head.

"And this, gentlemen," the fierce-eyed Colonel was snapping, "is one of the more warmly dressed of my third platoon." The Colonel, his ear bleeding from an old frostbite, made a derisive gesture. "I give you Private Hacker, sirs, as a Christmas present from our beloved and patriotic Congressmen!"

"What purpose to continue?" A heavy-set major in a patched and blood-stained gray watch cloak turned bitterly aside. "Have we not done all we can? During two long years we have fought the good fight and there remains no strength in us. Tomorrow I resign…"

"And I, too, will send in my commission." The speaker wore the remains of a blue Delaware uniform. "My men are dying of the cold. There is nothing— no straw, no hay, not even fir boughs for them to lie on, let alone blankets."

A hard-pressed commissary officer spread plump hands in despair. "Gentlemen, gentlemen! Would to God I were a magician and could conjure you blankets, uniforms, and provisions out of grass and leaves, but I assure you I am not."

The officers departed sullenly silent or in harsh and bitter complaint. Sulphurous were the curses they laid on Congress and the hopeless inefficiency of the Transport Corps. Mightily depressed, Corporal Maddox returned his attention to the chief clerk. He was barely in time, for that harassed individual was holding out a square of paper sealed with a pale-blue wafer.

"For Brigadier-General George Weedon." He coughed. "Urgent: Shake your butt getting there, Corporal."

Outside, the wind tore at a man like harpy's claws, so Maddox halted long enough to tie a battered tricorn onto his head with the bright of a three-yard-long muffler. Right now he wouldn't have taken ten pounds of gold for that length of warm green wool.

The sun had almost disappeared but still managed to gild the tops of some hardwood trees towering above the General's marquee. Here and there it sketched bright streaks along the barrels of the guns in a park of artillery arranged along the edge of that great field which would, at a later date, become known as the Grand Parade.

Every few rods Maddox encountered little groups of soldiers stumping along, their heads tilted against the rising wind. Most were lugging armfuls of fagots, but quite a few were engaged in hauling hewn and notched lengths of log toward a row of huts rising among the stark black dogwood trees in back of Woodford's Virginia Continentals. Because during the day the snow had become trampled and hard-packed their progress was not too painful.

All the same, Tim Maddox proceeded gingerly because of his bad shoe. In all directions he discerned knots of soldiers in every manner of garb, sitting on logs, crouched shoulder to shoulder about smoky green wood campfires attempting to cook whatever scraps of food they had been able to discover.

High in the darkening heavens a faint, sibilant singing sound had made itself noticeable. Corporal Maddox recognized the phenomenon at once. Frost—snow, and lots of it, would soon start falling.

The snow beneath his feet commenced to creak—another bad sign. And to think that once, long, comfortable years ago, he, his brothers and sisters had prayed for snow on Christmas Eve!

The wind continued to increase, lashing pitilessly at rows of ribby nags tethered, forlorn and miserable, to the artillery picket lines. Gradually, the beasts were shifting to present their rumps to the impending blizzard. The darker it grew, the more effectively did fires tint the snow a pretty rose red and cast into silhouette the miserable artillerists.

While plodding on across a field tenanted by empty and abandoned baggage wagons the courier came upon three scarecrow figures. They were from Stirling's *New York Levies.* Their capes fluttering like a bird's broken wings, two of them bent over a third who lay motionless and inert across the ruts of mud created by the passage of some heavy caisson.

"Come on, Hans," one of them was pleading. "'Tain't much further to them fires—not above two hundred yard. Ye can do it, Hans. Then ye'll be nice and warm and maybe, because it's Christmas Eve, they'll give us some-thin' to eat."

The other shook the prostrate man's shoulder. "Hans," he cried, "rouse up. You can't lie here like this; ye'll freeze, sure fire. Hans, ain't you and me come all the way from Staten Island? We come all that distance, we can make another… Oh, blazes, it ain't above a hundred yards." But the man lying face downward in the snow only groaned.

Maddox saw why the soldier, Hans, was unable to rise. The soles of his naked feet had degenerated into a pulpy mass of mud, torn flesh, and sticky blood.

"You'll never get him up," he predicted. "Suppose you fellers take his shoulders and I'll lug his feet."

The New Yorkers looked up, hollow eyes ringed in numb surprise.

"What for you helpin' us? You ain't New York. What outfit are you from anyway?"

"Smallwood's Maryland Cavalry," Maddox announced in conscious pride.

"Shucks! Thought all you fancy Nancys had traipsed off south." The larger of the New Yorkers blew his nose with his fingers.

"They were ordered away. I'm a courier at Headquarters."

The smaller New Yorker's lip curled. "Oh, one of them fat cats? Good to know somebody gets something t' eat around here, eh, Job?"

A sharp resentment heated in Maddox's features, but he controlled him-self. "Come on, if you want me to help you. I've got a message to deliver."

The weight they lifted was slight, for the man Hans was hardly a man, but a boy roughly Maddox's own age—nineteen. Pretty soon they came up to a sagging tent marked Medical Service. Already it was jam packed, but they slid the semi-conscious Hans in on top of a fellow who looked more dead than alive.

"Thanks," was all the two soldiers said, but Maddox didn't expect any more. They were New Yorkers from whom none but a fool would have looked for any politeness.

Pretty soon Corporal Maddox reached the outer cantonments of Anthony Wayne's burly Pennsylvanians and, as he had fully expected, found them in considerably better case. There were enough sturdy German farmers among them to have built huts sufficient to shelter most of their number. In the next company street the courier slowed his pace.

Despite the wind and the penetrating chill, a group of Germans was engaged in dressing a small fir tree with whatever had come to hand. Brass buttons, bits of tarnished gold lace, lengths of soiled pink ribbon were being employed. A big-handed sergeant was, with great care, unraveling a worn-out red stocking. Another was laboriously cutting six pointed stars out of bits of foolscap.

Yes, the Pennsylvanians were mighty lucky; they'd a stone jug warming beside their roaring campfire.

Corporal Maddox would have liked to linger at least until the lice, chilled and dormant in the seams of his clothing, felt impelled to start feeding, but Weedon's troops lay encamped a good mile farther on.

HANDS CLENCHED behind him, Major-General Anthony Wayne tramped angrily back and forth over broken leaves, dead grass, and melting snow marking the grimy canvas flooring of the Commander-in-Chief's compartment.

"Your Excellency," he was growling, "there is no longer any purpose in continuing this campaign. Is it not now entirely plain that the Congress has traduced and abandoned us? To disperse at once is our only recourse. Even so hundreds will perish—to delay will cost still more lives. I assure you, sir, our rank and file are utterly dispirited and the officers disgusted. Yesterday alone four regimental surgeons packed up and rode off—no attempt at a by-your-leave. Possibly in spring, sir, a new army can be assembled, but at present our situation is hopeless—quite hopeless."

The big Pennsylvanian seated himself momentarily on a corner of a map chest. The once-brilliant red revers of his uniform lapels and cuffs looked more than ever faded, worn, and weather-beaten.

General Washington for some instants remained silent, his wide mouth immobile, its lips compressed. At length he said, "All that you say is only too true, old friend, and you never were a faint-heart. To you I will confess that I, too, find myself at my wit's end. How can our people elect such contempt-ible, self-seeking poltroons and scoundrels to the Congress?"

The Commander-in-Chief's steel-gray eyes lowered themselves until they came to rest on a litter of papers crowding his field desk.

"I have said my say, Your Excellency." Wayne got stiffly to his feet, fixed a look of deep affection upon his chief. "Whatever is your decision I shall abide by it—to the full limit of my ability." Wayne pulled his triple cape tighter about him. "And now a more immediate matter. Pray indulge me if I protest against your refusal to move into Mrs. Hewes' residence. You, sir, constitute the very soul of this army. Without you it would have dispersed long since. Promise at least to sup with me—'tis the eve of Christmas, after all."

The Commander-in-Chief hesitated, half smiled. He felt sorely tempted. Throughout the Continental Service Anthony Wayne had been long renowned for setting an excellent mess even in the midst of the most miserable campaigns.

"I will attempt to indulge you—and myself, Anthony. You may rely on it. If possible, I will appear by eight of this evening, otherwise, pray do not wait upon my arrival."

Wayne drew himself up, bowed. "May I wish you a Merry Christmas, sir? Would to God there were some hope of fulfillment!"

"There will be other Christmases," the General reminded, but the words fell heavily from his lips as, with a tired gesture, he turned back to that mound of documents awaiting his attention.

He heard Wayne lift the canvas barrier, heard the rhythmic *slap-slap!* of the guard's hands on his piece as he presented arms. As seldom before, the General felt very alone. Light penetrating the canvas was feeble indeed— nearly as dim as the prospects of this half-born Republic.

Mechanically, the General's chilled knuckles rubbed at eyes grown hot and weary from sleeplessness. Practically speaking, what hope remained to an army in a like situation? Even lion-hearts like Nat Greene and Tony Wayne were convinced that the end had come. The weight of massive bullion epaulettes dragged at George Washington's shoulders and his big body sagged on a camp stool until the silvery clamor of wild geese in the sky attracted his attention.

The Potomac must be full of them by now. Christmas Eve! Slaves in the quarters behind his long white mansion would be making merry, crying "Christmas gift!" —war or no war. He slumped still more on his stool, absently watched the gray mist of his breath go drifting across the tent. How long since he had ridden his beloved acres? Years. Years. Years.

Christmas at Mount Vernon was a wonderful season—it meant the presence of family, friends, and neighbors; good wines, fires, candles, and lovely women in dazzling silks and brocades.

Grimly, the General surveyed his surroundings. Yonder, only half seen in the gloom, stood a battered chest containing a few clothes, his field desk, and a mud-splashed gray riding cape flung across his folding camp bed. Why must this go on and on? Secretly loving America at the bottom of his heart, Lord Howe undoubtedly would grant the most lenient of terms.

Suddenly the Commander-in-Chief sat erect, selected a sheet of foolscap, and commenced to write.

In Camp at Valley Forge
December ye 24, 1777
To the President of Congress

Sir:
Conscious of the Fruitlessness of further Contest with the Enemy and aware that my Army has been Abandoned to starvation and neglect by the various State Authorities and by the Congress itself, I have, sir, the Honour herewith to tender my resigna—

The quill ceased its busy scratching. A distant clamor was making itself heard. The General stiffened, listening intently. So Wayne *had* been well informed—already a mutiny was breaking out.

Hastily closing the clasps on his long gray watch cloak, General Washington donned a rabbit's fur cap he favored in cold weather and strode into the anteroom.

"The Sergeant of the Guard and two soldiers will accompany me; no more."

Gray cloak billowing to his long stride, the General strode across the anteroom and, fearful of what awaited him in the wind-filled twilight, set off in that direction from which the uproar was arising so rapidly that the three enlisted men at his heels were forced to adopt a sort of dog-trot to keep up.

A keen northeast wind smote him, groped beneath his cloak and uniform like a cold hand equipped with chill fingers. Soon it would be wholly dark, but very pale yellow streaks in the west still marked the last of the daylight. Christmas Eve had indeed commenced.

The tumult had died away; it sounded, however, as if it had originated somewhere among Major-General Henry Knox's artillery regiments. The Commander-in-Chief halted a moment, listening. As he did so he felt the first gentle impact of falling snowflakes.

"God help us," he muttered. "More snow." More snow, and already this year of 1777 had proved to be the bitterest, snowiest fall and winter within living memory!

Probably children in the streets of Philadelphia were laughing to see the myriad soft white flakes come fluttering, tumbling down to spell good coasting for new Christmas sleds. But to the Valley Forge encampment snow meant blocked roads, ever increasing misery around the campfires, more sick in the hospitals, and less hope of supplies.

"Aye, Mark, when it starts dry and fine like this 'tis going to snow hard." The Sergeant of the Guard began cursing softly, and turned up his greasy collar against the chill blasts.

Head bowed against the snowy wind, General Washington made his way toward the nearest ring of campfires and noted that some of the batteries had rigged tarpaulins horizontally between gun carriages and caissons, thus improvising tents under which they huddled. A card game was in progress in one with the players employing bits of biscuit for stakes. A gust of laughter arose when a player's chilled fingers accidentally faced a card and so lost him a big piece of crust.

This, then, was the clamor he had feared. Smiling thinly, the General continued his tour. If mutiny impended, he meant to prepare against it, and at once.

Nearing the outer lines of defenses, the tall, erect figure heard, of all things, someone singing, singing an old English Christmas carol. The caroler proved to be a surprisingly aged soldier wearing the tatters of a faded brown uniform; accompanying him was a corporal in a very unsoldierly Quaker hat and some gentleman's long-abandoned dress coat. The garment was of vivid canary-yellow brocade and glowed as if burnished by the campfire's light.

This squad must have something special cooking in the pot, for, unobservant of their visitors, they all kept an eye on it. Vaguely, the General wondered what their prize could be. A moment later he passed, abandoned on the fresh fallen snow, the skins and heads of a pair of striped house cats.

Someone recognized him, immediately sang out, "Here's the General! Three cheers for the Commander-in-Chief. Huzzah! Huzzah!"

The first light layer of snowflakes fell from their clothes as they struggled into a line and stood to attention.

A sergeant, his rag-clad feet flopping and spraying the snow up to his knees, strode forward, saluted awkwardly. "Sorry, sir, I—I can't turn out my platoon no better. Comes another year, sir, we'll turn out fit to make the Royal Tyrant's own guards look like rag-pickers."

"Bravely spoken, Sergeant, and I am sure you will. I am profoundly regretful," Washington said in his big clear Southern voice, "that on this holy eve, you and your platoon enjoy so few of the necessities." He tried to sound encouraging. "You may pass the word that I have made the firmest of representations to the Congress."

"Don't concern yourself over us, Gen'ral," a weak voice hailed from the farther corner of the campfire. "We made out before, sir, and by God we'll make out this time, too. Won't we, lads?"

From the bed of a rickety farm wagon appeared two or three tousled heads. Feebly, they joined in the cheering.

"The sick?" General Washington inquired.

"No, sir," the Sergeant said uncomfortably. "It's only they ain't got no coats nor shirts so they're layin' together to keep warm." The Sergeant swayed a little.

"When did you last taste meat?" demanded the Commander-in-Chief; his brows, jutting in the falling snow, were catching a few fine flakes.

"Oh, not so long ago, sir."

"Answer me exactly, Sergeant."

"Why, sir, 'twere five, no, six days ago."

The snow fell thicker, and the wind commenced to rattle and toss the bare limbs of a hickory grove behind the caissons.

The General moved on. Sometimes he found the troops crouched like misshapen gnomes about the fires; they never even raised their heads. Their hats and backs gradually were becoming whitened. They looked, on occasion, like stumps in a burnt-over field.

A miserable company of Poor's command had built a roaring bonfire because their huts stood barely commenced.

Unrecognized here, General Washington circulated quietly. He noticed to one side a young man, a corporal by the green worsted knot on his shoulder, holding a cowhide knapsack on his knees and, of all things, attempting to write by the dancing firelight.

"May I obtrude on your privacy enough to inquire what prompts you to write on this cold and miserable evening?"

The boy, recognizing an officer, but not his identity, got up, his face pallid and worried-looking. "Why, why, sir, this being the eve of Christmas, I was thinking of home—and my parents."

"Your name and grade?"

"Corporal Richard Wheeler, sir, of Poor's New York Brigade."

"Your letter. I wish to inspect it."

The Corporal blinked eyes red and swollen from long exposure to acrid wood smoke. "Why, why, sir! I swear 'tis only a letter to my mother."

In response to the silent demand presented by the General's outstretched hand, Corporal Wheeler surrendered his rumpled bit of paper.

The General turned his back toward the flames in order to read:

December 24, 1777

Respected Madam,

This is to convey my Christmas love and duty to all at Home. I would not have you Credit certain unpatriotick Rumors concerning the true Situation of this Army. You need have no concern for we are very Comfortable, we are indeed living on the Fat of the Land—

The General swallowed hard and stared into the flying snow a moment before returning the letter. Then, to Corporal Wheeler's amazement this strange officer very gravely saluted him before stalking off into the wind-filled dark.

The next troops in position along the other perimeter of defenses proved to be Glover's Massachusetts brigade, a curious organization composed largely of fishermen and sailors which had proven itself useful under a hundred difficult circumstances. This particular half company was enjoying the music of a fiddle and the antics of a pair of gap-toothed and unshaven soldiers ridiculously attired in female garments. To a clapped accompaniment they were kicking up their heels in an old country dance. Subconsciously, the General wondered why this half company seemed extra gay. He beckoned a private, who by the half light also failed to recognize him.

"Why all this merriment? You would appear to have small cause for gaiety."

"Why, sir, have your forgot? This is Christmas Eve." The speaker winked, stepped closer. "Besides, us boys have stumbled on a bit of luck—monstrous good luck."

"Good luck?"

The bearded soldier slid an arm from under the woman's green shawl protecting his shoulders. "D'you mark yonder alder copse—and what's in it?"

The General shielded his eyes against hard-driven snowflakes, barely made out a large dark blur and a small one. "A horse, is it not, and a man on guard?"

"Aye, that's what they are, my friend. Just that."

"What is afoot?"

"Yonder stands a snot-nosed artillery-ist with a fixed bayonet."

The General raised his coat collar against the fine particles beginning to sift in.

"But why is he there, solider?"

"Like us, he's waiting for yonder old crowbait to fall." The speaker gave a great booming laugh and waved his arms. "So long as the nag stands, he belongs to dear General Knox's artillery, but once he falls and can't rise, he's ours, and then, my friend, we eat, by God! Ain't that cause for cheer?

"Hah! Did you mark how he swayed just then? Your pardon!" The speaker dashed off through the whirling snow.

Like winter wolves ringing a crippled moose, an irregular circle of hollow-eyed infantrymen moved to surround that little alder thicket in which stood the poor furry beast. So gaunt that every rib showed, the horse held its snow-powdered head so low that its loose nether lip almost brushed the ground. It began swaying more noticeably and heaving long, shuddering sighs.

Cursing, hurling obscenities at the gathering crowd, the lone artilleryman kept tramping back and forth, trying to keep warm. Why in hell wouldn't the miserable creature collapse? Satan alone knew where this wretched beast had found strength enough to wander thus far from its picket line. By this time what little there was to eat at his unit must have been consumed, which meant for him another long night on an empty belly.

On second thought, the sentry told himself he wouldn't go right back to his battery. He'd linger here and maybe share in the meat, for all it was certain to prove as tough and stringy as an old boot.

Once more the tall figure and his three followers moved on. The wind now was really roaring, and snow flying in fine particles like spume over the bow of a ship laboring through a storm. The Sergeant lengthened his stride, saluted anxiously.

"Begging the General's pardon, what with this storm worsening we're like to lose our way."

"Very well, but I will have a look at Learned's command on our route back to Headquarters."

The Rhode Islanders recognized their commander at once and ran to form a ragged double line in his honor, yelling all the while, "Long live Liberty!" "Long live the United States!" "Three cheers for the Commander-in-Chief!"

A lieutenant commanding the nearest platoon hurried up and saluted stiffly with his sword.

"Your Excellency, we... er... possess a trifle of Medford rum. We would deem ourselves mighty honored if you would give us your opinion of its worth. After all, sir, 'tis Christmas tomorrow." He beckoned forward a soldier who offered a steaming earthenware cup.

There was only a gallon jug among above two hundred rag-clad and blanket-wrapped Rhode Islanders. If each were lucky he might get a teaspoonful of the fiery spirit.

"Your health—fellow soldiers!" The General barely wet his lips, but made a great pretense of swallowing.

"Next Christmas," called a stumpy little soldier, "'twill *us* be eatin' roast goose in Philadelphia and the Lobster-backs settin' on their butts out in the cold."

"Perhaps. But have you not suffered enough?" the Commander inquired.

"It's been no bed of roses, sir," the Lieutenant said, "but having come this far we may as well go the rest of the distance. With you to lead us, we *can't* lose!"

The General was repassing Glover's position when there arose a wild yell, followed by delighted shouts of "Merry Christmas! Merry Christmas!"

"That poor skate must have fallen at last," grunted one of the body-guards. "Ain't they the lucky dogs?"

DURING THE GENERAL'S absence some holly branches and a larger amount of mistletoe had appeared and were being tied in place by Sergeant Toulmin. Fires had been built up at either end of the Headquarters marquee, and about them a motley assortment of junior officers, some of them French, stood warming their hands. Every now and then they shook themselves, dog-like, to rid their coats and cloaks of the whirling snow.

General Washington paused briefly, a thin smile curving his wide mouth.

"A good evening to you, Gentlemen. Pray seek your quarters and find what cheer you can. May God relieve your sufferings, if the Congress will not. A Merry Christmas to you all!"

Snow-powdered cape asway, the big Virginian turned, and reentered his compartment. His aide, darkly handsome young Major Alexander Hamilton, was working in obvious impatience between a pair of stump candles that drew brief flashes from his always well-polished buttons.

"Sir," he said, "General Wayne's compliments. He is dispatching a mount for your convenience at half after seven. He counts on you for supper."

Washington removed his cape and hung it carefully on its peg. "You will go in my place, Major," he announced. "I shall be too occupied with correspondence to take advantage of General Wayne's hospitality—much as I should enjoy it."

The young West Indian hesitated, his bold black eyes half closed. What was up? In arranging documents on the Commander-in-Chief's desk he had come across that incompleted letter to the President of Congress. General Washington's features, however, were enigmatic—and weary, oh, so weary.

"Do you wish to finish this... er... communication, sir?"

"Thank you. I will attend to it."

"There is nothing more, sir?"

"No, no, Major. Go and amuse yourself. You have earned the right."

Major Hamilton saluted and stepped outside, but lingered undecided until he was aware of a sudden flare of light beating through the canvas, a glow such as might be caused by a burning document.

The Rescue

* * * * * *

Cleveland Amory

From *The Cat Who Came for Christmas*

T o anyone who has ever been owned by a cat, it will come as no surprise
that there are all sorts of things about your cat you will never, as long
as you live, forget.

Not the least of these is your first sight of him or her.

That my first sight of mine, however, would ever be memorable seemed,
at the time, highly improbable. For one thing, I could hardly see him at all.
It was snowing, and he was standing some distance from me in a New York
City alley. For another thing, what I did see of him was extremely unprepos-
sessing. He was thin and he was dirty and he was hurt.

The irony is that everything around him, except him, was beautiful. It was
Christmas Eve, and although no one outside of New York would believe it on

a bet or a bible, New York City can, when it puts its mind to it, be beautiful. And that Christmas Eve some years ago was one of those times.

The snow was an important part of it—not just the snow, but the fact that it was still snowing, as it is supposed to but rarely does over Christmas. And the snow was beginning to blanket, as at least it does at first, a multitude of such everyday New York sins as dirt and noise and smells and potholes. Combined with this, the Christmas trees and lights and decorations inside the windows, all of which can often seem so ordinary in so many other places, seemed, in New York that night, with the snow outside, just right.

I am not going so far as to say that New York that night was O Little Town of Bethlehem, but it was at least something different from the kind of New York Christmas best exemplified by a famous Christmas card sent out by a New York garage that year to all its customers. "Merry Christmas from the boys at the garage," that card said. "Second Notice."

For all that, it was hardly going to be, for me, a Merry Christmas. I am no Scrooge, but I am a curmudgeon and the word *merry* is not in the vocabulary of any self-respecting curmudgeon you would care to meet—on Christmas or any other day. You would be better off with a New York cabdriver, or even a Yankee fan.

There were other reasons why that particular Christmas had little chance to be one of my favorites. The fact that it was after seven o'clock and that I was still at my desk spoke for itself. The anti-cruelty society which I had founded a few years before was suffering growing pains—frankly, it is still suffering them—but at that particular time, they were close to terminal. We were heavily involved in virtually every field of animal work, and although we were doing so on bare subsistence salaries—or on no salary at all for most of us—the society itself was barely subsisting. It had achieved some successes, but its major accomplishments were still in the future.

And so, to put it mildly, was coin of the realm. Even its name, The Fund for Animals, had turned out to be a disappointment. I had, in what I had thought of as a moment of high inspiration, chosen it because I was certain that it would, just by its mention, indicate we could use money. The name had, however, turned out not only not to do the job but to do just the opposite. Everybody thought that we already had the money.

Besides the Fund's exchequer being low that Christmas Eve, so was my own. My writing career, by which I had supported myself since before you were born, was far from booming. I was spending so much time getting the Fund off the ground that I was four years behind on a book deadline and so many months behind on two magazine articles that, having run out of all reasonable excuses, one of the things I had meant to do that day was to borrow a line from the late Dorothy Parker and tell the editor I had really tried to finish but someone had taken the pencil.

As for my personal life, that too left something to be desired. Recently divorced, I was living in a small apartment, and although I was hardly a hermit —I had a goodly choice of both office parties and even friends' parties to go to that evening—still, this was not going to be what Christmas is supposed to be. Christmas is, after all, not a business holiday or a friends' holiday, it is a family holiday. And my family, at that point, consisted of one beloved daughter who lived in Pittsburgh and had a perfectly good family of her own.

On top of it all, there was a final irony in the situation. Although I had had animals in my life for as far back as I could remember, and indeed had had them throughout my marriage—and although I was working on animal problems every day of my life—I had not a single creature to call my own. For an animal person, an animal-less home is no home at all. Furthermore, mine, I was sure, was fated to remain that way. I traveled on an average of more than two weeks a month, and was away from home almost as much as I was there. For me, an animal made even less sense than a wife. You do not, after all, have to walk a wife.

I HAD JUST TURNED from the pleasant task of watching the snow outside to the unpleasant one of surveying the bills when the doorbell rang. If there had been anyone else to answer it, I would have told them to say to whoever it was that we already gave at home. But there was no one, so I went myself.

The caller was a snow-covered woman whom I recognized as Ruth Dwork. I had known Miss Dwork for many years. A former schoolteacher, she is one of those people who, in every city, make the animal world go round. She is a rescuer and feeder of everything from dogs to pigeons and is a lifetime soldier in what I have called the Army of the Kind. She is, however, no private soldier in that army—she makes it to go round. In fact, I always called her Sergeant Dwork.

"Merry Christmas, Sergeant," I said. "What can I do you for?"

She was all business. "Where's Marian?" she asked. "I need her." Marian Probst, my longtime and longer-suffering assistant, is an experienced rescuer, and I know Miss Dwork had, by the very look of her, a rescue in progress. "Marian's gone," I told her. "She left about five-thirty, saying something about some people having Christmas Eve off. I told her she was a clock-watcher, but it didn't do any good."

Sergeant Dwork was unamused. "Well, what about Lia?" she demanded. Lia Albo is national coordinator of the Fund for Animals and an extremely expert rescuer. She, however, had left before Marian on—what else?—another rescue.

Miss Dwork was obviously unhappy about being down to me. "Well," she said, looking me over critically but trying to make the best of a bad bargain, "I need someone with long arms. Get your coat."

As I walked up the street with Sergeant Dwork, through the snow and biting cold, she explained that she had been trying to rescue a particular stray cat for almost a month, but that she had no success. She had, she said, tried everything. She had attempted to lure the cat into a Hav-a-Heart trap but, hungry as he was and successful as this method had been in countless other cases, it had not worked with this cat. He had simply refused to enter any enclosure that he could not see his way out of. Lately, she confessed, she had abandoned such subtleties for a more direct approach. And, although she had managed to get the cat to come close to the rail fence at the end of the alley, and even to take bite-sized chunks of cheese from her outstretched fingers, she had never been able to get him to come quite close enough so that she could catch him. When she tried, he would jump away, and then she had to start all over the each-time-ever-more-difficult task of trying again to win his trust.

However, the very night before, Sergeant Dwork informed me, she had come the closest she had ever come to capturing the cat. That time, she said, as he devoured the cheese, he had not jumped away but had stood just where he was—nearer than he had ever been but still maddeningly just out of reach. Good as this news was, the bad news was that Miss Dwork now felt that she was operating against a deadline. The cat had been staying in the basement of the apartment building, and the superintendent of the building had now received orders to get rid of it before Christmas or face the consequences. And now the other workers in the building, following their super's orders, had joined in the war against the cat. Miss Dwork herself had seen someone, on her very last visit, throw something at him and hit him.

WHEN WE ARRIVED at our destination, there were two alleyways. "He's in one or the other," Sergeant Dwork whispered. "You take that one, I'll take this." She disappeared to my left and I stood there, hunched in my coat with the snow falling, peering into the shaft of darkness and having, frankly, very little confidence in the whole plan.

The alley was a knife cut between two tall buildings filled with dim, dilapidated garbage cans, mounds of snowed-upon refuse, and a forbidding grate. And then, as I strained my eyes to see where, amongst all this dismal debris, the cat might be hiding, one of the mounds of refuse suddenly moved. It stretched and shivered and turned to regard me. I had found the cat.

As I said, that first sight was hardly memorable. He looked less like a real cat than like the ghost of a cat. Indeed, etched as he was against the whiteness of the snow all around him, he was so thin that he would have looked completely ghostlike, had it not been for how pathetically dirty he was. He was so dirty, in fact, that it was impossible even to guess as to what color he might originally have been.

When cats, even stray cats, allow themselves to get like that, it is usually a sign that they have given up. This cat, however, had not. He had not, even though, besides being dirty, he was wet and cold and he was hungry.

And, on top of everything else, you could tell by the kind of off-kilter way he was standing that his little body was severely hurt. There was something very wrong either with one of his back legs or perhaps with one of his hips. As for his mouth, that seemed strangely crooked, and he seemed to have a large cut across it.

But, as I said, he had not given up. Indeed, difficult as it must have been for him from that off-kilter position, he proceeded, while continuing to stare at me unwaveringly, to lift a front paw—and, snow or no snow, to lick it. Then the other front paw. And, when they had been attended to, the cat began the far more difficult feat of hoisting up, despite whatever it was that was amiss with his hips, first one back paw and then the other. Finally, after finishing, he did what seemed to me completely incredible—he performed an all-four-paw, ears-laid-back, straight-up leap. It looked to me as if he was, of all things in such a situation, practicing his pounce.

An odd image came to my mind—something, more years ago than I care to remember, that my first college tennis coach had drilled into our team about playing three-set matches. "In the third set," he used to say, "extra effort for ordinary results." We loathed the saying and we hated even more the fact that he made us, in that third set, just before receiving serve, jump vigorously up and down. He was convinced that this unwonted display would inform our opponents that we were fairly bursting with energy—whether that was indeed the fact or not. We did the jumping, of course, because we had to, but all of us were also convinced that we were the only players who ever had to do such a silly thing. Now when I see, without exception, every top tennis player in the world bouncing like cork into the third set, I feel like a pioneer and very much better about the whole thing.

And when I saw the cat doing his jumping, I felt better too—but this time, of course, about him. Maybe he was not as badly hurt as at first I had thought.

In a moment I noticed that Sergeant Dwork, moving quietly, had rejoined me. "Look at his mouth," she whispered. "I told you they have declared war on him!"

OURS WAS TO BE a war too—but one not against, but for, the cat. As Sergeant Dwork quietly imparted her battle plan, I had the uneasy feeling that she obviously regarded me as a raw recruit, and also that she was trying to keep my duties simple enough so that even a mere male could perform them. In any case, still whispering, she told me she would approach the fence with the cheese cubes, with which the cat was by now thoroughly familiar, in her outstretched hand, and that, during this period, I apparently should be crouching down behind her but nonetheless moving forward with her. Then, when she had gotten the cat to come as close as he would, she would step swiftly aside and I, having already thrust my arms above her through the vertical bars of the fence, was to drop to my knees and grab. The Sergeant was convinced that the cat was so hungry that, at that crucial moment, he would lose enough of his wariness to go for the bait—and the bite—which would seal his capture.

Slowly, with our eyes focused on our objective, we moved out and went over the top. And just as we did so, indeed as I was crouching into position behind Sergeant Dwork, I got for the first time a good look at the cat's eyes peering at us. They were the first beautiful thing I ever noticed about him. They were a soft and lovely radiant green.

As Sergeant Dwork went forward, she kept talking reassuringly to the cat, meanwhile pointedly removing the familiar cheese from her pocket and making sure he would be concentrating on it rather than the large something looming behind her. She did her job so well that we actually reached our battle station at almost the exact moment when the cat, still proceeding toward us, albeit increasingly warily, was close enough to take his first bite from the Sergeant's outstretched hand.

That first bite, however, offered us no chance of success. In one single incredibly quick but fluid motion, the cat grabbed the cheese, wolfed it down, and sprang back. Our second attempt resulted in exactly the same thing. Again the leap, the grab, the wolf, and the backward scoot. He was simply too adept at the game of eat and run.

By this time I was thoroughly convinced that nothing would come of the Sergeant's plan. But I was equally convinced that we had somehow to get that cat. I wanted to get over that fence and go for him.

The Sergeant, of course, would have none of such foolhardiness, and, irritated as this made me, I knew she was right. I could never have caught the cat that way. The Sergeant was, however, thinking of something else. Wordlessly she gave me the sign of how she was going to modify her tactics. This time she would offer the cat not one but two cubes of cheese—one in each of her two outstretched hands. But this time, she indicated, although she would push her right hand as far as it would go through the fence, she would keep her left hand well back. She obviously hoped that the cat would this time attempt both bites before the retreat. Once more we went over the top—literally in my case, because I already had my hands through the fence over the Sergeant. And this time, just as she had hoped, the cat not only took the first bite but also went for that second one. And, at just that moment, as he was mid-bite, Sergeant Dwork slid to one side and I dropped to my knees.

As my knees hit the ground, my face hit the grate. But I did not even feel it. For, in between my hands, my fingers underneath and my thumbs firmly on top, was cat. I had him.

Surprised and furious, he first hissed, then screamed, and finally, spinning off the ground to mid-air, raked both my hands with his claws. Again I felt nothing, because by then I was totally engrossed in a dual performance—not letting go of him and yet somehow managing to maneuver his skinny, desperately squirming body, still in my tight grasp, albeit for that split second in just one hand, through the narrow apertures of the rail fence. And now his thinness was all-important because, skin and bones as he was, I was able to pull him between the bars.

Still on my knees, I raised him up and tried to tuck him inside my coat. But in this maneuver I was either over-confident or under-alert, because somewhere between the raising and the tucking, still splitting fire, he got in one final rake of my face and neck. It was a good one.

As I struggled to my feet, Sergeant Dwork was clapping her hands in pleasure, but obviously felt the time had now come to rescue me. "Oh," she said. "Oh dear. Your face. Oh my." Standing there in the snow, she tried to mop me with her handkerchief. As she did so, I could feel the cat's little heart racing with fear as he struggled to get loose underneath my coat. But it was to no avail. I had him firmly corralled, and, once again, with both hands.

The Sergeant had now finished her mopping and became all Sergeant again. "I'll take him now," she said, advancing toward me. Involuntarily, I took a step backwards. "No, no, that's all right," I assured her. "I'll take him to my apartment." The Sergeant would have none of this. "Oh, no," she exclaimed. "Why, my apartment is very close." "So is mine," I replied, moving the cat even farther into the depths of my coat. "Really, it's no trouble at all. And anyway, it'll just be for tonight. Tomorrow, we'll decide—er, what to do with him."

Sergeant Dwork looked at me doubtfully as I started to move away. "Well then," she said, "I'll call you first thing in the morning." She waved a mittened hand. "Merry Christmas," she said. I wished her the same, but I couldn't wave back.

JOE, THE DOORMAN at my apartment building, was unhappy about my looks. "Mr. Amory!" he exclaimed. "What happened to your face? Are you all right?" I told him that not only was I all right, he ought to have seen the other guy. As he took me to the elevator, he was obviously curious about both the apparent fact that I had no hands and also the suspicious bulge inside my coat. Like all good New York City doormen, Joe is the soul of discretion—at least from tenant to tenant—but he has a bump of curiosity which would rival Mt. Everest. He is also, however, a good animal man, and he had a good idea that whatever I had, it was something alive. Leaning his head toward my coat, he attempted to reach in. "Let me pet it," he said. "No," I told him firmly. "Mustn't touch." "What is it?" he asked. "Don't tell anyone," I said, "but it's a saber-toothed tiger. Undeclawed, too." "Wow," he said. And then, just before the elevator took off, he told me that Marian was already upstairs.

I had figured that Marian would be there. My brother and his wife were coming over for a drink before we all went out to a party, and Marian, knowing I would probably be late, had arrived to admit them and hold, so to speak, the fort.

I kicked the apartment door. When Marian opened it, I blurted out the story of Sergeant Dwork and the rescue. She too wanted to know what had happened to my face and if I was all right. I tried the same joke I had tried on Joe. But Marian is a hard woman on old jokes. "The only 'other guy' I'm interested in," she said, "is in your coat." I bent down to release my prize, giving him a last hug to let him know that everything was now fine.

Neither Marian nor I saw anything. All we saw, before his paws ever hit the ground, was a dirty tan blur, which, crooked hips notwithstanding, literally flew around the apartment—seemingly a couple of feet off the ground and all the time looking frantically for an exit.

In the living room I had a modest Christmas tree. Granted, it was not a very big tree—he was not, at that time, a very big cat. Granted too, that this tree had a respectable pile of gaily wrapped packages around the base and even an animal figure attached to the top. Granted, even that it was festooned with lights, which, at rhythmic intervals, flashed on and off. To any cat, however, a tree is a tree and this tree, crazed as he was, was no exception. With one bound he cleared the boxes, flashed up through the branches, the lights, and the light cord and managed, somewhere near the top, to disappear again. "Now that's a good cat," I heard myself stupidly saying. "You don't have to be frightened. Nothing bad is going to happen to you here."

Walking toward the tree, I reached for where I thought he would be next, but it was no use. With one bound, he vanished down the far side and, flashing by my flailing arms, tried to climb up the inside of the fireplace. Fortunately the flue was closed, thus effectively foiling his attempt at doing a Santa Claus in reverse.

When he reappeared, noticeably dirtier than before, I was waiting for him. "Good boy," I crooned, trying to sound my most reasonable. But it was no use. He was gone again, this time on a rapid rampage through the bedroom—one which was in fact so rapid that not only was it better heard than seen but also, during the worst of it, both Marian and I were terrified that he might try to go through the window. When he finally materialized again in the hall, even he looked somewhat discouraged. Maybe, I thought desperately, I could reason with him now. Slowly I backed into the living room to get a piece of cheese from the hors d'oeuvre tray. This, I was sure, would inform him that he was among friends and that no harm would befall him. "He's gone," she said. "Gone," I said. "Gone where?" She shook her head and I suddenly realized that, for the first time in some time, there was no noise, there was no scurrying, there was no sound of any kind. There was, in fact, no cat.

We waited for a possible reappearance. When none was forthcoming, obviously we had no alternative but to start a systematic search. It is a comparatively small apartment and there are, or so Marian and I first believed, relatively few hiding places. We were wrong. For one thing, there was a wall-long bookshelf in the living room, and this we could not overlook, for the cat was so thin and so fast that it was eminently feasible that he found a way to clamber up and wedge himself behind a stack of books on almost any shelf. Book by book, we began opening holes.

But he was not here. Indeed, he was not anywhere. We turned out three closets. We moved the bed. We wrestled the sofa away from the wall. We looked under the tables. We canvassed the kitchen. And here, although it is such a small kitchen that it can barely accommodate two normal-sized adults at the same time, we opened every cupboard, shoved back the stove, peered into the microwave, and even poked about in the tiny space under the sink.

AT THAT MOMENT, the doorbell rang. Marian and I looked at each other—it had to be my brother and his wife, Mary. My brother is one of only three men who went into World War II as a private and came out as colonel in command of a combat division. He was, as a matter of fact, in the Amphibious Engineers, and made some fourteen opposed landings against the Japanese. He had also since served as deputy director of the CIA. A man obviously used to crises, he took one look at the disarray of the apartment. In such a situation, my brother doesn't talk, he barks. "Burglars," he barked. "It looks like a thorough job."

I explained to him briefly what was going on—and that the cat had now disappeared altogether. Not surprisingly, while Mary sat down, my brother immediately assumed command. He demanded to know where we had not looked. Only where he couldn't possibly go, I explained, trying to hold my ground. "I don't want theories," he barked. "Where *haven't* you looked?" Lamely, I named the very top shelves of the closet, the inside of the oven, and the dishwasher. "Right," he snapped, and advanced on first the closets, then the oven, and last the dishwasher. And, sure enough, at the bottom of the latter, actually curled around the machinery and wedged into the most impossible place to get to in the entire apartment, was the cat. "Ha!" said my brother, attempting to bend down and reach him.

I grabbed him from behind. I was not going to have my brother trust his luck with one more opposed landing. Bravely, I took his place. I was, after all, more expendable.

Actually, the fact was that none of us could get him out. And he was so far down in the machinery, even he couldn't get himself out. "Do you use it?" my brother demanded. I shook my head. "Dismantle it," he barked once more. Obediently, I searched for screwdriver, pliers, and hammer and, although I am not much of a mantler, I consider myself second to no one, not even my brother, as a dismantler. My progress, however, dissatisfied my brother. He brushed me aside and went over the top himself. I made no protest—with the dishwasher the Amphibious Engineer was, after all, at least close to being in his element.

When my brother had finished the job, all of us, Mary included, peered down at the cat. And, for the first time since my first sight of him in the alley, he peered back. He was so exhausted that he made no attempt to move, although he was now free to do so. "I would like to make a motion," Marian said quietly. "I move that we leave him right where he is, put out some food and water and a litter pan for him—and leave him be. What he needs now is peace and quiet."

The motion carried. We left out three bowls—of water, of milk, and of food—turned out all the lights, including the Christmas lights, and left him.

That night, when I got home, I tiptoed into the apartment. The three bowls were just where we had left them—and every one of them was empty.

There was, however, no cat. But this time I initiated no search. I simply refilled the dishes and went to bed. With the help of Sergeant, a colonel, and Marian, I now had, for better or for worse, for a few days at least, a Christmas cat.

The Gift of
LOVE

A Christmas Dinner Won in Battle

Stephen Crane

Tom had set up a plumbing shop in the prairie town of Levelville as soon as the people learned to care more about sanitary conditions than they did about the brand of tobacco smoked by the inhabitants of Mars. Nevertheless, he was a wise young man, for he was only one week ahead of the surveyors. A railroad, like a magic wand, was going to touch Levelville and change it into a great city. In an incredibly short time, the town had a hotel, a mayor, a board of alderman, and more than a hundred real estate agents, besides a blue print of the plans for a street railway three miles long. When the cowboys rode in with their customary noise to celebrate the fact that they had been paid, their efforts were discouraged by new policemen in uniform. Levelville had become a dignified city.

As the town expanded in marvelous circles out over the prairies, Tom bestrode the froth of the wave of progress. He was soon one of the first citizens. These waves carry men to fortune with sudden sweeping movements, and Tom had the courage, the temerity, and the assurance to hold his seat like a knight errant.

In the democratic and genial atmosphere of this primary boom, he became an intimate acquaintance of Colonel Fortman, the president of the railroad, and with more courage, temerity, and assurance, had already fallen violently in love with his daughter, the incomparable Mildred. He carried his intimacy with the colonel so far as to once save his life from the flying might of the 5:30 express. It seems that the colonel had ordered the engineer of the 5:30 to make his time under all circumstances—to make his time if he had to run through fire, flood, and earthquake. The engineer decided that the usual rule relating to the speed of trains when passing through freight yards could not concern an express that was ordered to slow down for nothing but the wrath of heaven and in consequence, at the time of this incident, the 5:30 was shrieking through the Levelville freight yard at fifty miles an hour, roaring over the switches and screaming along the lines of box cars. The colonel and Tom were coming from the shops. They had just rounded the corner of a car and stepped out upon the main track when this whirring, boiling, howling demon of an express came down upon them. Tom had an instant in which to drag his companion off the rails; the train whistled past them like an enormous projectile. "Damn that fellow—he's making his time," panted the old colonel gazing after the long speeding shadow with its two green lights. Later he said very soberly: "I'm much obliged to you for that, Tom old boy."

When Tom went to him a year later, however, to ask for the hand of Mildred, the colonel replied: "My dear man, I think you are insane. Mildred will have over a million dollars at my death, and while I don't mean to push the money part of it too far forward, yet Mildred with her beauty, her family name, and her wealth, can marry the finest in the land. There isn't anyone too great for her. So you see, my dear man, it is impossible that she could consider you for a moment."

Whereupon Tom lost his temper. He had the indignation of a good, sound-minded, fearless-eyed young fellow who is assured of his love and assured almost of the love of the girl. Moreover, it filled him with unspeakable rage to be called "My dear man."

They then accused each other of motives of which neither was guilty, and Tom went away. It was a serious quarrel. The colonel told Tom never to dare to cross his threshold. They passed each other on the street without a wink of an eye to disclose the fact that one knew that the other existed. As time went on the colonel became more massively aristocratic and more impenetrably stern. Levelville had developed about five grades of society, and the Fortmans mingled warily with the dozen families that formed the highest and iciest grades. Once, when the colonel and Mildred were driving through town, the girl bowed to a young man who passed them.

"Who the deuce was that?" said the colonel airily. "Seems to me I ought to know that fellow."

"That's the man that saved your life from the 5:30," replied Mildred.

"See here, young lady," cried the colonel angrily, "don't you take his part against me."

About a year later came the great railway strike. The papers of the city foreshadowed it vaguely from time to time, but no one apparently took the matter in a serious way. There had been threats and rumors of threats but the general public had seemed to view them as idle bombast. At last, however, the true situation displayed itself suddenly and vividly. Almost the entire force of the great P.C.C. and W.U. system went on strike. The people of the city awoke one morning to find the gray sky of dawn splashed with a bright crimson color. The strikers had set ablaze one of the company's shops in the suburbs and the light from it flashed out a red, ominous signal of warning foretelling the woe and despair of the struggle that was to ensue. Rumors came that the men, usually so sober, industrious and imperturbable, were running in a wild mob, raving and destroying. Whereupon, the people who had laughed to scorn any idea of being prepared for this upheaval began to assiduously abuse the authorities for not being ready to meet it.

That morning Tom, in his shirt sleeves, went into the back of his shop to direct some of his workmen about a certain job, and when he came out he was well covered by as honest a coating of grime and soot as was ever worn by a journeyman. He went to the sink to dispose of this adornment and while there he heard his men talking of the strike. One was saying: "Yes, sir; sure as th' dickens! They say they're goin' t' burn th' president's house an' everybody in it." Tom's body stiffened at these words. He felt himself turn cold. A moment later he left the shop forgetting his coat, forgetting his covering of soot and grime.

In the main streets of the city there was no evident change. The horses of the jangling street cars still slipped and strained in the deep mud into which the snow had been churned. The store windows were gay with the color of Christmas. Innumerable turkeys hung before each butcher's shop. Upon the walks the businessmen had formed into little eager groups discussing the domestic calamity. Against the leaden-hued sky, over the tops of the buildings, arose a great leaning pillar of smoke marking the spot upon which stood the burning shop.

Tom hurried on through that part of town which was composed of little narrow streets with tiny gray houses on either side. There he saw a concourse of Slavs, Polacs, Italians, and Hungarians, laborers of the company, floundering about in the mud and raving, conducting a riot in their own inimitable way. They seemed as blood-thirsty, pitiless, mad, as starved wolves. And Tom presented a figure no less grim as he ran through the crowd, coatless and now indeed hatless, with pale skin showing through the grime. He went until he came to a stretch of commons across which he could see the Fortman's house standing serenely, with no evidences of riot about it. He moderated his pace then.

When he had gone about half way across this little snow-covered common, he looked back, for he heard cries. Across the white fields, winding along the muddy road, there came a strange procession. It resembled a parade of Parisians at the time of the first revolution. Fists were wildly waving and at times hoarse voices rang out. It was as if this crowd was delirious from drink. As it came nearer Tom could see women—gaunt and ragged creatures with inflamed visages and rolling eyes. There were men with dark sinister faces whom Tom had never before seen. They had emerged from the earth, so to speak, to engage in this carousal of violence. And from this procession there came continual threatening ejaculations, shrill cries for revenge, and querulous voices of hate, that made a sort of barbaric hymn, a pagan chant of savage battle and death.

Tom waited for them. Those in the lead evidently considered him to be one of their number since his face was grimed and his garments disheveled. One gigantic man with bare and brawny arms and throat gave him invitation with a fierce smile. "Come ahn, Swipsey, while we go roast 'em."

A raving gray-haired woman, struggling in the mud, sang a song which consisted of one endless line:

"We'll burn th' foxes out,
We'll burn th' foxes out,
We'll burn th' foxes out."

As for the others, they babbled and screamed in a vast variety of foreign tongues. Tom walked along with them listening to the cries that came from the terrible little army, marching with clenched fists and with gleaming eyes fastened upon the mansion that upreared so calmly before them.

When they arrived, they hesitated a moment, as if awed by the impassive silence of the structure with closed shutters and barred doors, which stolidly and indifferently confronted them.

Then from the center of the crowd came the voice of the gray-headed old woman: "Break in th' door! Break in th' door!" And then it was that Tom displayed the desperation born of his devotion to the girl within the house. Although he was perhaps braver than most men, he had none of that magnificent fortitude, that gorgeous tranquility amid upheavals and perils which is the attribute of people in plays; but he stepped up on the porch and faced the throng. His face was wondrously pallid and his hands trembled but he said: "You fellows can't come in here."

There came a great sarcastic howl from the crowd. "Can't we?" They broke into laughter at this wildly ridiculous thing. The brawny, bare-armed giant seized Tom by the arm. "Get outta th' way, you yap," he said between his teeth. In an instant Tom was punched and pulled and knocked this way and that way, and amid the pain of these moments he was conscious that members of the mob were delivering thunderous blows upon the huge doors. Directly indeed they crashed down and he felt the crowd sweep past him and into the house. He clung to a railing; he had no more sense of balance than a feather. A blow in the head had made him feel that the ground swirled and heaved around him. He had no further interest in rioting and such scenes of excitement. Gazing out over the common he saw two patrol wagons, loaded with policemen, and the lashed horses galloping in the mud. He wondered dimly why they were in such a hurry.

But at that moment a scream rang from the house out through the open doors. He knew the voice, and like an electric shock it aroused him from his semi-stupor. Once more alive, he turned and charged into the house as valiant and as full of rage as a Roman. Pandemonium reigned within. There came yells and roars, splinterings, cracklings, crashings. The scream of Mildred again rang out; this time he knew it came from the dining room before whose closed door four men were as busy as miners with improvised pick and drill.

Tom grasped a heavy oaken chair that stood ornamentally in the hall and, elevating it about his head, ran madly at the four men. When he was almost upon them, he let the chair fly. It seemed to strike all of them. A heavy oak chair of the old English type is one of the most destructive of weapons. Still, there seemed to be enough of the men left for they flew at him from all sides like dragons. In the dark of the hallway, Tom put down his head and half-closed his eyes and plied his fists. He knew he had but a moment in which to stand up, but there was a sort of grim joy in knowing that the most terrific din of this affray was going straight through the dining room door, and into the heart of Mildred and when she knew that her deliverer was… He saw a stretch of blood-red sky flame under his lids and then sank to the floor, blind, deaf, and nerveless.

When the old colonel arrived in one of the patrol wagons, he did not wait to see the police attack in front but ran around to the rear. As he passed the dining room windows he saw his wife's face. He shouted, and when they opened a window he clambered with great agility into the room. For a minute they deluged each other with shouts of joy and tears. Then finally the old colonel said: "But they did not get in here. How was that?"

"Oh, Papa," said Mildred, "they were trying to break in when somebody came and fought dreadfully with them and made them stop."

"Heavens, who could it have been?" said the colonel. He went to the door and opened it. A group of police became visible hurrying about the wide hall but near the colonel's feet lay a body with a white still face.

"Why, it's… it's…" ejaculated the colonel in great agitation.

"It's Tom," cried Mildred.

When Tom came to his senses he found that his fingers were clasped tightly by a soft white hand which by some occult power of lovers he knew at once.

"Tom," said Mildred.

And the old colonel from farther away said, "Tom, my boy!"

But Tom was something of an obstinate young man. So as soon as he felt himself recovered sufficiently, he arose and went unsteadily toward the door.

"Tom, where are you going?" cried Mildred.

"Where are you going, Tom?" called the colonel.

"I'm going home," said Tom doggedly. "I didn't intend to cross this threshold. I…" He swayed unsteadily and seemed about to fall. Mildred screamed and ran toward him. She made a prisoner of him. "You shall not go home," she told him.

"Well," began Tom weakly yet persistently, "I…"

"No, no, Tom," said the colonel. "You are to eat a Christmas dinner with us tomorrow and then I wish to talk with you about… about…"

"About what?" asked Tom.

"About… about… damnitall, about marrying my daughter," cried the colonel.

Christmas Day
in the Morning

* * * * * *

Pearl S. Buck

He woke suddenly and completely. It was four o'clock, the hour at which his father had always called him to get up and help with the milking. Strange how the habits of his youth clung to him still! That was fifty years ago, and his father had been dead for thirty, yet he waked at four o'clock every morning. Over the years, he had trained himself to turn over and go to sleep, but this morning it was Christmas.

Why did he feel so awake tonight? He slipped back in time, as he did so easily nowadays. He was fifteen years old and still on his father's farm. He loved his father. He had not known it until one day a few days before Christmas, when he had overheard his father talking to his mother.

"Mary, I hate to wake Rob in the mornings. He's growing so fast and he needs his sleep. If you could see how hard he's sleeping when I go in to wake him up! I wish I could manage alone."

"Well, you can't, Adam." His mother's voice was brisk. "Besides, he isn't a child anymore. It's time he took his turn."

"Yes," his father said slowly. "But I sure do hate to wake him."

When he heard his father's words, something in him spoke: His father loved him! He had never thought of that before, simply taking for granted the tie of their blood. Neither his father nor his mother talked about loving their children—they had no time for such things. There was always so much to do on the farm.

Now that he knew his father loved him, there would be no loitering in the mornings and having to be called again. He always got up immediately after that. He stumbled blindly in his sleep and pulled on his clothes with his eyes shut, but he got up.

And then on the night before Christmas, that year when he was fifteen, he lay for a few minutes thinking about the next day. They were poor, and most of the excitement about Christmas was in the turkey they had raised themselves and the mince pies his mother had made. His sister sewed presents for everyone and his mother and father always bought him something he needed, like a warm jacket, but usually something more too, such as a book. And he saved and bought them each something, too.

He wished, that Christmas when he was fifteen, he had a better present for his father. As usual he had gone to the ten-cent store and bought a tie. It had seemed nice enough until he lay thinking the night before Christmas. As he gazed out of his attic window, the stars were bright.

"Dad," he had once asked when he was a little boy. "What is a stable?"

"It's just a barn," his father had replied, "like ours."

Then Jesus had been born in a barn, and to a barn the shepherds had come.

The thoughts struck him like a silver dagger. Why couldn't he give his father a special gift too, out there in the barn? He could get up early, earlier than four o'clock, and he could creep into the barn and do all the milking before his father even got out of bed. He'd do it all alone, milk the cows and clean up, and then when his father went in to start the milking he'd see it all was done. And he would know who had done it. He laughed to himself as he looked at the stars. It was what he would do! He mustn't sleep too sound and forget to get up early.

He must have waked twenty times, scratching a match each time to look at his old watch—midnight, half past one, then two o'clock.

At a quarter to three he got up and put on his clothes. He crept downstairs, careful to avoid the creaky boards, and let himself out. The cows looked at him, sleepy and surprised. It was early for them too.

He had never milked all alone before, but it seemed almost easy. He kept thinking about his father's surprise. His father would come in to get him, saying that he would get things started while Rob was getting dressed. He'd go to the barn, open the door, and then he'd go get the two big empty milk cans waiting to be filled. But they wouldn't be waiting or empty, they'd be standing in the milk house, filled.

"What on earth!" he could hear his father exclaiming.

He smiled and milked steadily, two strong streams rushing into the pail frothing and fragrant.

The task went more easily than he had ever known it to go before. For once, milking was not a chore. It was something else, a gift to his father who loved him. He finished, the two milk cans were full, and he covered them and closed the milk house door carefully, making sure to close the latch.

Back in his room he had only a minute to pull off his clothes in the darkness and jump into bed, for he heard his father up and moving around. He put the covers over his head to silence his quick breathing. The door opened.

"Rob," his father called. "We have to get up, son, even if it is Christmas."

"Aw-right," he said sleepily.

His father closed the door and he lay still, laughing to himself. In just a few minutes his father would know. His dancing heart was ready to jump from his body.

The minutes were endless—ten, fifteen, he did not know how many, it seemed like hours—and he heard his father's footsteps again. When his father opened the door he lay perfectly still.

"Rob!"

"Yes, Dad?"

His father was laughing, a strange sobbing sort of laugh.

"Thought you'd fool me, did you?" His father was standing by his bed, feeling for him, pulling away the covers.

"Merry Christmas, Dad!"

He found his father and clutched him in a great hug. He felt his father's arms wrap around him. It was dark and they could not see each other's faces.

"Son, I thank you. Nobody ever did a nicer thing…"

"Oh, Dad, I want you to know—I do want to be good!" The words broke from him of their own will. He did not know what to say. His heart was bursting with love.

He got up and pulled on his clothes again and they went down to the Christmas tree. Oh, what a Christmas, and how his heart had nearly burst again with shyness and pride as his father told his mother and sister how he, Rob, had got up all by himself and finished all the milking.

"The best Christmas gift I ever had, and I'll remember it, son, every year on Christmas morning, so long as I live."

They had both remembered it every year, and now that his father was dead, he remembered it alone: that blessed Christmas dawn when, alone with the cows in the barn, he had made his first gift of true love.

This Christmas he wanted to write a card to his wife and tell her how much he loved her. It had been a long time since he had really told her, although he loved her in a very special way, much more than he ever had when they were young. He had been fortunate that she had loved him. Ah, that was the true joy of life, the ability to love. Love was still alive in him; it still was.

It occurred to him suddenly that it was alive because long ago it had been born in him when he knew his father loved him. That was it: Love alone could awaken love. And he could give the gift again and again. This morning, this blessed Christmas morning, he would give it to his beloved wife. He would write it down in a letter for her to read and keep forever. He went to his desk and began to write: My dearest love…

Such a happy, happy, Christmas!

The Gift of the Magi

O. Henry

One dollar and eighty-seven cents. That was all. And sixty cents of it in pennies. Pennies saved one and two at a time by bulldozing the grocer and the vegetable man and the butcher until one's cheeks burned with the silent imputation of parsimony that such close dealing implied. Three times Della counted it. One dollar and eighty-seven cents. And the next day would be Christmas.

There was clearly nothing to do but flop down on the shabby little couch and howl. So Della did it. Which instigates the moral reflection that life is made up of sobs, sniffles, and smiles, with sniffles predominating.

While the mistress of the home is gradually subsiding from the first stage to the second, take a look at the home. A furnished flat at $8 per week. It did not exactly beggar description, but it certainly had that word on the lookout for the mendicancy squad.

In the vestibule below was a letter-box into which no letter would go, and an electric button from which no mortal finger could coax a ring. Also appertaining thereunto was a card bearing the name "Mr. James Dillingham Young."

The "Dillingham" had been flung to the breeze during a former period of prosperity when its possessor was being paid $30 per week. Now, when the income was shrunk to $20, the letters of "Dillingham" looked blurred, as though they were thinking seriously of contracting to a modest and unassuming D. But whenever Mr. James Dillingham Young came home and reached his flat above he was called "Jim" and greatly hugged by Mrs. James Dillingham Young, already introduced to you as Della. Which is all very good.

Della finished her cry and attended to her cheeks with the powder rag. She stood by the window and looked out dully at a grey cat walking a grey fence in a grey backyard. Tomorrow would be Christmas Day, and she had only $1.87 with which to buy Jim a present. She had been saving every penny she could for months, with this result. Twenty dollars a week doesn't go far. Expenses had been greater than she had calculated. They always were. Only $1.87 to buy a present for Jim. Her Jim. Many a happy hour she had spent planning for something nice for him. Something fine and rare and sterling—something just a little bit near to being worthy of the honour of being owned by Jim.

There was a pier-glass between the windows of the room. Perhaps you have seen a pier-glass in an $8 flat. A very thin and very agile person may, by observing his reflection in a rapid sequence of longitudinal strips, obtain a fairly accurate conception of his looks. Della, being slender, had mastered the art.

Suddenly she whirled from the window and stood before the glass. Her eyes were shining brilliantly, but her face had lost its colour within twenty seconds. Rapidly she pulled down her hair and let it fall to its full length.

Now, there were two possesssions of the James Dillingham Youngs in which they both took a mighty pride. One was Jim's gold watch that had been his father's and grandfather's. The other was Della's hair. Had the Queen of Sheba lived in the flat acrosss the airshaft, Della would have let her hair hang out the window some day to dry just to depreciate Her Majesty's jewels and gifts. Had King Solomon been the janitor, with all his treasures piled up in the basement, Jim would have pulled out his watch every time he passed, just to see him pluck at his beard from envy.

So now Della's beautiful hair fell about her, rippling and shining like a cascade of brown waters. It reached below her knee and made itself almost a garment for her. And then she did it up again nervously and quickly. Once she faltered for a minute and stood still while a tear or two splashed on the worn red carpet.

On went her old brown jacket; on went her old brown hat. With a whirl of skirts and with the brilliant sparkle still in her eyes, she fluttered out the door and down the stairs to the street.

Where she stopped the sign read: "Mme. Sofronie. Hair Goods of All Kinds." One flight up Della ran, and collected herself, panting. Madame, large, too white, chilly, hardly looked the "Sofronie."

"Will you buy my hair?" asked Della.

"I buy hair," said Madame. "Take yer hat off and let's have a sight at the looks of it."

Down rippled the brown cascade.

"Twenty dollars," said Madame, lifting the mass with a practised hand.

"Give it to me quick," said Della.

Oh, and the next two hours tripped by on wings. Forget the hashed metaphor. She was ransacking the stores for Jim's present.

She found it at last. It surely had been made for Jim and no one else. There was no other like it in any of the stores, and she had turned all of them inside out. It was a platinum fob chain simple and chaste in design, properly proclaiming its value by substance alone and not by meretricious ornamentation—as all good things should do. It was even worth of The Watch. As soon as she saw it she knew that it must be Jim's. It was like him. Quietness and value—the description applied to both. Twenty-one dollars they took from her for it, and she hurried home with 87 cents. With that chain on his watch Jim might be properly anxious about the time in any company. Grand as the watch was, he sometimes looked at it on the sly on account of the old leather strap that he used in place of a chain.

When Della reached home her intoxication gave way a little to prudence and reason. She got out her curling irons and lighted the gas and went to work repairing the ravages made by generosity added to love. Which is always a tremendous task, dear friends—a mammoth task.

Within forty minutes her head was covered with tiny, close-lying curls that made her look wonderfully like a truant schoolboy. She looked at her reflection in the mirror long, carefully, and critically.

"If Jim doesn't kill me," she said to herself, "before he takes a second look at me, he'll say I look like a Coney Island chorus girl. But what could I do—oh! what could I do with a dollar and eighty-seven cents?"

At 7 o'clock the coffee was made and the frying-pan was on the back of the stove hot and ready to cook the chops.

Jim was never late. Della doubled the fob chain in her hand and sat on the corner of the table near the door that he always entered. Then she heard his step on the stair away down on the first flight, and she turned white for just a moment. She had a habit of saying little silent prayers about the simplest everyday things, and now she whispered: "Please God, make him think I am still pretty."

The door opened and Jim stepped in and closed it. He looked thin and very serious. Poor fellow, he was only twenty-two—and to be burdened with a family! He needed a new overcoat and he was without gloves.

Jim stopped inside the door, as immovable as a setter at the scent of quail. His eyes were fixed upon Della, and there was an expression in them that she could not read, and it terrified her. It was not anger, nor surprise, nor disapproval, nor horrow, nor any of the sentiments that she had been prepared for. He simply stared at her fixedly with that peculiar expression on his face.

Della wriggled off the table and went for him.

"Jim, darling," she cried, "don't look at me that way. I had my hair cut off and sold it because I couldn't have lived through Christmas without giving you a present. It'll grow out again—you won't mind, will you? I just had to do it. My hair grows awfully fast. Say 'Merry Christmas!' Jim, and let's be happy. You don't know what a nice—what a beautiful, nice gift I've got for you."

"You've cut off your hair?" asked Jim, laborioulsy, as if he had not arrived at that patent fact yet even after the hardest mental labour.

"Cut if off and sold it," said Della. "Don't you like me just as well, anyhow? I'm me without my hair, ain't I?"

Jim looked about the room curiously.

"You say your hair is gone?" he said, with an air almost of idiocy.

"You needn't look for it," said Della. "It's sold, I tell you—sold and gone, too. It's Christmas Eve, boy. Be good to me, for it went for you. Maybe the hairs of my head were numbered," she went on with a sudden serious sweetness, "but nobody could ever count my love for you. Shall I put the chops on, Jim?"

Out of his trance Jim seemed quickly to wake. He enfolded his Della. For ten seconds let us regard with discreet scrutiny some inconsequential object in the other direction. Eight dollars a week or a million a year—what is the difference? A mathematician or a wit would give you the wrong answer. The magi brought valuable gifts, but that was not among the. This dark assertion will be illuminated later on.

"Don't make any mistake, Dell," he said, "about, me. I don't think there's anything in the way of a haircut or a shave or a shampoo that could make me like my girl any less. But if you'll unwrap that package you may see why you had me going a while at first."

White fingers and nimble tore at the string and paper. And then an ecstatic scream of joy; and then, alas! a quick feminine change to hysterical tears and wails, necessitating the immediate employment of all the comforting powers of the lord of the flat.

For there lay The Combs—the set of combs, side and back, that Della had worshipped for long in a Broadway window. Beautiful combs, pure tortoise shell, with jeweled rims—just the shade to wear in the beautiful vanished hair. They were expensive combs, she knew, and her heart had simply craved and yearned over them without the least hope of possession. And now, they were hers, but the tresses that should have adorned the coveted adornments were gone.

But she hugged them to her bosom, and at length she was able to look up with dim eyes and smile and say: "My hair grows so fast, Jim."

And then Della leaped up like a little singed cat and cried, "Oh, oh!"

Jim had not yet seen his beautiful present. She held it out to him eagerly upon her open palm. The dull precious metal seemed to flash with a reflection of her bright and ardent spirit.

"Isn't it a dandy, Jim? I hunted all over town to find it. You'll have to look at the time a hundred times a day now. Give me your watch. I want to see how it looks on it."

Instead of obeying, Jim tumbled down on the couch and put his hands under the back of his head and smiled.

"Dell," said he, "let's put our Christmas presents away and keep 'em a while. They're too nice to use just at present. I sold the watch to get the money to buy your combs. And now suppose you put the chops on."

The magi, as you know, were wise men—wonderfully wise men who brought gifts to the Babe in the manger. They invented the art of giving Christmas presents. Being wise, their gifts were no doubt wise ones, possibly bearing the privilege of exchange in case of duplication. And here I have lamely related to you the uneventful chronicle of two foolish children in a flat who most unwisely sacrificed for each other the greatest treasures of their house. But in a last word to the wise of these days let it be said that of all who give gifts these two were the wisest. Of all who give and receive gifts, such as they are wisest. Everywhere they are wisest. They are the magi.

The Gift of
GIVING

A Christmas Inspiration

Lucy Maud Montgomery

Well I really think Santa Claus has been very good to us all," said Jean Lawrence, pulling the pins out of her heavy coil of fair hair and letting it ripple over her shoulders.

"So do I," said Nellie Preston as well as she could with a mouthful of chocolates. "Those blessed home folks of mine seem to have divined by instinct the very things I most wanted."

It was the dusk of Christmas Eve and they were all in Jean Lawrence's room at No. 16 Chestnut Terrace. No. 16 was a boarding house, and boarding houses are not proverbially cheerful places in which to spend Christmas, but Jean's room, at least, was a pleasant spot, and all the girls had brought their Christmas presents in to show each other. Christmas came on Sunday that year and the Saturday evening mail at Chestnut Terrace had been an exciting one.

Jean had lighted the pink-globed lamp on her table and the mellow light fell over merry faces as the girls chatted about their gifts. On the table was a big white box heaped with roses, betokened a bit of Christmas extravagance on somebody's part. Jean's brother had sent them to her from Montreal, and all the girls were enjoying them in common.

No. 16 Chestnut Terrace was overrun with girls generally. But just now only five were left; all the others had gone home for Christmas, but these five could not go and were bent on making the best of it.

Belle and Olive Reynolds, who were sitting on the bed—Jean could never keep them off it—were High School girls; they were said to be always laughing, and even the fact that they could not go home for Christmas because a young brother had measles did not dampen their spirits.

Beth Hamilton, who was hovering over the roses, and Nellie Preston, who was eating candy, were art students, and their homes were too far away to visit. As for Jean Lawrence, she was an orphan, and had no home of her own. She worked on the staff of one of the big city newspapers and the other girls were a little in awe of her cleverness, but her nature was a "chummy" one and her room was a favorite rendezvous. Everybody liked frank, open-handed and -hearted Jean.

"It was so funny to see the postman when he came this evening," said Olive. "He just bulged with parcels. They were sticking out in every direction."

"We all got our share of them," said Jean with a sigh of content.

"Even the cooks got six—I counted."

"Miss Allen didn't get a thing—not even a letter," said Beth quickly. Beth had a trick of seeing things that other girls didn't.

"I forgot Miss Allen. No, I don't believe she did," answered Jean thoughtfully as she twisted up her pretty hair. "How dismal it must be to be so forlorn as that on Christmas Eve of all times. Ugh! I'm glad I have friends."

"I saw Miss Allen watching us as we opened our parcels and letters," Beth went on. "I happened to look up once, and such an expression as was on her face, girls! It was pathetic and sad and envious all at once. It really made me feel bad—for five minutes," she concluded honestly.

"Hasn't Miss Allen any friends at all?" asked Beth.

"No, I don't think she has," answered Jean. "She has lived here for fourteen years, so Mrs. Pickrell says. Think of that, girls! Fourteen years at Chestnut Terrace! Is it any wonder that she is thin and dried up and snappy?"

"Nobody ever comes to see her and she never goes anywhere," said Beth. "Dear me! She must feel lonely now when everybody else is being remembered by their friends. I can't forget her face tonight; it actually haunts me. Girls, how would you feel if you hadn't anyone belonging to you, and if nobody thought about you at Christmas?"

"Ow!" said Olive, as if the mere idea made her shiver.

A little silence followed. To tell the truth, none of them liked Miss Allen. They knew that she did not like them either, but considered them frivolous and pert, and complained when they made a racket.

"The skeleton at the feast," Jean called her, and certainly the presence of the pale, silent, discontented-looking woman at the No. 16 table did not tend to heighten its festivity.

Presently Jean said with a dramatic flourish, "Girls, I have an inspiration— a Christmas inspiration!"

"What is it?" cried four voices.

"Just this: Let us give Miss Allen a Christmas surprise. She has not received a single present and I'm sure she feels lonely. Just think how we would feel if we were in her place."

"That is true," said Olive thoughtfully. "Do you know, girls, this evening I went to her room with a message from Mrs. Pickrell, and I do believe she had been crying. Her room looked dreadfully bare and cheerless, too. I think she is very poor. What are we to do, Jean?"

"Let us each give her something nice. We can put the things just outside of her door so that she will see them whenever she opens it. I'll give her some of Fred's roses too, and I'll write a Christmassy letter in my very best style to go with them," said Jean, warming up to her ideas as she talked.

The other girls caught her spirit and entered into the plan with enthusiasm.

"Splendid!" cried Beth. "Jean, it is an inspiration, sure enough. Haven't we been horribly selfish—thinking of nothing but our own gifts and fun and pleasure? I feel really ashamed."

"Let us do the thing up the very best way we can," said Nellie, forgetting even her beloved chocolates in her eagerness. "The shops are open yet. Let us go uptown and invest."

Five minutes later, five capped and jacketed figures were scurrying up the street in the frosty, starlit December dusk. Miss Allen, in her cold little room, heard their gay voices and sighed. She was crying by herself in the dark. It was Christmas for everybody but her, she thought drearily.

In an hour the girls came back with their purchases.

"Now, let's hold a council of war," said Jean jubilantly. "I hadn't the faintest idea what Miss Allen would like so I just guessed wildly. I got her a lace handkerchief and a big bottle of perfume and a painted photograph frame—and I'll stick my own photo in it for fun. That was really all I could afford. Christmas purchases have left my purse dreadfully lean."

"I got her a glove box and a pin tray," said Belle, "and Olive got her a calendar and Whittier's poems. And besides we are going to give her half of that big plumy fruit cake Mother sent us from home. I'm sure she hasn't tasted anything so delicious for years, for fruit cakes don't grow on Chestnut Terrace and she never goes anywhere else for a meal."

Beth had bought a pretty cup and saucer and said she meant to give one of her pretty watercolors too. Nellie, true to her reputation, had invested in a big box of chocolate creams, a gorgeously striped candy cane, a bag of oranges, and a brilliant lampshade of rose-colored crepe paper to top it off with.

"It makes such a lot of show for the money," she explained. "I am bankrupt, like Jean."

"Well, we've got a lot of pretty things," said Jean in a tone of satisfaction. "Now we must do them up nicely. Will you wrap them in tissue paper, girls, and tie them with baby ribbon—here's a box of it—while I write that letter?"

While the others chatted over their parcels, Jean wrote her letter, and Jean could write delightful letters. She had a decided talent in that respect, and her correspondents all declared her letters to be things of beauty and joy forever. She put her best into Miss Allen's Christmas letter. Since then, she had written many bright and clever things, but I do not believe she ever in her life wrote anything more genuinely original and delightful than that letter.

Besides, it breathed the very spirit of Christmas, and all the girls declared that it was splendid.

"You must all sign it now," said Jean, "and I'll put it in one of those big envelopes. And, Nellie, won't you write her name on it in fancy letters?"

Which Nellie proceeded to do, and furthermore embellished the envelope by a border of chubby cherubs, dancing hand-in-hand around it, a sketch of No. 16 Chestnut Terrace in the corner in lieu of a stamp. Not content with this she hunted out a huge sheet of drawing paper and drew upon it an original pen-and-ink design after her own heart. A dudish cat—Miss Allen was fond on the No. 16 cat if she could be said to be fond of anything— was portrayed seated on a rocker arrayed in a smoking jacket and cap with a cigar waved airily aloft in one paw while the other held out a placard bearing the legend "Merry Christmas." A second cat in full street costume bowed politely, hat in paw, and waved a banner inscribed with "Happy New Year," while faintly suggested kittens gamboled around the border. The girls laughed until they cried over it and voted it to be the best thing Nellie had yet done in original work.

All this had taken time and it was past eleven o'clock. Miss Allen had cried herself to sleep long ago and everybody else in Chestnut Terrace was abed when five figures cautiously crept down the hall, headed by Jean with a dim lamp. Outside of Miss Allen's door the procession halted and the girls silently arranged their gifts on the floor.

"That's done," whispered Jean in a tone of satisfaction as they tiptoed back. "And now let us go to bed or Mrs. Pickrell, bless her heart, will be down on us for burning so much midnight oil. Oil has gone up, you know, girls."

It was in the early morning that Miss Allen opened her door. But early as it was, another door down the hall was half open too and five rosy faces were peering cautiously out. The girls had been up for an hour for fear they would miss the sight and were all in Nellie's room, which commanded a view of Miss Allen's door.

That lady's face was a study. Amazement, incredulity, wonder, chased each other over it, succeeded by a glow of pleasure. On the floor before her was a snug little pyramid of parcels topped by Jean's letter. On a chair behind it was a bowl of delicious hot-house roses and Nellie's placard.

Miss Allen looked down the hall but saw nothing, for Jean had slammed the door just in time. Half an hour later when they were going down to breakfast Miss Allen came along the hall with outstretched hands to meet them. She had been crying again, but I think her tears were happy ones; and she was smiling now. A cluster of Jean's roses were pinned on her breast.

"Oh, girls, girls," she said, with a little tremble in her voice. "I can never thank you enough. It was so kind and sweet of you. You don't know how much good you have done me."

Breakfast was an unusually cheerful affair at No. 16 that morning. There was no skeleton at the feast and everybody was beaming. Miss Allen laughed and talked like a girl herself.

"Oh, how surprised I was!" she said. "The roses were like a bit of summer, and those cats of Nellie's were so funny and delightful. And your letter too, Jean! I cried and laughed over it. I shall read it every day for a year."

After breakfast everyone went to Christmas service. The girls went uptown to the church they attended. The city was very beautiful in the morning sunshine.

There had been a white frost in the night and the tree-lined avenues and public square seemed like glimpses of fairyland.

"How lovely the world is," said Jean.

"This is really the very happiest Christmas morning I have ever known," declared Nellie. "I never felt so really Christmassy in my inmost soul before."

"I suppose," said Beth thoughtfully, "that it is because we have discovered for ourselves the old truth that it is more blessed to give than to receive. I've always known it, in a way, but I never realized it before."

"Blessing on Jean's Christmas inspiration," said Nellie. "But, girls, let us try to make it an all-the-year-round inspiration, I say. We can bring a little of our own sunshine into Miss Allen's life as long as we live with her."

"Amen to that!" said Jean heartily. "Oh, listen, girls—the Christmas chimes!"

And over all the beautiful city was wafted the grand old message of peace on earth and good will to all the world.

Christmas at Orchard House

Louisa May Alcott

I

"Christmas won't be Christmas without any presents," grumbled Jo, lying on the rug.

"It's so dreadful to be poor!" sighed Meg, looking down at her old dress.

"I don't think it's fair for some girls to have plenty of pretty things, and other girls nothing at all," added little Amy, with an injured sniff.

"We've got father and mother and each other," said Beth contentedly, from her corner.

The four young faces on which the firelight shone brightened at the cheerful words, but darkened again as Jo said sadly,

"We haven't got father, and shall not have him for a long time." She didn't say "perhaps never," but each silently added it, thinking of father far away, where the fighting was.

Nobody spoke for a minute; then Meg said in an altered tone, "You know the reason mother proposed not having any presents this Christmas was because it is going to be a hard winter for everyone; and she thinks we ought not to spend money for pleasure, when our men are suffering so in the army. We can't do much, but we can make our little sacrifices, and ought to do it gladly. But I'm afraid I don't." And Meg shook her head, as she thought regretfully of all the pretty things she wanted.

"But I don't think the little we should spend would do any good. We've each got a dollar, and the army wouldn't be much helped by our giving that. I agree not to expect anything from mother or you, but I do want to buy *Undine and Sintram* for myself; I've wanted to *so* long," said Jo, who was a bookworm.

"I planned to spend mine in new music," said Beth, with a little sigh, which no one heard but the hearth brush and kettle holder.

"I shall get a nice box of Faber's drawing pencils; I really need them," said Amy decidedly.

"Mother didn't say anything about our money, and she won't wish us to give up everything. Let's each buy what we want, and have a little fun; I'm sure we work hard enough to earn it," cried Jo, examining the heels of her shoes in a gentlemanly manner.

"I know *I* do—teaching those tiresome children nearly all day, when I'm longing to enjoy myself at home," began Meg, in the complaining tone again.

"You don't have half such a hard time as I do," said Jo. "How would you like to be shut up for hours with a nervous, fussy old lady, who keeps you trotting, is never satisfied, and worries you till you're ready to fly out of the window or cry?"

"It's naught to fret; but I do think washing dishes and keeping things tidy is the worst work in the world. It makes me cross; and my hands get so stiff, I can't practice well at all"; and Beth looked at her rough hands with a sigh that anyone could hear that time.

"I don't believe any of you suffer as I do," cried Amy; "for you don't have to go to school with impertinent girls, who plague you if you don't know your lessons, and laugh at your dresses, and label your father if he isn't rich, and insult you when your nose isn't nice."

"If you mean *libel*, I'd say so, and not talk about *labels*, as if papa was a pickle bottle," advised Jo, laughing.

"I know what I mean, and you needn't be *satirical* about it. It's proper to use good words, and improve your *vocabilary*," returned Amy, with dignity.

"Don't peck at one another, children. Don't you wish we had the money papa lost when we were little, Jo? Dear me! How happy and good we'd be, if we had no worries!" said Meg, who could remember better times.

"You said, the other day, you thought we were a deal happier than the King children, for they were fighting and fretting all the time, in spite of their money."

"So I did, Beth. Well, I think we are; for, though we do have to work, we make fun for ourselves, and are a pretty jolly set, as Jo would say."

"Jo does use such slang words!" observed Amy, with a reproving look at the long figure stretched on the rug. Jo immediately sat up, put her hands in her pockets, and began to whistle.

"Don't, Jo. It's so boyish!"

"That's why I do it."

"I detest rude, unladylike girls!"

"I hate affected, niminy-piminy chits!"

" 'Birds in their little nests agree,' " sang Beth, the peacemaker, with such a funny face that both sharp voices softened to a laugh, and the "pecking" ended for that time.

"Really, girls, you are both to be blamed," said Meg, beginning to lecture in her elder-sisterly fashion. "You are old enough to leave off boyish tricks, and to behave better, Josephine. It didn't matter so much when you were a little girl; but now you are so tall, and turn up your hair, you should remember that you are a young lady."

"I'm not! And if turning up my hair makes me one, I'll wear it in two tails till I'm twenty," cried Jo, pulling off her net, and shaking down a chestnut mane. "I hate to think I've got to grow up, and be Miss March, and wear long gowns, and look as prim as a China-aster! It's bad enough to be a girl, anyway, when I like boys' games and work and manners! I can't get over my disappointment in not being a boy; and it's worse than ever now, for I'm dying to go and fight with papa, and I can only stay at home and knit, like a poky old woman!" And Jo shook the blue army sock till the needles rattled like castanets, and her ball bounded across the room.

"Poor Jo! It's too bad, but it can't be helped; so you must try to be contented with making your name boyish, and playing brother to us girls," said Beth, stroking the rough head at her knee with a hand that all the dishwashing and dusting in the world could not make ungentle in its touch.

"As for you, Amy," continued Meg, "you are altogether too particular and prim. Your airs are funny now; but you'll grow up an affected little goose, if you don't take care. I like your nice manners and refined ways of speaking, when you don't try to be elegant; but your absurd words are as bad as Jo's slang."

"If Jo is a tomboy and Amy a goose, what am I, please?" asked Beth, ready to share the lecture.

"You're a dear, and nothing else," answered Meg warmly; and no one contradicted her, for the "Mouse" was the pet of the family.

As young readers like to know "how people look," we will take this moment to give them a little sketch of the four sisters, who sat knitting away in the twilight, while the December snow fell quietly without, and the fire crackled cheerfully within. It was a comfortable old room, though the carpet was faded and the furniture very plain; for a good picture or two hung on the walls, books filled the recesses, chrysanthemums and Christmas roses bloomed in the windows, and a pleasant atmosphere of home-peace pervaded it.

Margaret, the eldest of the four, was sixteen, and very pretty, being plump and fair, with large eyes, plenty of soft, brown hair, a sweet mouth, and white hands, of which she was rather vain. Fifteen-year-old Jo was very tall, thin, and brown, and reminded one of a colt; for she never seemed to know what to do with her long limbs, which were very much in her way. She had a decided mouth, a comical nose, and sharp, gray eyes, which appeared to see everything, and were by turns fierce, funny, or thoughtful. Her long, thick hair was her one beauty; but it was usually bundled into a net, to be out of her way. Round shoulders had Jo, big hands and feet, a fly-away look to her clothes, and the uncomfortable appearance of a girl who was rapidly shooting up into a woman, and didn't like it. Elizabeth—or Beth, as everyone called her—was a rosy, smooth-haired, bright-eyed girl of thirteen, with a shy manner, a timid voice, and a peaceful expression, which was seldom disturbed. Her father called her "Little Tranquility," and the name suited her excellently; for she seemed to live in a happy world of her own, only venturing out to meet the few whom she trusted and loved. Amy, though the youngest, was a most important person—in her own opinion at least. A regular snow-maiden, with blue eyes, and yellow hair, curling on her shoulders, pale and slender, and always carrying herself like a young lady mindful of her manners. What the characters of the four sisters were we will leave to be found out.

The clock struck six; and, having swept up the hearth, Beth put a pair of slippers down to warm. Somehow the sight of the old shoes had a good effect upon the girls; for mother was coming, and everyone brightened to welcome her. Meg stopped lecturing, and lighted the lamp. Amy got out of the easy chair without being asked, and Jo forgot how tired she was as she sat up to hold the slippers nearer to the blaze.

"They are quite worn out; Marmee must have a new pair."

"I thought I'd get her some with my dollar," said Beth.

"No, I shall!" cried Amy.

"I'm the oldest," began Meg, but Jo cut in with a decided—"I'm the man of the family now papa is away, and I shall provide the slippers, for he told me to take special care of mother while he was gone."

"I'll tell you what we'll do," said Beth. "Let's each get her something for Christmas, and not get anything for ourselves."

"That's like you, dear! What will we get?" exclaimed Jo.

Everyone thought soberly for a minute; then Meg announced, as if the idea was suggested by the sight of her own pretty hands, "I shall give her a nice pair of gloves."

"Army shoes, best to be had," cried Jo.

"Some handkerchiefs, all hemmed," said Beth.

"I'll get a little bottle of cologne; she likes it, and it won't cost much, so I'll have some left to buy my pencils," added Amy.

"How will we give the things?" asked Meg.

"Put them on the table, and bring her in and see her open the bundles. Don't you remember how we used to do on our birthdays?" answered Jo.

"I used to be *so* frightened when it was my turn to sit in the big chair with the crown on, and see you all come marching round to give presents, with a kiss. I liked the things and the kisses, but it was dreadful to have you sit looking at me while I opened the bundles," said Beth, who was toasting her face and the bread for tea, at the same time.

"Let Marmee think we are getting things for ourselves, and then surprise her. We must go shopping tomorrow afternoon, Meg; there is so much to do about the play for Christmas night," said Jo, marching up and down, with her hands behind her back and her nose in the air.

"I don't mean to act any more after this time; I'm getting too old for such things," observed Meg, who was as much a child as ever about "dressing-up" frolics. "You won't stop, I know, as long as you can trail round in a white gown with your hair down, and wear gold-paper jewelry. You are the best actress we've got, and there'll be an end of everything if you quit the boards," said Jo. "We ought to rehearse tonight. Come here, Amy, and do the fainting scene, for you are as stiff as a poker in that."

"I can't help it, I never saw anyone faint, and I don't choose to make myself all black and blue, tumbling flat as you do. If I can go down easily, I'll drop; if I can't, I shall fall into a chair and be graceful; I don't care if Hugo does come at me with a pistol," returned Amy, who was not gifted with dramatic power, but was chosen because she was small enough to be borne out shrieking by the villain of the piece.

"Do it this way: Clasp your hands so, and stagger across the room, crying frantically, 'Roderigo! Save me! Save me!' " and away went Jo, with a melodramatic scream which was truly thrilling.

Amy followed, but she poked her hands out stiffly before her, and jerked herself along as if she went by machinery; and her "Ow!" was more suggestive of pins being run into her than fear and anguish. Jo gave a despairing groan, and Meg laughed outright, while Beth let her bread burn as she watched the fun, with interest.

"It's no use! Do the best you can when the time comes, and if the audience laughs, don't blame me. Come on, Meg."

Then things went smoothly, for Don Pedro defied the world in a speech of two pages without a single break; Hagar, the witch, chanted an awful incantation over her kettleful of simmering toads, with weird effect; Roderigo rent his chains asunder manfully, and Hugo died in agonies of remorse and arsenic with a wild "Ha! Ha!"

"It's the best we've had yet," said Meg, as the dead villain sat up and rubbed his elbows.

"I don't see how you can write and act such splendid things, Jo. You're a regular Shakespeare!" exclaimed Beth, who firmly believed that her sisters were gifted with wonderful genius in all things.

"Not quite," replied Jo modestly. "I do think, 'The Witch's Curse, an Operatic Tragedy' is rather a nice thing; but I'd like to try 'Macbeth,' if we only had a trap door for Banquo. I always wanted to do the killing part. 'Is that a dagger that I see before me?' " muttered Jo, rolling her eyes and clutching at the air, as she had seen a famous tragedian do.

"No, it's the toasting fork, with mother's shoe on it instead of the bread. Beth's stage struck!" cried Meg, and the rehearsal ended in a general burst of laughter.

II

JO WAS THE FIRST to wake in the gray dawn of Christmas morning. No stockings hung at the fireplace, and for a moment she felt as much disappointed as she did long ago, when her little sock fell down because it was so crammed with goodies. Then she remembered her mother's promise, and, slipping her hand under her pillow, drew out a little crimson-covered book. She knew it very well, for it was that beautiful old story of the best life ever lived, and Jo felt that it was a true guidebook for any pilgrim going the long journey. She woke Meg with a "Merry Christmas," and bade her see what was under her pillow. A green-covered book appeared, with the same picture inside, and a few words written by their mother, which made their one present very precious in their eyes. Presently, Beth and Amy woke, to rummage and find their little books also—one dove-colored, the other blue; and all sat looking at and talking about them, while the East grew rosy with the coming day. In spite of her small vanities, Margaret had a sweet and pious nature, which unconsciously influenced her sisters, especially Jo, who loved her very tenderly, and obeyed her because advice was so gently given.

"Girls," said Meg seriously, looking from the tumbled head beside her to the two little night-capped ones in the room beyond, "mother wants us to read and love and mind these books, and we must begin at once. We used to be faithful about it; but since father went away, and all this war trouble unsettled us, we have neglected many things. You can do as you please, but *I* shall keep my book on the table here, and read a little every morning as soon as I wake, for I know it will do me good, and help me through the day."

Then she opened her new book and began to read. Jo put her arm round her, and, leaning cheek to cheek, read also, with the quiet expression so seldom seen on her restless face.

"How good Meg is! Come, Amy, let's do as they do. I'll help you with the hard words, and they'll explain things if we don't understand," whispered Beth, very much impressed by the pretty books and her sisters' example.

"I'm glad mine is blue," said Amy; and then the rooms were very still while the pages were softly turned, and the winter sunshine crept in to touch the bright heads and serious faces with a Christmas greeting.

"Where is mother?" asked Meg, as she and Jo ran down to thank her for their gifts, half an hour later.

"Goodness only knows. Some poor creeter come a-beggin', and your ma went straight off to see what was needed. There never *was* such a woman for givin' away vittles and drink, clothes and firin'," replied Hannah, who had lived with the family since Meg was born, and was considered by them all more as a friend than a servant.

"She will be back soon, I think; so fry your cakes, and have everything ready," said Meg, looking over the presents which were collected in a basket and kept under the sofa, ready to be produced at the proper time. "Why, where is Amy's bottle of cologne?" she added, as the little flask did not appear.

"She took it out a minute ago, and went off with it to put a ribbon on it, or some such notion," replied Jo, dancing about the room to take the first stiffness off the new army slippers.

"How nice my handkerchiefs look, don't they? Hannah washed and ironed them for me, and I marked them all myself," said Beth, looking proudly at the somewhat uneven letters which had cost her such labor.

"Bless the child! She's gone and put 'Mother' on them, instead of 'M. March.' How funny!" cried Jo, taking up one.

"Isn't it right? I thought it was better to do it so, because Meg's initials are 'M.M.' and I don't want anyone to use these but Marmee," said Beth, looking troubled.

"It's all right, dear, and a very pretty idea—quite sensible, too, for no one can ever mistake now. It will please her very much, I know," said Meg, with a frown for Jo and a smile for Beth.

"There's mother. Hide the basket, quick!" cried Jo, as a door slammed, and steps sounded in the hall.

Amy came in hastily, and looked rather abashed when she saw her sisters all waiting for her.

"Where have you been, and what are you hiding behind you?" asked Meg, surprised to see, by her hood and cloak, that lazy Amy had been out so early.

"Don't laugh at me, Jo! I didn't mean anyone should know till the time came. I only meant to change the little bottle for a big one, and I gave *all* my money to get it, and I'm truly trying not to be selfish anymore."

As she spoke, Amy showed the handsome flask which replaced the cheap one; and looked so earnest and humble in her little effort to forget herself that Meg hugged her on the spot, and Jo pronounced her "a trump," while Beth ran to the window, and picked her finest rose to ornament the stately bottle.

"You see I felt ashamed of my present, after reading and talking about being good this morning, so I ran round the corner and changed it the minute I was up: and I'm *so* glad, for mine is the handsomest now."

Another bang of the street door sent the basket under the sofa, and the girls to the table, eager for breakfast.

"Merry Christmas, Marmee! Many of them! Thank you for our books; we read some, and mean to every day," they cried, in chorus.

"Merry Christmas, little daughters! I'm glad you began at once, and hope you will keep on. But I want to say one word before we sit down. Not far away from here lies a poor woman with a little newborn baby. Six children are huddled into one bed to keep from freezing, for they have no fire. There is nothing to eat over there; and the oldest boy came to tell me they were suffering from hunger and cold. My girls, will you give them your breakfast as a Christmas present?"

They were all unusually hungry, having waited nearly an hour, and for a minute no one spoke; only a minute, for Jo exclaimed impetuously, "I'm so glad you came before we began!"

"May I go and help carry the things to the poor little children?" asked Beth eagerly.

"*I* shall take the cream and the muffins," added Amy, heroically giving up the articles she most liked.

Meg was already covering the buckwheats, and piling the bread onto one big plate.

"I thought you'd do it," said Mrs. March, smiling as if satisfied. "You shall all go and help me, and when we come back we will have bread and milk for breakfast, and make it up at dinnertime."

They were soon ready, and the procession set out. Fortunately it was early, and they went through back streets, so few people saw them, and no one laughed at the queer party.

A poor, bare, miserable room it was, with broken windows, no fire, ragged bedclothes, a sick mother, wailing baby, and a group of pale, hungry children cuddled under one old quilt, trying to keep warm.

How the big eyes stared and the blue lips smiled as the girls went in!

"Ach, mein Gott! It is good angels come to us!" said the poor woman, crying for joy.

"Funny angels in hoods and mittens," said Jo, and set them laughing.

In a few minutes it really did seem as if kind spirits had been at work there. Hannah, who had carried wood, made a fire, and stopped up the broken panes with old hats and her own cloak. Mrs. March gave the mother tea and gruel, comforted her with promises of help, while she dressed the little baby as tenderly as if it had been her own. The girls, meantime, spread the table, set the children round the fire, and fed them like so many hungry birds—laughing, talking, and trying to understand the funny broken English.

"Das ist gut!" "Die Engel-kinder!" cried the poor things, as they ate, and warmed their purple hands at the comfortable blaze.

The girls had never been called angel children before, and thought it very agreeable, especially Jo, who had been considered a "Sancho" ever since she was born. That was a very happy breakfast, though they didn't get any of it; and when they went away, leaving comfort behind, I think there were not in all the city four merrier people than the hungry little girls who gave away their breakfasts and contented themselves with bread and milk on Christmas morning.

"That's loving our neighbor better than ourselves, and I like it," said Meg, as they set out their presents, while their mother was upstairs collecting clothes for the poor Hummels.

Not a very splendid show, but there was a great deal of love done up in the few little bundles; and the tall vase of red roses, white chrysanthemums, and trailing vines, which stood in the middle, gave quite an elegant air to the table.

"She's coming! Strike up, Beth! Open the door, Amy! Three cheers for Marmee!" cried Jo, prancing about, while Meg went to conduct mother to the seat of honor.

Beth played her gayest march, Amy threw open the door, and Meg enacted escort with great dignity. Mrs. March was both surprised and touched; and smiled with her eyes full as she examined her presents, and read the little notes which accompanied them. The slippers went on at once, a new handkerchief was slipped into her pocket, well scented with Amy's cologne, the rose was fastened in her bosom, and the nice gloves were pronounced a "perfect fit."

There was a good deal of laughing and kissing and explaining, in the simple, loving fashion which makes these home-festivals so pleasant at the time, so sweet to remember long afterward, and then all fell to work.

How Santa Claus Came
to Simpson's Bar

Bret Harte

I t had been raining in the valley of the Sacramento. The North Fork had overflowed its banks and Rattlesnake Creek was impassable. The few boulders that had marked the summer ford at Simpson's Crossing were obliterated by a vast sheet of water stretching to the foothills. The up stage was stopped at Grangers; the last mail had been abandoned in the *tules*, the rider swimming for his life. "An area," remarked the *Sierra Avalanche*, with pensive local pride, "as large as the State of Massachusetts is now under water."

Nor was the weather any better in the foothills. The mud lay deep on the mountain road. Wagons that neither physical force nor moral objurgation could move from the evil ways into which they had fallen, encumbered the track, and the way to Simpson's Bar was indicated by broken-down teams

---

and hard swearing. And farther on, cut off and inaccessible, rained upon and bedraggled, smitten by high winds and threatened by high water, Simpson's Bar, on the eve of Christmas day, 1862, clung like a swallow's nest to the rocky entablature and splintered capitals of Table Mountain, and shook in the blast.

As night shut down on the settlement, a few lights gleamed through the mist from the windows of cabins on either side of the highway now crossed and gullied by lawless streams and swept by marauding winds. Happily, most of the population was gathered at Thompson's store, clustered around a red-hot stove, at which they silently spat in some accepted sense of social communion that perhaps rendered conversation unnecessary. Indeed, most methods of diversion had long since been exhausted on Simpson's Bar. High water had suspended the regular occupations on gulch and on river, and a consequent lack of money and whiskey had taken the zest from most illegitimate recreation. Even Mr. Hamlin was fain to leave the Bar with fifty dollars in his pocket—the only amount actually realized of the large sums won by him in the successful exercise of his arduous profession. "Ef I was asked," he remarked somewhat later, "ef I was asked to pint out a purty little village where a retired sport as didn't care for money could exercise hisself, frequent and lively, I'd say Simpson's Bar; but for a young man with a large family depending on his exertions, it don't pay." As Mr. Hamlin's family consisted mainly of female adults, this remark is quoted rather to show the breadth of his humor than the exact extent of his responsibilities.

Howbeit, the unconscious objects of this satire sat that evening in the listless apathy begotten of idleness and lack of excitement. Even the sudden splashing of hoofs before the door did not arouse them. Dick Bullen alone paused in the act of scraping out his pipe, and lifted his head, but no other one of the group indicated any interest in, or recognition of, the man who entered.

It was a figure familiar enough to the company, and known in Simpson's Bar as "the Old Man." A man of perhaps fifty years, grizzled and scant of hair, but still fresh and youthful of complexion. A face full of ready but not very powerful sympathy, with a chameleon-like aptitude for taking on the shade and color of contiguous moods and feelings. He had evidently just left some hilarious companions, and did not at first notice the gravity of the group, but clapped the shoulder of the nearest man jocularly, and threw himself into a vacant chair.

"Jest heard the best thing out, boys! Ye know Smiley, over yar—Jim Smiley, funniest man in the Bar? Well, Jim was jest telling the richest yarn about—"

"Smiley's a… fool," interrupted a gloomy voice.

"A particular… skunk," added another in sepulchral accents.

A silence followed these positive statements. The Old Man glanced quickly around the group. Then his face slowly changed. "That's so," he said reflectively, after a pause, "certainly a sort of skunk and suthin of a fool. In course." He was silent for a moment as in painful contemplation of the unsavoriness and folly of the unpopular Smiley. "Dismal weather, ain't it?" he added, now fully embarked on the current of prevailing sentiment. "Mighty rough papers on the boys, and no show for money this season. And tomorrow's Christmas."

There was a movement among the men at this announcement, but whether of satisfaction or disgust was not plain. "Yes," continued the Old Man in the lugubrious tone he had, within the last few moments, unconsciously adopted, "yes, Christmas, and tonight's Christmas eve. Ye see, boys, I kinder thought—that is, I sorter had an idee, jest passin' like, you know— that maybe ye'd all like to come over to my house tonight and have a sort of tear round. But I suppose, now, you wouldn't? Don't feel like it, maybe?" he added with anxious sympathy, peering into the faces of his companions.

"Well, I don't know," responded Tom Flynn with some cheerfulness. "P'r'aps we may. But how about your wife, Old Man? What does *she* say to it?"

The Old Man hesitated. His conjugal experience had not been a happy one, and the fact was known to Simpson's Bar. His first wife, a delicate, pretty little woman, had suffered keenly and secretly from the jealous suspicions of her husband, until one day he invited the whole Bar to his house to expose her infidelity. On arriving, the party found the shy, *petite* creature quietly engaged in her household duties, and retired abashed and discomfited. But the sensitive woman did not easily recover from the shock of this extraordinary outrage. It was with difficulty she regained her equanimity sufficiently to release her lover from the closet in which he was concealed and escape with him. She left a boy of three years to comfort her bereaved husband. The Old Man's present wife had been his cook. She was large, loyal, and aggressive.

Before he could reply, Joe Dimmick suggested with great directness that it was the "Old Man's house," and that, invoking the Divine Power, if the case were his own, he would invite whom he pleased, even if in so doing he imperiled his salvation. The Powers of Evil, he further remarked, should contend against him vainly. All this delivered with a terseness and vigor lost in this necessary translation.

"In course. Certainly. Thet's it," said the Old Man with a sympathetic frown. "That's no trouble about *thet*. It's my own house, built every stick on it myself. Don't you be afeard o' her, boys. She *may* cut up a trifle rough— ez wimmin do—but she'll come round." Secretly the Old Man trusted the exaltation of liquor and the power of courageous example to sustain him in such an emergency.

As yet, Dick Bullen, the oracle and leader of Simpson's Bar, had not spoken. He now took his pipe from his lips. "Old Man, how's that yer Johnny gettin' on? Seems to me he didn't look so peart last time I seed him on the bluff heavin' rocks at Chinamen. Didn't seem to take much interest in it. Thar was a gang of 'em by yar yesterday—drownded out up the river—and I kinder thought o' Johnny, and how he'd miss 'em! Maybe now, we'd be in the way ef he wuz sick?"

The father, evidently touched not only by this pathetic picture of Johnny's deprivation, but by the considerate delicacy of the speaker, hastened to assure him that Johnny was better and that a "little fun might 'liven him up." Whereupon Dick arose, shook himself, and saying, "I'm ready. Lead the way, Old Man. Here goes," himself led the way with a leap, a characteristic howl, and darted out into the night. As he passed through the outer room he caught up a blazing brand from the hearth. The action was repeated by the rest of the party, closely following and elbowing each other, and before the astonished proprietor of Thompson's grocery was aware of the intention of his guests, the room was deserted.

The night was pitchy dark. In the first gust of wind their temporary torches were extinguished, and only the red brands dancing and flitting in the gloom like drunken will-o -the-wisps indicated their whereabouts. Their way led up Pine-Tree Cañon, at the head of which a broad, low, bark-thatched cabin burrowed in the mountainside. It was the home of the Old Man, and the entrance to the tunnel in which he worked when he worked at all. Here the crowd paused for a moment, out of delicate deference to their host, who came up panting in the rear.

"P'r'aps ye'd better hold on a second out yer, whilst I go in and see thet things is all right," said the Old Man, with an indifference he was far from feeling. The suggestion was graciously accepted, the door opened and closed on the host, and the crowd, leaning their backs against the wall and cowering under the eaves, waited and listened.

For a few moments there was no sound but the dripping of water from the eaves, and the stir and rustle of wrestling boughs above them. Then the men became uneasy, and whispered suggestion and suspicion passed from the one to the other. "Reckon she's caved in his head the first lick!" "Decoyed him inter the tunnel and barred him up, likely." "Got him down and sittin' on him." "Prob'ly bilin suthin to heave on us. Stand clear the door, boys!" For just then the latch clicked, the door slowly opened, and a voice said, "Come in out o' the wet."

The voice was neither that of the Old Man nor of his wife. It was the voice of a small boy, its weak treble broken by that preternatural hoarseness which only vagabondage and the habit of premature self-assertion can give. It was the face of a small boy that looked up at theirs—a face that might have been pretty and even refined but that it was darkened by evil knowledge from within, and dirt and hard experience from without. He had a blanket around his shoulders and had evidently just risen from his bed. "Come on," he repeated, "and don't make no noise. The Old Man's in there talking to mar," he continued, pointing to an adjacent room which seemed to be a kitchen, from which the Old Man's voice came in deprecating accents. "Let me be," he added, querulously, to Dick Bullen, who had caught him up, blanket and all, and was affecting to toss him into the fire. "Let go o' me, you d—d old fool, d'ye hear?"

Thus adjured, Dick Bullen lowered Johnny to the ground with a smoth-ered laugh, while the men, entering quietly, ranged themselves around a long table of rough boards which occupied the center of the room. Johnny then gravely proceeded to a cupboard and brought out several articles which he deposited on the table. "Thar's whiskey. And crackers. And red herons. And cheese." He took a bite of the latter on his way to the table. "And sugar." He scooped up a mouthful *en route* with a small and very dirty hand. "And terbacker. Thar's dried appils too on the shelf, but I don't admire 'em. Appils is swellin'. Thar," he concluded, "now wade in, and don't be afeard. *I* don't mind the old woman. She don't b'long to *me*. S'long."

He had stepped to the threshold of a small room, scarcely larger than a closet, partitioned off from the main apartment, and holding in its dim recess a small bed. He stood there a moment looking at the company, his bare feet peeping from the blanket, and nodded.

"Hello, Johnny! You ain't goin' to turn in agin, are ye?" said Dick.

"Yes, I are," responded Johnny, decidedly.

"Why, wot's up, old fellow?"

"I'm sick."

"How sick?"

"I've got fevier. And childblains. And roomatiz," returned Johnny, and vanished within. After a moment's pause, he added in the dark, apparently from under the bedclothes, "And biles!"

There was an embarrassing silence. The men looked at each other, and at the fire. Even with the appetizing banquet before them, it seemed as if they might again fall into the despondency of Thompson's grocery, when the voice of the Old Man, incautiously lifted, came deprecatingly from the kitchen.

"Certainly! Thet's so. In course they is. A gang o' lazy drunken loafers, and that ar Dick Bullen's the ornariest of all. Didn't hev no more *sabe* than to come round yar with sickness in the house and no provision. Thet's what I said: 'Bullen,' sez I, 'it's crazy drunk you are, or a fool,' sez I, 'to think o' such a thing.' 'Staples,' I sez, 'be you a man, Staples, and 'spect to raise h—l under my roof and invalids lyin' round?' but they would come—they would. Thet's wot you must 'spect o' such trash as lays round the Bar."

A burst of laughter from the men followed this unfortunate exposure. Whether it was overheard in the kitchen, or whether the Old Man's irate companion had just then exhausted all other modes of expressing her contemptuous indignation, I cannot say, but a back door was suddenly slammed with great violence. A moment later and the Old Man reappeared, haply unconscious of the cause of the late hilarious outburst, and smiled blandly.

"The old woman thought she'd jest run over to Mrs. McFadden's for a sociable call," he explained, with jaunty indifference, as he took a seat at the board.

Oddly enough it needed this untoward incident to relieve the embarrassment that was beginning to be felt by the party, and their natural audacity with their host. I do not propose to record the convivialities of that evening. The inquisitive reader will accept the statement that the conversation was characterized by the same intellectual exaltation, the same cautious reverence, the same fastidious delicacy, the same rhetorical precision, and the same logical and coherent discourage somewhat later in the evening, which distinguish similar gatherings of the masculine sex in more civilized localities and under more favorable auspices. No glasses were broken in the absence of any; no liquor was uselessly spilled on the floor or table in the scarcity of that article.

It was nearly midnight when the festivities were interrupted. "Hush," said Dick Bullen, holding up his hand. It was the querulous voice of Johnny from his adjacent closet. "Oh, Dad!"

The Old Man arose hurriedly and disappeared in the closet. Presently he reappeared. "His rheumatiz is coming on agin bad," he explained, "and he wants rubbin'." He lifted the demijohn of whiskey from the table and shook it. It was empty. Dick Bullen put down his tin cup with an embarrassed laugh. So did the others. The Old Man examined their contents and said hopefully, "I reckon that's enough; he don't need much. You hold on all o' you for a spell, and I'll be back"; and vanished in the closet with an old flannel shirt and the whiskey. The door closed but imperfectly, and the following dialogue was distinctly audible.

"Now, sonny, whar does she ache worst?"

"Sometimes over yar and sometimes under yar; but it's most powerful from yer to yer. Rub yer, dad."

A silence seemed to indicate a brisk rubbing. Then Johnny:

"Hevin' a good time out yer, Dad?"

"Yes, sonny."

"Tomorrer's Chrismiss, ain't it?"

"Yes, sonny. How does she feel now?"

"Better. Rub a little furder down. Wot's Chrismiss, anyway? Wot's it all about?"

"Oh, it's a day."

This exhaustive definition was apparently satisfactory, for there was a silent interval of rubbing. Presently Johnny again: "Mar sez that everywhere else but yer everybody gives things to everybody Chrissmiss, and then she jist waded inter you. She sez thar's a man they call Sandy Claws, not a white man, you know, but a kind o' Chinemin, comes down the chimbley night afore Chrismiss and gives things to chillern—boys like me. Puts 'em in their butes! Thet's what she tried to play upon me. Easy now, Pop, whar are you rubbin' to—thet's a mile from the place. She jest made that up, didn't she, jest to aggrevate me and you? Don't rub thar... Why, Dad!"

In the great quiet that seemed to have fallen upon the house the sigh of the near pines and the drip of leaves without was very distinct. Johnny's voice, too, was lowered as he went on. "Don't you take on now, fur I'm gettin' all right fast. Wot's the boys doin' out thar?"

The Old Man partly opened the door and peered through. His guests were sitting there sociably enough, and there were a few silver coins and a lean buckskin purse on the table. "Bettin' on suthin—some little game or 'nother. They're all right," he replied to Johnny, and recommended his rubbing.

"I'd like to take a hand and win some money," said Johnny, reflectively, after a pause.

The Old Man glibly repeated what was evidently a familiar formula, that if Johnny would wait until he struck it rich in the tunnel he'd have lots of money, etc., etc.

"Yes," said Johnny, "but you don't. And whether you strike it or I win it, it's about the same. It's all luck. But it's mighty cur'o's about Chirsmiss, ain't it? Why do they call it Chrismiss?"

Perhaps from some instinctive deference to the overhearing of his guests, or from some vague sense of incongruity, the Old Man's reply was so low as to be inaudible beyond the room.

"Yes," said Johnny, with some slight abatement of interest, "I've heerd o' *him* before. Thar, that'll do, Dad. I don't ache near so bad as I did. Now wrap me tight in this yer blanket. So. Now," he added in a muffled whisper, "sit down yer by me till I go asleep." To assure himself of obedience, he disengaged one hand from the blanket and, grasping his father's sleeve, again composed himself to rest.

For some moments the Old Man waited patiently. Then the unwonted stillness of the house excited his curiosity, and without moving from the bed, he cautiously opened the door with his disengaged hand, and looked into the main room. To his infinite surprise it was dark and deserted. But even then a smoldering log on the hearth broke, and by the up-springing blaze he saw the figure of Dick Bullen sitting by the dying embers.

"Hello!"

Dick started, rose, and came somewhat unsteadily toward him.

"Whar's the boys?" said the Old Man.

Gone up the cañon on a little *pasear*. They're coming back for me in a minit. I'm waitin' round for 'em. What are you starin' at, Old Man?" he added with a forced laugh. "Do you think I'm drunk?"

The Old Man might have been pardoned the supposition, for Dick's eyes were humid and his face flushed. He loitered and lounged back to the chimney, yawned, shook himself, buttoned up his coat and laughed. "Liquor ain't so plenty as that, Old Man. Now don't you git up," he continued, as the Old Man made a movement to release his sleeve from Johnny's hand. "Don't you mind manners. Sit jest whar you be. I'm goin' in a jiffy. Thar, that's them now."

There was a low tap at the door. Dick Bullen opened it quickly, nodded "Good night" to his host, and disappeared. The Old Man would have followed him but for the hand that still unconsciously grasped his sleeve. He could have easily disengaged it—it was small, weak, and emaciated. But perhaps because it *was* small, weak, and emaciated, he changed his mind, and, drawing his chair closer to the bed, rested his head upon it. In this defenseless attitude the potency of his earlier potations surprised him. The room flickered and faded before his eyes, reappeared, faded again, went out, and left him—asleep.

Meantime, Dick Bullen, closing the door, confronted his companions. "Are you ready?" said Staples. "Ready," said Dick. "What's the time?" "Past twelve," was the reply. "Can you make it? It's nigh on fifty miles, the round trip hither and yon." "I reckon," returned Dick, shortly. "Whar's the mare?" "Bill and Jack's holdin' her at the crossin'." "Let 'em hold on a minit longer," said Dick.

He turned and reentered the house softly. By the light of the guttering candle and dying fire he saw that the door of the little room was open. He stepped toward it on the tiptoe and looked in. The Old Man had fallen back in his chair, snoring, his helpless feet thrust out in a line with his collapsed shoulders, and his hat pulled over his eyes. Beside him, on a narrow wooden bedstead, lay Johnny, muffled tightly in a blanket that hid all save a strip of forehead and a few curls damp with perspiration. Dick Bullen made a step forward, hesitated, and glanced over his shoulder into the deserted room. Everything was quiet. With a sudden resolution he parted his huge mustaches with both hands and stooped over the sleeping boy. But even as he did so a mischievous blast, lying in wait, swooped down the chimney, rekindled the hearth, and lit up the room with a shameless glow from which Dick fled in bashful terror.

His companions were already waiting for him at the crossing. Two of them were struggling in the darkness with some strange misshapen bulk, which as Dick came nearer took the semblance of a great yellow horse.

It was the mare. She was not a pretty picture. From her Roman nose to her rising haunches, from her arched spine hidden by the stiff *machillas* of a Mexican saddle, to her thick, straight, bony legs, there was not a line of equine grace. In her half-blind but wholly vicious white eyes, in her protruding under lip, in her monstrous color, there was nothing but ugliness and vice.

"Now then," said Staples, "stand cl'ar of her heels, boys, and up with you. Don't miss your first holt of her mane, and mind ye get your off stirrup *quick*. Ready!"

There was a leap, a scrambling struggle, a bound, a wild retreat of the crowd, a circle of flying hoofs, two springless leaps that jarred the earth, a rapid play and jingle of spurs, a plunge, and then the voice of Dick somewhere in the darkness, "All right!"

"Don't take the lower road back onless you're hard pushed for time! Don't hold her in downhill! We'll be at the ford at five. G'lang! Hoopa! Mula! GO!"

A splash, a spark struck from the ledge in the road, a clatter in the rocky cut beyond, and Dick was gone.

SING, O MUSE, the ride of Richard Bullen! Sing, O Muse of chivalrous men! The sacred quest, the doughty deeds, the battery of low churls, the fearsome ride and grewsome perils of the Flower of Simpson's Bar! Alack! She is dainty, this Muse! She will have none of this bucking brute and swaggering, ragged rider, and I must fain follow him in prose, afoot!

It was one o'clock, and yet he had only gained Rattlesnake Hill. For in that time Jovita had rehearsed to him all her imperfections and practiced all her vices. Thrice had she stumbled. Twice had she thrown up her Roman nose in a straight line with the reins, and, resisting bit and spur, struck out madly across the country. Twice had she reared, and, rearing, fallen backward; and twice had the agile Dick, unharmed, regained his seat before she found her vicious legs again. And a mile beyond them, at the foot of a long hill, was Rattlesnake Creek. Dick knew that here was the crucial test of his ability to perform his enterprise, set his teeth grimly, put his knees well into her flanks, and changed his defensive tactics to brisk aggression. Bullied and maddened, Jovita began the descent of the hill. Here the artful Richard pretended to hold her in with ostentatious objurgation and well-feigned cries of alarm. It is unnecessary to add that Jovita instantly ran away. Nor need I state the time made in the descent; it is written in the chronicles of Simpson's

Bar. Enough that in another moment, as it seemed to Dick, she was splashing on the overflowed banks of Rattlesnake Creek. As Dick expected, the momentum she had acquired carried her beyond the point of balking, and, holding her well together for a mightly leap, they dashed into the middle of the swiftly flowing current. A few moments of kicking, wading, and swimming, and Dick drew a long breath on the opposite bank.

The road from Rattlesnake Creek to Red Mountain was tolerably level. Either the plunge in Rattlesnake Creek had dampened her baleful fire, or the art which led to it had shown her the superior wickedness of her rider, for Jovita no longer wasted her surplus energy in wanton conceits. Once she bucked, but it was from force of habit. Once she shied, but it was from a new freshly painted meetinghouse at the crossing of the county road. Hollows, ditches, gravelly deposits, patches of freshly springing grasses, flew from beneath her rattling hoofs. She began to smell unpleasantly, once or twice she coughed slightly, but there was no abatement of her strength or speed. By two o'clock he had passed Red Mountain and begun the descent to the plain. Ten minutes later the driver of the fast Pioneer coach was overtaken and passed by a "man on a Pinto hoss"—an event sufficiently notable for remark. At half past two Dick rose in his stirrups with a great shout. Stars were glittering through the rifted clouds, and beyond him, out of the plain, rose two spires, a flagstaff, and a straggling line of black objects. Dick jingled his spurs and swung his *riata*, Jovita bounded forward, and in another moment they swept into Tuttleville and drew up before the wooden piazza of "The Hotel of All Nations."

What transpired that night at Tuttleville is not strictly a part of this record. Briefly I may state, however, that after Jovita had been handed over to a sleepy ostler, whom she at once kicked into unpleasant consciousness, Dick sallied out with the barkeeper for a tour of the sleeping town. Lights still gleamed from a few saloons and gambling houses; but, avoiding these, they stopped before several closed shops, and by persistent tapping and judicious outcry roused the proprietors from their beds, and made them unbar the doors of their magazines and expose their wares. Sometimes they were met by curses, but oftener by interest and some concern in their needs, and the interview was invariably concluded by a drink. It was three o'clock before this pleasantry was given over, and with a small waterproof bag of india-rubber strapped on his shoulders Dick returned to the hotel. But here he was waylaid by Beauty—Beauty opulent in charms, affluent in dress, persuasive in speech, and Spanish in accent! In vain she repeated the invitation in "Excelsior," happily scorned by all Alpine-climbing youth, and rejected by this child of the Sierras—a rejection softened in this instance by a laugh and his last gold coin. And then he sprang to the saddle and dashed down the lonely street and out into the lonelier plain, where presently the lights, the black line of houses, the spires, and the flagstaff sank into the earth behind him again and were lost in the distance.

The storm had cleared away, the air was brisk and cold, the outlines of adjacent landmarks were distinct, but it was half past four before Dick reached the meetinghouse and the crossing of the county road. To avoid the rising grade he had taken a longer and more circuitous road, in whose viscid mud Jovita sank fetlock deep at every bound. It was a poor preparation for a steady ascent of five miles more; but Jovita, gathering her legs under her, took it with her usual blind, unreasoning fury, and a half-hour later reached the long level that led to Rattlesnake Creek. Another half-hour would bring him to the creek. He threw the reins lightly upon the neck of the mare, chirruped to her, and began to sing.

Suddenly Jovita shied with a bound that would have unseated a less practiced rider. Hanging to her rein was a figure that had leaped from the bank, and at the same time from the road before her arose a shadowy horse and rider. "Throw up your hands," commanded this second apparition, with an oath.

Dick felt the mare tremble, quiver, and apparently sink under him. He knew what it meant and was prepared.

"Stand aside, Jack Simpson, I know you, you d—d thief. Let me pass or—"

He did not finish the sentence. Jovita rose straight in the air with a terrific bound, throwing the figure from her bit with a single shake of her vicious head, and charged with deadly malevolence down on the impediment before her. An oath, a pistol shot, horse and highwayman rolled over in the road, and the next moment Jovita was a hundred yards away. But the good right arm of her rider, shattered by a bullet, dropped helplessly at his side.

Without slacking his speed he shifted the reins to his left hand. But a few moments later he was obliged to halt and tighten the saddle-girths that had slipped in the onset. This, in his crippled condition, took some time. He had no fear of pursuit, but looking up he saw that the eastern stars were already paling, and that the distant peaks had lost their ghostly whiteness, and now stood out blackly against a lighter sky. Day was upon him. Then completely absorbed in a single idea, he forgot the pain of his wound, and mounting again dashed on toward Rattlesnake Creek. But now Jovita's breath came broken by gasps, Dick reeled in his saddle, and brighter and brighter grew the sky.

Ride, Richard; run, Jovita; linger, O day!

For the last few rods there was a roaring in his ears. Was it exhaustion from loss of blood, or what? He was dazed and giddy as he swept down the hill, and did not recognize his surroundings. Had he taken the wrong road, or was this Rattlesnake Creek?

It was. But the brawling creek he had swam a few hours before had risen, more than doubled its volume, and now rolled a swift and resistless river between him and Rattlesnake Hill. For the first time that night Richard's heart sank within him. The river, the mountain, the quickening east, swam before his eyes. He shut them to recover his self-control. In that brief interval, by some fantastic mental process, the little room at Simpson's Bar and the figures of the sleeping father and son rose upon him. He opened his eyes wildly, cast off his coat, pistol, boots, and saddle, bound his precious pack tightly to his shoulders, grasped the bare flanks of Jovita with his bared knees, and with a shout dashed into the yellow water. A cry rose from the opposite bank as the head of a man and horse struggled for a few moments against the battling current, and then were swept away amidst uprooted trees and whirling driftwood.

THE OLD MAN STARTED and woke. The fire on the hearth was dead, the candle in the outer room flickering in its socket, and somebody was rapping at the door. He opened it, but fell back with a cry before the dripping, half-naked figure that reeled against the doorpost.

"Dick?"

"Hush! Is he awake yet?"

"No, but, Dick—"

"Dry up, you old fool! Get me some whiskey *quick!*" The Old Man flew and returned with—an empty bottle! Dick would have sworn, but his strength was not equal to the occasion. He staggered, caught at the handle of the door, and motioned to the Old Man.

"Thar's suthin' in my pack yer for Johnny. Take it off. I can't."

The Old Man unstrapped the pack and laid it before the exhausted man.

"Open it, quick!"

He did so with trembling fingers. It contained only a few poor toys— cheap and barbaric enough, goodness knows, but bright with paint and tinsel. One of them was broken; another, I fear, was irretrievably ruined by water; and on the third—ah me! There was a cruel spot.

"It don't look like much, that's a fact," said Dick, ruefully. "But it's the best we could do… Take 'em, Old Man, and put 'em in his stocking, and tell him—tell him, you know—hold me, Old Man—" The Old Man caught at his sinking figure. "Tell him," said Dick, with a weak little laugh, "tell him Sandy Claus has come."

AND EVEN SO, bedraggled, ragged, unshaven, and unshorn, with one arm hanging helplessly at his side, Santa Claus came to Simpson's Bar and fell fainting on the first threshold. The Christmas dawn came slowly after, touching the remoter peaks with the rosy warmth of ineffable love. And it looked so tenderly on Simpson's Bar that the whole mountain, as if caught in a generous action, blushed to the skies.

A Christmas Carol in Prose

AN EXCERPT

Charles Dickens

Stave Four
THE LAST OF THE SPIRITS

The Phantom slowly, gravely, silently, approached. When it came near him, Scrooge bent down upon his knee; for in the very air through which this Spirit moved it seemed to scatter gloom and mystery.

It was shrouded in a deep black garment, which concealed its head, its face, its form, and left nothing of it visible, save one outstretched hand. But for this it would have been difficult to detach its figure from the night, and separate it from the darkness by which it was surrounded.

He felt that it was tall and stately when it came beside him, and that its mysterious presence filled him with a solemn dread. He knew no more, for the Spirit neither spoke nor moved.

"I am in the presence of the Ghost of Christmas Yet to Come?" said Scrooge. The Spirit answered not, but pointed onward with its hand.

"You are about to show me shadows of the things that have not happened, but will happen in the time before us," Scrooge pursued. "Is that so, Spirit?"

The upper portion of the garment was contracted for an instant in its folds, as if the Spirit had inclined its head. That was the only answer he received.

Although well used to ghostly company by this time, Scrooge feared the silent shape so much that his legs trembled beneath him, and he found that he could hardly stand when he prepared to follow it. The Spirit paused a moment, as observing his condition, and giving him time to recover.

But Scrooge was all the worse for this. It thrilled him with a vague uncertain horror, to know that behind the dusky shroud there were ghostly eyes intently fixed upon him, while he, though he stretched his own to the utmost, could see nothing but a spectral hand and one great heap of black.

"Ghost of the Future!" he exclaimed. "I fear you more than any specter I have seen. But as I know your purpose is to do me good, and as I hope to live to be another man from what I was, I am prepared to bear you company, and do it with a thankful heart. Will you not speak to me?"

It gave him no reply. The hand was pointed straight before them.

"Lead on!" said Scrooge. "Lead on! The night is waning fast, and it is precious time to me, I know. Lead on, Spirit!"

The Phantom moved away as it had come toward him. Scrooge followed in the shadow of its dress, which bore him up, he thought, and carried him along.

They scarcely seemed to enter the city; for the city rather seemed to spring up about them, and encompass them of its own act. But there they were in the heart of it; on 'Change, amongst the merchants; who hurried up and down, and chinked the money in their pockets, and conversed in groups, and looked at their watches, and trifled thoughtfully with their great gold seals, and so forth as Scrooge had seen them often.

The Spirit stopped beside one little knot of businessmen. Observing that the hand was pointed to them, Scrooge advanced to listen to their talk.

"No," said a great fat man with a monstrous chin, "I don't know much about it either way. I only know he's dead."

"When did he die?" inquired another.

"Last night, I believe."

"Why, what was the matter with him?" asked a third, taking a vast quantity of snuff out of a very large snuff box. "I thought he'd never die."

"God knows," said the first, with a yawn.

"What has he done with his money?" asked a red-faced gentleman with a pendulous excrescence on the end of his nose, which shook like the gills of a turkey cock.

"I haven't heard," said the man with the large chin, yawning again. "Left it to his company, perhaps. He hasn't left it to *me*. That's all I know."

This pleasantry was received with a general laugh.

"It's likely to be a very cheap funeral," said the same speaker, "for upon my life I don't know of anybody to go to it. Suppose we make up a party and volunteer?"

"I don't mind going if a lunch is provided," observed the gentleman with the excrescence on his nose. "But I must be fed if I make one."

Another laugh.

"Well, I am the most disinterested among you, after all," said the first speaker, "for I never wear black gloves, and I will never eat lunch. But I'll offer to go, if anybody else will. When I come to think of it, I'm not at all sure that I wasn't his most particular friend; for we used to stop and speak whenever we met. Bye, bye!"

Speakers and listeners strolled away, and mixed with other groups. Scrooge knew the men, and looked toward the Spirit for an explanation.

The Phantom glided on into a street. Its finger pointed to two persons meeting. Scrooge listened again, thinking that the explanation might lie here.

He knew these men, also, perfectly. They were men of business, very wealthy and of great importance. He had made a point of always standing well in their esteem; in a business point of view, that is, strictly in a business point of view.

"How are you?" said one.

"How are you?" returned the other.

"Well!" said the first. "Old Scratch has got his own at last, hey?"

"So I am told," returned the second. "Cold, isn't it?"

"Seasonable for Christmastime. You are not a skater, I suppose?"

"No. No. Something else to think of. Good morning!"

Not another word. That was their meeting, their conversation, and their parting.

Scrooge was at first inclined to be surprised that the Spirit should attach importance to conversations apparently so trivial; but feeling assured that they must have some hidden purpose, he set himself to consider what it was likely to be. They could scarcely be supposed to have any bearing on the death of Jacob, his old partner, for that was Past, and this Ghost's province was the Future. Nor could he think of anyone immediately connected with himself to whom he could apply them. But nothing doubting that to whomsoever they applied they had some latent moral for his own improvement, he resolved to treasure up every word he heard, and everything he saw; and especially to observe the shadow of himself when it appeared. For he had an expectation that the conduct of his future self would give him the clue he missed, and would render the solution of these riddles easy.

He looked about in that very place for his own image; but another man stood in his accustomed corner, and though the clock pointed to his usual time of day for being there, he saw no likeness of himself among the multitudes that poured in through the Porch. It gave him little surprise, however, for he had been revolving in his mind a change of life, and thought and hoped he saw his newborn resolutions carried out in this.

Quiet and dark, beside him stood the Phantom, with its outstretched hand. When he roused himself from his thoughtful quest, he fancied from the turn of the hand, and its situation in reference to himself, that the Unseen Eyes were looking at him keenly. It made him shudder, and feel very cold.

They left the busy scene, and went into an obscure part of the town, where Scrooge had never penetrated before, although he recognized its situation and its bad repute. The ways were foul and narrow; the shops and houses wretched; the people half-naked, drunken, slipshod, ugly. Alleys and archways, like so many cesspools, disgorged their offences of smell, and dirt, and life, upon the straggling streets; and the whole quarter reeked with crime, with filth and misery.

Far in this den of infamous resort, there was a low-browed, beetling shop, below a penthouse roof, where iron, old rags, bottles, bones, and greasy offal were bought. Upon the floor within were piled up heaps of rusty keys, nails, chains, hinges, files, scales, weights, and refuse iron of all kinds. Secrets that few would like to scrutinize were bred and hidden in mountains of unseemly rags, masses of corrupted fat, and sepulchers of bones. Sitting in among the wares he dealt in, by a charcoal stove made of old bricks, was a gray-haired rascal, nearly seventy years of age; who had screened himself from the cold air without by a frowsy curtaining of miscellaneous tatters hung upon a line, and smoked his pipe in all the luxury of calm retirement.

Scrooge and the Phantom came into the presence of this man, just as a woman with a heavy bundle slunk into the shop. But she had scarcely entered, when another woman, similarly laden, came in, too; and she was closely followed by a man in faded black, who was no less startled by the sight of them than they had been upon the recognition of each other. After a short period of blank astonishment, in which the old man with the pipe had joined them, they all three burst into a laugh.

"Let the charwoman alone to be first!" said she who had entered first. "Let the laundress alone to be the second; and let the undertaker's man alone to be the third. Look here, old Joe, here's a chance! If we haven't all three met here without meaning it!"

"You couldn't have met in a better place," said old Joe, removing his pipe from his mouth. "Come into the parlor. You were made free of it long ago, you know; and the other two ain't strangers. Stop till I shut the door of the shop. Ah! How it squeaks! There ain't such a rusty bit of metal in the place as its own hinges, I believe, and I'm sure there's no such old bones here as mine. Ha, ha! We're all suitable to our calling, we're well matched. Come into the parlor. Come into the parlor."

The parlor was the space behind the screen of rags. The old man raked the fire together with an old stair rod, and, having trimmed his smoky lamp (for it was night) with the stem of his pipe, put it into his mouth again.

While he did this the woman who had already spoken threw her bundle on the floor and sat down in a flaunting manner on a stool; crossing her elbows on her knees, and looking with a bold defiance at the other two.

"What odds, then! What odds, Mrs. Dilber?" said the woman. "Every person has a right to take care of themselves. *He* always did!"

"That's true, indeed!" said the laundress. "No man more so."

"Why, then, don't stand staring as if you was afraid, woman. Who's the wiser? We're not going to pick holes in each other's coats, I suppose?"

"No, indeed!" said Mrs. Dilber and the man together. "We should hope not."

"Very well, then!" cried the woman. "That's enough. Who's the worse for the loss of a few things like these? Not a dead man, I suppose?"

"No, indeed," said Mrs. Dilber, laughing.

"If he wanted to keep 'em after he was dead, a wicked old screw," pursued the woman, "why wasn't he natural in his lifetime? If he had been, he'd have had somebody to look after him when he was struck with Death, instead of lying gasping out his last there, alone by himself."

"It's the truest word that ever was spoke," said Mrs. Dilber. "It's a judgment on him."

"I wish it was a little heavier judgment," replied the woman. "And it should have been, you may depend upon it, if I could have laid my hands on anything else. Open that bundle, old Joe, and let me know the value of it. Speak out plain. I'm not afraid to be the first, nor afraid for them to see it. We knew pretty well that we were helping ourselves, before we met here, I believe. It's no sin. Open the bundle, Joe."

But the gallantry of her friends would not allow of this; and the man in faded black, mounting the breach firs, produced *his* plunder. It was not extensive. A seal or two, a pencil case, a pair of sleeve buttons, and a brooch of no great value, were all. They were severally examined and appraised by old Joe, who chalked the sums he was disposed to give for each, upon the wall, and added them up into a total when he found that there was nothing more to come.

"That's your account," said Joe, "and I wouldn't give another sixpence, if I was to be boiled for not doing it. Who's next?"

Mrs. Dilber was next. Sheets and towels, a little wearing apparel, two old-fashioned silver teaspoons, a pair of sugar tongs, and a few boots. Her account was stated on the wall in the same manner.

"I always give too much to ladies. It's a weakness of mine, and that's the way I ruin myself," said old Joe. "That's your account. If you asked me for another penny and made it an open question, I'd repent of being so liberal and knock off half a crown."

"And now undo *my* bundle, Joe," said the first woman.

Joe went down on his knees for the great convenience of opening it, and having unfastened a great many knots, dragged out a large heavy roll of some dark stuff.

"What do you call this?" said Joe. "Bed curtains?"

"Ah!" returned the woman, laughing, and leaning forward on her crossed arms. "Bed curtains!"

"You don't mean to say you took 'em down, rings and all, with him lying there?" said Joe.

"Yes, I do," replied the woman. "Why not?"

"You were born to make your fortune," said Joe, "and you'll certainly do it."

"I certainly shan't hold my hand, when I can get anything in it by reaching it out, for the sake of such a man as he was, I promise you, Joe," returned the woman coolly. "Don't drop that oil upon the blankets, now."

"His blankets?" asked Joe.

"Who else's do you think?" replied the woman. "He isn't likely to take cold without 'em, I dare say."

"I hope he didn't die of anything catching? Eh?" said old Joe, stopping in his work, and looking up.

"Don't you be afraid of that," returned the woman. "I ain't so fond of his company that I'd loiter about him for such things, if he did. Ah! You may look through that shirt till your eyes ache, but you won't find a hole in it, nor a threadbare place. It's the best he had, and a fine one too. They'd have wasted it, if it hadn't been for me."

"What do you call wasting of it?" asked old Joe.

"Putting it on him to be buried in, to be sure," replied the woman, with a laugh. "Somebody was fool enough to do it, but I took it off again. If calico ain't good enough for such a purpose, it isn't good enough for anything. It's quite as becoming to the body. He can't look uglier than he did in that one."

Scrooge listened to this dialogue in horror. As they sat grouped about their spoil, in the scanty light afforded by the old man's lamp, he viewed them with a detestation and disgust, which could hardly have been greater, as though they had been obscene demons, marketing the corpse itself.

"Ha, ha!" laughed the same woman, when old Joe, producing a flannel bag with money in it, told out their several gains upon the ground. "This is the end of it, you see?

He frightened every one away from him when he was alive, to profit us when he was dead! Ha, ha, ha!"

"Spirit!" said Scrooge, shuddering from head to foot. "I see, I see. The case of this unhappy man might be my own. My life tends that way, now. Merciful Heaven, what is this?"

He recoiled in terror, for the scene had changed, and now he almost touched a bed—a bare, uncurtained bed, on which, beneath a ragged sheet, there lay a something covered up, which, though it was dumb, announced itself in awful language.

The room was very dark, too dark to be observed with any accuracy, though Scrooge glanced round it in obedience to a secret impulse, anxious to know what kind of room it was. A pale light rising in the outer air, fell straight upon the bed, and on it, plundered and bereft, unwatched, unwept, uncared for, was the body of this man.

Scrooge glanced toward the Phantom. Its steady hand was pointed to the head. The cover was so carelessly adjusted that the slightest raising of it, the motion of a finger upon Scrooge's part, would have disclosed the face. He thought of it, felt how easy it would be to do, and longed to do it; but had no more power to withdraw the veil than to dismiss the specter at his side.

Oh, cold, cold, rigid, dreadful Death, set up thine altar here, and dress it with such terrors as thou hast at thy command, for this is thy dominion! But of the loved, revered, and honored head, thou can not turn one hair to thy dread purposes, or make one feature odious. It is not that the hand is heavy and will fall down when released; it is not that the heart and pulse are still; but that the hand was open, generous, and true; the heart brave, warm, and tender; and the pulse a man's. Strike, Shadow, strike! And see his good deeds springing from the wound, to sow the world with life immortal!

No voice pronounced these words in Scrooge's ears, and yet he heard them when he looked upon the bed. He thought, if this man could be raised up now, what would be his foremost thoughts? Avarice, hard-dealing, griping cares? They have brought him to a rich end, truly!

He lay, in the dark, empty house, with not a man, a woman, or a child, to say he was kind to me in this or that, and for the memory of one kind word I will be kind to him. A cat was tearing at the door, and there was a sound of gnawing rats beneath the hearthstone. What *they* wanted in the room of death, and why they were so restless and disturbed, Scrooge did not dare to think.

"Spirit!" he said, "this is a fearful place. In leaving it, I shall not leave its lesson, trust me. Let us go!"

Still the Ghost pointed with an unmoved finger to the head.

"I understand you," Scrooge returned, "and I would do it if I could. But I have not the power, Spirit. I have not the power."

Again it seemed to look upon him.

"If there is any person in the town who feels emotion caused by this man's death," said Scrooge, quite agonized, "show that person to me, Spirit, I beseech you!"

The Phantom spread its dark robe before him for moment, like a wing, and withdrawing it, revealed a room by daylight, where a mother and her children were.

She was expecting someone, and with anxious eagerness; for she walked up and down the room; started at every sound; looked out from the window; glanced at the clock; tried, but in vain, to work with her needle; and could hardly bear the voices of her children in their play.

At length the long, expected knock was heard. She hurried to the door and met her husband—a man whose face was care-worn and depressed, though he was young. There was a remarkable expression in it now, and a kind of serious delight of which he felt ashamed, and which he struggled to repress.

He sat down to the dinner that had been hoarding for him by the fire, and when she asked him faintly what news (which was not until after a long silence), he appeared embarrassed how to answer.

"Is it good," she said, "or bad?"—to help him.

"Bad," he answered.

"We are quite ruined?"

"No. There is hope yet, Caroline."

"If *he* relents," she said, amazed, "there is! Nothing is past hope, if such a miracle has happened."

"He is past relenting," said her husband. "He is dead."

She was a mild and patient creature, if her face spoke truth; but she was thankful in her soul to hear it, and she said so, with clasped hands. She prayed forgiveness the next moment, and was sorry, but the first was the emotion of her heart.

"What the half-drunken woman, whom I told you of last night, said to me, when I tried to see him and obtain a week's delay, and what I thought was a mere excuse to avoid me, turns out to have been quite true. He was not only very ill, but dying, then."

"To whom will our debt be transferred?"

"I don't know. But before that time we shall be ready with the money; and even though we were not, it would be bad fortune indeed to find so merciless a creditor in his successor. We may sleep tonight with light hearts, Caroline!"

Yes. Soften it as they would, their hearts were lighter. The children's faces, hushed and clustered round to hear what they so little understood, were brighter; and it was a happier house for this man's death! The only emotion that the ghost could show him, caused by the event, was one of pleasure.

"Let me see some tenderness connected with a death," said Scrooge, "or that dark chamber, Spirit, which we left just now, will be forever present to me."

The Ghost conducted him through several streets familiar to his feet, and as they went along, Scrooge looked here and there to find himself, but nowhere was he to be seen. They entered poor Bob Cratchit's house, the dwelling he had visited before, and found the mother and the children seated round the fire.

Quiet. Very quiet. The noisy little Cratchits were still as statues in one corner, and sat looking up at Peter, who had a book before him. The mother and her daughters were engaged in sewing. But surely they were very quiet!

"'And he took a child, and set him in the midst of them.'"

Where had Scrooge heard those words? He had not dreamed them. The boy must have read them out, as he and the Spirit crossed the threshold. Why did he not go on?

The mother laid her work upon the table, and put her hand up to her face. "The color hurts my eyes," she said.

The color? Ah, poor Tiny Tim!

"They're better now again," said Cratchit's wife. "It makes them weak by candlelight, and I wouldn't show weak eyes to your father when he comes home, for the world. It must be near his time."

"Past it rather," Peter answered, shutting up his book. "But I think he has walked a little slower than he used, these few last evenings, mother."

They were very quiet again. At last she said, and in a steady, cheerful voice, that only faltered once: "I have known him walk with—I have known him walk with Tiny Tim upon his shoulder, very fast indeed."

"And so have I," cried Peter. "Often."

"And so have I," exclaimed another. So had all.

"But he was very light to carry," she resumed intent upon her work, "and his father loved him so, that it was no trouble; no trouble. And there is your father at the door!"

She hurried out to meet him; and little Bob in his comforter—he had need of it, poor fellow—came in. His tea was ready for him on the hob, and they all tried who should help him to it most. Then the two young Cratchits got upon his knees and laid, each child, a little cheek against his face, as if they said, "Don't mind it, father." "Don't be grieved!"

Bob was very cheerful with them, and spoke pleasantly to all the family. He looked at the work upon the table, and praised the industry and speed of Mrs. Cratchit and the girls. They would be done long before Sunday, he said.

"Sunday! You went today, then, Robert?" said the wife.

"Yes, my dear," returned Bob. "I wish you could have gone. It would have done you good to see how green a place it is. But you'll see it often. I promised him that I would walk there on a Sunday. My little, little child!" cried Bob. "My little child!"

He broke down all at once. He couldn't help it. If he could have helped it, he and his child would have been farther apart perhaps than they were.

He left the room, and went upstairs into the room above, which was lighted cheerfully, and hung with Christmas. There was a chair set close behind the child, and there were signs of someone having been there, lately. Poor Bob sat down in it, and when he had thought a little and composed himself, he kissed the little face. He was reconciled to what had happened, and went down again quite happy.

They drew about the fire, and talked; the girls and mother working still. Bob told them of the extraordinary kindness of Mr. Scrooge's nephew, whom he had scarcely seen but once, and who, meeting him in the street that day, and seeing that he looked a little—"just a little down you know," said Bob, inquired what had happened to distress him. "On which," said Bob, "for he is the pleasantest-spoken gentleman you ever heard, I told him. 'I am heartily sorry for it, Mr. Cratchit,' he said, 'and heartily sorry for your good wife.' By the bye, how he ever knew *that* I don't know."

"Knew what, my dear?"

"Why, that you were a good wife," replied Bob.

"Everybody knows that!" said Peter.

"Very well observed, my boy!" cried Bob. "I hope they do. 'Heartily sorry,' he said, 'for your good wife. If I can be of service to you in any way,' he said, giving me his card, 'that's where I live. Pray come to me.' Now, it wasn't," cried Bob, "for the sake of anything he might be able to do for us, so much as for his kind way, that this was quite delightful. It really seemed as if he had known our Tiny Tim, and felt with us."

"I'm sure he's a good soul!" said Mrs. Cratchit.

"You would be sure of it, my dear," returned Bob, "if you saw and spoke to him. I shouldn't be at all surprised—mark what I say!—if he got Peter a better situation."

"Only hear that, Peter," said Mrs. Cratchit.

"And then," cried one of the girls, "Peter will be keeping company with someone, and setting up for himself."

"Get along with you!" reported Peter, grinning.

"It's just as likely as not," said Bob, "one of these days, though there's plenty of time for that, my dear. But however and whenever we part from one another, I am sure we shall none of us forget poor Tiny Tim—shall we—or this first parting that there was among us?"

"Never, father!" cried they all.

"And I know," said Bob, "I know, my dears, that when we recollect how patient and how mild he was, although he was a little, little child, we shall not quarrel easily among ourselves, and forget poor Tiny Tim in doing it."

"No, never, father!" they all cried again.

"I am very happy," said little Bob. "I am very happy!"

Mrs. Cratchit kissed him, his daughters kissed him, the two young Cratchits kissed him, and Peter and himself shook hands. Spirit of Tiny Tim, thy childish essence was from God!

"Specter," said Scrooge, "something informs me that our parting moment is at hand. I know it, but I know not how. Tell me what man that was whom we saw lying dead?"

The Ghost of Christmas Yet to Come conveyed him, as before—though at a different time, he thought; indeed, there seemed no order in these latter visions, save that they were in the Future—into the resorts of businessmen, but showed him not himself. Indeed, the Spirit did not stay for anything, but went straight on, as to the end just now desired, until besought by Scrooge to tarry for a moment.

"This court," said Scrooge, "through which we hurry now, is where my place of occupation is, and has been for a length of time. I see the house. Let me behold what I shall be, in days to come."

The Spirit stopped. The hand was pointed elsewhere.

"The house is yonder," Scrooge exclaimed. "Why do you point away?"

The inexorable finger underwent no change.

Scrooge hastened to the window of his office, and looked in. It was an office still, but not his. The furniture was not the same, and the figure in the chair was not himself. The Phantom pointed as before.

He joined it once again, and wondering why and whither he had gone, accompanied it until they reached an iron gate. He paused to look round before entering.

A churchyard. Here, then, the wretched man whose name he had now to learn lay underneath the ground. It was a worthy place. Walled in by houses; overrun by grass and weeds, the growth of vegetation's death, not life; choked up with too much burying; fat with repleted appetite. A worthy place!

The Spirit stood among the graves, and pointed down to One. He advanced toward it trembling. The Phantom was exactly as it had been, but he dreaded that he saw new meaning in its solemn shape.

"Before I draw nearer to that stone to which you point," said Scrooge, "answer me one question. Are these the shadows of the things that Will be, or are they shadows of the things that May be, only?"

Still the Ghost pointed downward to the grave by which it stood.

"Men's courses will foreshadow certain ends, to which, if persevered in, they must lead," said Scrooge. "But if the courses be departed from, the ends will change. Say it is thus with what you show me!"

The Spirit was immovable as ever.

Scrooge crept toward it, trembling as he went, and following the finger, read upon the stone of the neglected grave his own name, EBENEZER SCROOGE.

"Am I that man who lay upon the bed?" he cried, upon his knees.

The finger pointed from the grave to him, and back again.

"No, Spirit! Oh, no, no!"

The finger still was there.

"Spirit!" he cried, tight clutching at its robe. "Hear me! I am not the man I was. I will not be the man I must have been but for this intercourse. Why show me this, if I am past all hope?"

For the first time the hand appeared to shake.

"Good Spirit," he pursued, as down upon the ground he fell before it. "Your nature intercedes for me, and pities me. Assure me that I yet may change these shadows you have shown me, by an altered life?"

The kind hand trembled.

"I will honor Christmas in my heart, and try to keep it all the year. I will live in the Past, the Present, and the Future. The Spirits of all Three shall strive within me. I will not shut out the lessons that they teach. Oh, tell me I may sponge away the writing on this stone?"

In his agony, he caught the spectral hand. It sought to free itself, but he was strong in his entreaty, and detained it. The Spirit, stronger yet, repulsed him.

Holding up his hands in a last prayer to have his fate reversed, he saw an alteration in the Phantom's hood and dress. It shrunk, collapsed, and dwindled down into a bedpost.

Stave Five
THE END OF IT

Yes! And the bedpost was his own. The bed was his own; the room was his own. Best and happiest of all, the time before him was his own, to make amends in!

"I will live in the Past, the Present, and the Future!" Scrooge repeated, as he scrambled out of bed. "The Spirits of all Three shall strive within me. Oh Jacob Marley! Heaven and the Christmastime be praise for this! I say it on my knees, old Jacob; on my knees!"

He was so fluttered and so glowing with his good intentions that his broken voice would scarcely answer to his call. He had been sobbing violently in his conflict with the Spirit, and his face was wet with tears.

"They are not torn down," cried Scrooge, folding one of his bed curtains in his arms. "They are not torn down, rings and all. They are here—I am here—the shadows of the things that would have been may be dispelled.

They will be. I know they will!"

His hands were busy with his garments all this time; turning them inside out, putting them on upside down, tearing them, mislaying them, making them parties to every kind of extravagance.

"I don't know what to do!" cried Scrooge, laughing and crying in the same breath; and making a perfect Laocoön of himself with his stockings. "I am light as a feather. I am as happy as an angel. I am as merry as a schoolboy. I am as giddy as a drunken man. A merry Christmas to everybody! A happy New Year to all the world! Hallo here! Whoop! Hallo!"

He had frisked into the sitting room, and was now standing there, perfectly winded.

"There's the saucepan that the gruel was in!" cried Scrooge, starting off again, and going round the fireplace. "There's the door by which the Ghost of Jacob Marley entered! There's the corner where the Ghost of a Christmas Present sat! There's the window where I saw the wandering Spirits! It's all right, it's all true, it all happened. Ha, ha, ha!"

Really, for a man who had been out of practice for so many years, it was a splendid laugh, a most illustrious laugh. The father of a long, long line of brilliant laughs!

"I don't know what day of the month it is," said Scrooge. "I don't know how long I have been among the Spirits. I don't know anything. I'm quite a baby. Never mind—I don't care. I'd rather be a baby. Hallo! Whoop! Hallo here!"

He was checked in his transports by the churches ringing out the lustiest peals he had ever heard. Clash, clash, hammer; ding, ding, bell. Bell, dong, ding; hammer, clang, clash! Oh, glorious, glorious!

Running to the window, he opened it, and put out his head. No fog, no mist; clear, bright, jovial, stirring, cold; cold, piping for the blood to dance to; golden sunlight; Heavenly sky; sweet fresh air; merry bells. Oh, glorious, glorious!

"What's today?" cried Scrooge, calling downward to a boy in Sunday clothes, who perhaps had loitered in to look about him.

"Eh?" returned the boy, with all his might of wonder.

"What's today, my fine fellow?" said Scrooge.

"Today?" replied the boy. "Why, CHRISTMAS DAY."

"It's Christmas Day!" said Scrooge to himself. "I haven't missed it. The Spirits have done it all in one night. They can do anything they like. Of course they can. Of course they can. Hallo, my fine fellow!"

"Hallo!" returned the boy.

"Do you know the poulterer's, in the next street but one, at the corner?" Scrooge inquired.

"I should hope I did," replied the lad.

"An intelligent boy!" said Scrooge. "A remarkable boy! Do you know whether they've sold the prize Turkey that was hanging up there? Not the little prize Turkey, the big one?"

"What, the one as big as me?" returned the boy.

"Is it?" said Scrooge. "Go and buy it."

"Walk 'ER?" exclaimed the boy.

"No, no," said Scrooge, "I am in earnest. Go and buy it, and tell 'em to bring it here, that I may give them the directions where to take it. Come back with the man, and I'll give you a shilling. Come back with him in less than five minutes, and I'll give you half a crown!"

The boy was off like a shot. He must have had a steady hand at a trigger who could have got a shot off half so fast.

"I'll send it to Bob Cratchit's," whispered Scrooge, rubbing his hands, and splitting with a laugh. "He shan't know who sends it. It's twice the size of Tiny Tim. Joe Miller never made such a joke as sending it to Bob's will be!"

The hand in which he wrote the address was not a steady one; but write it he did, somehow, and went downstairs to open the street door, ready for the coming of the poulterer's man. As he stood there, waiting his arrival, the knocker caught his eye.

"I shall love it as long as I live!" cried Scrooge, patting it with his hand. "I scarcely ever looked at it before. What an honest expression it has in its face! It's a wonderful knocker! Here's the Turkey. Hallo! Whoop! How are you? Merry Christmas!"

It *was* a Turkey! He never could have stood upon his legs, that bird. He would have snapped 'em short off in a minute, like sticks of sealing wax.

"Why, it's impossible to carry that to Camden Town," said Scrooge. "You must have a cab."

The chuckle with which he said this, and the chuckle with which he paid for the Turkey, and the chuckle with which he paid for the cab, and the chuckle with which he recompensed the boy were only to be exceeded by the chuckle with which he sat down breathless in his chair again, and chuckled till he cried.

Shaving was not an easy task, for his hand continued to shake very much; and shaving requires attention, even when you don't dance while you are at it. But if he had cut the end of his nose off, he would have put a piece of sticking plaster over it, and been quite satisfied.

He dressed himself "all in his best," and at last got out into the streets. The people were by this time pouring forth, as he had seen them with the Ghost of Christmas Present; and walking with his hands behind him, Scrooge regarded every one with a delighted smile. He looked so irresistibly pleasant, in a word, that three or four good-humored fellows said, "Good morning, sir! A merry Christmas to you!" And Scrooge said often afterward that, of all the blithe sounds he had ever heard, those were the blithest in his ears.

He had not gone far, when coming on toward him he beheld the portly gentleman who had walked into his counting-house the day before, and said "Scrooge and Marley's, I believe?" It sent a pang across his heart to think how this old gentleman would look upon him when they met, but he knew what path lay straight before him, and he took it.

"My dear sir," said Scrooge, quickening in his pace, and taking the old gentleman by both his hands. "How do you do? I hope you succeeded yesterday. It was very kind of you. A merry Christmas to you, sir!"

"Mr. Scrooge?"

"Yes," said Scrooge. "That is my name, and I fear it may not be pleasant to you. Allow me to ask your pardon. And will you have the goodness"—here Scrooge whispered in his ear.

"Lord bless me!" cried the gentleman, as if his breath were taken away. "My dear Mr. Scrooge, are you serious?"

"If you please," said Scrooge. "Not a farthing less. A great many back-payments are included in it, I assure you. Will you do me that favor?"

"My dear sir," said the other, shaking hands with him, "I don't know what to say to so munifi…"

"Don't say anything, please," retorted Scrooge. "Come and see me. Will you come and see me?"

"I will!" cried the old gentleman. And it was clear he meant to do it.

"Thankee," said Scrooge. "I am much obliged to you. I thank you fifty times. Bless you!"

He went to church, and walked about the streets, and watched the people hurrying to and fro, and patted the children on the head, and questioned beggars, and looked down into the kitchens of houses, and up to the windows, and found that everything could yield him pleasure. He had never dreamed that any walk—that any thing—could give him so much happiness. In the afternoon he turned his steps toward his nephew's house.

He passed the door a dozen times before he had the courage to go up and knock. But he made a dash, and did it.

"Is your master at home, my dear?" said Scrooge to the girl. Nice girl! Very.

"Yes, sir."

"Where is he, my love?" said Scrooge.

"He's in the dining room, sir, along with mistress. I'll show you up the stairs, if you please."

"Thankee. He knows me," said Scrooge, with his hand already on the dining room lock. "I'll go in here, my dear."

He turned it gently, and sidled his face in, round the door. They were looking at the table (which was spread out in great array)—for these young housekeepers are always nervous on such points, and like to see that everything is right.

"Fred!" said Scrooge.

Dear heart alive, how his niece by marriage started! Scrooge had forgotten, for the moment, about her sitting in the corner with the footstool, or he wouldn't have done it, on any account.

"Why, bless my soul!" cried Fred. "Who's that?"

"It's I. Your Uncle Scrooge. I have come to dinner. Will you let me in, Fred?"

Let him in! It is a mercy he didn't shake his arm off. He was at home in five minutes. Nothing could be heartier. His niece looked just the same. So did Topper when *he* came. So did the plump sister, when *she* came. So did everyone when *they* came. Wonderful party, wonderful games, wonderful unanimity, won-der-ful happiness!

But he was early at the office next morning. Oh, he was early there. If he could only be there first, and catch Bob Cratchit coming late! That was the thing he had set his heart upon.

And he did it. Yes, he did! The lock struck nine. No Bob. A quarter past. No Bob. He was full eighteen minutes and a half behind his time. Scrooge sat with his door wide open, that he might see him come into the tank.

His hat was off, before he opened the door; his comforter too. He was on his stool in a jiffy; driving away with his pen as if he were trying to overtake nine o'clock.

"Hallo!" growled Scrooge, in his accustomed voice as near as he could feign it. "What do you mean by coming here at this time of day?"

"I am very sorry, sir," said Bob. "I *am* behind my time."

"You are!" repeated Scrooge. "Yes. I think you are. Step this way, sir, if you please."

"It's only once a year, sir," pleaded Bob, appearing from the tank. "It shall not be repeated. I was making rather merry yesterday, sir."

"Now, I'll tell you what, my friend," said Scrooge. I am not going to stand this sort of thing any longer. And therefore," he continued, leaping from his stool, and giving Bob such a dig in the waistcoat that he staggered back into the tank again. "And therefore I am about to raise your salary!"

Bob trembled, and got a little nearer to the ruler. He had a momentary idea of knocking Scrooge down with it, holding him, and calling to the people in the court for help and a strait-waistcoat.

"A merry Christmas, Bob!" said Scrooge, with an earnestness that could not be mistaken, as he clapped him on the back. "A merrier Christmas, Bob, my good fellow, than I have given you for many a year! I'll raise your salary, and endeavor to assist your struggling family, and we will discuss your affairs this very afternoon, over a Christmas bowl of smoking bishop, Bob! Make up the fires, and buy another coal-scuttle before you dot another *i*, Bob Cratchit!"

Scrooge was better than his word. He did it all, and infinitely more. And to Tiny Tim, who did NOT die, he was a second father. He became as good a friend, as good a master, as good a man, as the good old city knew, or any other good old city, town, or borough, in the good old world. Some people laughed to see the alteration in him, but he let them laugh, and little heeded them. For he was wise enough to know that nothing ever happened on this globe, for good, at which some people did not have their fill in laughter in the outset; and knowing that such as these would be blind anyway, he thought it quite as well that they should wrinkle up their eyes in grins, as have the malady in less attractive forms. His own heart laughed, and that was quite enough for him.

He had no further intercourse with the Spirits, but lived upon the Total Abstinence Principle, ever afterward; and it was always said of him that he knew how to keep Christmas well, if any many alive possessed the knowledge. May that be truly said of us, and all of us! And so, as Tiny Tim observed, God Bless Us, Every One!

The Tailor of Gloucester

Beatrix Potter

"I'll be at charges for a looking-glass;
and entertain a score or two of tailors."
—RICHARD III

In the time of swords and periwigs and full-skirted coats with flowered lappets—when gentlemen wore ruffles, and gold-laced waistcoats of paduasoy and taffeta—there lived a tailor in Gloucester. He sat in the window of a little shop in Westgate Street, cross-legged on a table, from morning till dark.

All day long while the light lasted he sewed and snippeted, piecing out his satin and pompadour, and lutestring; stuffs had strange names, and were very expensive in the days of the Tailor of Gloucester.

But although he sewed fine silk for his neighbors, he himself was very, very poor—a little old man in spectacles, with a pinched face, old crooked fingers, and a suit of thread-bare clothes.

He cut his coats without waste, according to his embroidered cloth; there were very small ends and snippets that lay about upon the table—"Too narrow breadths for nought—except waistcoats for mice," said the tailor.

One bitter cold day near Christmastime the tailor began to make a coat—a coat of cherry-colored corded silk embroidered with pansies and roses, and a cream-colored satin waistcoat—trimmed with gauze and green worsted chenille—for the Mayor of Gloucester.

The tailor worked and worked, and he talked to himself. He measured the silk, and turned it round and round, and trimmed it into shape with his shears; the table was all littered with cherry-colored snippets.

"No breadth at all, and cut on the cross; it is no breadth at all; tippets for mice and ribbons for mobs! For mice!" said the Tailor of Gloucester.

When the snowflakes came down against the small leaded windowpanes and shut out the light, the tailor had done all his day's work; all the silk and satin lay cut out upon the table.

There were twelve pieces for the coat and four pieces for the waistcoat; and there were pocket flaps and cuffs, and buttons all in order. For the lining of the coat there was fine yellow taffeta; and for the buttonholes of the waistcoat, there was cherry-colored twist. And everything was ready to sew together in the morning, all measured and sufficient—except that there was wanting just one single skein of cherry-colored twisted silk.

The tailor came out of his shop at dark, for he did not sleep there at nights; he fastened the window and locked the door, and took away the key. No one lived there at night but little brown mice, and they run in and out without any keys!

For behind the wooden wainscots of all the old houses in Gloucester, there are little mouse staircases and secret trap doors; and the mice run from house to house through those long, narrow passages; they can run all over the town without going into the streets.

But the tailor came out of his shop, and shuffled home through the snow. He lived quite near by in College Court, next to the doorway to College Green; and although it was not a big house, the tailor was so poor he only rented the kitchen.

He lived alone with his cat; it was called Simpkin.

Now all day long while the tailor was out at work, Simpkin kept house by himself; and he also was fond of the mice, though he gave them no satin for coats!

"Miaw?" said the cat when the tailor opened the door. "Miaw?"

The tailor replied—"Simpkin, we shall make our fortune, but I am worn to a raveling. Take this groat (which is our last fourpence) and Simpkin, take a china pipkin; buy a penn'orth of bread, a penn'orth of milk and a penn'orth of sausages. And oh, Simpkin, with the last penny of our fourpence buy me one penn'orth of cherry-colored silk. But do not lose the last penny of the fourpence, Simpkin, or I am undone and worn to a thread-paper, for I have NO MORE TWIST."

Then Simpkin again said, "Miaw?" and took the groat and the pipkin, and went out into the dark.

The tailor was very tired and beginning to be ill. He sat down by the hearth and talked to himself about that wonderful coat.

"I shall make my fortune—to be cut bias—the Mayor of Gloucester is to be married on Christmas Day in the morning, and he hath ordered a coat and an embroidered waistcoat—to be lined with yellow taffeta—and the taffeta sufficeth; there is no more left over in snippets than will serve to make tippets for mice—"

Then the tailor started; for suddenly, interrupting him, from the dresser at the other side of the kitchen came a number of little noises—

Tip tap, tip tap, tip tap tip!

"Now, what can that be?" said the Tailor of Gloucester, jumping up from his chair. The dresser was covered with crockery and pipkins, willow pattern plates, and teacups and mugs.

The tailor crossed the kitchen, and stood quite still beside the dresser, listening, and peering through his spectacles. Again from under a teacup, came those funny little noises—

Tip tap, tip tap, tip tap tip!

"This is very peculiar," said the Tailor of Gloucester; and he lifted up the teacup which was upside down.

Out stepped a little live lady mouse, and made a curtsey to the tailor! Then she hopped away down off the dresser, and under the wainscot.

The tailor sat down again by the fire, warming his poor cold hands, and mumbling to himself—

"The waistcoast is cut out from peach-coloured satin—tambour stitch and rose-buds in beautiful floss silk. Was I wise to entrust my last fourpence to Simpkin? One-and-twenty button-holes of cherry-coloured twist!"

Tip tap, tip tap, tip tap tip!

"This is passing extraordinary!" said the Tailor of Gloucester, and turned over another tea-cup, which was upside down.

Out stepped a little gentleman mouse, and made a bow to the tailor!

And then from all over the dresser came a chorus of little tappings, all sounding together, and answering one another, like watch-beetles in an old worm-eaten window-shutter—

Tip tap, tip tap, tip tap tip!

And out from under teacups and from under bowls and basins, stepped other and more little mice who hopped away down off the dresser and under the wainscot.

The tailor sat down, close over the fire, lamenting—"One-and-twenty button-holes of cherry-colored silk! To be finished by noon of Saturday: and this is Tuesday evening. Was it right to let loose those mice, undoubtedly the property of Simpkin? Alack, I am undone, for I have no more twist!"

The little mice came out again, and listened to the tailor; they took notice of the pattern of that wonderful coat. They whispered to one another about the taffeta lining, and about little mouse tippets.

And then all at once they all ran away together down the passage behind the wainscot, squeaking and calling to one another, as they ran from house to house; and not one mouse was left in the tailor's kitchen when Simpkin came back with the pipkin of milk!

Simpkin opened the door and bounced in, with an angry "G-r-r-miaw!" like a cat that is vexed: for he hated the snow, and there was snow in his ears, and snow in his collar at the back of his neck. He put down the loaf and the sausages upon the dresser, and sniffed.

"Simpkin," said the tailor, "where is my twist?"

But Simpkin set down the pipkin of milk upon the dresser, and looked suspiciously at the teacups. He wanted his supper of a little fat mouse!

"Simpkin," said the tailor, "where is my TWIST?"

But Simpkin hid a little parcel privately in the teapot, and spit and growled at the tailor; and if Simpkin had been able to talk, he would have asked: "Where is my MOUSE?"

"Alack, I am undone!" said the Tailor of Gloucester, and went sadly to bed.

All that night long Simpkin hunted and searched through the kitchen, peeping into cupboards and under the wainscot, and into the teapot where he had hidden that twist; but still he found never a mouse!

Whenever the tailor muttered and talked in his sleep, Simpkin said, "Miaw-ger-r-w-s-s-ch!" and made strange horrid noises, as cats do at night.

For the poor old tailor was very ill with a fever, tossing and turning in his four-post bed; and still in his dreams he mumbled—"No more twist! No more twist!"

All that day he was ill, and the next day, and the next; and what should become of the cherry-colored coat? In the tailor's shop in Westgate Street the embroidered silk and satin lay cut out upon the table—one-and-twenty buttonholes—and who should come to sew them, when the window was barred, and the door was fast locked?

But that does not hinder the little brown mice; they run in and out without any keys through all the old houses in Gloucester!

Out of doors the market folks went trudging through the snow to buy their geese and turkeys, and to bake their Christmas pies; but there would be no Christmas dinner for Simpkin and the poor old Tailor of Gloucester.

The tailor lay ill for three days and nights; and then it was Christmas Eve, and very late at night. The moon climbed up over the roofs and chimneys, and looked down over the gateway into College Court. There were no lights in the windows, nor any sound in the house; all the city of Gloucester was fast asleep under the snow.

And still Simpkin wanted his mice, and he mewed as he stood beside the four-post bed.

But it is in the old story that all the beasts can talk, in the night between Christmas Eve and Christmas Day in the morning (though there are very few folk who can hear them, or know what it is they say).

When the Cathedral clock struck twelve there was an answer—like an echo of the chimes—and Simpkin heard it, and came out of the tailor's door, and wandered about in the snow.

From all the roofs and gables and old wooden houses in Gloucester came a thousand merry voices singing the old Christmas rhymes—all the old songs that ever I heard of, and some that I don't know, like Whittington's bells.

First and loudest the cocks cried out: "Dame, get up, and bake your pies!"

"Oh, dilly, dilly, dilly!" sighed Simpkin.

And now in a garret there were lights and sounds of dancing, and cats came from over the way.

"Hey, diddle, diddle, the cat and the fiddle! All the cats in Gloucester—except me," said Simpkin.

Under the wooden eaves the starlings and sparrows sang of Christmas pies; the jack-daws woke up in the Cathedral tower; and although it was the middle of the night the throstles and robins sang; the air was quite full of little twittering tunes.

Particularly he was vexed with some little shrill voices from behind a wooden lattice. I think that they were bats, because they always have very small voices—

especially in a black frost, when they talk in their sleep, like the Tailor of Gloucester.

They said something mysterious that sounded like—

"Buz, quoth the blue fly; hum, quoth the bee;
Buz and hum they cry, and so do we!"

and Simpkin went away shaking his ears as if he had a bee in his bonnet.

From the tailor's shop in Westgate came a glow of light; and when Simpkin crept up to peep in at the window it was full of candles. There was a snippeting of scissors, and snappeting of thread; and the little mouse voices sang loudly and gaily—

"Four-and-twenty tailors
Went to catch a snail,
The best man amongst them
Durst not touch her tail;
She put out her horns
Like a little kyloe cow,
Run, tailors, run! or she'll have you all e'en now!"

Then without a pause the little mouse voices went on again—

"Sieve my lady's oatmeal,
Grind my lady's flour,

Put it in a chestnut,
Let it stand an hour——"

"Mew! Mew!" interrupted Simpkin, and he scratched at the door. But the key was under the tailor's pillow, he could not get in.

The little mice only laughed, and tried another tune—

"Three little mice sat down to spin,
Pussy passed by and she peeped in.
What are you at, my fine little men?
Making coats for gentlemen.
Shall I come in and cut off your threads?
Oh, no, Miss Pussy, you'd bite off our heads!"

"Mew! Mew!" cried Simpkin. "Hey diddle dinketty?" answered the little mice—

"Hey diddle dinketty, poppetty pet!
The merchants of London they wear scarlet;
Silk in the collar, and gold in the hem,
So merrily march the merchantmen!"

They clicked their thimbles to mark the time, but none of the songs pleased Simpkin; he sniffed and mewed at the door of the shop.

"And then I bought
A pipkin and a popkin,
A slipkin and a slopkin,
All for one farthing——

and upon the kitchen dresser!" added the rude little mice.

"Mew! Scratch! Scratch!" scuffled Simpkin on the windowsill; while the little mice inside sprang to their feet, and all began to shout at once in little twittering voices: "No more twist! No more twist!" And they barred up the window shutters and shut out Simpkin.

But still through the nicks in the shutters he could hear the click of thimbles, and little mouse voices singing—

"No more twist! No more twist!"

Simpkin came away from the shop and went home, considering in his mind. He found the poor old tailor without fever, sleeping peacefully.

Then Simpkin went on tip-toe and took a little parcel of silk out of the teapot, and looked at in the moonlight; and he felt quite ashamed of his badness compared with those good little mice!

When the tailor awoke in the morning, the first thing which he saw upon the patchwork quilt, was a skein of cherry-colored twisted silk, and beside his bed stood the repentant Simpkin!

"Alack, I am worn to a ravelling," said the Tailor of Gloucester, "but I have my twist!"

The sun was shining on the snow when the tailor got up and dressed, and came out into the street with Simpkin running before him.

The starlings whistled on the chimney stacks, and the throstles and robins sang—but they sang their own little noises, not the words they had sung in the night.

"Alack," said the tailor, "I have my twist; but no more strength—nor time—than will serve to make me one single buttonhole; for this is Christmas Day in the Morning! The Mayor of Gloucester shall be married by noon—and where is his cherry-colored coat?"

He unlocked the door of the little shop in Westgate Street, and Simpkin ran in, like a cat that expects something.

But there was no one there! Not even one little brown mouse!

The boards were swept clean; the little ends of thread and the little silk snippets were all tided away, and gone from off the floor.

But upon the table—oh joy! the tailor gave a shout—there, where he had left plain cuttings of silk—there lay the most beautiful coat and embroidered satin waistcoat that were ever worn by a Mayor of Gloucester.

There were roses and pansies upon the facings of the coat; and the waistcoat was worked with poppies and corn-flowers.

Everything was finished except just one single cherry-colored buttonhole; and where that buttonhole was wanting there was pinned a scrap of paper with these words—in little teeny weeny writing—

NO MORE TWIST

And from then began the luck of the Tailor of Gloucester; he grew quite stout, and he grew quite rich.

He made the most wonderful waistcoats for all the rich merchants of Gloucester, and for all the fine gentlemen of the country round.

Never were seen such ruffles, or such embroidered cuffs and lappets! But his buttonholes were the greatest triumph of it all.

The stitches of those buttonholes were so neat—*so* neat—I wonder how they could be stitched by an old man in spectacles, with crooked old fingers, and a tailor's thimble.

The stitches of those buttonholes were so small—*so* small—they looked as if they had been made by little mice!

Christmas; or, the Good Fairy

❄ ❄ ❄ ❄ ❄ ❄

Harriet Beecher Stowe

From *Stories, Sketches, and Studies*

Oh, dear! Christmas is coming in a fortnight, and I have got to think up presents for everybody!" said young Ellen Stuart, as she leaned languidly back in her chair. "Dear me, it's so tedious! Everybody has got everything that can be thought of."

"Oh, no," said her confidential adviser, Miss Lester, in a soothing tone. "You have means of buying everything you can fancy; and when every shop and store is glittering with all manner of splendors, you cannot surely be at a loss."

"Well, now, just listen. To begin with, there's mamma. What can I get for her? I have thought of ever so many things. She has three card cases, four gold thimbles, two or three gold chains, two writing desks of different patterns; and then as to rings, brooches, boxes, and all other things, I should think she might be sick of the sight of them. I am sure I am," said she, languidly gazing on her white and jeweled fingers.

This view of the case seemed rather puzzling to the adviser and there was silence for a few minutes, when Ellen, yawning, resumed:

"And then there's cousins Jane and Mary. I suppose they will be coming down on me with a whole load of presents. And Mrs. B. will send me something—she did last year. And then there's cousins William and Tom—I must get them something; and I would like to do it well enough, if I only knew what to get."

"Well," said Eleanor's aunt, who had been sitting quietly rattling her knitting needles during this speech, "it's a pity that you had not such a subject to practice on as I was when I was a girl. Presents did not fly about in those days as they do now. I remember, when I was ten years old, my father gave me a most marvelously ugly sugar dog for a Christmas gift, and I was perfectly delighted with it. The very idea of a present was so new to us."

"Dear Aunt, how delighted I should be if I had any such fresh, unsophisticated body to get presents for! But to get and get for people that have more than they know what to do with now; to add pictures, books, and gilding when the center tables are loaded with them now, and rings and jewels when they are a perfect drug! I wish myself that I were not sick, and sated, and tired with having everything in the world given to me."

"Well, Eleanor," said her aunt, "if you really do want unsophisticated subjects to practice on, I can put you in the way of it. I can show you more than one family to whom you might seem to be a very good fairy, and where such gifts as you could give with all ease would seem like a magic dream."

"Why, that would really be worth while, Aunt."

"Look over in that back alley," said her aunt. "You see those buildings?"

"That miserable row of shanties? Yes."

"Well, I have several acquaintances there who have never been tired of Christmas gifts or gifts of any other kind. I assure you, you could make quite a sensation over there."

"Well, who is there? Let us know."

"Do you remember Owen, who used to make your shoes?"

"Yes, I remember something about him."

"Well, he has fallen into a consumption, and cannot work anymore; and he, and his wife, and three little children live in one of the rooms."

"How do they get along?"

"His wife takes in sewing sometimes, and sometimes goes out washing. Poor Owen! I was over there yesterday. He looks thin and wasted, and his wife was saying that he was parched with constant fever, and had very little appetite. She had, with great self-denial, and by restricting herself almost of necessary food, got him two or three oranges; and the poor fellow seemed so eager after them."

"Poor fellow!" said Eleanor, involuntarily.

"Now," said her aunt, "suppose Owen's wife should get up on Christmas morning and find at the door a couple dozen of oranges, and some of those nice white grapes, such as you had at your party last week. Don't you think it would make a sensation?"

"Why, yes, I think very likely it might. But who else, Aunt? You spoke of a great many."

"Well, on the lower floor there is a neat little room, that is always kept perfectly trim and tidy. It belongs to a young couple who have nothing beyond the husband's day wages to live on. They are, nevertheless, as cheerful and chipper as a couple of wrens; and she is up and down half a dozen times a day, to help poor Mrs. Owen. She has a baby of her own about five months old, and of course does all the cooking, washing, and ironing for herself and husband; and yet, when Mrs. Owen goes out to wash, she takes her baby, and keeps it whole days for her."

"I'm sure she deserves that the good fairies should smile on her," said Eleanor. "One baby exhausts my stock of virtues very rapidly."

"But you ought to see her baby," said Aunt E., "so plump, so rosy, and good-natured, and always clean as a lily. This baby is a sort of household shrine; nothing is too sacred or too good for it; and I believe the little thrifty woman feels only one temptation to be extravagant, and that is to get some ornaments to adorn this little divinity."

"Why, did she ever tell you so?"

"No, but one day, when I was coming downstairs, the door of their room was partly open, and I saw a peddler there with an open box. John, the husband, was standing with a little purple cap in his hand, which he was regarding with mystified, admiring air, as if he didn't quite comprehend it; and trim little Mary gazing at it with longing eyes.

" 'I think we might get it,' said John.

" 'Oh no,' said she, regretfully, 'yet I wish we could, it's so pretty!' "

"Say no more, Aunt. I see the good fairy must pop a cap into the window on Christmas morning. Indeed, it shall be done. How they will wonder where it came from, and talk about it for months to come!"

"Well, then," continued her aunt, "in the next street to ours there is a miserable building, that looks as if it were just going to topple over; and away up in the third story, in a little room just under the eaves, live two poor, lonely old women. They are both nearly on to ninety. I was in there the day before yesterday. One of them is constantly confined to her bed with rheumatism; the other, weak and feeble, with failing sight and trembling hands, totters about, her only helper; and they are entirely dependent on charity."

"Can't they do anything? Can't they knit?" said Eleanor.

"You are young and strong, Eleanor, and have quick eyes and nimble fingers. How long would it take you to knit a pair of stockings?"

"I?" said Eleanor. "What an idea! I never tried, but I think I could get a pair done in a week, perhaps."

"And if somebody gave you twenty-five cents for them, and out of this you had to get food, and pay room rent, and buy coal for your fire, and oil for your lamp—"

"Stop, Aunt, for pity's sake!"

"Well, I will stop; but they can't. They must pay so much every month for that miserable shell they live in, or be turned into the street. The meal and flour that some kind person sends goes off for them just as it does for others, and they must get more or starve; and coal is now scarce and high priced."

"Oh Aunt, I'm quite convinced, I'm sure. Don't run me down and annihilate me with all these terrible realities. What shall I do to play good fairy to these old women?"

"If you will give me full power, Eleanor, I will put up a basket to be sent to them that will give them something to remember all winter."

"Oh, I certainly will. Let me see if I can't think of something myself."

"Well, Eleanor, suppose, then, some fifty or sixty years hence, if you were old, and your father, and mother, and aunts, and uncles, now so thick around you, lay cold and silent in so many graves—you have somehow got away off to a strange city, where you were never known—you live in a miserable garret, where snow blows at night through the cracks, and the fire is very apt to go out in the old cracked stove. You sit crouching over the dying embers the evening before Christmas—nobody to speak to you, nobody to care for you, except another poor old soul who lies moaning in the bed. Now, what would you like to have sent to you?"

"Oh Aunt, what a dismal picture!"

"And yet, Ella, all poor, forsaken old women are made of young girls, who expected it in their youth as little as you do, perhaps."

"Say no more, Aunt. I'll buy—let me see—a comfortable warm shawl for each of these poor women. And I'll send them—let me see—oh, some tea—nothing goes down with old women like tea. And I'll make John wheel some coal over to them. And, Aunt, it would not be a very bad thought to send them a new stove. I remember, the other day, when mamma was pricing stoves, I saw some such nice ones for two or three dollars."

"For a new hand, Ella, you work up the idea very well," said her aunt.

"But how much ought I to give, for any one case, to these women, say?"

"How much did you give last year for any single Christmas present?"

"Why, six or seven dollars for some. Those elegant souvenirs were seven dollars. That ring I gave Mrs. B. was twenty."

"And do you suppose Mrs. B. was any happier for it?"

"No, really, I don't think she cared much about it. But I had to give her something, because she had sent me something the year before, and I did not want to send a paltry present to one in her circumstances."

"Then, Ella, give the same to any poor, distressed, suffering creature who really needs it, and see in how many forms of good such a sum will appear. That one hard, cold, glittering ring, that now cheers nobody, and means nothing, that you must give because you must, and she takes because she must, might, if broken up into smaller sums, send real warm and heartfelt gladness through many a cold and cheerless dwelling, through many an aching heart."

"You are getting to be an orator, Aunt. But don't you approve of Christmas presents, among friends and equals?"

"Yes, indeed," said her aunt, fondly stroking her head. "I have had some Christmas presents that did me a world of good—a little book mark, for instance, that a certain niece of mine worked for me, with wonderful secrecy, three years ago, when she was not a young lady with a purse full of money. That book mark was a true Christmas present. And my young couple across the way are plotting a profound surprise to each other on Christmas morning. John has contrived, by an hour of extra work every night, to lay by enough to get Mary a new calico dress; and she, poor soul, has bargained away the only thing in the jewelry line she ever possessed, to be laid out on a new hat for him.

"I know, too, a washerwoman who has a poor lame boy—a patient, gentle little fellow—who has lain quietly for weeks and months in his little crib, and his mother is going to give him a splendid Christmas present."

"What is it, pray?"

"A whole orange! Don't laugh. She will pay ten whole cents for it; for it shall be none of your common oranges, but a picked one of the very best going! She has put by the money, a cent at a time, for a whole month; and nobody knows which will be happiest in it, Willie or his mother. These are such Christmas presents as I like to think of—gifts coming from love, and tending to produce love. These are the appropriate gifts of the day."

"But don't you think that it's right for those who *have* money to give expensive presents, supposing always, as you say, they are given from real affection?"

"Sometimes, undoubtedly. The Savior did not condemn her who broke an alabaster box of ointment—very precious—simply as a proof of love, even although the suggestion was made: 'This might have been sold for three hundred pence, and given to the poor.' I have thought He would regard with sympathy the fond efforts which human love sometimes make to express itself by gifts, the rarest and most costly. How I rejoiced with all my heart, when Charles Elton gave his poor mother that splendid Chinese shawl and gold watch! Because I knew they came from the very fullness of his heart to a mother whom he could not do too much for—a mother who has done and suffered everything for him. In some such cases, when resources are ample, a costly gift seems to have a graceful appropriateness; but I cannot approve of it if it exhausts all the means of doing for the poor. It is better, then, to give a simple offering, and to do something for those who really need it."

Eleanor looked thoughtful; her aunt laid down her knitting, and said, in a tone of gentle seriousness, "Whose birth does Christmas commemorate, Ella?"

"Our Savior's, certainly, Aunt."

"Yes," said her aunt. "And when and how was He born? In a stable! Laid in a manger—thus born, that in all ages He might be known as the brother and friend of the poor. And surely, it seems but appropriate to commemorate His birthday by an especial remembrance of the lowly, the poor, the outcast, and distressed; and if Christ should come back to our city on a Christmas day, where should we think it most appropriate to His character to find Him? Would He be carrying splendid gifts to splendid dwellings, or would He be gliding about in the cheerless haunts of the desolate, the poor, the forsaken, and the sorrowful?"

And here the conversation ended.

"WHAT SORT OF CHRISTMAS presents is Ella buying?" said Cousin Tom, as the servant handed in a portentous-looking package, which had been just rung in at the door.

"Let's open it," said saucy Will. "Upon my word, two great gray blanket shawls! These must be for you and me, Tom! And what's this? A great bolt of cotton flannel and gray yarn stockings!"

The door bell rang again, and the servant brought in another bulky parcel, and deposited it on the marble-topped center table.

"What's here?" said Will, cutting the cord. "Whew! A perfect nest of packages! Oolong tea! Oranges! Grapes! White sugar! Bless me, Ella must be going to housekeeping!"

"Or going crazy!" said Tom. "And on my word," said he, looking out of the window, "there's a drayman ringing at our door, with a stove, with a tea kettle set in the top of it!"

"Ella's cook stove, of course," said Will. And just at this moment the young lady entered, with her purse hanging gracefully over her hand.

"Now, boys, you are too bad!" she exclaimed, as each of the mischievous youngsters was gravely marching up and down, attired in a gray shawl.

"Didn't you get them for us? We thought you did," said both.

"Ella, I want some of that cotton flannel, to make me a pair of pantaloons," said Tom.

"I say, Ella," said Will, "when are you going to housekeeping? Your cooking stove is standing down in the street; 'pon my word, John is loading some coal on the dray with it."

"Ella, isn't that going to be sent to my office?" said Tom. "Do you know I do so languish for a new stove with a tea kettle in the top, to heat a fellow's shaving water!"

Just then, another ring at the door, and the grinning servant handed in a small brown paper parcel for Miss Ella. Tom made a dive at it, and tearing off the brown paper, discovered a jaunty little purple velvet cap, with silver tassels.

"My smoking cap, as I live!" said he. "Only I shall have to wear it on my thumb, instead of my head—too small entirely," said he, shaking his head gravely.

"Come, you saucy boys," said Aunt E., entering briskly. "What are you teasing Ella for?"

"Why, do see this lot of things, Aunt! What in the world is Ella going to do with them?"

"Oh, I know!"

"You know? Then I can guess, Aunt, it is some of your charitable works. You are going to make a juvenile Lady Bountiful of El, eh?"

Ella, who had colored to the roots of her hair at the *exposé* of her very unfashionable Christmas preparations, now took heart, and bestowed a very gentle and salutary little cuff on the saucy head that still wore the purple cap, and then hastened to gather up her various purchases.

"Laugh away," said she, gaily, "and a good many others will laugh, too, over these things. I got them to make people laugh—people who are not in the habit of laughing!"

"Well, well, I see into it," said Will. "And I tell you I think right well of the idea, too. There are worlds of money wasted, at this time of the year, in getting things that nobody wants, and nobody cares for after they are got; and I am glad, for my part, that you are going to get up a variety in this line. In fact, I should like to give you one of these stray leaves to help on," said he, dropping a ten dollar note into her paper. "I like to encourage girls to think of something besides breast pins and sugar candy."

But our story spins on too long. If anybody wants to see the results of Ella's first attempts at *good fairyism*, they can call at the doors of two or three old buildings on Christmas morning, and they shall hear all about it.

Christmas for Sassafrass, Cypress & Indigo

Ntozke Shange

From *Sassafrass, Cypress & Indigo*

Hilda Effania couldn't wait till Christmas. The Christ Child was born. Hallelujah. Hallelujah. The girls were home. The house was humming. Hilda Effania justa singing, cooking up a storm. Up before dawn. Santa's elves barely up the chimney. She chuckled. This was gonna be some mornin'. Yes, indeed. There was nothing too good for her girls. Matter of fact, what folks never dreamed of would only just about do. That's right, all her babies come home for Christmas Day. Hilda Effania cooking up a storm. Little Jesus Child lyin' in his manger. Praise the Lord for all these gifts. Hilda Effania justa singin':

Poor little Jesus Child, Born in a Manger
Sweet little Jesus Child
and they didn't know who you were.

BREAKFAST WITH HILDA EFFANIA AND
HER GIRLS ON CHRSTMAS MORNING

HILDA'S TURKEY HASH
1 pound diced cooked turkey meat (white and dark)
2 medium onions, diced
1 red sweet pepper, diced
1 full boiled potato, diced
1 tablespoon cornstarch
3 tablespoons butter
Salt to taste, pepper too
(A dash of corn liquor, optional)

In a heavy skillet, put your butter. Sauté your onions and red pepper. Add your turkey, once your onions are transparent. When the turkey's sizzling, add your potato. Stir. If consistency is not to your liking, add the cornstarch to thicken, the corn liquor to thin. Test to see how much salt and pepper you want, and don't forget your cayenne.

CATFISH / THE WAY ALBERT LIKED IT
1/2 cup flour
1/2 cup cornmeal

Salt
Pepper
1/2 cup buttermilk
3 beaten eggs
Oil for cooking
Lemons
6 fresh catfish

Sift flour and cornmeal. Season with your salt and pepper. Mix the beaten eggs well with the buttermilk. Dip your fish in the egg and milk. Then roll your fish in the cornmeal-flour mix. Get your oil spitting hot in a heavy skillet. Fry your fish, not too long, on both sides. Your lemon wedges are for your table.

TRIO MARMALADE

1 tangerine
1 papaya
1 lemon
Sugar
Cold water

Delicately grate rinds of fruits. Make sure you have slender pieces of rind. Chop up your pulp, leaving the middle section of each fruit. Put the middles of the fruits and the seeds somewhere else in a cotton wrap. Add three times the amount of pulp and rind. That's the measure for your water. Keep this sitting overnight. Get up the next day and boil this for a half-hour. Drop your wrapped seed bag in there. Boil that, too. And mix in an exact equal of your seed bag with your sugar (white or brown). Leave it be for several hours. Come back. Get it boiling again. Don't stop stirring. You can test it and test it, but you'll know when it jells. Put on your table or in jars you seal while it's hot.

Now you have these with your hominy grits. (I know you know how to make hominy grits.) Fried eggs, sunny-side up. Ham-sliced bacon, butter rolls and Aunt Haydee's Red Pimiento Jam. I'd tell you that receipt, but Aunt Haydee never told nobody how it is you make that. I keep a jar in the pantry for special occasions. I get one come harvest.

MAMA'S BREAKFAST SIMMERING way downstairs drew the girls out of their sleep. Indigo ran to the kitchen. Sassafrass turned back over on her stomach to sleep a while longer, there was no House Mother ringing a cowbell. Heaven. Cypress brushed her hair, began her daily pliés and leg stretches. Hilda Effania sat at her kitchen table, drinking strong coffee with Magnolia Milk, wondering what the girls would think of her tree.

"Merry Chrstimas, Mama." Indigo gleamed. "May I please have some coffee with you? Nobody else is up yet. Then we can go see the tree, can't we, when they're all up. Should I go get 'em?" Indigo was making herself this coffee as quickly as she could, before Hilda Effania said "no." But Hilda was so happy Indigo could probably have had a shot of bourbon with her coffee.

"Only half a cup, Indigo. Just today." Hilda watched Indigo moving more like Cypress. Head erect, back stretched tall, with some of Sassafrass's easy coyness.

"So you had a wonderful time last night at your first party?"

"Oh, yes, Mama." Indigo paused. "But you know what?" Indigo sat down by her mother with her milk tinged with coffee. She stirred her morning treat, serious as possible. She looked her mother in the eyes. "Mama, I don't think boys are as much fun as everybody says."

"What do you mean, darling?"

"Well, they dance and I guess eventually you marry 'em. But I like my fiddle so much more. I even like my dolls better than boys. They're fun, but they can't talk about important things."

Hilda Effania giggled. Indigo was making her own path at her own pace. There'd be not one more boy-crazy, obsessed-with-romance child in her house. This last one made more sense out of the world than either of the other two. Alfred would have liked that. He liked independence.

"Good morning, Mama. Merry Christmas." Sassafrass was still tying her bathrobe as she kissed her mother.

"Merry Christmas, Indigo. I see Santa left you a cup of coffee."

"This is not my first cup of coffee. I had some on my birthday, too."

"Oh, pardon me. I didn't realize you were so grown. I've been away, you know?" Sassafrass was never very pleasant in the morning. Christmas was no exception. Indigo and her mother exchanged funny faces. Sassafrass wasn't goin' to spoil this day.

"Good morning. Good morning. Good morning, everyone." Cypress flew through the kitchen: *coupé jeté en tournant.*

"Merry Christmas, Cypress," the family shouted in unison.

"Oh, Mama, you musta been up half the night cooking what all I'm smelling." Cypress started lifting pot tops, pulling the oven door open.

"Cypress, you know I can't stand for nobody to be looking in my food till I serve it. Now, come on away from my stove."

Cypress turned to her mama, smiling. "Mama, let's go look at the tree."

"I haven't finished my coffee," Sassafrass yawned.

"You can bring it with you. That's what I'm gonna do," Indigo said with sweet authority.

The tree glistened by the front window of the parlor. Hilda Effania had covered it, of course, with cloth and straw. Satin ribbons of scarlet, lime, fushsia, bright yellow, danced on the far limbs of the pine. Tiny straw angels of dried palm swung from the upper branches. Apples shining, next to candy canes and gingerbread men, brought shouts of joy and memory from the girls, who recognized their own handiwork. The black satin stars with appliqués of the Christ Child Cypress had made when she was ten. Sassafrass fingered the lyres she fashioned for the children singing praises of the little Jesus: little burlap children with lyres she'd been making since she could thread a needle, among the miniatures of Indigo's dolls. Hilda Effania had done something else special for this Christmas, though. In silk frames of varied pastels were the baby pictures of her girls and one of her wedding day: Hilda Effania and Alfred, November 30, 1946.

Commotion. Rustling papers. Glee and surprise. Indigo got a very tiny laced brassiere from Cypress. Sassafrass had given her a tiny pair of earrings, dangling golden violins. Indigo had made for both her sisters dolls in their very own likenesses. Both five feet fall, with hips and bras. Indigo had dressed the dolls in the old clothes Cypress and Sassafrass had left at home.

"Look in their panties," Indigo blurted. Cypress felt down in her doll's panties. Sassafrass pulled her doll's drawers. They both found velvet sanitary napkins with their names embroidered across the heart of silk.

"Oh, Indigo. You're kidding. You're not menstruating, are you?"

"Indigo, you got your period?"

"Yes, she did." Hilda Effania joined, trying to change the subject. She'd known Indigo was making dolls, but not that the dolls had their period.

"Well, what else did you all get?" Hilda asked provocatively.

Cypress pulled out an oddly shaped package wrapped entirely in gold sequins. "Mama, this is for you." The next box was embroidered continuously with Sassafrass's name. "Here, guess whose?" Cypress held Indigo's shoulders. Indigo had on her new bra over her nightgown. Waiting for her mother and sister to open their gifts, Cypress did *tendues*. "Hold still, Indigo. If you move, my alignment goes off."

"Oh, Cypress, this is just lovely." Hilda Effania didn't know what else to say. Cypress had given her a black silk negligee with a very revealing bed jacket. "I certainly have to think when I could wear this and you all won't be home to see it."

"Aw, Mama. Try it on," Cypress pleaded.

"Yeah, Mama. Put that on. It looked so nasty." Indigo squinched up her face, giggled.

"Oh, Cypress, these are so beautiful, I can hardly believe it." Sassafrass held the embroidered box open. In the box lined with beige raw silk were seven cherry-wood hand-carved crochet needles of different gauges.

"Bet not one white girl up to the Callahan School has ever in her white life laid eyes on needles like that!" Cypress hugged her sister, flexed her foot.

"Indigo, you got to put that bra on under your clothes, not on top of 'em. Mama, would you look at this little girl?"

Hilda Effania had disappeared. "I'm trying on this scandalous thing, Cypress. You all look for your notes at the foot of the tree." She shouted from her bedroom, thinking she looked pretty good for a widow with three most grown girls.

Hilda Effania always left notes for the girls, explaining where their Christmas from Santa was. This practice began the first year Sassafrass had doubted that a fat white man came down her chimney to bring her anything. Hilda solved that problem by leaving notes from Santa Claus for all the children. That way they had to go search the house, high and low, for their gifts. Santa surely had to have been there. Once school chums and reality interfered with this myth, Hilda continued the practice of leaving her presents hidden away. She liked the idea that each child experienced her gift in privacy. The special relationship she nurtured with each was protected from rivalries, jokes, and Christmas confusions. Hilda Effania loved thinking that she'd managed to give her daughters a moment of their own.

My Oldest Darling, Sassafrass,

In the back of the pantry is something from Santa. In a red box by the attic window is something your father would want you to have. Out by the shed in a bucket covered with straw is a gift from your Mama.

Love to you,
Mama

Darling Cypress,

Underneath my hat boxes in the second-floor closet is your present from Santa. Look behind the tomatoes I canned last year for what I got you in your Papa's name. My own choice for you is under your bed.

XOXOX,
Mama

Sweet Little Indigo,

This is going to be very simple. Santa left you something outside your violin. I left you a gift by the outdoor stove on the right-hand side. Put your coat on before you go out there. And the special something I got you from your Daddy is way up in the china cabinet. Please, be careful.

I love you so much,
Mama

IN THE BACK of the pantry between the flour and rice, Sassafrass found a necklace of porcelain roses. Up in the attic across from Indigo's mound of resting dolls, there was a red box all right, with a woven blanket of mohair, turquoise, and silver. Yes, her father would have wanted her to have a warm place to sleep. Running out to the shed, Sassafrass knocked over the bucket filled with straw. There on the ground lay eight skeins of her mother's finest spun cotton, dyed so many colors. Sassafrass sat out in the air feeling her yarns.

Cypress wanted her mother's present first. Underneath her bed, she felt tarlatan. A tutu. Leave it to Mama. Once she gathered the whole thing out where she could see it, Cypress started to cry. A tutu *juponnage*, reaching to her ankles, rose and lavender. The waist was a wide sash with the most delicate needlework she'd ever seen. Tiny toe shoes in white and pink graced brown ankles tied with ribbons. Unbelievable. Cypress stayed in her room dancing in her tutu till lunchtime. Then she found *The Souls of Black Folk* by Du Bois near the tomatoes from her Papa's spirit. She was the only one who'd insisted on calling him Papa, instead of Daddy or Father. He didn't mind. So she guessed he wouldn't mind now. "Thank you so much, Mama and Papa." Cypress slowly went to the second-floor closet where she found Santa had left her a pair of opal earrings. To thank her mother Cypress did a complete *port de bras*, in the Cecchetti manner, by her mother's vanity. The mirrors inspired her.

Indigo had been very concerned that anything was near her fiddle that she hadn't put there. Looking at her violin, she knew immediately what her gift from Santa was. A brand-new case. No secondhand battered thing from Uncle John. Indigo approached her instrument slowly. The case was of crocodile skin, lined with white velvet. Plus, Hilda Effania had bought new rosin, new strings. Even cushioned the fiddle with cleaned raw wool. Indigo carried her new case with her fiddle outside to the stove where she found a music stand holding *A Practical Method for Violin* by Nicolas Laoureux. "Oh, my. She's right about that. Mama would be real mad if I never learned to read music." Indigo looked through the pages, understanding nothing. Whenever she was dealing with something she didn't understand, she made it her business to learn. With great difficulty, she carried her fiddle, music stand, and music book into the house.

Up behind the wine glasses that Hilda Effania rarely used, but dusted regularly, was a garnet bracelet from the memory of her father. Indigo figured the bracelet weighed so little, she would definitely be able to wear it every time she played her fiddle. Actually, she could wear it while conversing with the Moon.

Hilda Effania decided to chance fate and spend the rest of the morning in her fancy garb from Cypress. The girls were silent when she entered the parlor in black lace. She looked like she did in those hazy photos from before they were born. Indigo rushed over to the easy chair and straightened the pillows.

"Mama, I have my present for you." Hilda Effania swallowed hard. There was no telling what Indigo might bring her.

"Well, Sweetheart. I'm eager for it. I'm excited, too."

Indigo opened her new violin case, took out her violin, made motions of tuning it (which she'd already done). In a terribly still moment, she began "My Buddy," Hilda Effania's mother's favorite song. At the end, she bowed to her mother. Her sisters applauded.

Sassafrass gave her mother two things: a woven hanging of twined ika using jute and raffia, called "You Know Where We Came From, Mama," and six amethysts with holes drilled through, for her mother's creative weaving.

"Mama, you've gotta promise me you won't have a bracelet or a ring or something made from them. Those are for your very own pieces." Sassafrass wanted her mother to experience weaving as an expression of herself, not as something the family did for Miz Fitzhugh. Hilda Effania was still trying to figure out where in the devil she should put this "hanging," as Sassafrass called it.

"Oh, no, dear. I wouldn't dream of doing anything with these stones but what you intended."

When the doorbell rang, Hilda Effania didn't know what to do with herself. Should she run upstairs? Sit calmly? Run and get her house robe? She had no time to do any of that. Indigo opened the door.

"Merry Christmas, Miz Fitzhugh. Won't you come in?" Hilda sank back in the easy chair. Cypress casually threw her mother an afghan to cover herself. Miz Fitzhugh in red wool suit, tailored green satin shirt, red tam, all Hilda's design, and those plain brown pumps white women like, wished everyone a "Merry Christmas." She said Mathew, her butler, would bring some sweetbreads and venison over later, more toward the dinner hour. Miz Fitzhugh liked Sassafrass the best of the girls. That's why she'd sponsored her at the Callahan School. The other two, the one with the gall to want to be a ballerina and the headstrong one with the fiddle, were much too much for Miz Fitzhugh. They didn't even wanta be weavers. What was becoming of the Negro, refusing to ply an honorable trade.

Nevertheless, Miz Fitzhugh hugged each one with her frail blue-veined arms, gave them their yearly checks for their savings accounts she'd established when each was born. There'd be no talk that her Negroes were destitute. What she didn't know was that Hilda Effania let the girls use that money as they pleased. Hilda believed every family needed only one mother. She was the mother to her girls. That white lady was mighty generous, but she wasn't her daughters' mama or manna from Heaven. If somebody needed taking care of, Hilda Effania determined that was her responsibility; knowing in her heart that white folks were just peculiar.

"Why, Miz Fitzhugh, that's right kindly of you," Hilda honeyed.

"Why, Hilda, you know I feel like the girls were my very own," Miz Fitzhugh confided. Cypress began a series of violent *ronds de jambe*. Sassafrass picked up all the wrapping papers as if it were the most important thing in the world. Indigo felt some huge anger coming over her. Next thing she knew, Miz Fitzhugh couldn't keep her hat on. There was a wind justa pushing, blowing Miz Fitzhugh out the door. Because she had blue blood or blue veins, whichever, Indigo knew Miz Fitzhugh would never act like anything strange was going on. She'd let herself be blown right out the door with her white kid gloves, red tailored suit and all. Waving good-bye, shouting, "Merry Christmas," Miz Fitzhugh vanished as demurely as her station demanded.

Sucha raucous laughing and carrying on rarely came out of Hilda Effania's house like it did after Miz Fitzhugh'd been blown away. Hilda Effania did an imitation of her, hugging the girls.

"But Miz Fitzhugh, do the other white folks know you touch your Negroes?" Hilda responded, "Oh, I don't tell anyone!"

Eventually they all went to their rooms, to their private fantasies and preoccupations. Hilda was in the kitchen working the fat off her goose, fiddling with the chestnut stuffing, wondering how she would handle the house when it was really empty again. It would be empty; not even Indigo would be home come January.

"Yes, Alfred. I think I'm doing right by 'em. Sassafrass is in that fine school with rich white children. Cypress is studying classical ballet with Effie in New York City. Imagine that? I'm sending Indigo out to Difuskie with Aunt Haydee. Miz Fitzhugh's promised me a tutor for her. She doesn't want the child involved in all this violence 'bout the white and the colored going to school together, the integration. I know you know what I mean, 'less up there's segregated too.

"No, Alfred, I'm not blaspheming. I just can't imagine another world. I'm trying to, though. I want the girls to live the good life. Like what we planned.

Nice husbands. Big houses. Children. Trips to Paris and London. Going to the opera. Knowing nice people for friends. Remember we used to say we were the nicest, most interesting folks we'd ever met? Well, I don't want it to be that way for our girls. You know, I'm sort of scared of being here by myself. I can always talk to you, though. Can't I?

"I'ma tell Miz Fitzhugh that if she wants Indigo in Difuskie, that tutor will have to be a violin teacher. Oh, Alfred, you wouldn't believe what she can do on that fiddle. If you could only see how Cypress dances. Sassafrass's weavings. I wish you were here sometimes, so we could tell the world to look at what all we, Hilda Effania and Alfred, brought to this world."

Once her Chirstmas supper was organized in the oven, the refrigerator, and the sideboard, Hilda Effania slept in her new negligee, Alfred's WWII portrait close to her bosom.

The Adventure of the Blue Carbuncle

Sir Arthur Conan Doyle

I had called upon my friend Sherlock Holmes upon the second morning after Christmas, with the intention of wishing him the compliments of the season. He was lounging upon the sofa in a purple dressing gown, a pipe-rack within his reach upon the right, and a pile of crumpled morning papers, evidently newly studied, near at hand. Beside the couch was a wooden chair, and on the angle of the back hung a very seedy and disreputable hard-felt hat, much the worse for wear, and cracked in several places. A lens and a forceps lying upon the seat of the chair suggested that the hat had been suspended in this manner for the purpose of examination.

"You are engaged," said I. "Perhaps I interrupt you."

"Not at all. I am glad to have a friend with whom I can discuss my results. The matter is a perfectly trivial one"—he jerked his thumb in the direction of the old hat—"but there are points in connection with it which are not entirely devoid of interest and even of instruction."

I seated myself in his armchair and warmed my hands before his crackling fire, for a sharp frost had set in, and the windows were thick with the ice crystals. "I suppose," I remarked, "that, homely as it looks, this thing has some deadly story linked onto it—that it is the clue which will guide you in the solution of some mystery and the punishment of some crime."

"No, no. No crime," said Sherlock Holmes, laughing. "Only one of those whimsical little incidents which will happen when you have four million human beings all jostling each other within the space of a few square miles. Amid the action and reaction of so dense a swarm of humanity, every possible combination of events may be expected to take place, and many a little problem will be presented which may be striking and bizarre without being criminal. We have already had experience of such."

"So much so," I remarked, "that of the last six cases which I have added to my notes, three have been entirely free of any legal crime."

"Precisely. You allude to my attempt to recover the Irene Adler papers, to the singular case of Miss Mary Sutherland, and to the adventure of the man with the twisted lip. Well, I have no doubt that this small matter will fall into the same innocent category. You know Peterson, the commissionaire?"

"Yes."

"It is to him that this trophy belongs."

"It is his hat."

"No, no; he found it. Its owner is unknown. I beg that you will look upon it not as a battered billycock but as an intellectual problem. And, first, as to how it came here. It arrived upon Christmas morning, in company with a good fat goose, which is, I have no doubt, roasting at this moment in front of Peterson's fire. The facts are these: about four o'clock on Christmas morning, Peterson, who, as you know, is a very honest fellow, was returning from a small jollification and was making his way homeward down Tottenham Court Road. In front of him he saw, in the gaslight, a tallish man, walking with a slight stagger, and carrying a white goose slung over his shoulder. As he reached the corner of Goodge Street, a row broke out between this stranger and a little knot of roughs. One of the latter knocked off the man's hat, on which he raised his stick to defend himself and, swinging it over his head, smashed the shop window behind him. Peterson had rushed forward to protect the stranger from his assailants; but the man, shocked at having broken the window, and seeing an official-looking person in uniform rushing toward him, dropped his goose, took to his heels, and vanished amid the labyrinth of small streets which lie at the back of the Tottenham Court Road. The roughs had also fled at the appearance of Peterson, so that he was left in possession of the field of battle, and also of the spoils of victory in the shape of this battered hat and a most unimpeachable Christmas goose."

"Which surely he restored to their owner?"

"My dear fellow, there lies the problems. It is true that 'For Mrs. Henry Baker' was printed upon a small card which was tied to the bird's left leg, and it is also true that the initials 'H.B.' are legible upon the lining of this hat; but as there are some thousands of Bakers, and some hundreds of Henry Bakers in this city of ours, it is not easy to restore lost property to any one of them."

"What, then, did Peterson do?"

"He brought round both hat and goose to me on Christmas morning, knowing that even the smallest problems are of interest to me. The goose we retained until this morning, when there were signs that, in spite of the slight frost, it would be well that it should be eaten without unnecessary delay. Its finder has carried it off, therefore, to fulfill the ultimate destiny of a goose, while I continue to retain the hat of the unknown gentleman who lost his Christmas dinner.

"Did he not advertise?"

"No."

"Then, what clue could you have as to his identity?"

"Only as much as we can deduce."

"From his hat?"

"Precisely."

"But you are joking. What can you gather from this old battered felt?"

"Here is my lens. You know my methods. What can you gather yourself as to the individuality of the man who has worn this article?"

I took the tattered object in my hands and turned it over rather ruefully. It was a very ordinary black hat of the usual round shape, hard and much the worse for wear. The lining had been of red silk, but was a good deal discolored. There was no maker's name; but, as Holmes had remarked, the initials "H.B." were scrawled upon one side. It was pierced in the brim for a hat-securer, but the elastic was missing. For the rest, it was cracked, exceedingly dusty, and spotted in several places, although there seemed to have been some attempt to hide the discolored patches by smearing them with ink.

"I can see nothing," said I, handing it back to my friend.

"On the contrary, Watson, you can see everything. You fail, however, to reason from what you see. You are too timid in drawing your inferences."

"Then, pray tell me what it is that you can infer from this hat?"

He picked it up and gazed at it in the peculiar introspective fashion which was characteristic of him. "It is perhaps less suggestive than it might have been," he remarked, "and yet there are few inferences which are very distinct, and a few others which represent at least a strong balance of probability. That the man was intellectual is of course obvious upon the face of it, and also that he was fairly well-to-do within the last three years, although he has now fallen upon evil days. He had foresight, but has less now than formerly, pointing to a moral retrogression, which, when taken with the decline of his fortunes, seems to indicate some evil influence, probably drink, and work upon him. This may account also for the obvious fact that his wife has ceased to love him."

"My dear Holmes!"

"He has, however, retained some degree of self-respect," he continued, disregarding my remonstrance. "He is a man who leads a sedentary life, goes out a little, is out of training entirely, is middle-aged, has grizzled hair which he has had cut within the last few days, and which he anoints with lime cream. There are the more patent facts which are to me deduced from his hat. Also, by the way, that it is extremely improbable that he has gas laid on in his house.

"You are certainly joking, Holmes."

"Not in the least. Is it possible that even now, when I give you these results, you are unable to see how they are attained?"

"I have no doubt that I am very stupid, but I must confess that I am unable to follow you. For example, how did you deduce that this man was intellectual?"

For answer Holmes clapped the hat upon his head. It came right over the forehead and settled upon the bridge of his nose. "It is a question of cubic capacity," said he. "A man with so large a brain must have something in it."

"The decline of his fortunes, then?"

"This hat is three years old. These flat brims curled at the edge came in then. It is a hat of the very best quality. Look at the band of ribbed silk and the excellent lining. If this man could afford to buy so expensive a hat three years ago, and has had no hat since, then he has assuredly gone down in the world."

"Well, that is clear enough, certainly. But how about the foresight and the moral retrogression?"

Sherlock Holmes laughed. "Here is the foresight," said he, putting his finger upon the little disc and loop of the hat-securer. "They are never sold upon hats. If this man ordered one, it is a sign of a certain amount of foresight, since he went out of his way to take this precaution against the wind. But since we see that he has broken the elastic and has not troubled to replace it, it is obvious that he has less foresight now than formerly, which is a distinct proof of a weakening nature. On the other hand, he has endeavored to conceal some of these stains upon the felt by daubing them with ink, which is a sign that he has not entirely lost his self-respect."

"Your reasoning is certainly plausible."

"The further points, that he is middle-aged, that his hair is grizzled, that it has been recently cut, and that he uses lime cream, are all to be gathered from a close examination of the lower part of the lining. The lens discloses a large number of hair ends, clean cut by the scissors of a barber. They all appear to be adhesive, and there is a distinct odor of lime cream. This dust, you will observe, is not the gritty, gray dust of the street but the fluffy brown dust of the house, showing that is has been hung up indoors most of the time; while the marks of moisture upon the inside are proof positive that the wearer perspired very freely, and could, therefore, hardly be in the best of training."

"But his wife—you said that she had ceased to love him."

"This hat has not been brushed for weeks. When I see you, my dear Watson, with a week's accumulation of dust upon your hat, and when your wife allows you to go out in such a state, I shall fear that you also have been unfortunate enough to lose your wife's affection."

"But he might be a bachelor."

"Nay, he was bringing home the goose as a peace offering to his wife. Remember the card upon the bird's leg?"

"You have an answer to everything. But how on earth do you deduce that the gas is not laid on in his house?"

"One tallow stain, or even two, might come by chance; but when I see no less than five, I think that there can be little doubt that the individual must be brought into frequent contact with anything burning tallow—walks upstairs at night probably with his hat in one hand and a guttering candle in the other. Anyhow, he never got tallow stains from a gas jet. Are you satisfied?"

"Well, it is very ingenious," said I, laughing, "but since, as you said just now, there has been no crime committed, and no harm done save the loss of a goose, all this seems to be rather a waste of energy."

Sherlock Holmes had opened his mouth to reply, when the door flew open, and Peterson, the commissionaire, rushed into the apartment with flushed cheeks and the face of a man who is dazed with astonishment.

"The goose, Mr. Holmes! The goose, sir!" he gasped.

"Eh? What of it, then? Has it returned to life and flapped off through the kitchen window?" Holmes twisted himself round upon the sofa to get a fairer view of the man's excited face.

"See here, sir! See what my wife found in its crop!" He held out his hand and displayed upon the center of the palm, a brilliantly scintillating blue stone, rather smaller than a bean in size, but of such purity and radiance that it twinkled like an electric point in the dark hollow of his hand.

Sherlock Holmes sat up with a whistle. "By Jove, Peterson!" said he. "This is treasure trove indeed. I suppose you know what you have got?"

"A diamond, sir? A precious stone. It cuts into glass as though it were putty."

"It's more than a precious stone. It is *the* precious stone."

"Not the Countess of Morcar's blue carbuncle!" I ejaculated

"Precisely so. I ought to know its size and shape, seeing that I have read the advertisement about it in *The Times* every day lately. It is absolutely unique, and its value can only be conjectured, but the reward offered of £1,000 is certainly not within a twentieth part of the market price."

"A thousand pounds! Great Lord of mercy!" The commissionaire plumped down into a chair and stared from one to the other of us.

"That is the reward, and I have reason to know that there are sentimental considerations in the background which would induce the Countess to part with half her fortune if she could but recover the gem."

"It was lost, if I remember aright, at the Hotel Cosmopolitan," I remarked. "Precisely so, on December 22nd, just five days ago. John Horner, a plumber, was accused of having abstracted it from the lady's jewel case. The evidence against him was so strong that the case has been referred to the Assizes. I have some account of the matter here, I believe." He rummaged amid his newspapers, glancing over the dates, until at last he smoothed one out, doubled it over, and read the following paragraph:

Hotel Cosmopolitan Jewel Robbery. John Horner, 26, plumber, was brought up upon the charge of having upon the 22nd inst. abstracted from the jewel-case of the Countess of Morcar the valuable gem known as the blue carbuncle. James Ryder, upper-attendant at the hotel, gave his evidence to the effect that he had shown Horner up to the dressing-room of the Countess of Morcar upon the day of the robbery in order that he might solder the second bar of the gate, which was loose. He had remained with Horner some little time, but had finally been called away. On returning, he found that Horner had disappeared, that the bureau had been forced open, and that the small morocco casket in which, as it afterwards transpired, the Countess was accustomed to keep her jewel, was lying empty upon the dressing table. Ryder instantly gave the alarm, and Horner was arrested the same evening; but the stone could not be found either upon his person or in his rooms. Catherine Cusack, maid to the Countess, deposed to having heard Ryder's cry of dismay on discovering the robbery, and to having rushed into the room, where she found matters as described by the last witness. Inspector Bradstreet, B division, gave evidence as to the arrest of Horner, who struggled frantically, and protested his innocence in the strongest terms. Evidence of a previous conviction for robbery having been given against the prisoner, the magistrate refused to deal summarily with the offence, but referred it to the Assizes. Horner, who had shown signs of intense emotion during the proceedings, fainted away at the conclusion and was carried out of court.

"Hum! So much for the police court," said Holmes thoughtfully, tossing aside the paper. "The question for us now to solve is the sequence of events leading from a rifled jewel case at one end of the crop to a goose in Tottenham Court Road at the other. You see, Watson, our little deductions have suddenly assumed a much more important and less innocent aspect. Here is the stone; the stone came from the goose, and the goose came from Mr. Henry Baker, the gentleman with the bad hat and all the other characteristics with which I have bored you. So now we must set ourselves very seriously to finding this gentleman and ascertaining what part he has played in this little mystery. To do this, we must try the simplest means first, and these lie undoubtedly in an advertisement in the evening papers. If this fails, I shall have recourse to other methods."

"What will you say?"

"Give me a pencil and that slip of paper. Now, then:

Found at the corner of Goodge Street, a goose and a black felt hat. Mr. Henry Baker can have the same by applying at 6:30 this evening at 221B, Baker Street.

This is clear and concise."

"Very. But will he see it?"

"Well, he is sure to keep an eye on the papers, since, to a poor man, the loss was a heavy one. He was clearly so scared by his mischance in breaking the window and by the approach of Peterson that he thought of nothing but flight, but since then he must have bitterly regretted the impulse which caused him to drop his bird. Then, again, the introduction of his name will cause him to see it, for everyone who knows him will direct his attention to it. Here you are, Peterson, run down to the advertising agency and have this put in the evening papers."

"In which, sir?"

"Oh, in the *Globe, Star, Pall Mall, St. James's, Evening News Standard, Echo,* and any others that occur to you."

"Very well, sir. And this stone?"

"Ah, yes, I shall keep the stone. Thank you. And, I say, Peterson, just buy a goose on your way back and leave it here with me, for we must have one to give to this gentleman in place of the one which your family is now devouring."

When the commissionaire had gone, Holmes took up the stone and held it against the light. "It's a bonny thing," said he. "Just see how it glints and sparkles. Of course it is a nucleus and focus of crime. Every good stone is. They are the devil's pet baits. In the larger and older jewels every facet may stand for a bloody deed. This stone is not yet twenty years old. It was found in the banks of the Amoy River in southern China and is remarkable in having every characteristic of the carbuncle, save that it is blue in shade instead of ruby red. In spite of its youth, it has already a sinister history. There have been two murders, a vitriol-throwing, a suicide, a several robberies brought about for the sake of this forty-grain weight of crystallized charcoal. Who would think that so pretty a toy would be a purveyor to the gallows and the prison? I'll lock it up in my strong box now and drop a line to the Countess to say that we have it."

"Do you think that this man Horner is innocent?"

"I cannot tell."

"Well, then, do you imagine that this other one, Henry Baker, had anything to do with the matter?"

"It is, I think, much more likely that Henry Baker is an absolutely innocent man, who had no idea that the bird which he was carrying was of considerably more value than if it were made of solid gold. That, however, I shall determine by a very simple test if we have an answer to our advertisement."

"And you can do nothing until then?"

"Nothing."

"In that case I shall continue my professional round. But I shall come back in the evening at the hour you have mentioned, for I should like to see the solution of so tangled a business."

"Very glad to see you. I dine at seven. There is a woodcock, I believe. By the way, in view of recent occurrences, perhaps I ought to ask Mrs. Hudson to examine its crop."

I had been delayed at a case, and it was a little after half-past six when I found myself in Baker Street once more. As I approached the house I saw a tall man in a Scotch bonnet with a coat which was buttoned up to his chin waiting outside in the bright semicircle which was thrown from the fanlight. Just as I arrived the door was opened, and we were shown up together to Holmes's room.

"Mr. Henry Baker, I believe," said he, rising from his armchair and greeting his visitor with the easy air of geniality which he could so readily assume. "Pray take this chair by the fire, Mr. Baker. It is a cold night, and I observe that your circulation is more adapted for summer than for winter. Ah, Watson, you have just come at the right time. Is that your hat, Mr. Baker?"

"Yes, sir, that is undoubtedly my hat."

He was a large man with rounded shoulders, a massive head, and a broad, intelligent face, sloping down to a pointed beard of grizzled brown. A touch of red in the nose and cheeks, with a slight tremor of his extended hand, recalled Holmes's surmise as to his habits. His rusty black frock-coat was buttoned right up in front, with the collar turned up, and his lank wrists protruded from his sleeves without a sign of cuff or shirt. He spoke in a slow staccato fashion, choosing his words with care, and gave the impression generally of a man of learning and letters who had had ill-usage at the hands of fortune.

"We have retained these things for some days," said Holmes, "because we expected to see an advertisement from you giving your address. I am at a loss to know now why you did not advertise."

Our visitor gave a rather shamefaced laugh. "Shillings have not been so plentiful with me as they once were," he remarked. "I had no doubt that the gang of roughs who assaulted me had carried off both my hat and the bird. I did not care to spend more money in a hopeless attempt at recovering them."

"Very naturally. By the way, about the bird, we were compelled to eat it."

"To eat it!" Our visitor half rose from his chair in his excitement.

"Yes, it would have been of no use to anyone had we not done so. But I presume that this other goose upon the sideboard, which is about the same weight and perfectly fresh, will answer your purpose equally well?"

"Oh, certainly, certainly," answered Mr. Baker with a sigh of relief.

"Of course, we still have the feathers, legs, crop, and so on of your own bird, so if you wish—"

The man burst into a hearty laugh. "They might be useful to me as relics of my adventure," said he, "but beyond that I can hardly see what use the *disjecta membra* of my late acquaintance are going to be to me. No, sir, I think that, with your permission, I will confine my attentions to the excellent bird which I perceive upon the sideboard."

Sherlock Holmes glanced sharply across at me with a slight shrug of his shoulders.

"There is your hat, then, and there your bird," said he. "By the way, would it bore you to tell me where you got the other one from? I am somewhat of a fowl fancier, and I have seldom seen a better-grown goose."

"Certainly, sir," said Baker, who had risen and tucked his newly gained property under his arm. "There are a few of us who frequent the Alpha Inn, near the Museum—we are to be found in the Museum itself during the day, you understand. This year our good host, Windigate by name, instituted a goose club, by which, on consideration of some few pence every week, we were each to receive a bird at Christmas. My pence were duly paid, and the rest is familiar to you. I am much indebted to you, sir, for a Scotch bonnet is fitted neither to my years nor my gravity." With a comical pomposity of manner he bowed solemnly to both of us and strode off upon his way.

"So much for Mr. Henry Baker," said Holmes when he had closed the door behind him. "It is quite certain that he knows nothing whatever about the matter. Are you hungry, Watson?"

"Not particularly."

"Then I suggest that we turn our dinner into a supper and follow up this clue while it is still hot."

"By all means."

It was a bitter night, so we drew on our ulsters and wrapped cravats about our throats. Outside, the stars were shining coldly in a cloudless sky, and the breath of the passersby blew out into smoke like so many pistol shots. Our footfalls rang out crisply and loudly as we swung through the doctors' quarter, Wimpole Street, Harley Street, and so through Wigmore Street into Oxford Street. In a quarter of an hour we were in Bloomsbury at the Alpha Inn, which is a small public house at the corner of one of the streets which runs down into Holborn. Holmes pushed open the door of the private bar and ordered two glasses of beer from the ruddy-faced, white-aproned landlord.

"Your beer should be excellent if it is as good as your geese," said Holmes.

"My geese!" The man seemed surprised.

"Yes. I was speaking only half an hour ago to Mr. Henry Baker, who was a member of your goose club."

"Ah yes, I see. But you see, sir, them's not *our* geese."

"Indeed! Whose, then?"

"Well, I got the two dozen from a salesman in Covent Garden."

"Indeed? I know some of them. Which was it?"

"Breckinridge is his name."

"Ah! I don't know him. Well, here's to your good health, landlord, and prosperity to your house. Goodnight.

"Now for Mr. Breckinridge," he continued, buttoning up his coat as we came out into the frosty air. "Remember, Watson, that though we have so homely a thing as a goose at one end of this chain, we have at the other a man who will certainly get seven years' penal servitude unless we can establish his innocence. It is possible that our inquiry may but confirm his guilt; but, in any case, we have a line of investigation which has been missed by the police, and which a singular chance has placed in our hands. Let us follow it out to the bitter end. Faces to the south, then, and quick march!"

We passed across Holborn, down Endell Street, and so through a zigzag of slums to the Covent Garden Market. One of the largest stalls bore the name of Breckinridge upon it, and the proprietor, a horsy-looking man, with a sharp face and trim side-whiskers, was helping a boy to put up the shutters.

"Good evening. It's a cold night," said Holmes.

The salesman nodded and shot a questioning glance at my companion.

"Sold out of geese, I see," continued Holmes, pointing at the bare slabs of marble.

"Let you have five hundred tomorrow morning."

"That's no good."

"Well, there are some on the stall with the gas flare."

"Ah, but I was recommended to you."

"Who by?"

"The landlord of the Alpha."

"Oh, yes. I sent him a couple of dozen."

"Fine birds they were, too. Now where did you get them from?"

To my surprise the question provoked a burst of anger from the salesman.

"Now, then, mister," said he, with his head cocked and his arms akimbo, "what are you driving at? Let's have it straight, now."

"It is straight enough. I should like to know who sold you the geese which you supplied to the Alpha."

"Well, then, I shan't tell you. So now!"

"Oh, it is a matter of no importance, but I don't know why you should be so warm over such a trifle."

"Warm? You'd be as warm, maybe, if you were as pestered as I am. When I pay good money for a good article there should be an end of the business; but it's 'Where are the geese?' and 'Who did you sell the geese to?' and 'What will you take for the geese?' One would think they were the only geese in the world, to hear the fuss that is made over them."

"Well, I have no connection with any other people who have been making inquiries," said Holmes carelessly. "If you won't tell us the bet is off, that is all. But I'm always ready to back my opinion on a matter of fowls, and I have a fiver on it that the bird I ate is country bred."

"Well, then, you've lost your fiver, for it's town bred," snapped the salesman.

"It's nothing of the kind."

"I say it is."

"I don't believe it."

"D'you think you know more about fowls than I, who have handled them ever since I was a nipper? I tell you, all those birds that went to the Alpha were town bred."

"You'll never persuade me to believe that."

"Will you bet, then?"

"It's merely taking your money, for I know that I am right. But I'll have a sovereign on with you, just to teach you not to be obstinate."

The salesman chuckled grimly. "Bring me the books, Bill," said he.

The small boy brought round a small thin volume and a great greasy-backed one, laying them out together beneath the hanging lamp.

"Now then, Mr. Cocksure," said the salesman, "I thought that I was out of geese, but before I finish you'll find that there is still one left in my shop. You see this little book?"

"Well?"

"That's the list of the folk from whom I buy. D'you see? Well, then, here on this page are the country folk, and the numbers after their names are where their accounts are in the big ledger. Now, then! You see this other page in red ink? Well, that is a list of my town suppliers. Now, look at that third name. Just read it out to me."

"'Mrs. Oakshott, 117 Brixton Road—249,'" read Holmes.

"Quite so. Now turn that up in the ledger."

Holmes turned to the page indicated. "Here you are, 'Mrs. Oakshott, 117 Brixton Road, egg and poultry supplier.'"

"Now, then, what's the last entry?"

" 'December 22nd. Twenty-four geeze at 7*s*. 6*d*.'"

"Quite so. There you are. And underneath?"

" 'Sold to Mr. Windigate of the Alpha, at 12*s*.'"

"What have you to say now?"

Sherlock Holmes looked deeply chagrined. He drew a sovereign from his pocket and threw it down upon the slab, turning away with the air of a man whose disgust is too deep for words. A few yards off he stopped under a lamp-post and laughed in the hearty, noiseless fashion which was peculiar to him.

"When you see a man with whiskers of that cut and the 'pink'un' protruding out of his pocket, you can always draw him by a bet," said he. I daresay that if I had put £100 down in front of him, that man would not have given me such complete information as was drawn from him by the idea that he was doing me on a wager. Well, Watson, we are, I fancy, nearing the end of our quest, and the only point which remains to be determined is whether we should go on to this Mrs. Oakshott tonight, or whether we should reserve it for tomorrow. It is clear from what that surly fellow said that there are others besides ourselves who are anxious about the matter, and I should—"

His remarks were suddenly cut short by a loud hubbub which broke out from the stall which we had just left. Turning round we saw a little rat-faced fellow standing in the center of the circle of yellow light which was thrown by the swinging lamp, while Breckinridge the salesman, framed in the door of his stall, was shaking his fists fiercely at the cringing figure.

"I've had enough of you and your geese," he shouted. "I wish you were all at the devil together. If you come pestering me any more with your silly talk I'll set the dog at you. You bring Mrs. Oakshott here and I'll answer her, but what have you to do with it? Did I buy the geese off you?"

"No, but one of them was mine all the same," whined the little man.

"Well, then, ask Mrs. Oakshott for it."

"She told me to ask you."

"Well, you can ask the King of Proosia, for all I care. I've had enough of it. Get out of this!" He rushed fiercely forward, and the inquirer flitted away into the darkness.

"Ha! This may save us a visit to Brixton Road," whispered Holmes. "Come with me, and we will see what is to be made of this fellow." Striding through the scattered knots of people who lounged round the flaring stalls, my companion speedily overtook the little man and touched him upon the shoulder. He sprang round, and I could see in the gas light that every vestige of color had been driven from his face.

"Who are you, then? What do you want?" he asked in a quavering voice.

"You will excuse me," said Holmes blandly, "but I could not help overhearing the questions which you put to the salesman just now. I think that I could be of assistance to you."

"You? Who are you? How could you know anything of the matter?"

"My name is Sherlock Holmes. It is my business to know what other people don't know."

"But you can know nothing of this?"

"Excuse me, I know everything of it. You endeavoring to trace some geese which were sold by Mrs. Oakshott, of Brixton Road, to a salesman named Breckinridge, by him in turn to Mr. Windigate, of the Alpha, and by him to his club, of which Mr. Henry Baker is a member."

"Oh, sir, you are the very man whom I have longed to meet," cried the little fellow, with outstretched hands and quivering fingers. "I can hardly explain to you how interested I am in this matter."

Sherlock Holmes hailed a four-wheeler which was passing. "In that case we had better discuss it in a cozy room rather than in this wind-swept marketplace," said he. "But pray tell me, before we go farther, who it is that I have the pleasure of assisting."

The man hesitated for an instant. "My name is John Robinson," he answered with a sidelong glance.

"No, no; the real name," said Holmes sweetly. "It is always awkward doing business with an alias."

A flush sprang to the white cheeks of the stranger. "Well, then," said he, "my real name is James Ryder."

"Precisely so. Head attendant at the Hotel Cosmopolitan. Pray step into the cab, and I shall soon be able to tell you everything which you would wish to know."

The little man stood glancing from one to the other of us with half-frightened, half-hopeful eyes, as one who is not sure whether he is on the verge of a windfall or of a catastrophe. Then he stepped into the cab, and in half an hour we were back in the sitting room at Baker Street. Nothing had been said during our drive, but the high, thin breathing of our new companion, and the claspings and unclaspings of his hands, spoke of the nervous tension within him.

"Here we are!" said Holmes cheerily as we filed into the room. "The fire looks very seasonable in this weather. You look cold, Mr. Ryder. Pray take the basket chair. I will just put on my slippers before we settle this little matter of yours. Now, then! You want to know what became of those geese?"

"Yes, sir."

"Or rather, I fancy, of that goose. It was one bird, I imagine, in which you were interested—white, with a black bar across the tail."

Ryder quivered with emotion. "Oh, sir," he cried, "can you tell me where it went to?"

"It came here."

"Here?"

"Yes, and a most remarkable bird it proved. I don't wonder that you should take an interest in it. It laid an egg after it was dead—the bonniest, brightest little blue egg that ever was seen. I have it here in my museum."

Our visitor staggered to his feet and clutched the mantel piece with his right hand. Holmes unlocked his strong box and held up the blue carbuncle, which shone out like a star, with a cold, brilliant, many-pointed radiance. Ryder stood glaring with a drawn face, uncertain whether to claim or to disown it.

"The game's up, Ryder," said Holmes quietly. "Hold up, man, or you'll be into the fire! Give him an arm back into his chair, Watson. He's not got blood enough to go in for felony with impunity. Give him a dash of brandy. So! Now he looks a little more human. What a shrimp it is, to be sure!"

For a moment he had staggered and nearly fallen, but the brandy brought a tinge of color into his cheeks, and he sat staring with frightened eyes at his accuser.

"I have almost every link in my hands, and all the proofs which I could possibly need, so there is little which you need tell me. Still, that little may as well be cleared up to make the case complete. You had heard, Ryder, of this blue stone of the Countess of Morcar's?"

"It was Catherine Cusack who told me of it," said he in a crackling voice.

"I see—her ladyship's waiting maid. Well, the temptation of sudden wealth so easily acquired was too much for you, as it has been for better men before you; but you were not very scrupulous in the means you used. It seems to me, Ryder, that there is the making of a very pretty villain in you. You knew that this man Horner, the plumber, had been concerned in some such matter before, and that suspicion would rest the more readily upon him. What did you do, then? You made some small job in my lady's room—you and your confederate Cusack—and you managed that he should be the man sent for. Then, when he had left, you rifled the jewel case, raised the alarm, and had this unfortunate man arrested. You then—"

Ryder threw himself down suddenly upon the rug and clutched at my companion's knees. "For God's sake, have mercy!" he shrieked. "Think of my father! Of my mother! It would break their hearts. I never went wrong before! I never will again. I swear it. I'll swear it on a Bible. Oh, don't bring it into court! For Christ's sake, don't!"

"Get back into your chair!" said Holmes sternly. "It is very well to cringe and crawl now, but you thought little enough of this poor Horner in the dock for a crime of which he knew nothing."

"I will fly, Mr. Holmes. I will leave the country, sir. Then the charge against him will break down."

"Hum! We will talk about that. And now let us hear a true account of the next act. How came the stone into the goose, and how came the goose into the open market? Tell us the truth, for there lies your only hope of safety."

Ryder passed his tongue over his parched lips. "I will tell you it just as it happened, sir," said he. "When Horner had been arrested, it seemed to me that it would be best for me to get away with the stone at once, for I did not know at what moment the police might not take it into their heads to search me and my room. There was no place about the hotel where it would be safe. I went out, as if on some commission, and I made for my sister's house. She had married a man named Oakshott, and lived in Brixton Road, where she fattened fowls for the market. All the way there every man I met seemed to me to be a policeman or a detective; and, for all that it was a cold night, the sweat was pouring down my face before I came to the Brixton Road. My sister asked me what was the matter, and why I was so pale; but I told her that I had been upset by the jewel robbery at the hotel. Then I went into the back yard and smoked a pipe, and wondered what it would be best to do.

"I had a friend once called Maudsley, who went to the bad, and has just been serving his time in Pentonville. One day he had met me, and fell into talk about the ways of thieves, and how they could get rid of what they stole. I knew that he would be true to me, for I knew one or two things about him; so I made up my mind to go right on to Kilburn, where he lived, and take him into my confidence. He would show me how to turn the stone into money. But how to get to him in safety? I thought of the agonies I had gone through in coming from the hotel. I might at any moment be seized and searched, and there would be the stone in my waistcoat pocket. I was leaning against the wall at the time and looking at the geese which were waddling about round my feet, and suddenly an idea came into my head which showed me how I could beat the best detective that ever lived.

"My sister had told me some weeks before that I might have the pick of her geese for a Christmas present, and I knew that she was always as good as her word. I would take my goose now, and in it I would carry my stone to Kilburn.

There was a little shed in the yard, and behind this I drove one of the birds—a fine big one, white, with a barred tail. I caught it, and, prying its bill open, I thrust the stone down its throat as far as my finger could reach. The bird gave a gulp, and I felt the stone pass along its gullet and down into its crop. But the creature flapped and struggled, and out came my sister to know what was the matter. As I turned to speak to her the brute broke loose and fluttered off among the others.

" 'Whatever were you doing with that bird, Jem?' said she.

" 'Well,' said I, 'you said you'd give me one for Christmas, and I was feeling which was the fattest.'

"'Oh,' says she, 'we've set yours aside for you—Jem's bird we call it. It's the big white one over yonder. There's twenty-six of them, which makes one for you, and one for us, and two dozen for the market.'

"'Thank you, Maggie,' says I, 'but if it is all the same to you, I'd rather have that one I was handling just now.'

"'The other is a good three pounds heavier,' said she, 'and we fattened it expressly for you.'

"'Never mind. I'll have the other, and I'll take it now,' said I.

"'Oh, just as you like,' said she, a little huffed. 'Which is it you want, then?'

"'That white one with the barred tail, right in the middle of the flock.'

"'Oh, very well. Kill it and take it with you.'

"Well, I did what she said, Mr. Holmes, and I carried the bird all the way to Kilburn. I told my pal what I had done, for he was a man that it was easy to tell a thing like that to. He laughed until he choked, and we got a knife and opened the goose. My heart turned to water, for there was no sign of the stone, and I knew that some terrible mistake had occurred. I left the bird, rushed back to my sister's, and hurried into the back yard. There was not a bird to be seen there.

"'Where are they all, Maggie?' I cried.

"'Gone to the dealer's, Jem.'

"'Which dealer's?'

"'Breckinridge, of Covent Garden.'

"'But was there another with a barred tail?' I asked. 'The same as the one I chose?'

"'Yes, Jem, there were two barred-tailed ones, and I could never tell them apart.'

"Well, then, of course I saw it all, and I ran off as hard as my feet would carry me to this man Breckinridge, but he had sold the lot at once, and not one word would he tell me as to where they had gone. You heard him yourselves tonight. Well, he has always answered me like that. My sister thinks that I am going mad. Sometimes I think that I am myself. And now—and now I am myself a branded thief, without ever having touched the wealth for which I sold my character. God help me! God help me!" He burst into convulsive sobbing, with his face buried in his hands.

There was a long silence, broken only by his heavy breathing, and by the measured tapping of Sherlock Holmes's fingertips upon the edge of the table. Then my friend rose and threw open the door.

"Get out!" said he.

"What, sir! Oh, Heaven bless you!"

"No more words. Get out!"

And no more words were needed. There was a rush, a clatter upon the stairs, the bang of a door, and the crisp rattle of running footfalls from the street.

"After all, Watson," said Holmes, reaching up his hand for his clay pipe, "I am not retained by the police to supply their deficiencies. If Horner were in danger it would be another thing; but this fellow will not appear against him, and the case must collapse. I suppose that I am commuting a felony, but it is just possible that I am saving a soul. This fellow will not go wrong again; he is too terribly frightened. Send him to jail now, and you make him a jailbird for life. Besides, it is the season of forgiveness. Chance has put in our way a most singular and whimsical problem, and its solution is its own reward. If you will have the goodness to touch the bell, Doctor, we will begin another investigation, in which, also, a bird will be the chief feature."

Christmas Every Day

William Dean Howells

From *Christmas Every Day and Other Stories Told for Children*

The little girl came into her papa's study, as she always did Saturday morning before breakfast, and asked for a story. He tried to beg off that morning, for he was very busy, but she would not let him. So he began:

"Well, once there was a little pig—"

She put her hand over his mouth and stopped him at the word. She said she had heard little pig stories till she was perfectly sick of them.

"Well, what kind of story *shall* I tell, then?"

"About Christmas. It's getting to be the season. It's past Thanksgiving already."

"It seems to me," her papa argued, "that I've told as often about Christmas as I have about little pigs."

"No difference! Christmas is more interesting."

"Well!" Her papa roused himself from his writing by a great effort. "Well, then, I'll tell you about the little girl who wanted it Christmas every day in the year. How would you like that?"

"First rate!" said the little girl, and she nestled into a comfortable shape in his lap, ready for listening.

"Very well, then, this little pig—Oh, what are you pounding me for?"

"Because you said little pig instead of little girl."

"I should like to know what's the difference between a little pig and a little girl who wanted it Christmas every day!"

"Papa," said the little girl, warningly, "if you don't go on, I'll *give* it to you!" And at this her papa darted off like lightning, and began to tell the story as fast as he could.

WELL, ONCE THERE WAS a little girl who liked Christmas so much that she wanted it to be Christmas every day in the year; and as soon as Thanksgiving was over she began to send postal cards to the old Christmas Fairy to ask if she mightn't have it. But the old Fairy never answered any of the postals; and after a while the little girl found out that the Fairy was pretty particular, and wouldn't notice anything but letters—not even correspondence cards in envelopes; but real letters on sheets of paper, and sealed outside with a monogram—or your initial, anyway. So, then, she began to send her letters; and in about three weeks—or just the day before Christmas, it was—she got a letter from the Fairy, saying she might have it Christmas every day for a year, and then they would see about having it longer.

The little girl was a good deal excited already, preparing for the old-fashioned, once-a-year Christmas that was coming the next day, and perhaps the Fairy's promise didn't make such an impression on her as it would have made at some other time. She just resolved to keep it to herself, and surprise everybody with it as it kept coming true; and then it slipped out of her mind altogether.

She had a splendid Christmas. She went to bed early, so as to let Santa Claus have a chance at the stockings, and in the morning she was up the first of anybody and went and felt them, and found hers all lumpy with packages of candy, and oranges and grapes, and pocketbooks and rubber balls, and all kinds of small presents, and her big brother's with nothing but the tongs in them, and her young lady sister's with a new silk umbrella, and her papa's and mamma's with potatoes and pieces of coal wrapped up in tissue paper, just as they always had every Christmas. Then she waited around till the rest of the family were up and she was the first to burst into the library, when the doors were opened, and look at the large presents laid out on the library table—books, and portfolios, and boxes of stationery, and breastpins, and dolls, and little stoves, and dozens of handkerchiefs, and inkstands, and skates, and snow shovels, and photograph frames, and little easels, and boxes of watercolors, and Turkish paste, and nougat, and candied cherries, and dolls' houses, and waterproofs—and the big Christmas tree, lighted and standing in a wastebasket in the middle.

She had a splendid Christmas all day. She ate so much candy that she did not want any breakfast; and the whole forenoon the presents kept pouring in that the expressman had not had time to deliver the night before;

and she went round giving the presents she had got for other people, and plum pudding and nuts and raisins and oranges and more candy, and then went out and coasted, and came in with a stomach ache, crying; and her papa said he would see if his house was turned into that sort of fool's paradise another year; and they had a light supper, and pretty early everybody went to bed cross.

Here the little girl pounded her papa in the back, again.

"Well, what now? Did I say pigs?"

"You made them *act* like pigs."

"Well, didn't they?"

"No matter; you oughtn't to put it into a story."

"Very well, then, I'll take it all out."

Her father went on:

The little girl slept very heavily, and she slept very late, but she was wakened at last by the other children dancing round her bed with their stockings full of presents in their hands.

"What is it?" said the little girl, and she rubbed her eyes and tried to rise up in bed.

"Christmas! Christmas! Christmas!" they all shouted, and waved their stockings.

"Nonsense! It was Christmas yesterday."

Her brothers and sisters just laughed. "We don't know about that. It's Christmas today, anyway. You come into the library and see."

Then all at once it flashed on the little girl that the Fairy was keeping her promise, and her year of Christmases was beginning. She was dreadfully sleepy, but she sprang up like a lark—a lark that had overeaten itself and gone to bed cross—and darted into the library. There it was again! Books, and portfolios, and boxes of stationery, and breastpins—

"You needn't go over it all, papa; I guess I can remember just what was there," said the little girl.

Well, and there was the Christmas tree blazing away, and the family picking out their presents, but looking pretty sleepy, and her father perfectly puzzled, and her mother ready to cry. "I'm sure I don't see how I'm to dispose of all these things," said her mother, and her father said it seemed to him they had had something just like it the day before, but he supposed he must have dreamed it. This struck the little girl as the best kind of a joke; and so she ate so much candy she didn't want any breakfast, and went round carrying presents, and had turkey and cranberry for dinner, and then went out and coasted, and came in with a—

"Papa!"
"Well, what now?"
"What did you promise, you forgetful thing?"
"Oh! Oh yes!"

Well, the next day, it was just the same thing over again, but everybody getting crosser; and at the end of a week's time so many people had lost their tempers that you could pick up lost tempers anywhere; they perfectly strewed the ground. Even when people tried to recover their tempers they usually got somebody else's, and it made the most dreadful mix.

The little girl began to get frightened, keeping the secret all to herself; she wanted to tell her mother, but she didn't dare to; and she was ashamed to ask the Fairy to take back her gift, it seemed ungrateful and ill-bred, and she thought she would try to stand it, but she hardly knew how she could, for a whole year. So it went on and on, and it was Christmas on St. Valentine's Day and Washington's Birthday, just the same as any day, and it didn't skip even the First of April, though everything was counterfeit that day, and that was some *little* relief.

After a while coal and potatoes began to be awfully scarce, so many had been wrapped up in tissue paper to fool papas and mammas with. Turkeys got to be about a thousand dollars apiece—

"Papa!"

"Well, what?"

"You're beginning to fib."

"Well, *two* thousand, then."

And they got to passing off almost anything for turkeys—half-grown humming birds, and even rocs out of the *Arabian Nights*—the real turkeys were so scarce. And cranberries—well, they asked a diamond apiece for cranberries. All the woods and orchards were cut down for Christmas trees, and where the woods and orchards used to be it looked just like a stubble-field, with the stumps. After a while they had to make Christmas trees out of rags, and stuff them with bran, like old-fashioned dolls; but there were plenty of rags, because people got so poor, buying presents for one another, that they couldn't get any new clothes, and they just wore their old ones to tatters. They got so poor that everybody had to go to the poor house, except the confectioners, and the fancy-store keepers, and the picture-book sellers, and the expressmen; and *they* all got so rich and proud that they would hardly wait upon a person when he came to buy. It was perfectly shameful!

Well, after it had gone on about three or four months, the little girl, whenever she came into the room in the morning and saw those great ugly, lumpy stockings dangling at the fireplace, and the disgusting presents around everywhere, used to just sit down and burst out crying. In six months she was perfectly exhausted; she couldn't even cry any more; she just lay on the lounge and rolled her eyes and panted. About the beginning of October she took to sitting down on dolls wherever she found them—French dolls, or any kind—she hated the sight of them so; and by Thanksgiving she was crazy, and just slammed her presents across the room.

By that time people didn't carry presents around nicely anymore. They flung them over the fence, or through the window, or anything; and, instead of running their tongues out and taking great pains to write "For dear Papa," or "Mamma," or "Brother," or "Sister," or "Susie," or "Sammie," or "Billie," or "Bobbie," or "Jimmie," or "Jennie," or whoever it was, and troubling to get the spelling right, and signing their names, and "Xmas, 18—," they used to write in the gift books, "Take it, you horrid old thing!" and then go and bang it against the front door. Nearly everybody had built barns to hold their presents, but pretty soon the barns overflowed, and then they used to let them lie out in the rain, or anywhere. Sometimes the police used to come and tell them to shovel their presents off the sidewalk, or they would arrest them.

"I thought you said everybody had gone to the poor house," interrupted the little girl.

"They did go, at first," said her papa, "but after a while the poor houses got so full that they had to send the people back to their own houses. They tried to cry, when they got back, but they couldn't make the least sound."

"Why couldn't they?"

"Because they had lost their voices, saying 'Merry Christmas' so much. Did I tell you how it was on the Fourth of July?"

"No. How was it?" And the little girl nestled closer, in expectation of something uncommon.

Well, the night before, the boys stayed up to celebrate, as they always do, and fell asleep before twelve o'clock, as usual, expecting to be wakened by the bells and cannon. But it was nearly eight o'clock before the first boy in the United States woke up, and then he found out what the trouble was. As soon as he could get his clothes, he ran out of the house and smashed a big cannon-torpedo down on the pavement, but it didn't make any more noise than a damp wad of paper, and after he tried about twenty or thirty more, he began to pick them up and look at them. Every single torpedo was a big raisin! Then he just streaked it upstairs, and examined his firecrackers and toy pistol and two-dollar collection of fireworks, and found that they were nothing but sugar and candy painted up to look like fireworks! Before ten o'clock every boy in the United States found out that this Fourth of July things had turned into Christmas things; and then they just sat down and cried—they were so mad. There are about twenty million boys in the United States, and so you can imagine what a noise they made. Some men got together before night, with a little powder that hadn't turned into people sugar yet, and they said they would fire off *one* cannon, anyway. But the cannon burst into a thousand pieces, for it was nothing but rock candy, and some of the men nearly got killed. The Fourth of July orations all turned into Christmas carols, and when anybody tried to read the Declaration, instead of saying, "When in the course of human events it becomes necessary," he was sure to sing, "God rest you, merry gentlemen." It was perfectly awful.

The little girl drew a deep sigh of satisfaction.

"And how was it at Thanksgiving?"

Her papa hesitated. "Well, I'm almost afraid to tell you. I'm afraid you'll think it's wicked."

"Well, tell, anyway," said the little girl.

Well, before it came Thanksgiving it had leaked out who had caused all these Christmases. The little girl had suffered so much that she had talked about it in her sleep; and after that hardly anybody would play with her. People just perfectly despised her, because if it had not been for her greediness it wouldn't have happened. And now, when it came Thanksgiving, and she wanted them to go to church, and then have squash pie and turkey, and show their gratitude, they said that all the turkeys had been eaten up for her old Christmas dinners, and if she would stop the Christmases, they would see about the gratitude. Wasn't it dreadful? And the very next day the little girl began to send letters to the Christmas Fairy, and then telegrams, to stop it. But it didn't do any good; and then she got to calling at the Fairy's house, but the girl who came to the door always said, "Not at home," or "Engaged," or "At dinner," or something like that; and so it went on till it came to the old once-a-year Christmas Eve. The little girl fell asleep, and when she woke up in the morning—

"She found it was all nothing but a dream," suggested the little girl.

"No, indeed!" said her papa. "It was all every bit true!"

"Well, what *did* she find out, then?"

"Why, that it wasn't Christmas at last, and wasn't ever going to be, anymore. Now it's time for breakfast."

The little girl held her papa fast around the neck.

"You shan't go if you're going to leave it *so*!"

"How do you want it left?"

"Christmas once a year."

"All right," said her papa, and he went on again.

Well, there was the greatest rejoicing all over the country, and it extended clear up into Canada. The people met together everywhere, and kissed and cried for joy. The city carts went around and gathered up all the candy and raisins and nuts, and dumped them into the river; and it made the fish perfectly sick; and the whole United States, as far out as Alaska, was one blaze of bonfires, where the children were burning up their gift books and presents of all kinds. They had the greatest *time!*

The little girl went to thank the old Fairy because she had stopped its being Christmas, and she said she hoped she would keep her promise and see that Christmas never, never came again. Then the Fairy frowned, and asked if she was sure she knew what she meant; and the little girl asked her, Why not? and the old Fairy said that now she was behaving just as greedily as ever, and she'd better look out. This made the little girl think it all over carefully again, and she said she would be willing to have it Christmas about once in a thousand years; and then she said a hundred, and then she said ten, and at last she got down to one. Then the Fairy said that was the good old way that had pleased people ever since Christmas began, and she was agreed. Then the little girl said, "What're your shoes made of?" And the Fairy said, "Leather." And the little girl said, "Bargain's done forever," and skipped off, and hippity-hopped the whole way home, she was so glad.

"How will that do?" asked the papa.

"First rate!" said the little girl, but she hated to have the story stop, and was rather sober.

However, her mamma put her head in at the door, and asked her papa, "Are you never coming to breakfast? What have you been telling that child?"

"Oh, just a moral tale."

The little girl caught him around the neck again.

"*We* know! Don't you tell *what,* papa! Don't you tell *what!*"

Christmas Is a Sad Season for the Poor

* ❄ * * ❄ * ❄ ❄ *

John Cheever

Christmas is a sad season. The phrase came to Charlie an instant after the alarm clock had waked him, and named for him an amorphous depression that had troubled him all the previous evening. The sky outside his window was black. He sat up in bed and pulled the light chain that hung in front of his nose. Christmas is a very sad day of the year, he thought. Of all the millions of people in New York, I am practically the only one who has to get up in the cold black of 6 a.m. on Christmas Day in the morning; I am practically the only one.

He dressed, and when he went downstairs from the top floor of the rooming house in which he lived, the only sounds he heard were the coarse sounds of sleep; the only lights burning were lights that had been forgotten. Charlie ate some breakfast in an all-night lunchwagon and took an elevated train uptown. From Third Avenue, he walked over to Sutton Place. The neighborhood was dark. House after house put into the shine of the street lights a wall of black windows. Millions and millions were sleeping, and this general loss of consciousness generated an impression of abandonment, as if this were the fall of the city, the end of time. He opened the iron-and-glass doors of the apartment building where he had been working for six months as an elevator operator, and went through the elegant lobby to a locker room at the back. He put on a striped vest with brass buttons, a false ascot, a pair of pants with a light-blue stripe on the seam, and a coat. The night elevator man was dozing on the little bench in the car. Charlie woke him. The night elevator man told him thickly that the day doorman had been taken sick and wouldn't be in that day. With the doorman sick, Charlie wouldn't have any relief for lunch, and a lot of people would expect him to whistle for cabs.

CHARLIE HAD BEEN on duty a few minutes when 14 rang—a Mrs. Hewing, who, he happened to know, was kind of immoral. Mrs. Hewing hadn't been to bed yet, and she got into the elevator wearing a long dress under her fur coat. She was followed by her two funny-looking dogs. He took her down and watched her go out into the dark and take her dogs to the curb. She was outside for only a few minutes. Then she came in and he took her up to 14 again. When she got off the elevator, she said, "Merry Christmas, Charlie."

"Well, it isn't much of a holiday for me, Mrs. Hewing," he said. "I think Christmas is a very sad season of the year. It isn't that people around here ain't generous—I mean, I got plenty of tips—but, you see, I live alone in a furnished room and I don't have any family or anything, and Christmas isn't much of a holiday for me."

"I'm sorry, Charlie," Mrs. Hewing said. "I don't have any family myself. It is kind of sad when you're alone, isn't it?" She called her dogs and followed them into her apartment. He went down.

It was quiet then, and Charlie lighted a cigarette. The heating plant in the basement encompassed the building at that hour in a regular and profound vibration, and the sullen noises of arriving steam heat began to resound, first in the lobby and then to reverberate up through all the sixteen stories, but this was a mechanical awakening, and it didn't lighten his loneliness or his petulance. The black air outside the glass doors had begun to turn blue, but the blue light seemed to have no source; it appeared in the middle of the air. It was a tearful light, and as it picked out the empty street he wanted to cry. Then a cab drove up, and the Walsers got out, drunk and dressed in evening clothes, and he took them up to their penthouse. The Walsers got him to brooding about the difference between his life in a furnished room and the lives of the people overheard. It was terrible.

Then the early churchgoers began to ring, but there were only three of these that morning. A few more went off to church at eight o'clock, but the majority of the building remained unconscious, although the smell of bacon and coffee had begun to drift into the elevator shaft.

At a little after nine, a nursemaid came down with a child. Both the nursemaid and the child had a deep tan and had just returned, he knew, from Bermuda. He had never been to Bermuda. He, Charlie, was a prisoner, confined eight hours a day to a six-by-eight elevator cage, which was confined, in turn, to a sixteen-story shaft. In one building or another, he had made his living as an elevator operator for ten years. He estimated the average trip at about an eighth of a mile, and when he thought of the thousands of miles he had traveled, when he thought that he might have driven the car through the mists above the Caribbean and set it down on some coral beach in Bermuda, he held the narrowness of his travels against his passengers, as if it were not the nature of the elevator but the pressure of their lives that confined him; as if they had clipped his wings.

He was thinking about this when the DePauls, on 9, rang. They wished him a merry Christmas.

"Well, it's nice of you to think of me," he said as they descended, "but it isn't much of a holiday for me. Christmas is a sad season when you're poor. I live alone in a furnished room. I don't have any family."

"Who do you have dinner with, Charlie?" Mrs. DePaul asked.

"I don't have any Christmas dinner," Charlie said. "I just get a sandwich."

"Oh, Charlie!" Mrs. DePaul was a stout woman with an impulsive heart, and Charlie's plaint struck at her holiday mood as if she had been caught in a cloudburst. "I do wish we could share our Christmas dinner with you, you know," she said. "I come from Vermont, you know, and when I was a child, you know, we always used to have a great many people at our table. The mailman, you know, and the schoolteacher, and just anybody who didn't have any family of their own, you know, and I wish we could share our dinner with you the way we used to, you know, and I don't see any reason why we can't. We can't have you at the table, you know, because you couldn't leave the elevator—could you?—but just as soon as Mr. DePaul has carved the goose,

I'll give you a ring, and I'll arrange a tray for you, you know, and I want you to come up and at least share our Christmas dinner."

Charlie thanked them, and their generosity surprised him, but he wondered if, with the arrivals of friends and relatives, they wouldn't forget their offer.

Then old Mrs. Gadshill rang, and when she wished him a merry Christmas, he hung his head.

"It isn't much of a holiday for me, Mrs. Gadshill," he said. "Christmas is a sad season if you're poor. You see, I don't have any family. I live alone in a furnished room."

"I don't have any family either, Charlie," Mrs. Gadshill said. She spoke with a pointed lack of petulance, but her grace was forced. "That is, I don't have any children with me today. I have three children and seven grandchildren, but none of them can see their way to coming East for Christmas with me. Of course, I understand their problems. I know that it's difficult to travel with children during the holidays, although I always seemed to manage it when I was their age, but people feel differently, and we mustn't condemn them for the things we can't understand. But I know how you feel, Charlie. I haven't any family either. I'm just as lonely as you."

Mrs. Gadshill's speech didn't move him. Maybe she was lonely, but she had a ten-room apartment and three servants and bucks and bucks and diamonds and diamonds, and there were plenty of poor kids in the slums who would be happy at a chance at the food her cook threw away. Then he thought about poor kids. He sat down on a chair in the lobby and thought about them.

They got the worst of it. Beginning in the fall, there was all this excitement about Christmas and how it was a day for them. After Thanksgiving, they couldn't miss it. It was fixed so they couldn't miss it. The wreaths and decorations everywhere, and bells ringing, and trees in the park, and Santa Clauses on every corner, and pictures in the magazines and newspapers and on every wall and window in the city told them that if they were good, they would get what they wanted. Even if they couldn't read, they couldn't miss it. They couldn't miss it even if they were blind. It got into the air the poor kids inhaled. Every time they took a walk, they'd see all the expensive toys in the store windows, and they'd write letters to Santa Claus, and their mothers and fathers would promise to mail them, and after the kids had gone to sleep, they'd burn the letters in the stove. And when it came Christmas morning, how could you explain it, how could you tell them that Santa Claus only visited the rich, that he didn't know about the good? How could you face them when all you had to give them was a balloon or a lollipop?

On the way home from work a few nights earlier, Charlie had seen a woman and a little girl going down Fifty-ninth Street. The little girl was crying. He guessed she was crying—he knew she was crying—because she'd seen all the things in the toy store windows and couldn't understand why none of them were for her. Her mother did housework, he guessed, or maybe was a waitress, and he saw them going back to a room like his, with green walls and no heat, on Christmas Eve, to eat a can of soup. And he saw the little girl hang up her ragged stocking and fall asleep, and he saw the mother looking through her purse for something to put into the stocking. This reverie was interrupted by a bell on 11. He went up, and Mr. and Mrs. Fuller were waiting. When they wished him a merry Christmas, he said, "Well, it isn't much of a holiday for me, Mrs. Fuller. Christmas is a sad season when you're poor."

"Do you have any children, Charlie?" Mrs. Fuller asked.

"Four living," he said. "Two in the grave." The majesty of his lies overwhelmed him. "Mrs. Leary's a cripple," he added.

"How sad, Charlie," Mrs. Fuller said. She started out of the elevator when it reached the lobby, and then she turned. "I want to give your children some presents, Charlie," she said. "Mr. Fuller and I are going to pay a call now, but when we come back, I want to give you some things for your children."

He thanked her. Then the bell rang on 4, and he went up to get the Westons.

"It isn't much of a Christmas for me," he told them when they wished him a merry Christmas. "Christmas is a sad season when you're poor. You see, I live alone in a furnished room."

"Poor Charlie," Mrs. Weston said. "I know just how you feel. During the war, when Mr. Weston was away, I was all alone at Christmas. I didn't have any Christmas dinner or tree or anything. I just scrambled myself some eggs and sat there and cried." Mr. Weston, who had gone into the lobby, called impatiently to his wife. "I know just how you feel, Charlie," Mrs. Weston said.

BY NOON, THE CLIMATE in the elevator shaft had changed from bacon and coffee to poultry and game, and the house, like an enormous and complex homestead, was absorbed in the preparations for a domestic feast. The children and their nursemaids had all returned from the Park. Grandmothers and aunts were arriving in limousines. Most of the people who came through the lobby were carrying packages wrapped in colored paper, and were wearing their best furs and new clothes. Charlie continued to complain to most of the tenants when they wished him a merry Christmas, changing his story from the lonely bachelor to the poor father and back again, as his mood changed, but this outpouring of melancholy, and the sympathy it aroused, didn't make him feel any better.

At half past one, 9 rang, and when he went up, Mr. DePaul was standing in the door of their apartment holding a cocktail shaker and a glass. "Here's a little Christmas cheer, Charlie," he said, and he poured Charlie a drink. Then a maid appeared with a tray of covered dishes, and Mrs. DePaul came out of the living room. "Merry Christmas, Charlie," she said. "I had Mr. DePaul carve the goose early, so that you could have some, you know. I didn't want to put the dessert on the tray, because I was afraid it would melt, you know, so when we have our dessert, we'll call you."

"And what is Christmas without presents?" Mr. DePaul said, and he brought a large, flat box from the hall and laid it on top of the covered dishes.

"You people make it seem like a real Christmas to me," Charlie said. Tears started into his eyes. "Thank you, thank you."

"Merry Christmas! Merry Christmas!" they called, and they watched him carry his dinner and his present into the elevator. He took the tray and the box into the locker room when he got down. On the tray, there was a soup, some kind of creamed fish, and a serving of goose. The bell rang again, but before he answered it, he tore open the DePaul's box and saw that it held a dressing gown. Their generosity and their cocktail had begun to work on his brain, and he went jubilantly up to 12. Mrs. Gadshill's maid was standing in the door with a tray, and Mrs. Gadshill stood behind her. "Merry Christmas, Charlie!" she said. He thanked her, and tears came into his eyes again. On the way down, he drank off the glass of sherry on Mrs. Gadshill's tray. Mrs. Gadshill's contribution was a mixed grill. He ate the lamb chop with his fingers. The bell was ringing again, and he wiped his face with a paper towel and went up to 11. "Merry Christmas, Charlie," Mrs. Fuller said, and she was standing in the door with her arms full of packages wrapped in silver paper, just like a picture in an advertisement, and Mr. Fuller was beside her with an arm around her, and they both looked as if they were going to cry. "Here are some things I want you to take home to your children," Mrs. Fuller said. "And here's something for Mrs. Leary and here's something for you. And if you want to take these things out to the elevator, we'll have your dinner ready for you in a minute." He carried the things into the elevator and came back for the tray. "Merry Christmas, Charlie!" both of the Fullers called after him as he closed the door. He took their dinner and their presents into the locker room and tore open the box that was marked for him. There was an alligator wallet in it, with Mr. Fuller's initials in the corner. Their dinner was also goose, and he ate a piece of the meat with his fingers and was washing it down with a cocktail when the bell rang. He went up again. This time it was the Westons. "Merry Christmas, Charlie!" they said, and they gave him a cup of eggnog, a turkey dinner, and a present. Their gift was also a dressing gown. Then 7 rang, and when he went up, there was another dinner and some more toys. Then 14 rang, and when he went up, Mrs. Hewing was standing in the hall, in a kind of negligee, holding a pair of riding boots in one hand and some neckties in the other. She had been crying and drinking. "Merry Christmas, Charlie," she said tenderly. "I wanted to give you something, and I've been thinking about you all morning, and I've been all over the apartment, and these are the only things I could find that a man might want. These are the only things that Mr. Brewer left. I don't suppose you'd have any use for the riding boots, but wouldn't you like the neckties?" Charlie took the neckties and thanked her and hurried back to the car, for the elevator bell had run three times.

BY THREE O'CLOCK, Charlie had fourteen dinners spread on the table and the floor of the locker room, and the bell kept ringing. Just as he started to eat one, he would have to go up and get another, and he was in the middle of the Parsons' roast beef when he had to go up and get the DePaul's dessert. He kept the door of the locker room closed, for he sensed that the quality of charity is exclusive and that his friends would have been disappointed to find that they were not the only ones to try to lessen his loneliness. There were goose, turkey, chicken, pheasant, grouse, and pigeon. There were trout and salmon, creamed scallops and oysters, lobster, crab meat, whitebait, and clams. There were plum puddings, mince pies, mousses, puddles of melted ice cream, layer cakes, *Torten*, éclairs, and two slices of Bavarian cream pie. He had dressing gowns, neckties, cuff links, socks, and handkerchiefs, and one of the tenants had asked for his neck size and then given him three green shirts. There were a glass teapot filled, the label said, with jasmine honey, four bottles of after-shave lotion, some alabaster bookends, and a dozen steak knives. The avalanche of charity he had precipitated filled the locker room and made him hesitant, now and then, as if he had touched some wellspring in the female heart that would bury him alive in food and dressing gowns. He had made almost no headway on the food, for all the servings were preternaturally large, as if loneliness had been counted on to generate in him a brutish appetite. Nor had he opened any of the presents that had been given to him for his imaginary children, but he had drunk everything they sent down and around him were the dregs of Martinis, Manhattans, Old-Fashioneds, champagne-and-raspberry-shrub cocktails, eggnogs, Bronxes, and Side Cars.

His face was blazing. He loved the world, and the world loved him. When he thought back over his life, it appeared to him in a rich and wonderful light, full of astonishing experiences and unusual friends. He thought that his job as an elevator operator—cruising up and down through hundreds of feet of perilous space—demanded the nerve and the intellect of a birdman. All the constraints of his life—the green walls of his room and the months of unemployment—dissolved. No one was ringing, but he got into the elevator and shot it at full speed up to the penthouse and down again, up and down, to test his wonderful mastery of space.

A bell rang on 12 while he was cruising, and he stopped in his flight long enough to pick up Mrs. Gadshill. As the car started to fall, he took his hands off the controls in a paroxysm of joy and shouted, "Strap on your safety belt, Mrs. Gadshill! We're going to make a loop-the-loop!" Mrs. Gadshill shrieked. Then, for some reason, she sat down on the floor of the elevator. Why was her face so pale, he wondered. Why was she sitting on the floor? She shrieked again. He grounded the car gently, and cleverly, he thought, and opened the door. "I'm sorry if I scared you, Mrs. Gadshill," he said meekly. "I was only fooling." She shrieked again. Then she ran out into the lobby, screaming for the superintendent.

The superintendent fired Charlie and took over the elevator himself. The news that he was out of work stung Charlie for a minute. It was his first contact with human meanness that day. He sat down in the locker room and gnawed on a drumstick. His drinks were beginning to let him down, and while it had not reached him yet, he felt a miserable soberness in the offing. The excess of food and presents around him began to make him feel guilty and unworthy. He regretted bitterly the lie he had told about his children. He was a single man with simple needs. He had abused the goodness of the people upstairs. He was unworthy.

Then up through this drunken train of thought surged the sharp figure of his landlady and her three skinny children. He thought of them sitting in their basement room. The cheer of Christmas had passed them by. This image got him to his feet. The realization that he was in a position to give, that he could bring happiness easily to someone else, sobered him. He took a big burlap sack, which was used for collecting waste, and began to stuff it, first with his presents and then with the presents for his imaginary children. He worked with the haste of a man whose train is approaching the station, for he could hardly wait to see those long faces light up when he came in the door. He changed his clothes, and, fired by a wonderful and unfamiliar sense of power, he slung his bag over his shoulder like a regular Santa Claus, went out the back way, and took a taxi to the Lower East Side.

The landlady and her children had just finished off a turkey, which had been sent to them by the local Democratic Club, and they were stuffed and uncomfortable when Charlie began pounding on the door, shouting "Merry Christmas!" He dragged the bag in after him and dumped the presents for the children onto the floor. There were dolls and musical toys, blocks, sewing kits, an Indian suit, and a loom, and it appeared to him that, as he had hoped, his arrival in the basement dispelled its gloom. When half the presents had been opened, he gave the landlady a bathrobe and went upstairs to look over the things he had been given for himself.

NOW, THE LANDLADY'S children had already received so many presents by the time Charlie arrived that they were confused with receiving, and it was only the landlady's intuitive grasp of the nature of charity that made her allow the children to open some of the presents while Charlie was still in the room, but as soon as he had gone, she stood between the children and the presents that were still unopened. "Now, you kids have had enough already," she said. "You kids have got your share. Just look at the things you got there. Why, you ain't even played with half of them. Mary Anne, you ain't even looked at that doll the Fire Department give you. Now, a nice thing to do would be to take all this stuff that's left over to those poor people on Hudson Street—them Deckkers. They ain't got nothing." A beatific light came into her face when she realized that she could give, that she could bring cheer, that she could put a healing finger on a case needier than hers, and—like Mrs. DePaul and Mrs. Weston, like Charlie himself, and like Mrs. Deckker, when Mrs. Decker was to think, subsequently, of the poor Shannons—first love, then charity, and then a sense of power drove her. "Now, you kids help me get all this stuff together. Hurry, hurry, hurry," she said, for it was dark then, and she knew that we are bound, one to another, in licentious benevolence for only a single day, and that day was nearly over. She was tired, but she couldn't rest, she couldn't rest.

A Gift of the Heart

* * * * * *

Norman Vincent Peale

New York City, where I live, is impressive at any time, but as Christmas approaches it's overwhelming. Store windows blaze with lights and color, furs and jewels. Golden angels, 40 feet tall, hover over Fifth Avenue. Wealth, power, opulence… nothing in the world can match this fabulous display.

Through the gleaming canyons, people hurry to find last-minute gifts. Money seems to be no problem. If there's a problem, it's that the recipients so often have everything they need or want that it's hard to find anything suitable, anything that will really say, "I love you."

Last December, as Christ's birthday drew near, a stranger was faced with just that problem. She had come from Switzerland to live in an American home and perfect her English. In return, she was willing to act as secretary, mind the grandchildren, do anything she was asked. She was just a girl in her late teens. Her name was Ursula.

One of the tasks her employers gave Ursula was keeping track of Christmas presents as they arrived. There were many, and all would require acknowledgment. Ursula kept a faithful record, but with a growing sense of concern. She was grateful to her American friends; she wanted to show her gratitude by giving them a Christmas present. But nothing that she could buy with her small allowance could compare with the gifts she was recording daily. Besides, even without these gifts, it seemed to her that her employers already had everything.

At night from her window Ursula could see the snow expanse of Central Park and beyond it the jagged skyline of the city. Far below, taxis hooted and the traffic lights winked red and green. It was so different from the silent majesty of the Alps that at times she had to blink back tears of the homesickness she was careful never to show. It was in the solitude of her little room, a few days before Christmas, that her secret idea came to Ursula.

It was almost as if a voice spoke clearly, inside her head. "It's true," said the voice, "that many people in this city have much more than you do. But surely there are many who have far less. If you will think about this, you may find a solution to what's troubling you."

Ursula thought long and hard. Finally, on her day off, which was Christmas Eve, she went to a large department store. She moved slowly along the crowded aisles, selecting and rejecting things in her mind. At last she bought something and had it wrapped in gaily colored paper. She went out into the gray twilight and looked helplessly around. Finally, she went up to a doorman, resplendent in blue and gold. "Excuse, please," she said in her hesitant English, "can you tell me where to find a poor street?"

"A poor street, Miss?" said the puzzled man.

"Yes, a very poor street. The poorest in the city."

The doorman looked doubtful. "Well, you might try Harlem. Or down in the Village. Or the Lower East Side, maybe."

But these names meant nothing to Ursula. She thanked the doorman and walked along, threading her way through the stream of shoppers until she came to a tall policeman. "Please," she said, "can you direct me to a very poor street in... in Harlem?"

The policeman looked at her sharply and shook his head. "Harlem's no place for you, Miss." And he blew his whistle and sent the traffic swirling past.

Holding her package carefully, Ursula walked on, head bowed against the sharp wind. If a street looked poorer than the one she was on, she took it. But none seemed like the slums she had heard about. Once she stopped a woman, "Please, where do the very poor people live?" But the woman gave her a stare and hurried on.

Darkness came sifting from the sky. Ursula was cold and discouraged and afraid of becoming lost. She came to an intersection and stood forlornly on the corner. What she was trying to do suddenly seemed foolish, impulsive, absurd. Then, through the traffic's roar, she heard the cheerful tinkle of a bell. On the corner opposite, a Salvation Army man was making his traditional Christmas appeal.

At once Ursula felt better; the Salvation Army was a part of life in Switzerland too. Surely this man could tell her what she wanted to know. She waited for the light, then crossed over to him. "Can you help me? I'm looking for a baby. I have here a little present for the poorest baby I can find." And she held up the package with the green ribbon and the gaily colored paper.

Dressed in gloves and overcoat a size too big for him, he seemed a very ordinary man. But behind his steel-rimmed glasses his eyes were kind. He looked at Ursula and stopped ringing his bell. "What sort of present?" he asked.

"A little dress. For a small, poor baby. Do you know of one?"

"Oh, yes," he said. "Of more than one, I'm afraid."

"Is it far away? I could take a taxi, maybe?"

The Salvation Army man wrinkled his forehead. Finally he said, "It's almost six o'clock. My relief will show up then. If you want to wait, and if you can afford a dollar taxi ride, I'll take you to a family in my own neighborhood who needs just about everything."

"And they have a small baby?"

"A very small baby."

"Then," said Ursula joyfully, "I wait!"

The substitute bell-ringer came. A cruising taxi slowed. In its welcome warmth, Ursula told her new friend about herself, how she came to be in New York, what she was trying to do. He listened in silence, and the taxi driver listened too. When they reached their destination, the driver said, "Take your time, Miss. I'll wait for you."

On the sidewalk, Ursula stared up at the forbidding tenement, dark, decaying, saturated with hopelessness. A gust of wind, iron-cold, stirred the refuse in the street and rattled the ashcans. "They live on the third floor," the Salvation Army man said. "Shall we go up?"

But Ursula shook her head. "They would try to thank me, and this is not from me." She pressed the package into his hand. "Take it up for me, please. Say it's from... from someone who has everything."

The taxi bore her swiftly back from the dark streets to lighted ones, from misery to abundance. She tried to visualize the Salvation Army man climbing the stairs, the knock, the explanation, the package being opened, the dress on the baby. It was hard to do.

Arriving at the apartment house on Fifth Avenue where she lived, she fumbled in her purse. But the driver flicked the flag up. "No charge, Miss."

"No charge?" echoed Ursula, bewildered.

"Don't worry," the driver said. "I've been paid." He smiled at her and drove away.

Ursula was up early the next day. She set the table with special care. By the time she had finished, the family was awake, and there was all the excitement and laughter of Christmas morning. Soon the living room was a sea of gay discarded wrappings. Ursula thanked everyone for the presents she received. Finally, when there was a lull, she began to explain hesitantly why there seemed to be none from her. She told about going to the department store. She told about the Salvation Army man. She told about the taxi driver. When she finished, there was a long silence. No one seemed to trust himself to speak. "So you see," said Ursula, "I try to do a kindness in your name. And this is my Christmas present to you..."

How do I happen to know all this? I know it because ours was the home where Ursula lived. Ours was the Christmas she shared. We were like many Americans, so richly blessed that to this child from across the sea there seemed to be nothing she could add to the material things we already had. And so she offered something of far greater value: a gift of the heart, an act of kindness carried out in our name.

Strange, isn't it? A shy Swiss girl, alone in a great impersonal city. You would think that nothing she could do would affect anyone. And yet, by trying to give away love, she brought the true spirit of Christmas into our lives, the spirit of selfless giving. That was Ursula's secret—and she shared it with us all.

The Gift of
JOY

The Festival of St. Nicholas

Mary Mapes Dodge

From *Hans Brinker, or The Silver Skates*

Christmas Day is devoted by the Hollanders to church rites and pleasant family visiting. It is on Saint Nicholas' Eve that their young people became half wild with joy and expectation. To some of them it is a sorry time, for the saint is very candid, and if any of them have been bad during the past year, he is quite sure to tell them so. Sometimes he carries a birch rod under his arm and advises the parents to give them scoldings in place of confections, and floggings instead of toys.

It was well that the boys hastened to their abodes on that bright winter evening, for in less than an hour afterward, the saint made his appearance in half the homes of Holland. He visited the king's palace and in the self-same moment appeared in Annie Bouman's comfortable home. Probably one of our silver half-dollars would have purchased all that his saintship left at the peasant Bouman's; but a half-dollar's worth will sometimes do for the poor what hundreds of dollars may fail to do for the rich—it makes them happy and grateful, fills them with new peace and love.

Hilda van Gleck's little brothers and sisters were in a high state of excitement that night. They had been admitted into the grand parlor; they were dressed in their best, and had been given two cakes apiece at supper. Hilda was as joyous as any. Why not? Saint Nicholas would never cross a girl of fourteen from his list, just because she was tall and looked almost like a woman. On the contrary, he would probably exert himself to do honor to such an august-looking damsel. Who could tell? So she sported and laughed and danced as gaily as the youngest, and was the soul of all their merry games. Father, Mother, and Grandmother looked on approvingly; so did Grandfather, before he spread his large red handkerchief over his face, leaving only the top of his skullcap visible. This kerchief was his ensign of sleep.

Earlier in the evening all had joined in the fun. In the general hilarity, there had seemed to be a difference only in bulk between Grandfather and the baby. Indeed a shade of solemn expectation, now and then flitting across the faces of the younger members, had made them seem rather more thoughtful than their elders.

Now the spirit of fun reigned supreme. The very flames danced and capered in the polished grate. A pair of prim candles that had been staring at the astral lamp began to wink at other candles far away in the mirrors. There was a long bell-rope suspended from the ceiling in the corner, made of glass beads netted over a cord nearly as thick as your wrist. It generally hung in the shadow and made no sign; but tonight it twinkled from end to end. Its handle of crimson glass sent reckless dashes of red at the papered wall, turning its dainty blue stripes into purple. Passersby halted to catch the merry laughter floating, through curtain and sash, into the street, then skipped on their way with a startled consciousness that the village was wide awake. At last matters grew so uproarious that the grandsire's red kerchief came down from his face with a jerk. What a decent old gentleman could sleep in such a racket! Mynheer van Gleck regarded his children with astonishment. The baby even showed symptoms of hysterics. It was high time to attend to business. Madame suggested that if they wished to see the good Saint Nicholas they should sing the same loving invitation that had brought him the year before.

The baby stared and thrust his fist into his mouth as Mynheer put him down upon the floor. Soon he sat erect, and looked with a sweet scowl at the company. With his lace and embroideries, and his crown of blue ribbon and whalebone (for he was not quite past the tumbling age), he looked like the king of the babies.

The other children, each holding a pretty willow basket, formed at once in a ring, and moved slowly around the little fellow, lifting their eyes, meanwhile, for the saint to whom they were about to address themselves was yet in mysterious quarters.

Madame commenced playing softly upon the piano; soon as the voices rose—gentle, youthful voices—rendered all the sweeter for their tremor:

"Welcome, friend! Saint Nicholas, welcome!
  Bring no rod for us, tonight!
While our voices bid thee, welcome,
  Every heart with joy is light!

Tell us every fault and failing,
We will bear thy keenest railing,
So we sing—so we sing—
Thou shalt tell us everything!

Welcome, friend! Saint Nicholas, welcome!
  Welcome to this merry band!
Happy children greet thee, welcome!
  Thou art glad'ning all the land!

Fill each empty hand and basket,
'Tis thy little ones who ask it,
So we sing—so we sing—
Thou wilt bring us everything!"

During the chorus, sundry glances, half in eagerness, half in dread, had
been cast toward the polished folding doors. Now a loud knocking was heard.
The circle was broken in an instant. Some of the little ones, with a strange
mixture of fear and delight, pressed against their mother's knee. Grandfather
bent forward, with his chin resting upon his hand; Grandmother lifted

her spectacles; Mynheer van Gleck, seated by the fireplace, slowly drew his meerschaum from his mouth, while Hilda and the other children settled themselves beside him in an expectant group.

The knocking was heard again.

"Come in," said Madame softly.

The door slowly opened, and Saint Nicholas, in full array, stood before them. You could have heard a pin drop!

Soon he spoke. What a mysterious majesty in his voice! What kindliness in his tones!

"Karel van Gleck, I am pleased to greet thee, and thy honored vrouw Kathrine, and thy son and his good vrouw Annie!

"Children, I greet ye all! Hendrick, Hilda, Broom, Katy, Huygens, and Lucretia! And thy cousins, Wolfert, Diedrich, Mayken, Voost, and Katrina! Good children ye have been, in the main, since I last accosted ye. Diedrich was rude at the Haarlem fair last fall, but he has tried to atone for it since. Mayken has failed of late in her lessons, and too many sweets and trifles have gone to her lips, and too few stivers to her charity box. Diedrich, I trust, will be a polite, manly boy for the future, and Mayken will endeavor to shine as a student. Let her remember, too, that economy and thrift are needed in the foundation of a worthy and generous life. Little Katy has been cruel to the cat more than once. Saint Nicholas can hear the cat cry when its tail is pulled. I will forgive her if she will remember from this hour that the smallest dumb creatures have feeling and must not be abused."

As Katy burst into a frightened cry, the saint graciously remained silent until she was soothed.

"Master Broom," he resumed, "I warn thee that boys who are in the habit of putting snuff upon the foot stove of the schoolmistress may one day be discovered and receive a flogging—but thou art such an excellent scholar, I shall make thee no further reproof.

"Thou, Hendrick, didst distinguish thyself in the archery match last spring, and hit the Doel, though the bird was swung before it to unsteady thine eye. I give thee credit for excelling in manly sport and exercise—though I must not unduly countenance thy boat racing since it leaves thee too little time for thy proper studies.

"Lucretia and Hilda shall have a blessed sleep tonight. The consciousness of kindness to the poor, devotion in their souls, and cheerful, hearty obedience to household rule will render them happy.

"With one and all I avow myself well content. Goodness, industry, benevolence, and thrift have prevailed in your midst. Therefore, my blessing upon you—and may the New Year find all treading the paths of obedience, wisdom, and love. Tomorrow you shall find more substantial proofs that I have been in your midst. Farewell!"

With these words came a great shower of sugarplums, upon a linen sheet spread out in front of the doors. A general scramble followed. The children fairly tumbled over each other in their eagerness to fill their baskets. Madame cautiously held the baby down in their midst, till the chubby little fists were filled. Then the bravest of the youngsters sprang up and burst open the closed doors—in vain they peered into the mysterious apartment—but Saint Nicholas was nowhere to be seen.

A Kidnapped Santa Claus

L. Frank Baum

From *The Delineator*, Vol. LXIV

Santa Claus lives in the Laughing Valley, where stands the big rambling castle in which his toys are manufactured. His workmen, selected from the ryls, knooks, pixies, and fairies, live with him, and everyone is as busy as can be from one year's end to another.

It is called the Laughing Valley because everything there is happy and gay. The brook chuckles to itself as it leaps rollicking between its green banks; the wind whistles merrily in the trees; the sunbeams dance lightly over the soft grass; and the violets and wildflowers look smiling up from their green nests. To laugh, one needs to be happy; to be happy, one needs to be content. And throughout the Laughing Valley of Santa Claus, contentment reigns supreme.

On one side is the mighty Forest of Burzee. At the other side stands the huge mountain that contains the Caves of the Daemons. And between them the Valley lies smiling and peaceful.

One would think that our good old Santa Claus, who devotes his days to making children happy, would have no enemies on all the earth; and, as a matter of fact, for a long period of time he encountered nothing but love wherever he might go.

But the Daemons who live in the mountain caves grew to hate Santa Claus very much, and all for the simple reason that he made children happy.

The Caves of the Daemons are five in number. A broad pathway leads up to the first cave, which is a finely arched cavern at the foot of the mountain, the entrance being beautifully carved and decorated. In it resides the Daemon of Selfishness. Behind this is another cavern inhabited by the Daemon of Envy. The cave of the Daemon of Hatred is next in order, and through this, one passes to the home of the Daemon of Malice—situated in a dark and fearful cave in the very heart of the mountain. I do not know what lies beyond this. Some say there are terrible pitfalls leading to death and destruction, and this may very well be true. However, from each one of the four caves mentioned there is a small, narrow tunnel leading to the fifth cave—a cozy little room occupied by the Daemon of Repentance. And as the rocky floors of these passages are well worn by the track of passing feet, I judge that many wanderers in the Caves of the Daemons have escaped through the tunnels to the abode of the Daemon of Repentance, who is said to be a pleasant sort of fellow who gladly opens for one a little door admitting you into fresh air and sunshine again.

Well, these Daemons of the Caves, thinking that they had great cause to dislike old Santa Claus, held a meeting one day to discuss the matter.

"I'm really getting lonesome," said the Daemon of Selfishness. "For Santa Claus distributes so many pretty Christmas gifts to all the children that they become happy and generous, through his example, and keep away from my cave."

"I'm having the same trouble," rejoined the Daemon of Envy. "The little ones seem quite content with Santa Claus, and there are few, indeed, that I can coax to become envious."

"And that makes it bad for me!" declared the Daemon of Hatred. "For if no children pass through the caves of Selfishness and Envy, none can get to *my* cavern."

"Or to mine," added the Daemon of Malice.

"For my part," said the Daemon of Repentance, "it is easily seen that if children do not visit your caves they have no need to visit mine; so I am quite as neglected as you are."

"And all because of this person they call Santa Claus!" exclaimed the Daemon of Envy. "He is simply ruining our business, and something must be done at once."

To this they readily agreed; but what to do was another and more difficult matter to settle. They knew that Santa Claus worked all through the year at his castle in the Laughing Valley, preparing the gifts he was to distribute on Christmas Eve; and at first they resolved to try to tempt him into their caves, that they might lead him on to the terrible pitfalls that ended in destruction.

So the very next day, while Santa Claus was busily at work, surrounded by his little band of assistants, the Daemon of Selfishness came to him and said, "These toys are wonderfully bright and pretty. Why do you not keep them for yourself? It's a pity to give them to those noisy boys and fretful girls, who break and destroy them so quickly."

"Nonsense!" cried the old graybeard, his bright eyes twinkling merrily as he turned toward the tempting Daemon. "The boys and girls are never so noisy and fretful after receiving my presents, and if I can make them happy for one day in the year I am quite content."

So the Daemon went back to the others, who awaited him in their caves, and said, "I have failed, for Santa Claus is not at all selfish."

The following day the Daemon of Envy visited Santa Claus. Said he, "The toy shops are full of playthings quite as pretty as these you are making. What a shame it is that they should interfere with your business! They make toys by machinery much quicker than you can make them by hand; and they sell them for money, while you get nothing at all for your work."

But Santa Claus refused to be envious of the toy shops.

"I can supply the little ones but once a year—on Christmas Eve," he answered. "For the children are many, and I am but one. And as my work is one of love and kindness I would be ashamed to receive money for my little gifts. But throughout all the year the children must be amused in some way, and so the toy shops are able to bring much happiness to my little friends. I like the toy shops, and am glad to see them prosper."

In spite of this second rebuff, the Daemon of Hatred thought he would try to influence Santa Claus. So the next day he entered the busy workshop and said, "Good morning, Santa! I have bad news for you."

"Then run away, like a good fellow," answered Santa Claus. "Bad news is something that should be kept secret and never told."

"You cannot escape this, however," declared the Daemon. "For in the world are a good many who do not believe in Santa Claus, and these you are bound to hate bitterly, since they have so wronged you."

"Stuff and rubbish!" cried Santa.

"And there are others who resent your making children happy and who sneer at you and call you a foolish old rattlepate! You are quite right to hate such base slanderers, and you ought to be revenged upon them for their evil words."

"But I *don't* hate 'em!" exclaimed Santa Claus, positively. "Such people do me no real harm, but merely render themselves and their children unhappy. Poor things! I'd much rather help them any day than injure them."

Indeed, the Daemons could not tempt old Santa Claus in any way. On the contrary, he was shrewd enough to see that their object in visiting him was to make mischief and trouble. So the Daemons abandoned honeyed words and determined to use force.

It is well known that no harm can come to Santa Claus while he is in the Laughing Valley, for the fairies, and ryls, and knooks all protect him. But on Christmas Eve he drives his reindeer out into the big world, carrying a sleigh-load of toys and pretty gifts to children; and this was the time and the occasion when his enemies had the best chance to injure him. So the Daemons laid their plans and awaited the arrival of Christmas Eve.

The moon shone big and white in the sky, and the snow lay crisp and sparkling on the ground as Santa Claus cracked his whip and sped away out of the Valley into the great world beyond. The roomy sleigh was packed full with huge sacks of toys, and as the reindeer dashed onward our jolly old

Santa laughed and whistled and sang for very joy. For in all his merry life this was the one day in the year when he was happiest—the day he lovingly bestowed the treasures of his workshop upon the little children.

It would be a busy night for him, he well knew. As he whistled and shouted and cracked his whip again, he reviewed in his mind all the towns and cities and farmhouses where he was expected, and figured that he had just enough presents to go around and make every child happy. The reindeer knew exactly what was expected of them, and dashed along so swiftly that their feet scarcely seemed to touch the snow-covered ground.

Suddenly a strange thing happened: A rope shot through the moonlight and a big noose that was at the end of it settled over the arms and body of Santa Claus and drew tight. Before he could resist or even cry out, he was jerked from the seat of the sleigh and tumbled head foremost into a snow-bank, while the reindeer rushed onward with the load of toys and carried it quickly out of sight and sound.

Such a surprising experience confused old Santa for a moment, and when he had collected his senses he found that the wicked Daemons had pulled him from the snowdrift and bound him tightly with many coils of the stout rope. And then they carried the kidnapped Santa Claus away to their mountain, where they thrust the prisoner into a secret cave and chained him to the rocky wall so that he could not escape.

"Ha, ha!" laughed the Daemons, rubbing their hands together with cruel glee. "What will the children do now? How they will cry and scold and storm when they find there are no toys in their stockings and no gifts on their Christmas trees! And what a lot of punishment they will receive from their parents, and how they will flock to our caves of Selfishness, and Envy, and Hatred, and Malice! We have done a mighty clever thing, we Daemons of the Caves!"

NOW IT SO CHANCED that on this Christmas Eve the good Santa Claus had taken with him in his sleigh Nuter the Ryl, Peter the Knook, Kilter the Pixie, and a small fairy named Wisk—his four favorite assistants. These little people he had often found very useful in helping him to distribute his gifts to the children, and when their master was so suddenly dragged from the sleigh they were all snugly tucked underneath the seat, where the sharp wind could not reach them.

The tiny immortals knew nothing of the capture of Santa Claus until some time after he had disappeared. But finally they missed his cheery voice, and as their master always sang or whistled on his journeys, the silence warned them that something was wrong.

Little Wisk stuck out his head from underneath the seat and found Santa Claus gone and no one to direct the flight of the reindeer.

"Whoa!" he called out, and the deer obediently slackened speed and came to a halt.

Peter and Nuter and Kilter all jumped upon the seat and looked back over the track made by the sleigh. But Santa Claus had been left miles and miles behind.

"What shall we do?" asked Wisk, anxiously, all the mirth and mischief banished from his wee face by this great calamity.

"We must go back at once and find our master," said Nuter the Ryl, who thought and spoke with much deliberation.

"No, no!" exclaimed Peter the Knook, who, cross and crabbed though he was, might always be depended upon in an emergency. "If we delay, or go back, there will not be time to get the toys to the children before morning; and that would grieve Santa Claus more than anything else."

"It is certain that some wicked creatures have captured him," added Kilter, thoughtfully, "and their object must be to make the children unhappy. So our first duty is to get the toys distributed as carefully as if Santa Claus were himself present. Afterward, we can search for our master and easily secure his freedom."

This seemed such good and sensible advice that the others at once resolved to adopt it. So Peter the Knook called to the reindeer, and the faithful animals again sprang forward and dashed over hill and valley, through forest and plain, until they came to the houses wherein children lay sleeping and dreaming of the pretty gifts they would find on Christmas morning.

The little immortals had set themselves a difficult task; for although they had assisted Santa Claus on many of his journeys, their master had always directed and guided them and told them exactly what he wished them to do. But now they had to distribute the toys according to their own judgment, and they did not understand children as well as did old Santa. So it is no wonder they made some laughable errors.

Mamie Brown, who wanted a doll, got a drum instead; and a drum is of no use to a girl who loves dolls. And Charlie Smith, who delights to romp and play out of doors, and who wanted some new rubber boots to keep his feet dry, received a sewing box filled with colored worsteds and threads and needles, which made him so provoked that he thoughtlessly called our dear Santa Claus a fraud.

Had there been many such mistakes the Daemons would have accomplished their evil purpose and made the children unhappy. But the little friends of their absent Santa Claus labored faithfully and intelligently to carry out their master's ideas, and they made fewer errors than might be expected under such unusual circumstances.

And, although they worked as swiftly as possible, day had begun to break before the toys and other presents were all distributed; so for the first time in many years the reindeer trotted into the Laughing Valley, on their return, in broad daylight, with the brilliant sun peeping over the edge of the forest to prove they were far behind their accustomed hour.

Having put the deer in the stable, the little folk began to wonder how they might rescue their master; and they realized they must discover, first of all, what had happened to him and where he was.

So Wisk, that fairy, transported himself to the bower of the Fairy Queen, which was located deep in the heart of the Forest of Burzee; and once there, it did not take him long to find out all about the naughty Daemons and how they had kidnapped the good Santa Claus to prevent his making children happy. The Fairy Queen also promised her assistance, and then, fortified by this powerful support, Wisk flew back to where Nuter and Peter and Kilter awaited him, and the four counseled together and laid plans to rescue their master from his enemies.

IT IS POSSIBLE THAT Santa Claus was not as merry as usual during the night that succeeded his capture. For although he had faith in the judgment of his little friends he could not avoid a certain amount of worry, and an anxious look would creep at times into his kind old eyes as he thought of the disappointment that might await his dear little children. And the Daemons, who guarded him by turns, one after another, did not neglect to taunt him with contemptuous words in his helpless condition.

When Christmas Day dawned the Daemon of Malice was guarding the prisoner, and his tongue was sharper than that of any of the others.

"The children are waking up, Santa!" he cried. "They are waking up to find their stockings empty! Ho, ho! How they will quarrel, and wail, and stamp their feet in anger! Our caves will be full today, old Santa! Our caves are sure to be full!"

But to this, as to other like taunts, Santa Claus answered nothing. He was much grieved by his capture, it is true; but his courage did not forsake him. And, finding that the prisoner would not reply to his jeers, the Daemon of Malice presently went away, and sent the Daemon of Repentance to take his place.

This last personage was not so disagreeable as the others. He had gentle and refined features, and his voice was soft and pleasant in tone.

"My brother Daemons do not trust me over much," said he, as he entered the cavern, "but it is morning, now, and the mischief is done. You cannot visit the children again for another year."

"That is true," answered Santa Claus, almost cheerfully. "Christmas Eve is past, and for the first time in centuries I have not visited my children."

"The little ones will be greatly disappointed," murmured the Daemon of Repentance, almost regretfully, "but that cannot be helped now. Their grief is likely to make the children selfish and envious and hateful, and if they come to the Caves of the Daemons today I shall get a chance to lead some of them to my Cave of Repentance."

"Do you never repent, yourself?" asked Santa Claus, curiously.

"Oh, yes, indeed," answered the Daemon. "I am even now repenting that I assisted in your capture. Of course it is too late to remedy the evil that has been done; but repentance, you know, can come only after an evil thought or deed, for in the beginning there is nothing to repent of."

"So I understand," said Santa Claus. "Those who avoid evil need never visit your cave."

"As a rule, that is true," replied the Daemon. "Yet you, who have done no evil, are about to visit my cave at once; for to prove that I sincerely regret my share in your capture I am going to permit you to escape."

This speech greatly surprised the prisoner, until he reflected that it was just what might be expected of the Daemon of Repentance. The fellow at once busied himself untying the knots that bound Santa Claus and unlocking the chains that fastened him to the wall. Then he led the way through a long tunnel until they both emerged in the Cave of Repentance.

"I hope you will forgive me," said the Daemon, pleadingly. "I am not really a bad person, you know; and I believe I accomplished a great deal of good in the world."

With this he opened a back door that let in a flood of sunshine, and Santa Claus sniffed the fresh air gratefully.

"I bear no malice," said he to the Daemon, in a gentle voice. "And I am sure the world would be a dreary place without you. So, good morning, and a Merry Christmas to you!"

With these words he stepped out to greet the bright morning, and a moment later he was trudging along, whistling softly to himself, on his way to his home in the Laughing Valley.

Marching over the snow toward the mountain was a vast army, made up of the most curious creatures imaginable. There were numberless knooks from the forest, as rough and crooked in appearance as the gnarled branches of the trees they ministered to. And there were dainty ryls from the fields, each one bearing the emblem of the flower or plant it guarded. Behind these were many ranks of pixies, gnomes, and nymphs, and in the rear a thousand beautiful fairies floating along in gorgeous array.

This wonderful army was led by Wisk, Peter, Nuter, and Kilter, who had assembled it to rescue Santa Claus from captivity and to punish the Daemons who had dared to take him away from his beloved children.

And, although they looked so bright and peaceful, the little immortals were armed with powers that would be very terrible to those who had incurred their anger. Woe to the Daemons of the Caves if this mighty army of vengeance ever met them!

But lo! Coming to meet his loyal friends appeared the imposing form of Santa Claus, his white beard floating in the breeze and his bright eyes sparkling with pleasure at this proof of the love and veneration he had inspired in the hearts of the most powerful creatures in existence.

And while they clustered around him and danced with glee at his safe return, he gave them earnest thanks for their support. But Wisk, and Nuter, and Peter, and Kilter, he embraced affectionately.

"It is useless to pursue the Daemons," said Santa Claus to the army. "They have their place in the world, and can never be destroyed. But that is a great pity, nevertheless," he continued, musingly.

So the fairies, and knooks, and pixies, and ryls all escorted the good man to his castle, and there left him to talk over the events of the night with his little assistants.

Wisk had already rendered himself invincible and flown through the big world to see how the children were getting along on this bright Christmas morning; and by the time he returned, Peter had finished telling Santa Claus of how they had distributed the toys.

"We really did very well," cried the fairy, in a pleased voice. "For I found little unhappiness among the children this morning. Still, you must not get captured again, my dear master, for we might not be so fortunate another time in carrying out your ideas."

He then related the mistakes that had been made, and which he had not discovered until his tour of inspection. And Santa Claus at once sent him with rubber boots for Charlie Smith, and a doll for Mamie Brown; so that even those two disappointed ones became happy.

As for the wicked Daemons of the Caves, they were filled with anger and chagrin when they found that their clever capture of Santa Claus had come to naught. Indeed, no one on that Christmas Day appeared to be at all selfish, or envious, or hateful. And, realizing that while the children's saint had so many powerful friends it was folly to oppose him, the Daemons never again attempted to interfere with his journeys on Christmas Eve.

Christmas Eve

* ❄ ❄ ❄ ❄ ❄

Washington Irving

From *The Sketch Book*

It was a brilliant moonlight night, but extremely cold; our chaise whirled rapidly over the frozen ground; the post-boy smacked his whip incessantly, and a part of the time his horses were on a gallop. "He knows where he is going," said my companion, laughing, "and is eager to arrive in time for some of the merriment and good cheer of the servants' hall. My father, you must know, is a bigoted devotee of the old school, and prides himself upon keeping up something of old English hospitality. He is a tolerable specimen of what you will rarely meet with nowadays in its purity, the old English country gentleman; for our men of fortune spend so much of their time in town, and fashion is carried so much into the country, that the strong rich peculiarities of ancient rural life are almost polished away. My father, however, from early years, took honest Peacham for his text book, instead of Chesterfield. He determined, in his own mind, that there was no condition more truly honorable and enviable than that of a country gentleman on his paternal lands, and, therefore, passes the whole of his time on his estate. He is a strenuous advocate for the revival of the old rural games and holiday observances, and is deeply read in the writers, ancient and modern, who have treated on the subject. Indeed, his favorite range of reading is among the authors who flourished at least two centuries since; who, he insists, wrote and thought more like true Englishmen than any of their successors. He even regrets sometimes that he had not been born a few centuries earlier, when England was itself, and had its peculiar manner and customs. As he lives at some distance from the main road, in a rather lonely part of the country, without any rival gentry near him, he has that most enviable of all blessings to an Englishman, an opportunity of indulging the bent of his own humor without molestation. Being a representative of the oldest family in the neighborhood, and a great part of the peasantry being his tenants, he is much looked up to and, in general, is known simply by the appellation of 'The Squire'; a title which has been accorded to the head of the family since time immemorial. I think it best to give you these hints about my worthy old father, to prepare you for any little eccentricities that might otherwise appear absurd."

We had passed for some time along the wall of a park, and at length the chaise stopped at the gate. It was in a heavy magnificent old style, of iron bars, fancifully wrought at the top into flourishes and flowers. The huge square columns that supported the gate were surmounted by the family crest. Close adjoining was the porter's lodge; sheltered under dark fir trees, and almost buried in shrubbery.

The post-boy rang a large porter's bell, which resounded through the still frosty air, and was answered by the distant barking of dogs with which the mansion-house seemed garrisoned. An old woman immediately appeared at the gate. As the moonlight fell strongly upon her, I had quite a full view of a little primitive dame, dressed very much in the antique taste, with a neat kerchief and stomacher, and her silver hair peeping from under a cap of snowy whiteness. She came curtseying forth, with many expressions of simple joy at seeing her young master. Her husband, it seems, was up at the house keeping Christmas eve in the servants' hall; they could not do without him, as he was the best hand at a song and story in the household.

My friend proposed that we should alight and walk through the park to the hall, which was at no great distance, while the chaise should follow on. Our road wound through a noble avenue of trees, among the naked branches of which the moon glittered as she rolled through the deep vault of a cloudless sky. The lawn beyond was sheeted with a slight covering of snow, which here and there sparkled as the moonbeams caught a frosty crystal; and at a distance might be seen a thin transparent vapor, stealing up from the low grounds, and threatening gradually to shroud the landscape.

My companion looked round him with transport: "How often," said he, "have I scampered up this avenue, on returning home on school vacations! How often have I played under these trees when a boy! I feel a degree of filial reverence for them, as we look up to those who have cherished us in childhood. My father was always scrupulous in exacting our holidays, and having us around him on family festivals. He used to direct and superintend our games with strictness that some parents do the studies of their children. He was very particular that we should play the old English games according to their original form; and consulted old books for precedent and authority for every 'merrie disport'; yet I assure you there never was pedantry so delightful. It was the policy of the good old gentleman to make his children feel that home was the happiest place in the world; and I value this delicious home-feeling as one of the choicest gifts a parent can bestow."

We were interrupted by a clangor of a troop of dogs of all sorts and sizes, "mongrel, puppy, whelp and hound, and curs of low degree," that, disturbed by the ringing of the porter's bell, and the rattling of the chaise, came bounding, open-mouthed, across the lawn.

"The little dogs and all,
Tray, Blanch, and Sweetheart—see they bark at me!"

cried Bracebridge, laughing. At the sound of his voice the bark was changed into a yelp of delight, and in a moment he was surrounded and almost over-powered by the caresses of the faithful animals.

We had now come in full view of the old family mansion, partly thrown in deep shadow, and partly lit up by the cold moonshine. It was an irregular building of some magnitude, and seemed to be of the architecture of different periods. One wing was evidently very ancient, with heavy stone-shafted bow windows jutting out and overrun with ivy, from among the foliage of which the small diamond-shaped panes of glass glittered with the moonbeams. The rest of the house was in the French taste of Charles the Second's time, having been repaired and altered, as my friend told me, by one of his ancestors, who returned with that monarch at the Restoration. The grounds about the house were laid out in the old formal manner of artificial flower beds, clipped shrubberies, raised terraces, and heavy stone balustrades, ornamented with urns, a leaden statue or two, and a jet of water. The old gentleman, I was told, was extremely careful to preserve this obsolete finery in all its original state. He admired this fashion in gardening; it had an air of magnificence, was courtly and noble, and befitting good old family style. The boasted imitation of nature in modern gardening had sprung up with modern republican notions, but did not suit a monarchical government; it smacked of the leveling system. I could not help smiling at this introduction of politics into gardening, though I expressed some apprehension that I should find the old gentleman rather intolerant in his creed. Frank assured me, however, that it was almost the only instance in which he had ever heard his father meddle with politics; and he believed that he had got this notion from a member of parliament who once passed a few weeks with him. The Squire was glad of any argument to defend his clipped yew trees and formal terraces, which had been occasionally attacked by modern landscape gardeners.

As we approached the house, we heard the sound of music, and now and then a burst of laughter from one end of the building. This, Bracebridge said, must proceed from the servants' hall, where a great deal of revelry was permitted, and even encouraged, by the Squire throughout the twelve days of Christmas, provided everything was done conformably to ancient usage. Here were kept up the old games of hoodman blind, shoe the wild mare, hot cockles, steal the white loaf, bob apple, and snap dragon: The Yule log and Christmas candle were regularly burnt, and the mistletoe, with its white berries, hung up to the imminent peril of all the pretty housemaids.

So intent were the servants upon their sports, that we had to ring repeatedly before we could make ourselves heard. On our arrival being announced, the Squire came out to receive us, accompanied by his two other sons; one a young officer in the army, home on leave of absence; the other an Oxonian, just from the university. The Squire was a fine, healthy-looking old gentleman, with silver hair curling lightly round an open florid countenance; in which a physiognomist, with the advantage, like myself, of a previous hint or two, might discover a singular mixture of whim and benevolence.

The family meeting was warm and affectionate; as the evening was far advanced, the Squire would not permit us to change our traveling dresses, but ushered us at once to the company, which was assembled in a large, old-fashioned hall. It was composed of different branches of a numerous family connection, where there were the usual proportion of uncles and aunts, comfortably married dames, superannuated spinsters, blooming country cousins, half-fledged striplings, and bright-eyed boarding-school hoydens. They were variously occupied—some at round game of cards, others conversing around the fireplace. At one end of the hall was a group of the young folks, some nearly grown up, others of a more tender and budding age, fully engrossed by a merry game; and a profusion of wooden horses, penny trumpets, and tattered dolls, about the floor, showed traces of a troop of little fairy beings, who having frolicked through a happy day, had been carried off to slumber through a peaceful night.

While the mutual greetings were going on between Bracebridge and his relatives, I had time to scan the apartment. I have called it a hall, for so it had certainly been in old times, and the Squire had evidently endeavored to restore it to something of its primitive state. Over the heavy projecting fireplace was suspended a picture of a warrior in armor, standing by a white horse, and on the opposite wall hung helmet, buckler, and lance. At one end, an enormous pair of antlers were inserted in the wall, the branches serving as hooks on which to suspend hats, whips, and spurs; and in the corners of the apartment were fowling pieces, fishing rods, and other sporting implements. The furniture was of the cumbrous workmanship of former days, though some articles of modern convenience had been added, and the oaken floor had been carpeted; so that the whole presented an odd mixture of parlor and hall.

The grate had been removed from the wide overwhelming fireplace, to make way for a fire of wood, in the midst of which was an enormous log glowing and blazing, and sending forth a vast volume of light and heat; this I understood was the Yule log, which the Squire was particular in having brought in and illumined on a Christmas eve, according to ancient custom.

It was really delightful to see the old Squire seated in his hereditary elbow-chair by the hospitable fireside of his ancestors, and looking around him like the sun of a system, beaming warmth and gladness to every heart. Even the very dog that lay stretched at his feet, as he lazily shifted his position and yawned, would look fondly up in his master's face, wag his tail against the floor, and stretch himself again to sleep, confident of kindness and protection. There is an emanation from the heart in genuine hospitality which cannot be described, but is immediately felt, and puts the stranger at once at his ease. I had not been seated many minutes by the comfortable hearth of the worthy cavalier before I found myself as much at home as if I had been one of the family.

Supper was announced shortly after our arrival. It was served up in a spacious oaken chamber, the panels of which shone with wax, and around which were several family portraits decorated with holly and ivy. Beside the accustomed lights, two great wax tapers, called Christmas candles, wreathed with greens, were placed on a highly polished buffet among the family plate. The table was abundantly spread with substantial fare; but the Squire made his supper of frumenty, a dish made of wheat cakes boiled in milk with rich spices, being a standing dish in old times for Christmas eve. I was happy to find my old friend, minced pie, in the retinue of the feast; and finding him to be perfectly orthodox, and that I need not be ashamed of my predilection, I greeted him with all the warmth wherewith we usually greet an old and very genteel acquaintance.

The mirth of the company was greatly promoted by the humors of an eccentric personage whom Mr. Bracebridge always addressed with the quaint appellation of Master Simon. He was a tight, brisk little man, with the air of an arrant old bachelor. His nose was shaped like the bill of a parrot; his face slightly pitted with the smallpox, with a dry perpetual bloom on it, like a frost-bitten leaf in autumn. He had an eye of great quickness and vivacity, with a drollery and lurking waggery of expression that was irresistible. He was evidently the wit of the family, dealing very much in sly jokes and innuendoes with the ladies, and making infinite merriment by harpings upon old themes; which, unfortunately, my ignorance of the family chronicles did not permit me to enjoy. It seemed to be his great delight during supper to keep a young girl next to him in a continual agony of stifled laughter, in spite of her awe of the reproving looks of her mother, who sat opposite. Indeed, he was the idol of the younger part of the company, who laughed at everything he said or did, and at every turn of his countenance. I could not wonder at it; for he must have been a miracle of accomplishments in their eyes. He could imitate Punch and Judy; make an old woman of his hand, with the assistance of a burnt cork and pocket-handkerchief; and cut an orange into such a ludicrous caricature, that the young folks were ready to die with laughing.

I was let briefly into his history by Frank Bracebridge. He was an old bachelor of a small independent income, which by careful management was sufficient for all his wants. He revolved through the family system like a vagrant comet in its orbit; sometimes visiting one branch, and sometimes another quite remote; as is often the case with gentlemen of extensive connections and small fortunes in England. He had a chirping, buoyant disposition, always enjoying the present moment; and his frequent change of scene and company prevented his acquiring those rusty unaccommodating habits with which old bachelors are so uncharitably charged. He was a complete family chronicle, being versed in the genealogy, history, and intermarriages of the whole house of Bracebridge, which made him a great favorite with the old folks. He was a beau of all the elder ladies and superannuated spinsters, among whom he was habitually considered rather a young fellow, and he was a master of the revels among the children; so that there was not a more popular being in the sphere in which he moved than Mr. Simon Bracebridge. Of late years he had resided almost entirely with the Squire, to whom he had become a factotum, and whom he particularly delighted by jumping with his humor in respect to old times, and by having a scrap of an old song to suit every occasion. We had presently a specimen of his last-mentioned talent; for no sooner was supper removed, and spiced wines and other beverages peculiar to the season introduced, than Master Simon was called on for a good old Christmas song. He bethought himself for a moment, and then, with a sparkle of the eye, and a voice that was by no means bad, excepting that it ran occasionally into a falsetto, like the notes of a split reed, he quavered forth a quaint old ditty:

"Now Christmas is come,
Let us beat up the drum,
And call all our neighbors together;
And when they appear,
Let us make them such cheer
As will keep out the wind and the weather," etc.

The supper had disposed everyone to gaiety, and an old harper was summoned from the servants' hall, where he had been strumming all the evening, and to all appearance comforting himself with some of the Squire's homebrewed. He was a kind of hanger-on, I was told, of the establishment, and though ostensibly a resident of the village, was oftener to be found in the Squire's kitchen than his own home, the old gentleman being fond of the sound of "harp in hall."

The dance, like most dances after supper, was a merry one; some of the older folks joined in it, and the Squire himself figured down several couples with a partner with whom he affirmed he had danced at every Christmas for nearly half a century. Master Simon, who seemed to be a kind of connecting link between the old times and the new, and to be withal a little antiquated in the taste of accomplishments, evidently piqued himself on his dancing, and was endeavoring to gain credit by the heel and toe, rigadoon, and other graces of the ancient school; but he had unluckily assorted himself with a little romping girl from boarding-school, who, by her wild vivacity, kept him continually on the stretch, and defeated all his sober attempts at elegance—such are the ill-assorted matches to which antique gentlemen are unfortunately prone!

The young Oxonian, on the contrary, had led out one of his maiden aunts, on whom the rogue played a thousand little knaveries with impunity; he was full of practical jokes, and his delight was to tease his aunts and cousins; yet, like all madcap youngsters, he was a universal favorite among the women. The most interesting couple in the dance was the young officer and a ward of the Squire's, a beautiful blushing girl of seventeen. From several shy glances which I had noticed in the course of the evening, I suspected there was a little kindness growing up between them; and, indeed, the young soldier was just the hero to captivate a romantic girl. He was tall, slender, and handsome, and like most young British officers of late years, had picked up various small accomplishments on the Continent—he could talk French and Italian, draw landscapes, sing very tolerably, dance divinely; but, above all, he had been wounded at Waterloo. What girl of seventeen, well read in poetry and romance, could resist such a mirror of chivalry and perfection?

The moment the dance was over, he caught up a guitar, and lolling against the old marble fireplace, in an attitude which I am half inclined to suspect was studied, began the little French air of the Troubadour. The Squire, however, exclaimed against having anything on Christmas eve but good old English; upon which the young minstrel, casting up his eye for a moment, as if in an effort of memory, struck into another strain, and, with a charming air of gallantry, gave Herrick's "Night-Piece to Julia":

"Her eyes the glow-worm lend thee,
The shooting stars attend thee,
    And the elves also,
    Whose little eyes glow
Like the sparks of fire, befriend thee.

No Will-o'-the-Wisp mislight thee;
Nor snake or glow-worm bite thee;
    But on, on thy way,
    Not making a stay,
Since ghost there is none to affright thee.

Then let not the dark thee cumber;
What though the moon does slumber,
    The stars of the night
    Will lend thee their light,
Like tapers clear without number.

Then, Julia, let me woo thee,
Thus, thus to come unto me;
    And when I shall meet
    Thy silvery feet,
My soul I'll pour into thee."

The song might have been intended in compliment to the fair Julia, for so I found his partner was called, or it might not; she, however, was certainly unconscious of any such application, for she never looked at the singer, but kept her eyes cast upon the floor. Her face was suffused, it is true, with a beautiful blush, and there was a gentle heaving of the bosom, but all that was doubtless caused by the exercise of the dance; indeed, so great was her indifference, that she was amusing herself with plucking to pieces a choice bouquet of hothouse flowers, and by the time the song was concluded, the nosegay lay in ruins on the floor.

The party now broke up for the night with the kind-hearted old custom of shaking hands. As I passed through the hall, on the way to my chamber, the dying embers of the Yule log still sent forth a dusky glow; and had it not been the season when "no spirit dares stir abroad," I should have been half tempted to steal from my room at midnight, and peep whether the fairies might not be at their revels about the hearth.

My chamber was in the old part of the mansion, the ponderous furniture of which might have been fabricated in the days of the giants. The room was paneled with cornices of heavy carved work, in which flowers and grotesque faces were strangely intermingled; and a row of black-looking portraits stared mournfully at me from the walls. The bed was of rich though faded damask, with a lofty tester, and stood in a niche opposite a bow window. I had scarcely got into bed when a strain of music seemed to break forth in the air just below the window. I listened, and found it proceeded from a band, which I concluded to be the waits from some neighboring village. They went round the house, playing under the windows. I drew aside the curtains, to hear them more distinctly. The moonbeams fell through the upper part of the casement, partially lighting up the antiquated apartment. The sounds, as they receded, became more soft and aerial, and seemed to accord with quiet and moonlight. I listened and listened—they became more and more tender and remote, and, as they gradually died away, my head sank upon the pillow and I fell asleep.

Mr. Edwards Meets Santa Claus

Laura Ingalls Wilder

From *Little House® on the Prairie*

The days were short and cold, the wind whistled sharply, but there was no snow. Cold rains were falling. Day after day the rain fell, pattering on the roof and pouring from the eaves.

Mary and Laura stayed close by the fire, sewing their nine-patch quilt blocks, or cutting paper dolls from scraps of wrapping-paper, and hearing the wet sound of the rain. Every night was so cold that they expected to see snow next morning, but in the morning they only saw sad, wet grass.

They pressed their noses against the squares of the glass in the windows that Pa had made, and they were glad they could see out. But they wished they could see snow.

Laura was anxious because Christmas was near, and Santa Claus and his reindeer could not travel without snow. Mary was afraid that, even if it snowed, Santa Claus could not find them, so far away in Indian Territory. When they asked Ma about this, she said she didn't know.

"What day is it?" they asked her, anxiously. "How many more days till Christmas?" And they counted off the days on their fingers, till there was only one more day left.

Rain was still falling that morning. There was not one crack in the gray sky. They felt almost sure there would be no Christmas. Still, they kept hoping.

Just before noon the light changed. The clouds broke and drifted apart, shining white in a clear blue sky. The sun shone, birds sang, and thousands of drops of water sparkled on the grasses. But when Ma opened the door to let in the fresh, cold air, they heard the creek roaring.

They had not thought about the creek. Now they knew they would have no Christmas, because Santa Claus could not cross that roaring creek.

Pa came in, bringing a big fat turkey. If it weighed less than twenty pounds, he said, he'd eat it, feathers and all. He asked Laura, "How's that for a Christmas dinner? Think you can manage one of those drumsticks?"

She said, yes, she could. But she was sober. Then Mary asked him if the creek was going down, and he said it was still rising.

Ma said it was too bad. She hated to think of Mr. Edwards eating his bachelor cooking all alone on Christmas day. Mr. Edwards had been asked to eat Christmas dinner with them, but Pa shook his head and said a man would risk his neck, trying to cross that creek now.

"No," he said. "That current's too strong. We'll just have to make up our minds that Edwards won't be here tomorrow."

Of course that meant that Santa Claus could not come, either.

Laura and Mary tried not to mind too much. They watched Ma dress the wild turkey, and it was a very fat turkey. They were lucky little girls, to have a good house to live in, and a warm fire to sit by, and such a turkey for their Christmas dinner. Ma said so, and it was true. Ma said it was too bad that Santa Claus couldn't come this year, but they were such good girls that he hadn't forgotten them; he would surely come next year.

Still, they were not happy.

After supper that night they washed their hands and faces, buttoned their red-flannel nightgowns, tied their night-cap strings, and soberly said their prayers. They lay down in bed and pulled the covers up. It did not seem at all like Christmas time.

Pa and Ma sat silent by the fire. After a while Ma asked why Pa didn't play the fiddle, and he said, "I don't seem to have the heart to, Caroline."

After a longer while, Ma suddenly stood up.

"I'm going to hang up your stockings, girls," she said. "Maybe something will happen."

Laura's heart jumped. But then she thought again of the creek and she knew nothing could happen.

Ma took one of Mary's clean stockings and one of Laura's, and she hung them from the mantel shelf, on either side of the fireplace. Laura and Mary watched her over the edge of their bed covers.

"Now go to sleep," Ma said, kissing them good night. "Morning will come quicker if you're asleep."

She sat down again by the fire and Laura almost went to sleep. She woke up a little when she heard Pa say, "You've only made it worse, Caroline." And she thought she heard Ma say, "No, Charles. There's the white sugar." But perhaps she was dreaming.

Then she heard Jack growl savagely. The door latch rattled and someone said, "Ingalls! Ingalls!" Pa was stirring up the fire, and when he opened the door Laura saw that it was morning. The outdoors was gray.

"Great fishhooks, Edwards! Come in, man! What's happened?" Pa exclaimed.

Laura saw the stockings limply dangling, and she scrooged her shut eyes into the pillow. She heard Pa piling wood on the fire, and she heard Mr. Edwards say he had carried his clothes on his head when he swam the creek. His teeth rattled and his voice shivered. He would be all right, he said, as soon as he got warm.

"It was too big a risk, Edwards," Pa said. "We're glad you're here, but that was too big a risk for a Christmas dinner."

"Your little ones had to have a Christmas," Mr. Edwards replied. "No creek could stop me, after I fetched them their gifts from Independence."

Laura sat straight up in bed. "Did you see Santa Claus?" she shouted.

"I sure did," Mr. Edwards said.

"Where? When? What did he look like? What did he say? Did he really give you something for us?" Mary and Laura cried.

"Wait, wait a minute!" Mr. Edwards laughed. And Ma said she would put the presents in the stockings, as Santa Claus intended. She said they mustn't look.

Mr. Edwards came and sat on the floor by their bed, and he answered every question they asked him. They honestly tried not to look at Ma, and they didn't quite see what she was doing.

When he saw the creek rising, Mr. Edwards said, he had known that Santa Claus could not get across it. ("But you crossed it," Laura said. "Yes," Mr. Edwards replied, "but Santa Claus is too old and fat. He couldn't make it, where a long, lean razorback like me could do so.") And Mr. Edwards reasoned that if Santa Claus couldn't cross the creek, likely he would come no farther south than Independence. Why should he come forty miles across the prairie, only to be turned back? Of course he wouldn't do that!

So Mr. Edwards had walked to Independence. ("In the rain?" Mary asked. Mr. Edwards said he wore his rubber coat.) And there, coming down the street in Independence, he had met Santa Claus. ("In the daytime?" Laura asked. She hadn't thought that anyone could see Santa Claus in the daytime. No, Mr. Edwards said; it was night, but light shone out across the street from the saloons.)

Well, the first thing Santa Claus said was, "Hello, Edwards!" ("Did he know you?" Mary asked, and Laura asked, "How did you know he was really Santa Claus?" Mr. Edwards said that Santa Claus knew everybody. And he had recognized Santa at once by his whiskers. Santa Claus had the longest, thickest, whitest set of whiskers west of the Mississippi.)

So Santa Claus said, "Hello, Edwards! Last time I saw you, you were sleeping on a cornshuck bed in Tennessee." And Mr. Edwards well remembered the little pair of red-yarn mittens that Santa Claus had left for him that time.

Then Santa Claus said, "I understand you're living now down along the Verdigris River. Have you ever met up, down yonder, with two little young girls named Mary and Laura?"

"I surely am acquainted with them," Mr. Edwards replied.

"It rests heavy on my mind," said Santa Claus. "They are both of them sweet, pretty, good little young things, and I know they are expecting me. I surely do hate to disappoint two good little girls like them. Yet with the water up the way it is, I can't ever make it across that creek. I can figure no way whatsoever to get to their cabin this year. Edwards," Santa Claus said, "would you do me the favor to fetch them their gifts this one time?"

"I'll do that, and with pleasure," Mr. Edwards told Santa.

Then Santa Claus and Mr. Edwards stepped across the street to the hitching posts where the pack mule was tied. ("Didn't he have his reindeer?" Laura asked. "You know he couldn't," Mary said. "There isn't any snow." Exactly, said Mr. Edwards. Santa Claus traveled with a pack mule in the southwest.)

And Santa Claus uncinched the pack and looked through it, and he took out the presents for Mary and Laura.

"Oh, what are they?" Laura cried; but Mary asked, "Then what did he do?"

Then he shook hands with Mr. Edwards, and he swung up on his fine bay horse. Santa Claus rode well for a man of his weight and build. And he tucked his long, white whiskers under his bandana. "So long, Edwards," he said, and he rode away on the Fort Dodge trail, leading his pack mule and whistling.

Laura and Mary were silent an instant, thinking of that.

Then Ma said, "You may look now, girls."

Something was shining bright in the top of Laura's stocking. She squealed and jumped out of bed. So did Mary, but Laura beat her to the fireplace. And the shining thing was a glittering new tin cup.

Mary had one exactly like it.

These new tin cups were their very own. Now they each had a cup to drink out of. Laura jumped up and down and shouted and laughed, but Mary stood still and looked with shining eyes at her own tin cup.

Then they plunged their hands into the stockings again. And they pulled out two long, long sticks of candy. It was peppermint candy, striped red and white. They looked and looked at the beautiful candy, and Laura licked her stick, just one lick. But Mary was not so greedy. She didn't take even one lick of her stick.

Those stockings weren't empty yet. Mary and Laura pulled out two small packages. They unwrapped them, and each found a little heart-shaped cake. Over their delicate brown tops was sprinkled white sugar. The sparkling grains lay like tiny drifts of snow.

The cakes were too pretty to eat. Mary and Laura just looked at them. But at last Laura turned hers over, and she nibbled a tiny nibble from underneath, where it wouldn't show. And the inside of the little cake was white!

It had been made of pure white flour, and sweetened with white sugar.

Laura and Mary never would have looked in their stockings again. The cups and the cakes and the candy were almost too much. They were too happy to speak. But Ma asked if they were sure the stockings were empty.

Then they put their hands down inside them, to make sure.

And in the very toe of each stocking was a shining bright, new penny!

They had never even thought of such a thing as having a penny. Think of having a whole penny for your very own. Think of having a cup and a cake and a stick of candy and a penny.

There never had been such a Christmas.

Now of course, right away, Laura and Mary should have thanked Mr. Edwards for bringing those lovely presents all the way from Independence. But they had forgotten all about Mr. Edwards. They had even forgotten Santa Claus. In a minute they would have remembered, but before they did, Ma said, gently, "Aren't you going to thank Mr. Edwards?"

"Oh, thank you, Mr. Edwards! Thank you!" they said, and they meant it with all their hearts. Pa shook Mr. Edwards' hand, too, and shook it again. Pa and Ma and Mr. Edwards acted as if they were almost crying, Laura didn't know why. So she gazed again at her beautiful presents.

She looked up again when Ma gasped. And Mr. Edwards was taking sweet potatoes out of his pockets. He said they had helped to balance the package on his head when he swam across the creek. He thought Pa and Ma might like them, with the Christmas turkey.

There were nine sweet potatoes. Mr. Edwards had brought them all the way from town, too. It was just too much. Pa said so. "It's too much, Edwards," he said. They never could thank him enough.

Mary and Laura were too excited to eat breakfast. They drank the milk from their shining new cups, but they could not swallow the rabbit stew and cornmeal mush.

"Don't make them, Charles," Ma said. "It will soon be dinner time."

For Christmas dinner there was the tender, juicy, roasted turkey. There were the sweet potatoes, baked in the ashes and carefully wiped so that you could eat the good skins, too. There was a loaf of salt-rising bread made from the last of the white flour.

And after all that there were stewed dried blackberries and little cakes.

But these little cakes were made with brown sugar and they did not have white sugar sprinkled over their tops.

Then Pa and Ma and Mr. Edwards sat by the fire and talked about Christmas times back in Tennessee and up north in the Big Woods. But Mary and Laura looked at their beautiful cakes and played with their pennies and drank their water out of their new cups. And little by little they licked and sucked their sticks of candy, till each stick was sharp-pointed on one end.

That was a happy Christmas.

A Brooklyn Christmas

Betty Smith

From *A Tree Grows in Brooklyn*

Christmas was a charmed time in Brooklyn. It was in the air, long before it came. The first hint of it was Mr. Morton going around the schools teaching Christmas carols, but the first sure sign was the store windows.

You have to be a child to know how wonderful is a store window filled with dolls and sleds and other toys. And this wonder came free to Francie. It was nearly as good as actually having the toys to be permitted to look at them through the glass window.

Oh, what a thrill there was for Francie when she turned a street corner and saw another store all fixed up for Christmas! Ah, the clean shining window with cotton batting sprinkled with star dust for a carpet! There were flaxen-haired dolls and others which Francie liked better who had hair the color of good coffee with lots of cream in it. Their faces were perfectly tinted and they wore clothes the likes of which Francie had never seen on earth. The dolls stood upright in flimsy cardboard boxes. They stood with the help of a bit of tape passed around the neck and ankles and through holes at the back of the box. Oh, the deep blue eyes framed by thick lashes that stared straight into a little girl's heart and the perfect miniature hands extended, appealingly asking, "Please, won't *you* be my mama?" And Francie had never had a doll except a two-inch one that cost a nickel.

And the sleds! (Or, as the Williamsburg children called them, the sleighs.) There was a child's dream of heaven come true! A new sled with a flower someone had dreamed up painted on it—a deep blue flower with bright green leaves—the ebony-black painted runners, the smooth steering bar made of hard wood and gleaming varnish over all! And the names painted on them! "Rosebud!" "Magnolia!" "Snow King!" "The Flyer!" Thought Francie, "If I could only have one of those, I'd never ask God for another thing as long as I live."

There were roller skates made of shining nickel with straps of good brown leather and silvered nervous wheels, tensed for rolling, needing but a breath to start them turning, as they lay crossed one over the other, sprinkled with mica snow on a bed of cloud-like cotton.

There were other marvelous things. Francie couldn't take them all in. Her head spun and she was dizzy with the impact of all the seeing, all the making up for stories about the toys in the shop windows.

THE SPRUCE TREES began coming into the neighborhood the week before Christmas. Their branches were corded to hold back the glory of their spreading and probably to make shipping easier. Vendors rented space on the curb before a store and stretched a rope from pole to pole and leaned the trees against it. All day they walked up and down this one-sided avenue of aromatic leaning trees, blowing on stiff ungloved fingers and looking with bleak hope at those people who paused. A few ordered a tree set aside for the day; others stopped to price, inspect, and conjecture. But most came just to touch the boughs and surreptitiously pinch a fingerful of spruce needles together to release the fragrance. And the air was cold and still, and full of the pine smell and the smell of tangerines which appeared in the stores only at Christmas time and the mean street was truly wonderful for a little while.

THERE WAS A CRUEL custom in the neighborhood. It was about the trees still unsold when midnight of Christmas Eve approached. There was a saying that if you waited until then, you wouldn't have to buy a tree; that "they'd chuck 'em at you." This was literally true.

At midnight on the Eve of our dear Savior's birth, the kids gathered where there were unsold trees. The man threw each tree in turn, starting with the biggest. Kids volunteered to stand up against the throwing. If a boy didn't fall down under the impact, the tree was his. If he fell, he forfeited his chance at winning a tree. Only the roughest boys and some of the young men elected to be hit by the big trees. The others waited shrewdly until a tree came up that they could stand against. The little kids waited for the tiny, foot-high trees and shrieked in delight when they won one.

On the Christmas Eve when Francie was ten and Neeley nine, Mama consented to let them go down and have their first try for a tree. Francie had picked out her tree earlier in the day. She had stood near it all afternoon and evening praying that no one would buy it. To her joy, it was still there at midnight. It was the biggest tree in the neighborhood and its price was so high that no one could afford to buy it. It was ten feet high. Its branches were bound with new white rope and it came to a sure, pure point at the top.

The man took this tree out first. Before Francie could speak up, a neighborhood bully, a boy of eighteen known as Punky Perkins, stepped forward and ordered the man to chuck the tree at him. The man hated the way Punky was so confident. He looked around and asked:

"Anybody else wanna take a chance on it?"

Francie stepped forward. "Me, Mister."

A spurt of derisive laughter came from the tree man. The kids snickered. A few adults who had gathered to watch the fun, guffawed.

"Aw g'wan. You're too little," the tree man objected.

"Me and my brother—we're not too little together."

She pulled Neeley forward. The man looked at them—a thin girl of ten with starveling hollows in her cheeks but with the chin still baby-round. He looked at the little boy with his fair hair and round blue eyes—Neeley Nolan, all innocence and trust.

"Two ain't fair," yelped Punky.

"Shut your lousy trap," advised the man who held all power in that hour. "These here kids is got nerve. Stand back, the rest of yous. These kids is goin' to have a show at this tree."

The others made a wavering lane. Francie and Neeley stood at one end of it and the big man with the big tree at the other. It was a human funnel with Francie and her brother making the small end of it. The man flexed his great arms to throw the great tree. He noticed how tiny the children looked at the end of the short lane. For the split part of a moment, the tree thrower went through a kind of Gethsemane.

"Oh, Jesus Christ," his soul agonized, "why don't I just give 'em the tree, say Merry Christmas and let 'em go? What's the tree to me? I can't sell it no more this year and it won't keep till next year." The kids watched him solemnly as he stood there in his moment of thought. "But then," he rationalized, "if I did that, all the others would expect to get 'em handed to 'em. And next year nobody a-tall would buy a tree off of me. They'd all wait to get 'em handed to 'em on a silver plate. I ain't a big enough man to give this tree away for nothin'. No, I ain't big enough. I ain't big enough to do a thing like that. I gotta think of myself and my own kids." He finally came to his conclusion. "Oh, what the hell! Them two kids is gotta live in this world. They *got* to get used to it. They got to learn to give and to take punishment. And by Jesus, it ain't give but *take, take, take* all the time in this God-damned world." As he threw the tree with all his strength, his heart wailed out, "It's a God-damned, rotten, lousy world!"

Francie saw the tree leave his hands. There was a split bit of being when time and space had no meaning. The whole world stood still as something dark and monstrous came through the air. The tree came toward her blotting out all memory of her ever having lived. There was nothing—nothing but pungent darkness and something that grew and grew as it rushed at her. She staggered as the tree hit them. Neeley went to his knees but she pulled him up fiercely before he could go down. There was a mighty swishing sound as the tree settled. Everything was dark, green, and prickly. Then she felt a sharp pain at the side of her head where the trunk of the tree had hit her. She felt Neeley trembling.

When some of the older boys pulled the tree away, they found Francie and her brother standing upright, hand in hand. Blood was coming from scratches on Neeley's face. He looked more like a baby than ever with his bewildered blue eyes and the fariness of his skin made more noticeable because of the clear red blood. But they were smiling. Had they not won the biggest tree in the neighborhood? Some of the boys hollered "Horray!" A few adults clapped. The tree man eulogized them by screaming, "And now get the hell out of here with your tree, you lousy bastards."

Francie had heard swearing since she had heard words. Obscenity and profanity had no meaning as such among those people. They were emotional expressions of inarticulate people with small vocabularies; they made a kind of dialect. The phrases could mean any thing according to the expression and tone used in saying them. So now, when Francie heard themselves called lousy bastards, she smiled tremulously at the kind man. She knew that he was really saying, "Good-bye—God bless you."

The Tree That Didn't Get Trimmed

Christopher Morley

If you walk through a grove of balsam trees you will notice that the young trees are silent; they are listening. But the old tall ones—especially the firs—are whispering. They are telling the story of The Tree That Didn't Get Trimmed. It sounds like a painful story, and the murmur of the old trees as they tell it is rather solemn; but it is an encouraging story for young saplings to hear. On warm autumn days when your trunk is tickled by ants and insects climbing, and the resin is hot and gummy in your knots, and the whole glade smells sweet, drowsy, and sad, and the hardwood trees are boasting the gay colors they are beginning to show, many a young evergreen has been cheered by it.

All young fir trees, as you know by that story of Hans Andersen's—if you've forgotten it, why not read it again?—dream of being a Christmas Tree some day. They dream about it as young girls dream of being a bride, or young poets of having a volume of verse published. With the vision of that brightness and gaiety before them they patiently endure the sharp sting of the ax, the long hours pressed together on a freight car. But every December there are more trees cut down that are needed for Christmas. And that is the story that no one—not even Hans Andersen—has thought to put down.

The tree in this story should never have been cut. He wouldn't have been, but it was getting dark in the Vermont woods, and the man with the ax said to himself, "Just one more." Cutting young trees with a sharp, beautifully balanced ax is fascinating; you go on and on; there's a sort of cruel pleasure in it. The blade goes through the soft wood with one whistling stroke and the boughs sink down with a soft swish.

He was a fine, well-grown youngster, but too tall for his age; his branches were rather scraggly. If he'd been left there he would have been an unusually big tree some day; but now he was in the awkward age and didn't have the tapering shape and the thick, even foliage that people like on Christmas trees. Worse still, instead of running up to a straight, clean spire, his top was a bit lopsided, with a fork in it.

But he didn't know this as he stood with many others, leaning against the side wall of the greengrocer's shop. In those cold December days he was very happy, thinking of the pleasures to come. He had heard of the delights of Christmas Eve: the stealthy setting-up of the tree, the tinsel balls and colored toys and stars, the peppermint canes and birds with spun-glass tails. Even that old anxiety of Christmas trees—burning candles—did not worry him, for he had been told that nowadays people use strings of tiny electric bulbs which cannot set one on fire. So he looked forward to the festival with a confident heart.

"I shall be very grand," he said. "I hope there will be children to admire me. It must be a great moment when the children hang their stockings on you!" He even felt sorry for the first trees that were chosen and taken away. It would be best, he considered, not to be bought until Christmas Eve. Then, in the shining darkness someone would pick him out, put him carefully along the running board of a car, and away they would go. The tire-chains would clack and jingle merrily on the snowy road. He imagined a big house with fire glowing on a hearth; the hushed rustle of wrapping paper and parcels being unpacked. Someone would say, "Oh, what a beautiful tree!" How erect and still he would brace himself in his iron tripod stand.

But day after day went by, one by one the other trees were taken, and he began to grow troubled. For everyone who looked at him seemed to have an unkind word. "Too tall," said one lady. "No, this one wouldn't do, the branches are too skimpy," said another. "If I chop off the top," said the greengrocer, "it wouldn't be so bad." The tree shuddered, but the customer had already passed on to look at others. Some of his branches ached where the grocer had bent them upward to make his shape more attractive.

Across the street was a Ten Cent Store. Its bright windows were full of scarlet odds and ends; when the doors opened he could see people crowded along the aisles, cheerfully jostling one another with bumpy packages. A buzz of talk, a shuffle of feet, a constant ringing of cash drawers came noisily out of that doorway. He could see flashes of marvelous color, ornaments for luckier trees. Every evening, as the time drew nearer, the pavements were more thronged. The handsomer trees, not so tall as he but more bushy and shapely, were ranked in front of him; as they were taken away he could see the gaiety only too well. Then he was shown to a lady who wanted a tree very cheap. "You can have this one for a dollar," said the grocer. This was only one-third of what the grocer had asked for him at first, but even so the lady refused him and went across the street to buy a little artificial tree at the toy store. The man pushed him back carelessly, and he toppled over and fell alongside the wall. No one bothered to pick him up. He was almost glad, for now his pride would be spared.

Now it was Christmas Eve. It was a foggy evening with a drizzling rain; the alley alongside the store was thick with trampled slush. As he lay there among broken boxes and fallen scraps of holly strange thoughts came to him. In the still northern forest already his wounded stump was buried in forgetful snow. He remembered the wintry sparkle of the woods, the big trees with crusts and clumps of silver on their broad boughs, the keen singing of the lonely wind. He remembered the strong, warm feeling of his roots reaching down into the safe earth. That is a good feeling; it means to a tree just what it means to you to stretch your toes down toward the bottom of a well-tucked bed. And he had given up all this to lie here, disdained and forgotten, in a littered alley. The splash of feet, the chime of bells, the cry of cars went past him. He trembled a little with self-pity and vexation. "No toys and stockings for me," he thought sadly, and shed some of his needles.

Late that night, after all the shopping was over, the grocer came out to clear away what was left. The boxes, the broken wreaths, the empty barrels, and our tree with one or two others that hadn't been sold, all were thrown through the side door into the cellar. The doors were locked and he lay there in the dark. One of his branches, doubled under him in the fall, ached so he thought it must be broken. "So this is Christmas," he said to himself.

All that day it was very still in the cellar. There was an occasional creak as one of the bruised trees tried to stretch itself. Feet went along the pavement overhead, and there was a booming of church bells, but everything had a slow, disappointed sound. Christmas is always a little sad, after such busy preparations. The unwanted trees lay on the stone floor, watching the furnace light flicker on a hatchet that had been left there.

The day after Christmas a man came in who wanted some green boughs to decorate a cemetery. The grocer took the hatchet, and seized the trees without ceremony. They were too disheartened to care. Chop, chop, chop, went the blade, and the sweet-smelling branches were carried away. The naked trunks were thrown into a corner.

And now our tree, what was left of him, had plenty of time to think. He no longer could feel anything, for trees feel with their branches, but they think with their trunks. What did he think about as he grew dry and stiff? He thought that it had been silly of him to imagine such a fine, gay career for himself, and he was sorry for other young trees, still growing in the fresh hilly country, who were enjoying the same fantastic dreams.

Now perhaps you don't know what happens to the trunks of leftover Christmas trees. You could never guess. Farmers come in from the suburbs and buy them at five cents each for bean-poles and grape arbors. So perhaps (here begins the encouraging part of this story) they are really happier, in the end, than the trees that get trimmed for Santa Claus. They go back in the fresh moist earth of spring, and when the sun grows hot and the quick tendrils of the vines climb up them and presently they are decorated with the red blossoms of the bean or the little blue globes of the grape, just as pretty as any Christmas trinkets.

So one day the naked, dusty fir-poles were taken out of the cellar, and thrown into a truck with many others, and made a rattling journey out into the land. The farmer unloaded them in his yard and was tacking them up by the barn when his wife came out to watch him.

"There!" she said. "That's just what I want, a nice long pole with a fork in it. Jim, put that one over there to hold up the clothesline." It was the first time that anyone had praised our tree, and his dried-up heart swelled with a tingle of forgotten sap. They put him near one end of the clothesline, with his stump close to a flower bed. The fork that had been despised <devised? designed?> for a Christmas star was just the thing to hold up a clothesline. It was a washday, and soon the farmer's wife began bringing out wet ferments to swing and freshen in the clean bright air. And the very first thing that hung near the top of the Christmas pole was a cluster of children's stockings.

That isn't quite the end of the story, as the old fir trees whisper it in the breeze. The Tree That Didn't Get Trimmed was so cheerful watching the stockings, and other gay little clothes that plumped out in the wind just as though waiting to be spanked, that he didn't notice what was going on—or going up—below him. A vine had caught hold of his trunk and was steadily twisting upward. And one morning, when the farmer's wife came out intending to shift him, she stopped and exclaimed. "Why, I mustn't move this pole," she said. "The morning glory has run right up it." So it had, and our bare pole was blue and crimson with color.

Something nice, the old firs believe, always happens to the trees that don't get trimmed. They even believe that some day one of the Christmas-tree bean-poles will be the starting point for another Magic Beanstalk, as in the fairy tale of the boy who climbed up the bean-tree and killed the giant. When that happens, fairy tales will begin all over again.

Letter from Santa Claus

* ❄ ❄ ❄ ❄ ❄

Mark Twain

SANTA CLAUS, WHOM PEOPLE SOMETIMES CALL THE MAN IN THE MOON:
My dear Susy Clemens:

I have received and read all the letters which you and your little sister have
written me by the hand of your mother and your nurses; I have also read
those which you little people have written me with your own hands—for
although you did not use any characters that are in grown people's alphabet,
you used the characters that all children in all lands on Earth and in the
twinkling stars use; and as all my subjects in the moon are children and use
no character but that, you will easily understand that I can read your and
your baby sister's jagged and fantastic marks without any trouble at all. But I
had trouble with those letters which you dictated through your mother and

the nurses, for I am a foreigner and cannot read English writing well. You will find that I made no mistakes about the things which you and the baby ordered in your own letters—I went down your chimney at midnight when you were asleep and delivered them all myself—and kissed both of you, too, because you are good children, well-trained, nice-mannered, and about the most obedient little people I ever saw. But in the letters which you dictated there were some words which I could not make out for certain, and one or two orders which I could not fill because we ran out of stock. Our last lot of kitchen-furniture for dolls has just gone to a very poor little child in the North Star away up in the cold country above the Big Dipper. Your mama can show you that star and you will say: "Little Snow Flake" (for that is the child's name), "I'm glad you got that furniture, for you need it more than I." That is, you must write that, with your own hand, and Snow Flake will write you an answer. If you only spoke it she wouldn't hear you. Make your letter light and thin, for the distance is great and the postage very heavy.

There was a word or two in your mama's letter which I couldn't be certain of. I took it to be "trunk full of doll's clothes." Is that it? I will call at your kitchen door about nine o'clock this morning to inquire. But I must not see anybody and I must not speak to anybody but you. When the kitchen doorbell rings George must be blindfolded and sent to open the door. Then he must go back to the dining room or the china closet and take the cook with him. You must tell George he must walk on tiptoe and not speak—otherwise he will die some day. Then you must go up to the nursery and stand on a chair or the nurse's bed and put your ear to the speaking-tube that leads down to the kitchen and when I whistle through it you must speak in the tube and say, "Welcome, Santa Claus!" Then I will ask whether it was a trunk you ordered or not. If you say it was, I shall ask you what color you want the trunk to be. Your mama will help you to name a nice color and then you must tell me every single thing in detail which you want the trunk to contain. Then when I say, "Goodbye and Merry Christmas to my little Susy Clemens," you must say, "Goodbye, good old Santa Claus, I thank you very much and please tell that little Snow Flake I will look at her star tonight and she must look down here—I will be right in the West bay window; and every fine night I will look at her star and say, 'I know somebody up there and like her, too.'" Then you must go down into the library and make George close all the doors that open into the main hall, and everybody must keep still for a little while. I will go to the moon and get those things and in a few minutes I will come down the chimney that belongs to the fireplace that is in the hall—if it is a trunk you want—because I couldn't get such a thing as a trunk down the nursery chimney, you know.

People may talk if they want, until they hear my footsteps in the hall. Then you tell them to keep quiet a little while till I go back up the chimney. Maybe you will not hear my footsteps at all—so you may go now and then and peep through the dining room doors, and by and by you will see that thing which you want, right under the piano in the drawing room—for I shall put it there. If I should leave any snow in the hall, you must tell George to sweep it into the fireplace, for I haven't time to do such things. George must not use a broom, but a rag—else he will die some day. You must watch George and not let him run into danger. If my boot shall leave a stain on the marble, George must not holy-stone it away. Leave it there always in memory of my visit; and whenever you look at it or show it to anybody you must let it remind you to be a good little girl. Whenever you are naught and somebody points to that mark which your good old Santa Claus's boot made on the marble, what will you say, little Sweetheart?

Goodbye for a few minutes, till I come down to the world and ring the kitchen doorbell.

Your loving Santa Claus
Palace of St. Nicholas in the Moon,
Christmas Morning

Is There a Santa Claus?

Francis P. Church

This famous editorial first appeared in *The New York Sun*, September 21, 1897

We take pleasure in answering at once and thus prominently the communication below, expressing at the same time our great gratification that its faithful author is numbered among the friends of *The Sun*:

Dear Editor:

I am 8 years old.
Some of my little friends say there is no Santa Claus.
Papa says "If you see it in The Sun it's so."
Please tell me the truth, is there a Santa Claus?

Virginia O'Hanlon, 115 West 95th Street

VIRGINIA, your little friends are wrong. They have been affected by the skepticism of a skeptical age. They do not believe except what they see. They think that nothing can be which is not comprehensible by their little minds. All minds, Virginia, whether they be men's or children's, are little. In this great universe of ours man is mere insect, an ant, in his intellect, as compared with the boundless world around him, as measured by the intelligence capable of grasping the whole of truth and knowledge.

Yes, Virginia, there is a Santa Claus. He exists as certainly as love and generosity and devotion exist, and you know that they abound and give to your life its highest beauty and joy. Alas! How dreary would be the world if there were no Santa Claus! It would be as dreary as if there were no Virginias. There would be no childlike faith then, no poetry, no romance to make tolerable this existence. We should have no enjoyment, except in sense and sight. The eternal light with which childhood fills the world would be extinguished.

Not believe in Santa Claus! You might as well not believe in fairies! You might get your papa to hire men to watch in all the chimneys on Christmas eve to catch Santa Claus, but even if they did not see Santa Claus coming down, what would that prove? Nobody sees Santa Claus. The most real things in the world are those that neither children nor men can see. Did you ever see fairies dancing on the lawn? Of course not, but that's no proof that they are not there. Nobody can conceive or imagine all the wonders there are unseen and unseeable in the world.

You tear apart the baby's rattle and see what makes the noise inside, but there is a veil covering the unseen world which not the strongest man, no even the united strength of all the strongest men that ever lived, could tear apart. Only faith, fancy, poetry, love, romance, can push aside that curtain and view and picture the supernal beauty and glory beyond. Is it all real? Ah, Virginia, in all this world there is nothing else real and abiding.

No Santa Claus! Thank God he lives, and he lives forever. A thousand years from now, Virginia, nay, ten times ten thousand years from now, he will continue to make glad the heart of childhood.

ACKNOWLEGDMENTS

"The Rescue" from *Cat Who Came for Christmas, The* by Cleveland Amory Trust. Text copyright © 1987 by Cleveland Amory. Illustrations copyright © 1987 by Edith Allard by permission of Little Brown & Company.

"Bless Me Father, For I Have Sinned" by Ray Bradbury originally published in *Woman's Day* December 11, 1984 copyright © 1984 by Ray Bradbury. By permission of Don Congdon Associates, Inc.

"Christmas Day in the Morning" by Pearl S. Buck originally published in *Collier's* December 23, 1955 copyright © 1955 by Pearl S. Buck. By permission of Harold Ober Associates, Inc.

" December Night " from *Death Comes For The Archbishop* by Willa Cather copyright © 1927, 1929 by Willa Cather and renewed 1955, 1957 by The Executors of the Estate of Willa Cather. By permission of Alfred A. Knopf, a division of Random House, Inc.

"Christmas is a Sad Season for the Poor" from *The Stories of John Cheever* by John Cheever copyright © 1978 by John Cheever. By permission of Alfred A. Knopf, a division of Random House, Inc.

"The Miraculous Staircase" by Arthur Gordon originally published in *Guideposts* December 1966 copyright © 1966 by Guideposts. By permission of Guideposts.

"Valley Forge: 24 December 1777" by F. Van Wyck Mason copyright © 1950 and renewed 1978 by F. Van Wyck Mason By permission of The Harold Matson Co., Inc.

INDEX OF AUTHORS

INDEX OF STORIES